PROJECT SUICIDE

To: Christi

JOHN BUKOWSKI

Thanks for the health!

PathBinder
Publishing
COLUMBUS,
INDIANA

Published by PathBinder Publishing
P.O. Box 2611
Columbus, IN 47202
www.PathBinderPublishing.com

Edited by Doug Showalter
Covers designed by Anna Perlich
Cover photo by Pexels

First published in 2022
Manufactured in the United States

ISBN: 978-1-955088-26-8
Library of Congress Control Number: 9781955088268

*To my beautiful wife, Susan, my most honest
critic and my biggest source of encouragement.*

Testimonials

"John Bukowski's debut thriller, *Project Suicide*, keeps you on the edge of your seat. I can't wait to read his next book."
— Larry D. Sweazy, multiple award-winning author
of *The Broken Bow*

"*Project Suicide* is a rollercoaster ride filled with unforeseen twists, dips, and dives right up to its stunning climax."
— Matthew Clemens, co-author of the
Reeder and Rogers thrillers

Introduction

Project Suicide is a work of fiction with fictional characters. Any resemblance to people living or dead is purely coincidental. Some of the locations are real places, although they may have been fictionalized for purposes of the story. Likewise, as with any techno-thriller, some of the science is real and some is BS; I'll leave it to the reader to judge which is which.

The first draft of this novel was written before the onset of COVID-19. Now, a few years and multiple drafts later, it was my feeling that people are tired enough of this pandemic to not want to read about it. Therefore, I have avoided references to it and its accoutrements, such as social distancing, masks, and more.

— John Bukowski

Chapter 1

Nelson Barzoon glanced at his Rolex and wondered if anyone else had died today. Pondering briefly the chances of getting venereal disease from a courtroom bench, he unbuttoned his Brooks Brothers jacket and sat down.

"All rise."

Barzoon stood with the rest of the ragtag gathering. All except a guy in his mid-thirties, softly snoring, feet propped on the front railing. A slap from the bailiff's hand shot the man's knockoff Nikes to the floor with a clap that brought mixed chuckles and cheers from the assorted hookers, dopers, and thieves.

"Quiet," the bailiff shouted. The large, uniformed cop grunted directly at the still-seated man. "*All* rise."

Unlike most of the denizens of Columbus, Ohio, municipal night court, the man in the front row met the bailiff's gaze without flinching. He rose slowly and continued staring until the cop frowned and blinked. The man grinned ever so slightly, then looked to the judge, now seating himself.

"This session of Municipal court 182 is back in session. The honorable Pleasant Webster presiding."

"Be seated," said Judge Webster, a big man whose black face and hands blended with his robe, giving the appearance of a mountain on the bench. "Call the next case." The judge waved his hand before his nose and added, "And open a window."

Barzoon sat erect as the bailiff called out, "People versus Deacon Creel." He was glad the case was next on the docket. Time was pressing, and he was in no mood to wait amidst the great unwashed. From his perch at the end of the second row, he watched as Webster turned his attention to the defendant.

Creel's face sported a forty-eight-hour shadow. His hair was long and greasy, not quite covering a prominent mole on the left side of his forehead. Barzoon studied the man's attire. Dirty jeans and hoodie that fit with those of the night-court citizenry. A funkiness wafted from him as he stretched, his odor outpacing even the dull stench of BO, farts, and general untidiness — smells unbowed by smatterings of hooker perfume and attorney aftershave. All the trappings of just another vagrant. Yet the steel-blue eyes were sharp and intelligent, the features lean and well-proportioned. The barest hint of a grin said, "I know something you don't, but I don't give a shit."

"Charges?" Webster asked.

"Driving while intoxicated and disorderly conduct," Prosecutor Steven Simonetti replied, rearranging his toupee. "On the night of August seventh, on or about nine P.M., Dr. Deacon Creel, DVM, MPH, PhD…"

The judge stopped him with a wave of his meaty hand. "Is this necessary?"

"Not my idea, your honor. Mr. Thompson requested I read these credentials into the record."

"Mr. Thompson?"

Richard Thompson, a skinny public defender in a shiny corduroy jacket rose. "Yes, your honor. I wanted the court to know that the defendant, a decorated former US Navy officer and federal employee, is a respected health professional who has served his country. He is well regarded in his field and in the community."

"Said well-respected professional having two previous arrests," Simonetti said. "Including assault and battery and urinating in a public place."

Laughter rose from the spectators, causing the judge's gavel to descend.

"Order." The judge cleared his throat. "If I want the arrest record, Mr. Simonetti, I'll ask for it. And as far as these credentials, Mr. Thompson, I think you're doing your client more harm than good. I'd expect a man with this level of training and service to exhibit some discipline and self-restraint, not to mention basic deportment. Now, let's finish reading the charges … without the fruit salad."

As Simonetti droned on, Barzoon watched the smile once again touch the corners of the defendant's mouth. Creel seemed as relaxed — and as bored — as anyone in the room, including the lawyers. Yet, Barzoon knew the guy under those dirty clothes was a decorated veteran. And one of the most brilliant minds on the planet.

"And finally, your honor. When asked by the arresting officer to place his hands behind his back, the defendant responded with an expletive."

Webster furrowed his brow. "What precisely did he *explete*?"

"Well, your honor. Specifically, Dr. Creel told officer Maitland to go ..."

"Your honor?" Barzoon rebuttoned his jacket as he stood. "May I address the court?"

"Who the hell are you?"

"Nelson Barzoon, your honor. I'd like to speak on behalf of Dr. Creel."

The judge looked at the prosecutor, who looked at the public defender, who shrugged.

"Are you a lawyer, sir?"

"I am, your honor."

"Have you been retained to represent Dr. Creel?"

"Not exactly, your honor. But I believe I have mitigating details that should be discussed in your chambers. If that's convenient?"

Judge Webster again looked at Simonetti, who again looked at Thompson, who looked at Creel. The defendant whispered something to the public defender, who whispered back.

"Something to say, Mr. Thompson?"

Thompson started to address the judge, then shook his head.

"Well, this is highly irregular, but we're almost at the dinner recess." Webster held his gavel raised in indecision, then brought it down once onto the maple block. "Case postponed until after the dinner recess. At which time I will meet with Mr. Simonetti, Mr. Thompson, and Mr. ..."

"Barzoon, your honor."

"Right. I'll meet with you all in chambers." He looked at Deacon and added, "Let's have the defendant there as well. Does that suit you, Mr. Barroom?"

"I guess it will have to, your honor."

Webster hollered, "Next case."

Nelson Barzoon's palate was attuned to five-star restaurants, not shabby municipal offices, but the smell of French fries still made his stomach grumble. It was grumbling now as Webster leaned over his scratched oak desk, took a mammoth bite of Big Mac, then swiped his face with a paper napkin.

"So, what's your story, counselor?"

"My card, your honor."

The judge wiped fingers on his robe and picked up the white vellum card. "Department of Homeland Security?"

"Yes, sir. And the department would appreciate it if Dr. Creel could be released into my custody."

"We are in the middle of an arraignment, son." Another bite of burger entered the judge's maw.

"I appreciate that, your honor. But some, shall we say, urgent matters have arisen that necessitate this request."

A snigger from the left caused the judge to look at Creel leaning back in a wooden chair, long legs stretched before him, hands laced over chest, eyes closed.

"You think this funny, sir?"

Without opening his eyes or losing his knowing grin, Deacon softly said, "Usually."

"Um, your honor?"

The judged looked back at Nelson Barzoon.

"I know this is irregular but seeing as the charge is a minor one."

The prosecutor adjusted his polyester tie and cleared his throat. "We take drunk driving very seriously in this community. Especially on an expired license."

Barzoon smiled. "I appreciate that. My apologies. Be that as it may, no one has been injured and no property was damaged. So ..." He looked expectantly at Webster.

The judge munched some fries, thought for a moment, then looked at the lawyers sitting to his left. "Well?"

"I have no objections," Thompson said.

"No doubt," Webster replied. "What do the *people* think, Mr. Simonetti?"

The prosecutor sat forward, hands on knees. "There is still the matter of the drunk-driving charge. The public has been placed in jeopardy by Mr. Creel's ..."

"Dr. Creel," Barzoon said.

"Corrected. Dr. Creel's reckless behavior. Once he has been arraigned on that charge, the people have no problem releasing him on minimal bail, perhaps five hundred dollars. He could be turned over to your custody at nine this morning. If that's agreeable."

All eyes turned back to Barzoon, except for Creel's, still hidden behind closed lids.

"Regrettably, it is not." Barzoon rose and removed a folded document from the inside pocket of his suit jacket. He handed it to the judge, who again wiped fingers to robe and peered at the contents.

"This authorizes me to take custody of Dr. Creel immediately."

The judge paused, full mouth agape, French fries poised in midair.

Barzoon pointed. "I trust you recognize the signature below the seal?"

"Son of a bitch," the judge mumbled.

Chapter 2

The black Mercedes turned smoothly off I-70 onto US 23, its halogen beams piercing the darkness. Traffic was light, befitting a time with sunrise several hours distant. The two passengers sat quietly in the back, one shuffling papers balanced atop a cowhide briefcase, the other with eyes closed, odor the only reminder of his presence. Barzoon assumed he was asleep, until a soft voice broke the silence.

"Why are we heading south? John Glenn is the other way."

"We're headed toward Rickenbacker, the Air National Guard base." Barzoon moved a personnel form to the bottom of the pile. "There's a C-130 waiting on the tarmac."

"Then?"

"Edwards. You have a meeting in Maryland at zero eight hundred."

Deacon sat up. "What if I don't want to go to Maryland?"

"I'm not sure you have a say in the matter, Dr. Creel. And don't forget, I got you out of jail."

Deacon stretched. "Don't expect too much for your money, Mr. Barzoon. You may have taken me to dinner, but don't assume that gets you breakfast, too."

"This is a national emergency, Dr. Creel."

Deacon grunted. "Everything *is* with you folks."

"Let us say you have a duty to your country. If that isn't enough, then let us say you have a debt to pay to the past."

A long silence filled the car. Then finally, rubbing his chin, Deacon said, "Will I get a chance to freshen up a little?"

"On the plane. A corpsman will shave you."

"I can shave myself."

Barzoon continued staring at his papers. "No doubt, but you look a little shaky this morning."

Deacon held out a hand, fingers splayed. None of them quivered.

"Be that as it may. The corpsman ... corpswoman in this case, will shave you, take your vitals, and load you up with B-complex and hot coffee. *Then* you can wash up."

Barzoon noticed Deacon smell the pit of his hoodie.

"There's a new suit in your size waiting on the plane. I'm assuming you can dress yourself?"

Deacon smiled. "It depends on what the corpswoman looks like."

"I would think you'd prefer a nap instead."

Deacon yawned. "I snatched twenty winks in the courtroom." Then he straightened in the leather seat. "What's this all about?"

"You'll be briefed at Fort Deidenbach."

"Let me rephrase the question, counselor. How bad is it?"

Barzoon paused, document in midair, then placed it on the pile. "I'm not at liberty to say."

"*That* bad," Deacon said, settling back into the plush leather. "Wake me when we're on the field."

The Lockheed C-130 leveled off at twenty thousand feet. Four Allison engines and a ten-knot tail wind pushed the plane eastward at three hundred and fifty miles per hour. Inside the pressurized cargo bay, Deacon sat in a jump seat sipping black coffee while a marine corpswoman took vital signs by the light of an overhead spot.

"Blood pressure, one eighteen over seventy. Pulse forty-five." Her voice filled the headphones that cancelled the noise of the big turboprops. "You've got the heart rate of a horse, doctor."

Deacon smiled as if to say, "that's not all."

"Any dizziness, nausea, breathing difficulties, or pain?"

"Just a little headache."

"I don't doubt it. Your chart indicates a blood alcohol of 0.20 when you were arrested."

"Just a number," Deacon said.

"A number that can get one thrown in jail. And almost did, I understand."

"Till you guys rescued me." He sipped and grimaced. "What's the chance of getting a Bloody Mary on this flight?"

"No can do, sir." The corpswoman drew brown fluid into a hypodermic needle. "But this should help." The cabin filled with the sharp odor of rubbing alcohol as she rolled up the sleeve of his hoodie and rubbed his arm with a moistened pad. He didn't flinch as the needle slid home.

"What's your name?"

"Robbins, sir. Fleet Marine Force Specialist Amy Robbins."

Deacon nodded in appreciation. "An FMF in one so young."

Robbins looked to be mid-twenties, with large dark eyes. She was compactly built, her movements suggesting taut muscle under the camouflage fatigues billowing over her arms and legs. Her black hair was cropped short. Although she wore no makeup, her cheeks flushed with a healthy glow. She noticed Deacon staring.

"Something, sir?"

He shook his head. "You just remind me of someone."

"Let me guess." Robbins smiled. "Linda Ronstadt."

Deacon hesitated, then smiled back. "I guess you get that a lot."

"Although usually from men over fifty. I think it's the eyes."

"Where have you served?"

"Combat assignments in both Afghanistan and Iraq," Robbins said.

He held out a hand. "Deacon Creel. Call me Deke."

She shook it. "Pleasure, sir, ah, Deke. Now, I have orders to shave you."

"Won't let me handle a razor? Am I on suicide watch?"

Robbins smiled at his smile. She had an honest smile.

"Let's just say I'm following orders and that my superiors don't want anything to happen to you."

As Robbins turned to gather shaving things, Nelson Barzoon entered from the crew compartment. Jacket off, he was dressed in white shirt and power tie, identical headphones over his thinning head of grey hair.

"Better hurry along," Barzoon said into the mic almost brushing his lips. "We'll be touching down in less than thirty minutes."

"Considering the urgency you seem to place on getting me there, I'm surprised we're not on a Lear or Bombardier. We'd be there by now."

"Perhaps," Barzoon said. "Business jets may be faster, but they are not as *stealthy*. This Hercules travels under military secrecy." He smiled ten-thousand-dollars-worth of dental work. "And it can fly on one engine and land in a farmer's field, if needs be."

"Looks like I'm pretty valuable cargo these days."

"Turn to me, please, sir," Robbins said.

"Deke," he said, as her fingers spread shaving gel on his cheeks.

Barzoon stepped to the rear to retrieve a charcoal grey suit covered in clear plastic. "This should make you presentable once you've cleaned up. Toiletries are by the aft head." He pointed to a camouflage privacy curtain draped around an olive-drab metal box. A sheet of polished steel was anchored to the wall for a mirror. Barzoon patted the plastic-covered suit. "Paperwork in the pocket restores your security clearances and your rank, *Commander*."

"You think of everything," Deacon said.

"One tries."

"Turn to me please, sir."

Deacon looked into the dark eyes before him, attractive features scrunched in concentration, sure hands gently and methodically clearing off his whiskers. Then he smiled at Barzoon. "I think I might need help changing."

"No time for that." The lawyer smiled. "Or a nap either."

"I'll ask Warrant Officer Ramirez to come back," Robbins said. "He can assist you with changing. It won't add any time, sir, ah, Deke."

Their eyes met. "Never mind," Deacon said.

Deacon fidgeted with his collar, the tie feeling like a noose after months of relaxed, if not gracious living. He sat in a small, underground conference room. Most of Building 13 was underground, with the surface level of the grey blockhouse reserved for administration and other mundane matters. As one descended, matters became more serious — and more secret.

Seated with him was Barzoon, once again in his Brooks Brothers jacket. Directly opposite Deacon was a small bald man of indeterminate middle age. He was outfitted similarly to Barzoon, but the expensive suit hung limply on a dumpy frame that matched his academic pallor and thick glasses. Whenever he looked at Josiah Metternich, Deacon thought of Dr. Bunsen Honeydew from the Muppets.

"Nice to see you again, Dr. Creel. Or may I still call you Deacon?"

Deacon stared, not nodding. "Dr. Metternich." There was no smile, handshake, or familiarity. "Or should I say Director Metternich. Still have your title I see."

Metternich smiled coolly. "No thanks to you, Deacon."

Deacon's answering smile was just as frosty. "I tried my best, Doctor."

Barzoon cleared his throat. "Gentlemen? May we get down to cases?"

Deacon and Metternich held a gaze of mutual animosity, then Metternich read from a folder in front of him. "Deacon Creel. Age thirty-five. Born Dayton, Ohio. Father died when you were nine. Mother died some years later." He looked up. "Overdose, wasn't it?"

Deacon did not answer.

"Photographic memory. IQ tested at 169. Graduated high school at fifteen, college at eighteen, veterinary school at twenty-one." He peered at Deacon above his glasses. "I've always wondered. Why veterinary school?"

"Best infectious disease program." Deacon smiled. "And hardest to get into."

Metternich shrugged. "Graduate training in public health, microbiology, physiology, pathology, and other 'ologies' too numerous to mention. Uniformed service with CDC before volunteering for Chemical, Biological, Radiation, and Nuclear duty overseas. One CBRN tour in Iraq before transferring to Fort Deidenbach. Assigned to Unit 13. Duties unspecified, subject to need-to-know clearance."

He looked up. "That takes us to last year, when you resigned your commission and disappeared. No doubt more pressing personal obligations."

Metternich raised his glasses and stared at another page. "Urinating in public, was it?"

"If I was going to *piss* on the public," Deacon hissed, "I figured I should do it *in* public."

Metternich shook his head. "One of the finest team leaders we ever had. Why, Deacon?"

"Maybe I didn't like the direction I was leading the team, Doctor." A chill passed over Deacon. "Or where it was leading me."

"You gave up so much."

"I lost even more."

"Um, Joe?" Barzoon said.

"Quite," Metternich replied. "The business at hand." He broke the seal on a second folder that had been lying under the first. "A man of your intelligence has probably surmised that we did not go to the trouble of finding you and bringing you here to discuss your record — either employment or criminal."

"Quite," Deacon said.

"You recall project Annulment, no doubt."

Deacon's face darkened. "I should."

Barzoon broke the long, pregnant pause. "I believe Dr. Creel headed up the project for a time. That is, until that story leaked to the media."

"Do you still maintain you had nothing to do with that?" Metternich asked.

Deacon grinned. "Perish the thought."

"Just like you didn't have anything to do with the lost files."

"Who, me?"

"Or destruction of the electronic data."

"Did someone scrub those hard disks?" Deacon asked, leaning forward. "I can't recall."

"Um, gentlemen?" Barzoon said.

"That was quite a problem for us, Deacon."

"I hope so, Dr. Metternich."

"Weeks dealing with questions, congressional testimony, budget cuts."

Barzoon again interrupted. "Ah, gentlemen?"

"You seem to have covered your ass alright, Joe."

"Spinning our wheels trying to duplicate your results."

Deacon smiled. "We do what we can, Doctor."

"Delayed Seppuku for months."

"You don't know how happy I am to hear ..." Deacon's fist slammed the table. "*Delayed*?"

It was Metternich's turn to grin. "Quite."

"You mean you crazy bastards went through with it?"

"Temper, temper, Deacon."

"Doctors!" Barzoon stood. "This bickering is pointless and counterproductive. This isn't some schoolyard scuffle. If it were, I'd suggest you go into the parking lot to settle it." He smiled. "But then, Dr. Metternich would be dead, and Dr. Creel would be arrested for murder. And who would solve our problem?" The tension dropped—slightly. "So, let's get down to business."

Deacon unclenched his fist. "Give me the who, what, where, when, and why."

Metternich handed him the folder. "I'm afraid that all I can provide with any certainty at the moment is the what."

Deacon threw down the folder. "You're telling me things I already know, Doctor."

Metternich nodded. "But did you know that Silas Burke was dead?"

"Yes. I read the newspapers, at least the front page and the comics. The death of a presidential advisor generally makes it to the former."

"But did you know *how* he died?"

"Car accident, wasn't it?"

"Yes indeed." Metternich paused. "That's what the media were told. What they were not told was that he was driving alone at two A.M.. His BMW ran into a concrete abutment at one hundred and five miles per hour."

"Was alcohol involved?"

"It was not. No drugs of any kind were found in his body, except for a statin he was prescribed for high cholesterol."

Deacon waved a dismissive hand. "Well, that sounds suspicious, granted. But *one* case ..."

"What about two cases?"

"Two?"

"Kristen Lebel," Metternich said.

"The party chair? But that was natural causes, wasn't it?" Deacon looked at Barzoon for confirmation. "Heart attack, I believe the paper said."

"Heart *failure*," Metternich corrected, "induced by an overdose of secobarbital. The toxicology findings were not mentioned, in deference to the family."

"Did she leave a note?"

"No."

"Well then, surely that could have been accidental."

"Perhaps," Metternich replied, his thumbs twiddling. "But Ms. Lebel was not in the habit of taking sleep aids. In fact, the drugs were not even prescribed to *her*. They'd been stolen from a friend's medicine cabinet the day before. Furthermore, she was newly engaged and in high spirits, by all accounts."

Deacon shook his head. "Again, suspicious, I grant you, but ..."

"And number three." Metternich removed folded papers from his breast pocket. "The honorable Scott Waters." He slid the papers across the table. "First year of his second congressional term. Won by thirty points as I recall. Rising political star. Already spoken of as a VP pick, possibly the youngest presidential candidate in history. Happily married, two young children."

"Gunshot?" Creel said, looking at the coroner's report. "Yesterday?"

"A single gunshot to the head." Metternich placed a pudgy finger under his double chin.

"Any chance he could have been, you know, cleaning his gun, as they say?"

"As they say, but not as they *mean*," Metternich said.

"Any common factors among the three?"

"They all belonged to the same political party,' Metternich said. "And they all seemed to have everything to live for."

"So, as you can see, Doctor Creel," Barzoon said. "While I think we can all agree that politics is a high-stakes game with more than its share of stress, it seems highly unlikely that three political stars, by all accounts well-adjusted rising stars whose stresses were just beginning, would die under such circumstances."

Deacon collected the papers into a neat pile and stared at it saying nothing. Then, still staring down, he said, "You want me to recreate the formula for Creel-1." He looked up. "Why should I?"

Metternich started to say something, but Deacon's eyes flashed him into silence. "For *you*, Doctor? Forgive me for saying it, but I'd prefer you be the next victim."

"Now, Dr. Creel," Barzoon said. "No need to get personal. This is an issue of national security."

Deacon laughed. "You can shove your national security. I've seen what passes for national security, and it doesn't give me confidence in the security of the nation."

"Deacon, my boy."

"Don't give me that *my boy*, crap, Doctor. I am not your boy. The fact that I ever was makes my skin crawl."

"Dr. Creel." Barzoon spoke calmly. "Deacon. No matter your history with Dr. Metternich or this project, innocent people have been dying."

"And don't give me that innocent people bullshit either. There are no innocent people in this town, present company included." He paused, eyes dark. "Well, there was one, but she died." A tear welled in his eye.

The room was quiet. Metternich concentrated on his pudgy, pink hands as if they might perform some amazing feat of prestidigitation. Deacon gazed straight ahead, not seeing anything in this world.

Barzoon stared at Deacon, then finally said, "Scott Waters had loved ones as well, a wife and two small children. She, they, didn't deserve what happened to him." Deacon continued to stare. "Other politicians have families as well." Barzoon paused. "So does the president."

Deacon turned to Barzoon, his eyes afire. "Don't give me any BS about ..."

Barzoon cut him off. "You of all people should *empathize*. You of all people should want to prevent this from happening again. To *atone* for it."

The fire in Deacon's eyes died as the older man held his stare.

"Do you?" Barzoon said.

Steely blue eyes stared at aging brown ones, neither blinking, neither turning away. The eyes locked in silent combat, a soundless pissing contest that neither wanted to lose. Finally, their ocular game of chicken ended with Deacon grabbing a notepad and pen from the table. As he wrote, he said, "I get to pick my own team."

"Within reason," Metternich said.

"And they'll need to be told everything."

"Again, within reason."

"*Everything*. Everything about the problem, 606, Creel-1, the unexpected deaths, the FBI investigation, everything."

"There is no reason for them to know about the deaths, 606, or the investigation," Metternich said.

"Fine," Deacon said, tossing the pen aside. "Just drop me at the bus station and I'll make my way home from there."

"You arrogant ..." Barzoon grabbed Metternich's sleeve and the director's voice dropped. "Why?"

"Maybe because I'm tired of operating in the dark with you people. Maybe because *you* don't want them to know. Maybe just so I can be a pain in the ass. How's that?"

Metternich started to say something, but Barzoon cut him off. "Very well."

Deacon resumed his writing. "Is Charley Hayes still at NIH?"

"No," Metternich said. "He transferred to analysis and countermeasures at USAMRIID last year."

"And Lisa?"

"Dr. Reilly?"

Deacon nodded, still writing.

"She's moved back to Allergy and Infectious Diseases. I offered her your old position, but she turned it down."

"Smart girl." Deacon looked over his list, added another name, then slid it to his old boss.

Barzoon snatched the legal pad from Metternich's pudgy fingers. "I'll see to it."

"And *I'll* need everything you have."

"Understood."

Barzoon's response seemed to end the discussion, yet it didn't. Something told Deacon there was more to say. He watched as the two men stared at each other then turned away to look at opposite ends of the room, like an arguing couple in a busy restaurant. He waited, but no one spoke.

"What aren't you telling me?" Deacon's eyes probed from Metternich to Barzoon, then back again. The two men looked ill at ease, sheepish, as if neither one wanted to tell dad about the broken headlight. "Well?"

Finally, Barzoon spoke. "It's possible we may know the *who*."

Chapter 3

Amy Reilly double counted as part of her standard checklist: five four-by-four gauze, two poly-backed white towels, one fenestrated drape, two steel medicine cups, one Adson thumb forceps, one straight Iris scissors, one curved mosquito forceps, and one Webster needle holder. Satisfied, she wrapped the drape material snuggly over the laceration pack, tucking the flap tightly into the fold for a secure fit. Like folding the flag at Arlington, she thought for the millionth time.

She had an errant desire to hurl the surgical pack against the wall. She smiled, recalling CPO Stan Hustick, the senior tech during her Basic Medical Technician Corpsman Program. 'Stan the man,' as he was known among the ratings, would choose a surgical pack at random and hurl it against the wall. If it came apart, the unhappy corpsman-to-be would need to pack three more, each subjected to the same test. Amy's pack had been chosen during the first week. Her humiliation as a pair of Iris scissors skittered across the floor was a better lesson than the triplicate repacks, none of which came undone.

Amy's father had been married to the corps until an IED annulled the union. Her grandfather had been killed at Khe Sanh. Her great-grandfather had been wounded at Iwo Jima. Then there was just Amy or her sister Jenifer to carry on the family trade. Jen had always preferred Barbie to GI Joe, so that left Amy. She smiled at what her father would have said when his baby enlisted. The little girl who nursed orphan animals. The peacemaker for family squabbles. But hers was not the corps that fought, hers was the corps that healed.

Wrapping autoclave tape around the pack, she placed it in the pile. Then she stiffened, hearing her name on the PA system.

"Robbins. Specialist Amy Robbins. Please report to Captain Higgins on the double."

"What now?"

Higgins looked up from his computer screen. "Stand easy, Robbins."

Amy laced fingers behind her back and let her shoulders sag.

"Pack your gear. New orders for you."

"Beg pardon, sir?"

"You're on detached service to CBRN."

"Me, sir?"

"I don't see anyone else standing there."

"Yes, sir. May I enquire about my new duties sir?"

"You're to be aide de camp to Lieutenant Commander Deacon Creel."

"Deacon Cree... Deke?"

"You now know as much as I do." He handed her some papers. "Report to Fort Deidenbach, Unit 13, at seventeen hundred hours."

"Today, sir?"

"Yes, today."

"Um, but ..."

He resumed studying his computer. "Dismissed."

Chapter 4

Carla sighed. She'd been scared when she'd entered the motel room. Really frightened. Ready to confess and take the consequences. Now she'd relaxed, safe in the arms of her lover, bodies cozied into two spoons.

One hand firmly cupped her ample breast, eliciting a shivery "ah." The other softly stroked frizzy hair that could never be called beautiful. She grasped the first hand, drawing it away to her lips. She kissed it once. Twice. Three times. "That last one was for luck," she said.

"Luck is the byproduct of careful planning. Haven't I always told you that?"

"Yes, I know you're right. You're always right." She kissed the fingers again. "But we didn't plan on them finding out." She shivered as lips nibbled her neck.

"*You* didn't plan on it. But I knew they would eventually."

"But what do we do now? Now that they know?"

"Shhh." The hands resumed exploring Carla's body. "Trust me, baby."

"Mmm," Carla murmured.

"You see, I knew they would search bank records."

Like a snake seeking a lair, fingers slithered lightly along Carla's hip to her abdomen.

"Yes," she cooed.

"Only *so* many people had the access, making for a reasonably focused search."

The deft fingers flicked back and forth, tickling her short hairs. Carla giggled, though not from mirth.

"Bank records are a good starting point. A *logical* starting point."

The fingers traveled farther south, exploring. Carla gasped at this inquisitive hand, thrusting her heavy bottom against her lover's body.

"I was sure they would find the deposit. One hundred thousand is a nice round figure. One sure to draw attention. Such a large sum. Appearing suddenly and unexplained in the midst of the paycheck deposits and car payments."

A thumb joined the fingers, ever so gently pinching the flesh between, over and over in quickening rhythm matched by Carla's bucking hips.

"I didn't need the money." Her voice was a mere whisper. "Only you." Her breath came in jagged hiccups. "Only you."

"You're sweet." Her lover's voice was calm and in control. "But it was important that you receive it, nonetheless."

The quickening fingers orchestrated her response. Like a skilled conductor, they led her. Adjusting the pace of her movements. Slowing then hurrying.

"Ahhh."

"Important that it be visible, there in the records. A beginning. A direction. A motive."

"Yes." Carla's voice gasped encouragement. "Please, yes." Words beyond voluntary communication. "Oh God, please, yes." Words coming directly from her body, bypassing the language centers of her brain.

"A wild goose to be pursued. A focus that distorts the closer it's examined. Truth but lie. Fact but fiction."

"Yes, God, yes." Carla bucked and writhed wildly, gasping nonsense between quickening breaths. "Argh. Please. Don't... don't stop. Please."

Her body surrendered, moving uncontrollably. Only her lover's grip kept her from sizzling off the bed like water on a hot griddle. The strong arms wrapped about her, pinioning yet caressing. Freeing yet controlling.

"A red herring."

Carla no longer heard the words—or did not register them. Her mind, body, soul, and spirit focused on the sensation. "God, yes, yes, yes... Oh God. Yes!"

With one final mighty thrust, her body leaped into her lover's hand. Then the fingers stopped, leaving only ebbing pleasure.

As they left, her mind returned. She returned.

Her lover's fingers skittered upward, tickling Carla's gooseflesh and sending a shudder through her.

"Hmm," Carla murmured as the fingers came to rest on her neck, where they were joined by those of the other hand, two sets of fingers gently massaging from either side. "Hmm."

"A cul de sac." The fingers wrapped about her throat. "A *dead* end."

"A secretary?" Deacon said.

"A *senior* admin," Metternich corrected. "With seventeen years government service."

"Oh, an *experienced* secretary," Deacon said. "That's so much better. How did an administrative assistant gain access to level four classified materials?"

"You don't understand. Carla Ortiz was a GS-13 with high-levels of clearance going back to Bush."

"Carla Ortiz? The same scatterbrain that used to work for *me*?"

"She'd served on the House Intelligence committee," Metternich added. "We had no reason to believe she would be a risk."

"How did *any* admin gain access to level four?"

Metternich shrugged. "The workload expanded. More administrative responsibilities. Ms. Ortiz was a long-term, well-respected civil servant. Her clearances were on a par with mine. It was only natural to delegate more responsibilities her way. Given recent budgetary concerns, it was also a cost-cutting measure."

"More time for the scientists to science?" Deacon said. He'd heard the argument before. Pass off routine matters to the bureaucracy. It was usually an excuse for laziness — and usually resulted in secret projects no longer being secret.

"Precisely. And she was Latina," Metternich said.

"Excuse me?"

"New regulatory directive," Barzoon chimed in, his voice taking on the tenor of a bureaucratic memorandum. "Whenever possible, department heads are to increase involvement of women and minorities in high-profile or high-priority projects." He smiled. "Ms. Ortiz being a Hispanic woman, well ..."

"Two birds, one stone?" Deacon finished.

"Precisely," Barzoon said.

"So, what you're telling me," Deacon said to Metternich, "is that people are dying for the sake of political correctness."

"I wouldn't go so far as ..."

Barzoon raised his hand, cutting Metternich off. "I think Dr. Creel has a basic grasp of the situation."

Barzoon was a pompous ass, but he cut through the crap. Deacon had to give him that. "You said you *may* know the who. Why the may?"

"It's only supposition at this point," Barzoon said. "A large deposit in her savings account. One-hundred thousand dollars to be exact." His tailored shoulders rose. "Perhaps a rich uncle left it to her. Or maybe she won the lottery. It's being checked by the FBI."

"It's her," Metternich said. The director's writhing hands looked like squirming white worms. "And now that we know the *who*, it should be a simple matter of finding Ortiz and sweating information on her accomplice or accomplices."

Deacon thought the good doctor had seen too many episodes of *Law and Order*. He directed his question to Barzoon. "You've lost track of her?"

"She's taken a leave of absence. Cited some personal issue. The FBI and capitol police have staked out her apartment in South Laurel and her mother's home in Baltimore. They even have a car outside her brother's house in Kansas City. All those with access to level four are under surveillance. A lot of phones are tapped." Barzoon shrugged. "She hasn't shown in thirty-six hours."

"That's immaterial," Metternich said. "We'll find her. She'll turn up somewhere, she *has* to. Everything's under control."

"Then why am I here?" Deacon said.

Metternich ignored him. "We'll find her. We'll get to the bottom of it."

"Only if she hasn't passed it on to someone else," Deacon said, finger raised. "And only if she talks."

"The FBI assures me they'll get the information. Who she's working with? Who *they're* working for, and why?" Deacon thought Metternich's grinning teeth should have an apple between them. "I'm told there's an old adage in the bureau. Your own mother isn't safe when you're facing twenty to life at Leavenworth."

Definitely too much *Law and Order*. Or maybe *Dragnet*. "You're forgetting an older adage, Doctor."

"Oh?"

"Two can keep a secret, when one of them is dead."

"We have a preliminary meeting scheduled with the FBI for one-thirty this afternoon," Barzoon said.

Deacon rose from his chair. "Reschedule it for five-thirty."

"But time is crucial," Metternich said.

"Sleep is crucial, Doctor," Deacon said, buttoning his jacket. "Clear heads are crucial. She's already got a day-and-a-half head start. A few hours won't make much difference."

"But we ..."

Barzoon raised a restraining hand. "As you say, Dr. Creel. Guest quarters are on level two."

"I remember."

Chapter 5

It was early spring of last year. Outside, chill wind nipped the air and mist melted March snow into April slush. Inside, the restaurant was warm and cozy, the smell of wet pavement replaced by garlic and marinara.

Siranella's was six blocks off the harbor. Just a little Italian place. Nothing special about it. Except it was *their* place. And that made it special.

"Good evening, Dr. Creel. Or should I say Lieutenant Commander Creel."

"Evening, Michael. News travels fast in this town."

The maître d's return smile held a hint of mischief.

"Ms. Adams. Always a pleasure. Let me take your wrap."

"Thanks, Michael."

Liz Adams handed over her dripping coat, revealing a black, cold-shoulder cocktail dress, its hem showing plenty of the sexiest legs Deacon had ever seen. He got a chill as she shook out her short-cropped black hair, drops spattering his face. Enormous eyes smiled at him.

"Sorry," she said.

He smiled back, then handed his coat to the maître d.

"Right this way," Michael said.

Deke paused a moment to watch his lady's four-inch heels strut off. Then he followed.

They passed a small alcove near the fire.

"Can't have our usual table?" Deacon asked.

"I'm sorry, no. Not tonight, Doctor."

"But it's empty. Reservation?"

He heard Liz giggle.

"Not exactly," Michael said.

"Why not, then?"

The head waiter stopped, grinned his knowing grin, and waved his arm. "Not enough room."

Two chairs were still open at a table set for eleven. Deke recognized Stan Karnofsky from genetics seated with his wife, Sue. His neighbors, Lee and Pete, were seated next to them. Two more couples from the base were there, including Lisa Reilly and her partner, Ruth. Lisa was his officemate before his promotion bumped him up to a single. Her Asian features were from her Laotian mother, and her tall lean body from her shanty-Irish father. She was also Deacon's best friend. At the head of the table, replete in his best rumpled suit, was Josiah Metternich, his sweat-slicked face glistening in the candlelight.

Metternich rose and raised a martini glass in his chubby mitt. The rest of the table rose as well, faces smiling with genuine (and alcohol-induced) pleasure. "To Doctor Deacon Creel, our newest Lieutenant Commander and our newest project leader."

"Here, here," resounded across the table, along with hearty "Congrats" and "You deserve it."

"Ms. Adams set it up," Michael said.

Deke looked at Liz, his face still puzzled, hers beaming. She leaned close and kissed his cheek. "I love you," she whispered in his ear. Then she added, "Sorry I had to include Joe."

He kissed her back and shrugged. Then he mouthed, "I love you, too."

"Liz?"

"Hmm," she answered sleepily, drifting off in the bedroom of her Germantown apartment.

The digital clock said it was one thirty in the morning, zero-one-thirty in military time. Deacon lay looking at the ceiling, unable to sleep despite the half-dozen drinks he'd consumed. Too full of life and the future to close his eyes on the present, on tonight.

The air smelled of sweat and musk, the sweet perfume of their recent lovemaking. He could still feel the heat of it, a warm dampness blending with the warmth radiating from the body next to him, the body of the woman he loved.

"How many kids do you want to have?"

"That's putting the cart before the horse, isn't it," she muttered. "You haven't even asked me to marry you."

"I'm thinking three," he said. "A boy, a girl, and a surprise."

"You know of a third alternative?" Her voice was losing some of its sleep husk as she rose toward consciousness.

"You know," he answered, "that unplanned one. The one that happens after a New Year's Eve party, or when Samantha and Tommy are at their aunt Sherri's for the weekend."

"First of all, I detest New Year's parties, all those people trying to get as drunk as possible like it's an Olympic event. Secondly, my sister would not want to take the kids for the weekend." She yawned, turning onto her back. "Besides, I don't like the name Tommy — sounds common and a little juvenile."

"He will be a *kid*, you know."

"What else do you see in your crystal ball?"

"Well, I'm thinking we'll get a little cape cod in Four Corners or maybe Chevy Chase."

"Chevy Chase? Pricey."

"Some place with good schools but not too far from the metro."

"Got it all planned out, hmm?" There was a smile in her voice as she scrunched her bare shoulders into the pillow. "Will I be permitted to work in this dream world of yours?"

"Sure. Part-time, telecommuting, that kind of thing. But these won't be latch-key kids. They won't come home to an empty house. Or find their mother passed out ..."

"Shhh," Liz said, her hand entwining with his, fingers gently massaging out the memory. No one spoke for a moment, then Liz said simply, "Yes."

"Yes?"

"Mmm hmm." She kissed him, her lips were soft and a little salty. "But Tom is out."

"How about Tomàs? You know, with a Spanish flair."

"We'll see, señor. Now shut up and come here."

Deacon woke suddenly, a roar from the hallway jerking him upright and bringing back his headache. The din sounded like a vacuum, its bag in need of changing. The number five glowed from a bedside clock sitting on an institutional, guest-quarters end table. The cleaning crew, he thought. Right on time. Nothing had changed in a year. Government bureaucracy marches on. He smiled to the empty room. Then he remembered the dream, and his smile faded. One thing had changed. A year ago, he had Liz. A year ago, he had a future. Now? What now?

Chapter 6

Amy knocked on the door for the second time today. She'd arrived at Building 13 at quarter of five, not wanting to chance being late on her first day as — as what? Aide de camp? Who used that term anymore? And why her? She was a medic, not a gopher.

It wasn't her first time at Deidenbach — the world of military medical being a small one. She'd passed Building 13 before but never thought much of the drab, grey structure. Nor knew much about what went on inside. But after her orders had been checked twice in five minutes, by two different security guards, she figured it was something pretty hush hush. She'd found the man in charge, the same big shot who'd been on the plane. He'd sent her on a wild goose chase to guest quarters. Now she was back and in danger of tardiness.

"Come in," said the voice behind the door.

"Yes, Mr., ah ..."

"Barzoon. Please call me Nelson." He smiled up from his paperwork. "Did you get lost? I did at first. This place is like an iceberg, little above the surface but a rabbit warren below."

"He wasn't there, sir."

"Beg pardon?"

"Commander Creel. He wasn't in guest room 2A."

"Hmm." Barzoon looked at his watch. "Perhaps he's in the commissary. I suspect he'd be hungry by this time. The commissary is ..."

"I checked the commissary, sir. Commander Creel wasn't there."

Barzoon reached for the phone. "Perhaps he's with Dr. Metternich." He lifted a grey handset. "Hello, Joe? Nelse

Barzoon. Is Creel with you?... Because he isn't in guest quarters, that's why. ... No, we checked there." He smiled at Amy. "Fine."

Barzoon pressed the plunger, then a red button. "I'll have security locate him." He smiled again. "We had a ... shall we say *hectic* meeting. He may have gone for a walk to cool off, um, relax." His smile vanished like a wisp of smoke. "Hello? This is Mr. Barzoon. Locate Dr. Deacon Creel. Yes, Lieutenant Commander Creel. He came in with Director Metternich and myself this morning. ...He what?"

For the first time, Amy saw cracks in the man's unflappable façade.

"You *let* him? Never mind your excuses. Find him. ... Search the base, idiot!"

Barzoon slammed down the phone. Just like that, Mr. Cool was back, but with a strained quality to the ever-ready smile.

"It appears that Commander Creel left the premises." His eyes pierced into Amy's. "It may take a moment to locate him. Why don't you wait in the commissary?"

"Yes, sir."

Amy took the stairs down to the second floor, wondering what she was getting herself into. She pushed the exit bar and turned right. The commissary was at the end of this corridor, past a set of double doors. She'd be glad to get there for a jolt of caffeine. She thought of Nelson Barzoon. She'd had COs like that before and learned not to trust that Dr. Jekyll smile. Yes, a jolt of caffeine was what she needed. "Or maybe a stiff scotch" Her words and footsteps bounced off the bright linoleum, till only the echoes remained.

Pausing, she thought about her arrival at the base, showing her ID and orders at the gate. She remembered passing a 7-Eleven as she turned off Amber Drive. A second building was kitty-corner to the convenience store, a line of cars in the lot and a line of off-duty personnel crossing the street to their favorite afterwork destination, located within one hundred yards of the gate, just three-quarters of a mile from Building 13. Walking distance. Then she thought about Deacon Creel — Deke — and their first meeting. Her feet pivoted back to the stairwell for the trip to ground level.

"Guitars, Cadillacs" blaring from the juke fit the bar nicely, its twangy rhythms and hillbilly vocals bemoaning a desperate man trying to hang on. Although this was no dive the Terminator was likely to visit.

There was no smoky haze, except where the diehards puffed away outside the entrance. The linoleum was faded but clean, the woodwork likewise. Instead of bikers and country shit kickers, the room was dressed in camouflage and business casual.

Although darker and older, Woody's Place wasn't that different from the officer's club, the nearest tavern to Building 13 and her first stop. The long bar at the O club had been almost as crowded, although the music was softer and the patrons wore nicer clothes. After running the gauntlet of stares given uniformed noncoms entering officer's country, she'd discovered that a man fitting Deke's description had been there. He'd showed orders proving he was indeed a lieutenant commander, downed his officer's club two-drink maximum in the form of a double bourbon, left a ten spot, and departed.

There were no disapproving stares at Woody's, just a few leers. Instead of the young barman at the O Club, the innkeeper behind Woody's bar was grey and overweight, but still had the buzzcut and hoorah gravitas of an ex-marine.

"Woody?" Amy shouted over the noise.

"Woodrow Samples," drawled the large black man. "What's yours, darlin."

"Information."

Woody smiled. "I'm married, if that's what you're after." He held forth a gold ring that looked tiny on his meaty left hand. "But if I wasn't?" He winked.

"Damn," Amy said. "My bad luck. But how about a second question?"

"Shoot."

"I'm looking for a man."

Woody filled a beer mug as he nodded toward the crowded tavern. "Take your pick. You'll do alright."

"No. This guy is about six foot, lean, dark hair, steel-grey eyes. Thirty-five or so. Dressed in a grey suit. Have you seen him?"

"What's this about? You don't look like an MP."

"I'm not."

"Wife, girlfriend?"

Amy shook her head. "I'm his ... assistant."

"Would you settle for assisting me?" said a young sergeant standing next to her.

"Thanks, but no thanks." Amy kept looking at Woody. "Have you seen him?"

The beefy barman paused for a moment, then said, "Yeah, I seen him." He pointed to a back booth hidden from the rest of the room. "Came in about seventeen-thirty hours."

"Thanks."

"Hey, darlin?" Amy turned back to the bar. "See if you can get him to go home. He's had two doubles and two beers in the last hour. I'd cut him off, but it don't show on him. He just gets smiley and wisecracks."

"Thanks," Amy said.

Deacon was slumped against the varnished wood, hands on a beer mug. The tie was gone, his suit jacket balled into a corner of the booth. Put him in jeans and a hoodie and he wouldn't look that different from when she first saw him, except darkness now replaced indifference. His dark mole peeked from dark hair that drooped into eyes staring darkly at the opposite empty seat. A hint of five-o'clock shadow darkened his cheeks.

"Commander Creel?"

He just stared ahead and took a swig from the half-empty mug.

Amy raised her voice. "Dr. Creel, sir?"

He drained the mug.

"Deke?"

He raised his glass to get the attention of the barmaid. Then he saw Amy. At first his eyes popped, as if he were seeing a ghost. Then reality returned with a weak smile.

"Specialist Robbins." He raised a forefinger. "Correction, Fleet Marine Force Specialist Robbins. How good of you to join me." He wasn't slurring, but he had the unmistakable tone of someone diving into the tank.

"Hello, Commander."

He held his finger up again. "Deke. That's an order, Specialist Robbins."

"Yes, sir, Deke." Amy smiled.

Deke pointed to the empty bench opposite him. "Please, have a seat." He again raised his empty glass. "Allow me to get you a libation."

"We should be going, Deke. You're late for your meeting."

He shook his head. "Meetings, meetings, meetings. How I missed meetings." He sniggered. "I'd tell them to go jump off a bridge with their meeting, but they'll most likely be doing that on their own soon enough." The grin died as he tried to gulp beer from the empty glass. Holding the mug over his head again, he shouted, "Jazzelle."

An attractive black girl of maybe twenty-one approached the table. Her features suggested she was some iteration of Woody.

"Another round for me. Double Makers and a Miller draft." His eyes pierced Amy's. "What will Specialist Robbins be having?"

"I'm fine," she said to Jazzelle.

"Nonsense," Deacon said. "I insist."

Amy didn't want to make a scene, so she smiled at the waitress. "Scotch and water." She held her thumb and fore finger a smidgeon apart for scotch and several inches for water.

"Single malt," Deacon said. "The best for Marine Force Specialist Robbins."

Jazzelle looked toward her father with question-mark eyes. Amy met the barkeep's gaze and nodded reassuringly. Woody paused before nodding back. Jazzelle saw the private exchange and hurried off.

"Don't worry about the cost," Deacon whispered. "I'm out of money anyway, so we might as well drink the best." She recognized the screw-'em grin she'd seen on the C130.

"Just one for the road. Okay, Deke?"

"The long road back," he said. "Back to the world where everything is spic and span on the surface, purulent underneath. One big pus pocket waiting to be lanced." He wiped his hands as if trying to erase a stain. "Where are those drinks? Jazzelle! Ah, there you are."

The waitress put the drinks on the table and met Amy's eyes. "Thank you," Amy said, her smile again reassuring that she'd handle it.

Deacon sipped his bourbon and cannonballed some beer.

"We better be getting back, Deke."

He nodded too vociferously. "Back. Back to the adding machine. The bureaucracy that adds up the body count then sticks a price tag on it." He gulped more beer. "Government efficiency."

She placed a hand on his. "Let's go, Deke."

He held her hand tenderly, then shook it off as if she were on fire. "Not yet. Can't go until I tell you a little story. A little tale about government efficiency." He sipped more liquor. "Not so long ago in a land not so far away." He drank more beer. "About a half mile. That's not far, is it?"

Amy shook her head.

"There was a not so young, not quite middle-aged man who shall remain nameless. He'd joined a hush hush little group with an unlucky title. He was a newly minted gold-leaf Commander who had served his country and had worked his way to a position of authority in the unlucky little group, a group built around truth, justice, and the American way. His parents were gone, but he had his work. And he was soon to be married to a woman who made the sun rise and set." Mist formed behind his steel-blue eyes. "Then he learned that the whole thing was a monstrous scam."

He gulped more liquor. "Our tale begins, or maybe ends, in the spring. The blossoms are in bloom. The world is rife with new life and new possibilities. Our not so young not so old hero is moving into new quarters that fit his new station." He knocked back the rest of the bourbon. "Yes, new possibilities. The world was his oyster. But there were no pearls in it. Only swine."

Deacon leaned back with a sigh and began his story ...

Chapter 7

Once upon a time less than a year ago, I was moving into my new digs. I heard knocking on my office door and looked up from the books I was placing on the shelf. A familiar soul was leaning in the doorway; a tall Asian woman in service khakis wagging her butch-cut head in disapproval.

"Still not moved in, Commander? This will reflect poorly on your fitness report," she said.

"As you were, Lieutenant. No need to salute me indoors."

Both she and I laughed.

"How's it hanging, Lisa? Have a nice weekend?"

"Okay, although Ruth has been on the rag about that trip to see her folks. I keep telling her that I need to clear leaves in advance. This isn't Walmart where you can just call in sick for a few days."

"She's still mad about that?"

"That and getting married."

I slid a copy of *Medical Aspects of Biological Warfare* next to *Modern Epidemiology*, then moved the second book to a higher shelf. "When *are* you two going to tie the knot?"

"I don't know. The way she nags I feel like I'm already married. Nice party on Friday. Were you really surprised?"

"Yep. Ms. Adams got me good."

"When are *you* two going to tie the knot?"

"Oh..." I placed *Entomology in Human and Animal Health* on the middle shelf. "As soon as I pick up the ring from the jeweler next week. And we set the date, of course."

"You son of a bitch." Lisa ran over and hugged me. "Congratulations! You popped the old question Friday night in between nooky."

"Don't be crude."

Lisa punched the shoulder of my khaki shirt. "I said nooky, not screwing. Was she surprised?"

"I suspect she suspected."

"Why don't you bring Herr Metternich along when you slip her the ring? That'd really surprise her." She shook her head. "That bad penny shows up everywhere."

"Let's cut Joe a little slack, okay?"

"Since when?"

I shrugged. "Maybe it's the promotion." Three more texts filled a gap on the top shelf. "Anyway, I think we're too hard on him. He's just doing his job."

"And making ours more difficult." She scrunched her face as if behind thick glasses, then mimicked our boss's nasal drone. "Let's have another meeting, people. Staff meetings, diversity meetings, conflict of interest meetings. Him and his meetings, a bunch of liberal, bureaucratic, bullshit time wasters."

I wagged a finger her way. "Remember the rule, no politics. Let's not turn this into a hostile work environment."

"Since when do you care about that, Commander Pacifist." Lisa crossed her arms. "That's something you don't see in the military every day — a pacifist war hero."

"Uniformed service," I corrected. "I wear the uniform, but don't think of myself as military. And I'm not a hero."

"They gave you a medal."

"That was reflex not bravery. Anyway, what about you? A conservative lesbian minority?"

Lisa laughed as her butt hit my desk. "That's probably why we get along so well. Two odd ducks in the same PC pond."

I slid the last book into an empty spot in the bookcase. "Anyhow, let's go easy on the big guy. He can't help it if he likes meetings — or has an odd personality."

"Odd personality? How about *no* personality? His parents must have excised it along with his foreskin. Speaking of meetings, we better get a wiggle on, or we'll miss the ten o'clock."

I dusted my hands and grabbed a legal pad. "What's this one about?"

"Big wig from industry gonna talk about some new drug." She glanced down the hall. "Speaking of big wigs, here comes Der Fuhrer. See you there."

"Good morning, Joe," she said as she left.

"Morning, Lisa." Josiah Metternich filled the doorway. He pointed at his watch. "Don't forget the ten o'clock meeting."

"On my way." Lisa's voice followed her footsteps down the hall.

Metternich turned to me. "Morning, Deacon. Lovely party Friday. Quite lovely. Thank you and Elizabeth for inviting me."

"Our pleasure, Joe." I looked at my watch. "Well, I better be off. Don't want to be late for the meeting."

"I'll walk down with you," Metternich said, patting me on the back. "Pay very close attention today, Deacon. Dr. Witt will be presenting very interesting new data. Data that will be of special interest to the unit." He patted my shoulder again, like a fat Father Flannigan at Boys Town. "And special interest to the new project you will be starting."

"New project?"

Metternich smiled. "To go with your new promotion. Yes, very interesting indeed. I think project-leader Creel will find it quite interesting."

The second-floor lecture hall was small as such places went — no more than a large conference room. But this morning it was packed full of khaki and white coats sitting in several dozen theater seats and standing in the back, all staring from the darkness at a well-lit podium. Metternich was seated to one side of the dais, nodding with interest as Dr. Harlan Witt held court. Witt was a balding man of late-fifties vintage. He had the same pale complexion as Metternich, suggesting long hours in artificial light. But his face had more character, as well as an intelligence and kindliness that Joe's could not duplicate.

"Alzheimer's disease is the most common form of dementia," Witt said, "accounting for twenty-four million cases worldwide. Approximately five percent of these have so-called early-onset disease, sapping the cognitive function from those as young as thirty years of age. These many millions of lost years of quality life are the true tragedy of AD."

"And a *true* jackpot for Snyder Labs," Lisa whispered, "if they can come up with a cure."

"Shh," I said. "I want to hear this."

Lisa snapped off a fake salute but kept her mouth shut.

My maternal grandmother had had dementia. I still recalled my shock the first time I ran to hug her only to have her say, "'Who are you, young man?"

"At its simplest," Witt continued, "AD is a disease of failed repair. Amyloid and tau proteins are found in normal brain tissue, but microglial cells scavenge these particles before they form protein bundles known as plaques, and brain-cell tangles that block neurotransmitters. It is the buildup of protein plaques and dendritic tangles that leads to the progressive nature of this insidious disease." With a click, a microscopic image of brain cells filled the screen. "Note the moth-eaten appearance of the many plaques and tangles in this brain tissue."

Another click and the screen filled with the familiar X-shape of a chromosome, one of the twenty-three little wonders that determine who and what we are.

"As with all diseases, Alzheimer's is associated with genetic patterns, although it would be more appropriate to call these genetic miscues. Errors at certain gene loci change a predisposition for the disease to an active case of dementia." He sipped water from a nearby glass. "Not all the genes responsible for AD are known, but early onset disease has been genetically mapped to two loci termed presenility genes one and two." His laser bounced back and forth, then steadied on chromosome fourteen. "Presenility-1 is the most common cause of early onset disease, accounting for up to half of all inherited cases."

The laser cut out and he faced his audience again, his gentle features haloed in the glow of the podium light. "This genetic information holds the hope for new and promising cures for this devastating illness, although none have been developed." His angelic features took on a devilish grin. "Until now."

"Cup of coffee, Harlan?" Metternich asked.

"Thank you, no, Joe. Caffeine and I have parted company."

"Deacon?"

"Thank you, Dr. Metternich."

"Black, isn't it?" Joe handed me a cup.

Metternich's office was as organized as its occupant was

rumpled. Everything was well ordered and tidy. There were no piles of papers or open texts. Books lined the shelves, neatly arranged along with photos of exotic places and a framed service award. Administration took place here, not science.

"Well, Deacon, my boy. What did you think of the lecture?"

"Interesting," I replied. "Very interesting. Fascinating in fact. One of the most promising AD treatments I've heard of. You and your people are to be congratulated, Dr. Witt."

"I would agree," Metternich said. He smiled his most becoming smile — something approximating the leer of an adolescent boy finding his first *Playboy*. "I've asked Dr. Creel to join us, Harlan, to discuss your little, um, shall we say problem?"

"Problem?" I asked.

"Let's say, rather, challenge." Witt smiled and folded his hands on his lap. "As I said during the lecture, we are quite excited about the possibilities associated with SL606. For the first time, there is a drug targeting the specific gene locus associated with early-onset disease. Phase I clinical studies in severely afflicted Alzheimer's patients have delayed progression by years and ..." He leaned forward, his voice more animated. "And, in two cases, have actually reversed the process, providing cognitive improvement that continued for weeks."

"But?" I asked.

Witt's shoulders slumped. "But, in both those instances, recovery was hampered by certain, well, side effects."

"What sort of side effects?"

"Well, as I said, SL606 binds to the Presenility-1 gene, thereby turning off production of amyloid protein. Natural repair mechanisms then begin to clean up accumulated plaques, and in some cases even dendritic tangles. It is quite remarkable."

"What side effects?" I repeated.

"Well, we have discovered that this binding site abuts another important gene locus. One directly involved with the fundamental urge for self-preservation. Therefore, as the patient improves, as cognition returns, so does self-awareness. With awareness of self and ..." He pointed around the room. "And of those around you, of, well, life in general, with this awareness comes thoughts of, shall I say ideation associated with ..."

"Suicide?" I'm sure my voice rose an octave. "Are you telling me they committed suicide?"

"In both cases," Witt said.

"How? What method?"

"Does it matter?" Metternich said.

"It was very disappointing," Witt said, shoulders slumping. "Devastating for the family members. To see the spark return to a loved one's eyes, then to have that spark extinguished at their own hand."

"Yes," I said. "I can imagine." I sipped my coffee, which was as bitter as thoughts of suicide. "But what does this have to do with me, with Unit 13?"

Witt pointed to Metternich. "I asked Joe to read a paper I've been working on, one which details our success and failure. He suggested that this might be a good area where we can cross-pollinate."

"Cross-pollinate?"

"Yes," Witt continued. "The possibility of a cooperative venture between industry and government."

"But why Unit 13?"

"For two reasons," Metternich said. "First, drug delivery."

"I'm not sure I understand."

"SL606 does not cross the blood-brain barrier," Witt said. "The protective, fatty layer that keeps most drugs and organisms from entering the central nervous system. We currently have been administering the drug via spinal puncture, placing it directly into the cerebrospinal fluid thereby bypassing the blood-brain barrier." He threw up his palms, which looked soft as veal. "That's fine for a phase I trial on terminal patients, but hardly amenable to larger-scale studies, or general therapy for that matter."

"This is an area where the unit's work could be quite useful," Metternich said. "Plasmids and other methods that are used to enhance the infectivity of certain biowarfare agents might be amenable to solving that problem. Perhaps piggybacking 606 onto a genetically modified virus or bacterium." His self-satisfied smile did not improve the adolescent leer.

"Fine," I said, putting down my cup. "I grant you that might be possible. But I don't see how that addresses the suicidal side effect. Or why Unit 13 would have a stake in this."

Metternich's smile vanished, replaced by a pompous academic scoff. "I'm surprised at you, Commander. Surely you must see the potential here."

I looked at both faces, then shrugged.

Metternich leaned in closer. "Deacon. Although SL606 holds promise as a cure for early-onset Alzheimer's Disease, perhaps all AD, this side effect also holds other, shall we say, more sinister possibilities." His voice dropped. "Consider, Commander Creel, what would happen if this drug were given to a healthy individual? One with normal cognitive ability?"

"SL606 would still bind to the gene locus," Witt said, "even though there was no abnormal protein to defend against. The binding would likewise turn off the adjacent SP-alpha, the gene linked to self-preservation." He raised the shoulders of his blue suit. "The target individual would then have ideation similar to that experienced by our test subjects."

"A suicide drug," Metternich said. "In the wrong hands, such would be a deadly weapon — an assassin's dream."

"But surely," I said, "getting someone to sit still for a spinal tap would be more difficult than slipping them poison — or a bullet to the head."

Metternich shook me off. "Delivery is a temporary obstacle. One which can, and will, be overcome. That does not concern me at the moment. My bigger concern is the potential as a biowarfare agent."

He leaned back, his smug grin returning. "We at Unit 13 are in the business of defending against such threats."

Pale thumbs twiddled over vested belly. "We blue sky such problems at *higher* levels."

He nodded toward me. "As you know. Various 'what if' scenarios. What would be possible? What would be likely?"

He leaned forward and pointed. "I believe this suicide drug would be both possible *and* likely."

His bulk resumed its slouch, his thumbs their twiddle. "I think I can convince my superiors of that. And ..." His finger rose toward heaven or maybe upper management. "This is an opportunity to ease the development of a life-saving new medication *while* serving our mission of protecting the public from biological threats."

He nodded. "Quite the feather in my, um, our caps. Win, win, win."

"I see," I said. "So, where do I come in? Do I pursue drug delivery?" Once again, pale hands waved me off.

"Don't concern yourself with that. As I said, delivery is a minor problem. One that other members of the unit can tackle. Your skills, my good Dr. Creel, are best directed at the larger issue. How do we divorce binding at the presenility site from that at the site for self-preservation?" He smiled. "How do we keep the marriage between 606 and PS-1, while annulling the bigamy with SP-alpha?"

"Nicely put, Joe."

Metternich beamed gratitude at Witt, then looked expectantly at me. "Build your team, my boy. Select whomever you like."

"Anyone?"

"Within reason. I'll clear it with the bureaucracy. But keep the number small. This is a need-to-know basis."

"Someone from Snyder should be there," Witt said.

"Naturally," Metternich said. "I'll arrange the clearance. We'll need someone from security as well."

"Security?" I asked.

"As I said, the potential threat from this agent is considerable. Secrecy is paramount."

I was still naive enough to find this strange. "Everyone at Unit 13 has top clearances, Dr. Metternich. That's about as secure as you can get."

"Be that as it may. You and your team will be on this full time."

It was clear that I was being dismissed, so I rose to leave.

"I want weekly progress reports," Metternich said.

I nodded.

"This is important work, Commander. Work that could land you an excellence award." He pointed to the plaque on his own wall. "Maybe even an eagle on your collar." The adolescent boy was back. "I have every confidence in you, my lad. Don't let me down."

I didn't know then that I was letting myself down.

Chapter 8

PROGRESS REPORT
Project Annulment: Week 8
Team Members:
Deacon Creel, U13 – Project leader
Lisa Reilly, U13 – Microbiology
Stanley Karnofsky, U13 – Genetics
Julia Sweeny, Snyder Laboratories, Molecular biology division
Baxter McCloud, U13 – Site security

Summary

As reported previously, this work has utilized the rodent model developed by Snyder Laboratories. In summary, Snyder genetically engineered a knockout strain of rats that replicate the suicidal behaviors of the drug in people. Rats receiving SL606 rapidly develop abnormal behaviors, including repeated head ramming, gnawing at cage wire, and obsessive consumption of undigestible bedding. In all cases, death has occurred within six days. Electron microscopy following necropsy confirm that the cause of these self-destructive behaviors is drug binding to the self-preservation gene, SP-alpha.

The Unit 13 efforts at removing this adverse effect continue to build on previous weeks, following two different avenues of approach.

(1)   Drs. Sweeny and Karnofsky and their team continue to explore methods of shortening the SL606 molecule to limit binding solely to the presenility gene, PS-1. However, this approach has not (as of yet) made significant progress due to the

close proximity of the PS-1 and SP-alpha codons. All efforts at shortening the molecular structure of SL606 have neither removed the suicidal events nor maintained drug efficacy. Cell-line cultures continue to express long-chain amyloid protein, suggesting that the shortened form of the drug would no longer be effective for treating Alzheimer's disease.

(2)   Drs. Creel and Reilly, et al., continue work to develop a protective molecule that binds to SP-alpha without triggering suicidal ideation. Initial experiments are promising. Knockout rats treated with the protective molecule (dubbed Creel-1) prior to SL606 administration develop no self-destructive behaviors. Unfortunately, the current form of Creel-1 likewise destroys the efficacy of SL606, so that additional work is needed before it would be a useful adjunct to SL606 therapy. However, Creel-1 does appear to provide protection from malevolent deployment of SL606 for criminal or biowarfare purposes.

Metternich dropped the folder among the uncharacteristic clutter on his desk, the shine in his eyes mirroring the sheen off his greasy skin.

"Excellent, Deacon. More than I could have hoped at this stage."

"Thank you, Joe." I actually felt warmed by the praise despite the pig-faced prig delivering it. "It's just preliminary. Much more work is needed before Creel-1 is ready for human studies. And considerably more work before it can be used to make SL606 a viable treatment."

"But in Creel-1," Metternich said, "we have the beginnings of a biodefense agent. A vaccine as it were to protect against accidental or deliberate exposure to 606."

"A *preliminary* one, perhaps. If 606 were ever weaponized, that is."

"Outstanding. How did you manage it?" Metternich seemed truly surprised and equally impressed. "Snyder has been working on this for months and weren't any closer than when they started. They were considering junking the whole thing, going back to formula and starting over before I suggested our little cross-pollination."

Believe it or not, I felt my face warm with the praise. "Well, I think they were too close to the problem. I saw it with fresh eyes. Snyder was focused on an agent that would stop the side effect while maintaining the efficacy of 606. When you..."

Metternich cut me off before I let the cat out of the bag. "Truly excellent, my boy."

"Thanks, Joe. There are still production issues, of course."

I leaned back, crossing my legs. Maybe it was the praise, but I'd begun to relax around Metternich. To think of him more as a colleague, not quite a friend but less of an adversary. As I said, I was still naive.

"Creel-1 is difficult to synthesize," I said, "We used up the initial sample in the rodent studies. And there's still the drug administration problem. We've been giving both SL606 and Creel-1 to rats intrathecally, injecting it directly into the spinal fluid. But the molecule is small enough that we should be able to attach it to something that gets into the central nervous system naturally, perhaps a modified encephalitis virus."

"That's being worked on, my boy. That's being worked on." Metternich snatched up the folder, his eyes delving deeper into the report.

"Well, if that's all, Joe. I better get back to work."

"Yes, don't let me keep you. Oh, Deacon?"

I turned back from the doorway.

"Are all these files in central records?"

"Not yet. We've only just identified the agent. I wanted to make sure we were onto something before formalizing things. I'd like to run another test first."

"Later, my boy. Later. For now, make sure I receive copies of all files and computerized data. I'd like to go over them at my leisure. And one can never have too many backups, not for something of this importance."

"Alright, Joe." His eagerness should have been a warning bell but, like I said.

I started leaving again when he called out.

"By the way, I want you to know that I've put you up for an excellence award. A well-deserved award, I might add."

"Thank you, Joe. Always nice to be recognized. But the rest of the team?"

"Oh, they'll be taken care of as well." He changed to a fatherly tone. "You know, my boy, it's not just the recognition. The award comes with a twenty-five-hundred-dollar stipend, which I'm sure a recently engaged fellow would find useful."

I returned his smile. "Yes, indeed, sir."

"And, um, Deacon?"

"Sir?"

"I might not be able to find that eagle I promised you. But I'm almost certain I can change that gold oakleaf on your collar to silver."

"So, von Ribbentrop was pleased?"

Lisa Reilly stood in my office, looking long and lean in her khakis. I often thought it a waste that her taut body was reserved for women, although I doubted Ruth felt that way.

"Yes indeed."

"Pleased? Or *very* pleased?"

I shoved a pile of folders away from the edge of my desk and leaned against it. "I'd say very, very pleased. Pleased enough to hand me an excellence award *and* the hat of a full commander."

"Lah ti fuckin' dah," Lisa said. "Did you happen to mention that your brilliance was aided and abetted by others?"

I placed a hand on my chin. "Hmm. I can't remember, I might have said *something*."

She punched my shoulder. "And?"

"And, Joe said, and I quote, 'They'll be taken care of.'"

"What does that mean?"

"I don't know, but I suspect more green in the pay envelope." I tapped the folders into some semblance of a stack. "Maybe a promotion or two. Depends on Joe's mood on any given day."

"Now you're talking," Lisa said. "Imagine if we'd done something really important."

Lisa is naturally a naysayer, but her off-hand dismissal took me by surprise. I put down the folders. "How so?"

"I mean, we've only identified an agent that protects *animals* against the side effects of a *human* drug while also *deactivating* that drug. You'd get the same result from not giving the drug in the first place."

She had a good point, but I was still high on praise and promotion. I shrugged. "It's a first step."

"Yeah, but you know as well as I do that first steps in drug development are often last steps. Journals like *Science* and *Nature* are full of promising new treatments every month. How many of them pan out?" She plopped into one of my institutionally grey metal chairs. "We've still got to refine Creel-1 so that it allows 606 to do its thing without Biggy Rat bashing his little brains out. Something that Snyder Labs has failed to do. Then we have to duplicate the same thing in people." She raised a finger. "Hoping that we haven't introduced new and even more fascinating side effects."

"Your skepticism is probably what makes you a good scientist, but it also makes you a pain in the ass."

"It's a gift. Why is Himmler so hot on this anyway? I mean, *another* AD drug under development?"

"A *promising* new AD drug." I shot her with a finger gun.

She shot me back. "Big whup. That and three-fifty buys you a latte. You think Joe has stock in Snyder Labs?"

Lisa had a way of taking the wind out of my sails, and I wasn't in the mood to listen. Instead of following her reasoning, I was looking for rationalizations.

"I know that the higher-ups are constantly looking for threats to guard against. How else are they going to increase funding for this place?" I raised my palms like a new blackjack dealer. "No threats, no Unit 13. I sat in on one of their *emerging issues* blue-sky sessions once."

"When was this?"

"A few weeks back. Joe invited me."

"Hanging out with the hoi polloi?"

"You aren't kidding. There was an undersecretary of defense, a brand-new congressman from the intelligence committee named Waters, a captain from Naval Intelligence, a high-profile woman from Homeland Security..."

"Who?"

"Cathleen Harris. Know her?"

"No, but I'd like to." Lisa's face lit up. "I saw her once on Fox. I'd like to take a swing at that."

"I didn't know she swang your way."

"I hear she's a switch hitter. Not to mention on everybody's short list for everything from attorney general to VP. But I digress. Continue."

I carried the folders behind my desk. "We spent two hours kicking over ideas."

"What kind of ideas?"

"What have we been talking about? Threats. *Emerging* threats. How likely is another outbreak of Spanish flu? Could it be weaponized by someone? Have we adequately protected the mail system from anthrax? How might bugs be better formulated to increase virulence and deliverability? On and on, ad nauseum, to infinity and beyond."

"Your tax dollars at work," Lisa said.

"They seemed to get most excited when an idea had PR legs."

"Meaning?"

"Something that captured the imagination of the media, and therefore the public."

"And therefore, funding?"

"Exactly. Alien organisms. New and more deadly forms of sexually transmitted infection."

"Kinky."

"This kind of thing must be right up their alley. A drug that causes the recipient to ... skreek." I cut my hand across my throat in a universal gesture. "A terrorist's dream."

"Or an assassin's," Lisa said.

"Hmm. That's just what Metternich said two months ago." Another warning bell that I ignored.

Lisa's lanky frame unfolded from the chair. "Well, such pleasant speculation has given me an appetite. Now that you are on the fast track to fame and fortune, what say you buy me lunch?"

"I'm your man. Just give me one minute." I walked the folders into the outer office. "Hey, Carla?"

"Yes, Dr. Creel."

"Please, Deke will do."

Carla Ortiz smiled. She was one of those women whom other women said would be really attractive if she lost the weight. I wondered if maybe that was why she was pushing forty and never married, or so office scuttlebutt opined. She'd just transferred to Unit 13 and was eager to please.

"Do me a favor and make photocopies of these. Then sign them back into the records vault."

"Right away, sir, I mean Deke." She had a pretty smile.

Lisa and I headed toward the commissary. "Oh, one more thing," I said, turning back. "Dr. Metternich has another file that will need to be copied and filed." I tapped the papers I'd just placed on Carla's desk. "It's in a folder like these, with the grey stripes."

"You bet, Deke. Right after lunch."

Liz raised her champagne glass. "To Commander Deacon Creel, the smartest, handsomest, most successful man in uniformed service."

There was no crowded table this night. No rounds of "here here" or "he's a jolly good fellow." This was a private celebration in our own special place. In fact, as the evening wore on, the small, midweek crowd at Siranella's had dwindled so that we were enjoying a cozy corner of what amounted to a private dining room. Liz was resplendent in a little black dress, a pearl enhancer glistening in the cleavage. The air was rife with the sharp smell of the guttering candle, the musk of her perfume, and the heady scent of the evening's possibilities.

"You forget sexiest," I said, taking her hand.

"That title requires a demonstration." She leaned across the table and kissed me.

"You don't know by now?"

"Well, it's one of those things in need of repetition. Let's call it continuing education, like keeping up with your journals." She pouted. "And I'm afraid you've been delinquent in that department lately.

I strummed my thumb along her satin skin. "Hmm. You're right of course. Practice makes perfect?"

"Precisely. Now you pay the check, and I'll take you home for a refresher course."

"What about dessert?"

"There's whipped cream in the fridge."

I check-marked the server as the insistent tone of a cell phone filled the air.

"You or me?" Liz asked.

"Me, I think." I recognized the number. "You better have a good reason for disturbing my dinner, Lieutenant." I held my hand over the phone and mouthed, "Lisa."

"Sorry, Deke. Hope I'm not interrupting your dessert," the voice on the phone said.

"Actually, we were just heading home for dessert." I winked at Liz.

"Whipped cream or Hershey's syrup?"

I had to laugh. "We may have been suite mates too long. What's up?"

"You asked me to remind you about that NIH meeting tomorrow in Bethesda."

"Is that tomorrow?"

"Oh-eight-thirty. Building 32. You're representing the unit, remember? Giving that talk for Herr Metternich. Remember?"

"Shit."

"Is that commanderial language?"

"No, it's what you say when something slipped your mind and you're looking at an early morning and seventy minutes of rush-hour traffic."

"Looks like you'll have to limit yourself to one helping of dessert. Use the whipped cream, it cleans up easier."

"F you."

"Aye, aye, sir. Don't do anything I wouldn't do."

"Not much danger of that. Thanks for reminding me about the lecture, Leese."

"De nada. Enjoy."

"What was the 'shit' and 'eff you' about?" Liz asked.

"Oh, nothing. Just something I say now and again."

"Nice."

I laid my credit card next to the bill, then signaled for the server. "Okay if we make a stop on the way back?"

"On your one night off?"

"I know. We haven't been able to spend much time together lately."

"Between your work and my schedule, I feel like I hardly see you. Is this what it's going to be like after were married?"

"Only if you start nagging." I kissed her. Not a fix for everything but always a pleasure. "Seriously, just one stop. I promise I'll make it up to you."

Now Liz kissed me — hard and deep. "I'm going to hold you to that promise, sir."

Her 'sex' voice made my heart race as it always did. "Tonight, I'm yours to command."

"Hmm. I like the sound of that."

"I just need to make a quick stop at the office for something."

"Something for your bumper-to-bumper drive tomorrow?"

"Yeah. Forgot I was giving a talk for Herr, ah, I mean Joe, in the morning. I have to be at NIH by eight-thirty."

"I thought you had a photographic memory?"

"I've been a little distracted lately." We kissed again. "And I'm better with visual stuff than meeting times. For example, the panties you're wearing are black with pink flowers in the white-lace waistband. I noticed when you got dressed this morning."

"I'm afraid your photographic memory has failed you again." She smiled. "I'm not wearing any panties."

"I'll make it a *really* quick stop." The server dropped the bill and thanked us.

"So, what are we stopping for?"

"I need to pick up the memory stick with the presentation on it." I signed the receipt and took my copy. "Me and my photographic memory could recite the whole thing for them, but they seem to prefer visual aids."

"So do *you*." Liz crossed her legs, the hem of her short skirt riding up.

My heart rate increased to feline proportions. "A really, really quick stop."

We stood before the security camera, waiting for the buzz. Then eleven steps on grey ceramic tile brought us to a reception desk bathed in the sterile glow of fluorescent light.

"Good evening, Dr. Creel. What brings you by this evening?" The civilian guard monitoring the security cameras noticed Liz's short dress and smiled, not too subtly I thought. "Ma'am."

"I just need to pick up something from my office, Tom. Sorry, I don't have my badge."

"That's alright sir. Just sign in, please." I signed the register and received a temporary security badge. "I'm afraid you'll have to stay up here, ma'am."

"We're only going down to two, Tom."

"Sorry, Dr. Creel. You know the rules. Only authorized personnel after six p.m. Sorry, ma'am."

"I feel like I'm at least seventy-five with all this ma'am-ing"

"Sorry, ah ..."

"Liz," Ms. Adams said, the dimples on her cheeks bringing a blush to young Tom's.

"Ah, okay, Liz. Have a seat. Can I get you anything? Coffee?"

"No thanks."

"I won't be long," I said. "Why don't you read a magazine?"

Liz scanned the rack as Tom scanned her legs. "Hmm. *Biology Today*, *Science*. How *will* I choose?"

I smiled. Liz was one of the brightest tax attorneys at The Treasury Department, but she had trouble understanding WebMD. "Sorry there's no *American Law and Economics*."

"How about *People*?"

I gave her a peck. "I'll be back in a few."

My footsteps echoed through the stairwell leading to sub-two. Without the swell of humanity and their chattering voices, the building took on a whole new feeling, a darker, more sinister quality. In the quiet of the night, the work we did hung in the air like the silence of the grave. It wasn't that long ago that these offices and laboratories were involved in planning for World War III, the bugs invented here key weapons in the cold war. Unit 13 was now tasked with combatting threats rather than creating them. Still, the hairs on my neck tickled as I descended.

The first swipe of the key card produced only a red flicker from the lock plate. After two more tries and a mild curse, the green light lit with a click. Another eighteen steps and I was at the admin station that served the four offices in this section. Rummaging for keys, I noted a familiar folder in plain sight on Carla's desk. If the grey stripes didn't give it away, the Top Secret stamped in red did.

"Jeez, Carla." I shook my head. "You're a senior admin, you're supposed to know better." I snatched up the confidential folder. "I'll have to have a little talk with Ms. Ortiz."

Once inside my office, I grabbed the memory stick from

the desk drawer and put the folder in its place. I paused after closing the drawer, then locked it for good measure. I locked my office door as well. In five quick minutes, I was back beside Liz.

"All set?" she asked.

"Let's go."

I grabbed her arm, but she shook off my hand, lacing hers around the sleeve of my jacket.

"What's the rush. We've got all night."

My heart beat fast again, thoughts of Carla Ortiz and misplaced files all but forgotten.

"Enjoy your evening," Tom said, signing me out.

I smiled, not knowing that joy would soon be a thing of the past.

Chapter 9

I threw my jacket on the chair and yawned. It was one of those days that made me realize I wasn't a kid anymore.

"You just getting back?" Lisa's long lines leaned in the doorway. Today, like me, she was dressed in civilian clothes, grey slacks replacing her khakis.

"Yep." I slumped into my chair. "Did you know Joe was going to be at that lecture?"

"Today's lecture?"

I nodded.

"At NIH? Herr Metternich?"

"Yep. I'm setting up and I glance at the crowd. There's Bunsen Honeydew smiling at me."

"I thought he had a staff meeting."

"That was this afternoon. I know this because he dragged me to it."

"I see," Lisa said. "So why did he have *you* give the lecture?"

"Beats the hell out of me."

"You think he wanted to see how you'd do? A test?"

"He's seen me lecture before."

Lisa placed thumbs in imaginary suspenders. "Maybe he was showing you off — his boy wonder. Lectures, staff meetings, rubbing elbows with the rich and famous."

"Three *hours* talking about budgets, yearly projections, funding gaps. Not to mention having lunch with him."

"Lunch too?"

"At the U club. Me, him, and Director Swensen. God, I hate chicken cordon rubber."

"Looks like someone is being groomed for bigger things." She puckered her lips. "Kiss, kiss, kiss."

"Don't you have something to do?"

"I do. Just wanted to check how things went." She held out a folder. "I also thought you might want to see the results of the pharmacokinetic study."

I took the manila cardboard. "Anything interesting?"

Lisa shrugged. "Creel-1 fits a standard two-compartment metabolic model. Classic liver conjugation and urinary excretion. Peak plasma concentration in six hours, eighteen-hour half-life. It's all in there." She pointed. "Still doesn't get it into the central nervous system though."

I imitated Joe's pompous squeak. "That's being worked on, my boy."

"Herr Director said that?"

I tapped my nose.

"I thought we were the only ones working on this problem. You know, with Stan and Sweeny."

I kept my nose buried in the metabolism report. "This may come as a surprise to you, but I don't think Joe tells us everything."

"I'm just heading out," Lisa said. "You coming?"

"I just got here." My thumb slid across the raised surface of the grey stripes applied to all Unit files. "Oh, Leese?"

Her short black hair popped back into the doorway. "You bellowed, liege lord?"

"Where's Carla?"

"Ms. Ortiz?"

I nodded.

Lisa pointed to her wristwatch. "She left at 3:45. Union hours. Why?"

I thought about the folder locked in my desk drawer. "Something for her to file. But I guess it can wait."

"Speaking of weight. She's got a nice face, don't you think? If she cut down on the Pringles."

I pointed to the door. "Go home."

Lisa saluted. "Aye, aye, Captain."

"Still only lieutenant commander."

"Give it time. Kiss, kiss, kiss."

"Go!"

She snapped off a second salute, gave me a guttural, "Sir," and was gone.

The wall clock read 8:05 when I logged off my computer. I figured I'd call Liz from the road, see if she wanted a late supper. Picking up the metabolism folder, I headed for the file room. Then I remembered the other file. Digging out my keys, I retrieved it from the drawer and plopped it on the desk, so my hands were free to return the key to my trousers. The folder flipped open as it hit the desktop. That's when I noticed the project number on the cover page — it wasn't one of the ones burnt into my photographic memory. All project numbers for my group began with a CR designation. This one began with ME.

"Must have grabbed the wrong file off Joe's desk. Jesus Petes, Carla. Two boners in one day." Things might have gone a lot different if I'd stopped there. But my eyes scanned the heading.

PROGRESS REPORT
Project Seppuku: Week 16
No team members were listed. I read on.
Summary

As reported previously, SL606 is a small molecule that might be attached to viruses able to cross the blood brain barrier. Initial efforts built upon the work of investigators at the California Institute of Technology, binding SL606 to their genetically engineered AAV-PHP.B virus. Following intravenous injection, the drug-vector complex successfully penetrated the central nervous system of knockout rats, producing the characteristic self-destructive behaviors peculiar to this drug. In all cases, death occurred within six days.

Given that IV administration is a suboptimal mode of weaponized delivery, parallel research has investigated drug binding to respiratory or entero viruses. To date, best results have been obtained with a modified parainfluenza virus carrier. The high level of respiratory infectivity of parainfluenza makes it ideally suited to delivery by aerosol or even skin contact (via the hand-to-mouth route). Furthermore, the mild illness produced by parainfluenza necessitates little attenuation. Infected rats showed no more than mild sniffles and conjunctivitis for 24-96 hours prior to onset of self-destructive behaviors. Similar results might be expected in human subjects.

Attenuated poliovirus has also shown promise as a carrier via the oral route. However, given that SL606 is destroyed by stomach acid, it has been necessary to enterically coat the 606-poliovirus complex. Enterically coated tablets survived the hostile environment of the stomach and succeeded in producing stereotypical self-destructive behaviors within three to five days. Prior to the onset of said behaviors, knockout rats remained clinically normal, with no outward signs such as vomiting, diarrhea, or loss of appetite.

Another promising route of delivery is sexual transmission via binding to HIV. The major impediment to this method is the need to reduce HIV pathogenicity without reducing infectivity. The severe illness associated with HIV is not a consideration for the target, given the short life expectancy following SL606 administration. Rather, the goal would be protection of the sexual-partner (assassin) carrier from subsequent HIV infection. Of course, this line of investigation assumes the existence of an antidote to SL606, with said antidote used to protect the assassin-carrier from suicidal ideation. Development of the antidote should be a top priority, given its importance to all stages of this project.

Animal studies should be completed within sixty days. Under the current environment, human trials are not possible. However, given the successful development of appropriate clearances and ...

My mind spun with the implications.
Weaponization?
Aerosol delivery?
Human trials?
Assassin-carriers?
An antidote? My brainchild being used to advance this ... abomination. Cold sweat stung my eyes as I looked back at the header.

Project Seppuku. Another word for hara-kiri.

Week 16. A full two-months before my team began work. Two months. Two fucking months.

The U.S. went out of the biowarfare business in the 1970s. Even rookies to CBRN knew that. The Biological Weapons

Convention of 1972 ended the production and stockpiling of offensive biowarfare agents, with thousands of tons of anthrax, tularemia, and botulinus toxin destroyed on both sides.

Rookies also knew that the Soviets had continued clandestine weaponization until the collapse of that evil empire. But the U.S. supposedly kept the bargain, with places like Fort Deidenbach (and Unit 13) focused only on defensive applications. After all, we Americans were the good guys. Well, maybe not all of us.

My mouth became the Sahara, my heart, hummingbird wings. Bands of steel wrapped my chest. I'd never had a panic attack before, not even when I found my mom. Now I knew what all the fuss was about.

I couldn't breathe. I couldn't speak. I couldn't pull my eyes away from the file, even as my vision grayed. I almost hoped that this was a heart attack — and that I'd die.

I found myself driving, the manila folder still hidden under my suit jacket, my government laptop under the front seat. For once, my photographic memory failed me; the trip from my office past two levels of security was a blank, as if I'd sponged the blackboard of my mind to clean away the chalk stain. But it was still there, a milky white smear over an evil blackness cold as slate.

I can't recall much emotion, not then. I was numb, my thoughts and sensations dulled as a drilled tooth. My mind wasn't registering much, at least trying not to. Not the enormity of what I'd just discovered. Certainly not the possibility of a twenty-year stretch in Leavenworth for sneaking top-secret documents out of a federal institution. Such rational thoughts were replaced by instinct, baser responses involving the need for action. The responses I'd discovered in Iraq. Responses we all had but seldom needed. Fight or flight.

They give you medals for that, but it's simple reflex, like the knee jerk. But instead of a rubber hammer, this reflex is fueled by adrenaline. Fight or flight. In Iraq, it had been fight. Now, I flew down Rosemont Avenue for the merge onto Route 15. Then … where?

"Calm down, Deke," Liz said. "You're not making any sense."

"The unit has gone, I mean they're planning, I mean, Metternich has."

Liz was right, I wasn't making much sense. The numbness had passed, along with a considerable quantity of adrenaline. Now I was nearing post-traumatic stress. My mind had walled off the event like an abscess. But such dams never hold — bitter experience and the death of both parents taught me that. Now the pus pocket ruptured, spilling the truth in long, nauseating waves. There was anger, the gut-wrenching anger of being lied to. There was betrayal, like walking in on a lover in the arms of your best friend. But mostly, there was disillusionment, the kind that hits when Santa Claus dies or that idolized athlete admits to steroids. Disillusionment that leaves a hole in what you considered the essence of your being.

On the drive to Liz's apartment, I kept thinking about when I was twelve; entering high school years ahead of kids my age. I remembered feeling that rollercoaster drop upon realizing the cute girl from Spanish class liked me only because I did her homework. I felt the same way then as I did now, twenty years later. Except this was adult disillusionment, with no childhood spackle of birthdays, graduations, and first times to fill the hole.

I poured a triple bourbon into a crystal glass, knocking back half of it in one gulp. I looked at the quiver in my normally composed fingers, steadying them against the cut glass. Then I tossed the folder on Liz's coffee table.

"Go ahead, read for yourself."

"What's this?" The grey stripes and project number on the file meant nothing to her. But she couldn't help but notice the words Top Secret stamped in red like a flashing alarm. "Are you …? Should I be seeing this? Should it even be outside building 13?"

"Read it."

Her bedazzled eyes stared at me. "I'm not allowed past the reception desk, but now it's okay to read top-secret files?"

I shook my head and finished the booze. "It doesn't matter anymore. Read it."

She hesitatingly touched the folder, her eyes once again seeking reassurance from me. I nodded.

"What's project seppuku?" She looked up.

"Project suicide," I said, pointing. "Read the summary."

As she read, I peeked through the drapes and scanned the empty street. No suspicious vehicles. No grey vans with tinted windows. Routine suburbia. But I still felt edgy, like I was being watched.

"I'm not sure I'm understanding all this," Liz said. "What's SL606?"

I put down the glass, some semblance of composure returning with the buzz of the liquor. "A drug under development by Snyder Labs. A new treatment for Alzheimer's. A wonder drug. Just one problem, the cure is worse than the disease."

"Self-destructive behaviors in rats?" She looked up again. "What kind of self-destructive behaviors?"

"Suicidal behaviors."

"Why do they want rats to commit suicide?"

"They don't. But the Alzheimer's patients Snyder gave the drug to *did*. My group was charged with coming up with a cure for this suicidal side effect."

"An antidote?" Liz asked.

I nodded. "Part of our mission at Unit 13 is coming up with preventives for potential bioterror threats."

"Like vaccines?"

"Vaccines, antidotes, decontamination procedures, so on, so forth. I found one that seemed to work against 606, at least in rats. It stopped the suicide but made the drug inactive."

"So, no cure for Alzheimer's."

I put my hand on the Jim Beam bottle, then thought better of it.

"What's with all the virus talk?"

"SL606 doesn't get into the brain easily, so they're piggybacking it onto something that does. A virus like polio or parainfluenza."

"I'm confused," Liz said, still reading. "If your job is preventing *bioterror* threats, why are you working on a commercial drug? And if the drug doesn't work and causes these suicidal behaviors, why are they trying to make it get into the brain easier? It seems to me that ... sexual transmission?"

page 67 of 312

She stopped, her mouth agape. Then she said just one word. "Assassin?" She looked at me, her eyes two dark lakes. "They're making an assassination drug." She spoke in a near whisper.

"Bingo."

"But, but, I thought we stopped offensive biowarfare research years ago."

"*We* did." I pointed to the file. "*They* didn't."

"Does Joe know about this?"

"Does *Joe* know? Look at the ME designation on the project number."

"ME Like in Metternich?"

I nodded. "Joe is the project leader."

Liz looked back at the folder, then she looked at me. "What are you going to do?"

My hands grasped the bourbon bottle again, this time pouring out two glasses. I handed one to Liz.

"I was thinking about that in the car." The plan had been hazy on the drive over, no more than a series of kaleidoscopic images. With time and liquor, it was crystallizing. "Not as a scientist or an officer, but as a human being."

"And?"

I brought my index and pinky fingers to my lips, producing a soft blast.

"Blow the whistle?"

I tapped my nose again. "I think the *Post* and the *Times* might like to know about this." I held up the summary report I'd smuggled out of Unit 13.

"What about your career?"

"Fuck my career!" I winced at the shock in Liz's eyes. "Sorry. But I can't worry about my career. This goes way past careers and pensions and loyalty oaths." I smiled. "Besides. What are they going to do, court martial me? I don't think Joe or his superiors would like having to explain what they were up to at a general court. And I think I can set it up so there is some doubt. At least enough to make them hesitate to dig up enough evidence to hang me." I sipped my liquor.

"I can get you a good lawyer." She smiled. It was good to see her smile.

"Thanks. But first, I have to make it impossible for them to continue with this hellish game."

"How?"

"I'll need to destroy the records. Force them to start from scratch with the media breathing down their neck."

"But do you have access to this ..." She pointed at the folder. "This assassination drug?"

"Not that – I'm talking about the antidote."

"How will that stop them from developing the assassination drug?"

"Because an antidote is top priority." I pointed to the file. "You read it yourself."

"But, why?"

I paced like one of our caged rats.

"Because that's how the biowarfare game is played. Before you develop a weapon, you develop a cure. Vaccination, antibiotics — they were the preamble to weaponizing anthrax and tularemia." I picked up the folder. "And Creel-1 is the key to weaponized 606."

"Creel-1?"

"The antidote."

"But they already have it, at least a start. You said you developed it."

"But all Joe has is a summary report. The rest is in secured storage down at the Unit. With any luck, he hasn't looked at the data yet." I thought about this. "No, I'm sure he hasn't. He was with me most of the day, then he said he had a dinner meeting."

"What about electronic data?"

"Dribs and drabs here and there among the bench tech's laptops. Impossible to pull it all together without the test results and details on synthesis."

"Where is that?"

"On the laptop in my car... and here." I reached into my pocket and held up a memory stick. "This I'll deposit in the nearest sewer. As for my laptop, I have a little program that'll scrub the hard disk cleaner than a surgeon's fingernails."

"But doesn't Lisa have the data?"

I kept pacing and shook my head. "I'm the project leader. Everything's with me and central records. She might be able to come up with some of it, but not all, certainly not the synthesis procedure. And once I talk to her, I think she'll develop amnesia."

"Is it stored anyplace else?"

I tapped my head. "In here. But I'm in charge of that."

"When are you going to do all this?"

I stopped and turned to her. "Tonight. It has to be tonight. Joe will probably gather up the files tomorrow. At least I can't take a chance that he won't. So, I'll need to destroy them tonight."

"Will they just let you walk them out?"

I put down my drink and met her eyes. She needed to understand. I needed her strength.

"No. They search all containers and briefcases. I took a real chance sneaking out the file and laptop under my coat, but Tom was distracted on the phone." I checked the curtains again. "I'll need help. Some type of diversion while I sneak in, disable the cameras, and work the documents-room shredder." I thought for a moment as I walked back. "Maybe I should call Lisa."

"How long will you need?"

"Let me see." I looked at my watch. "Shred two sets of documents, original and copies ... fifteen minutes might do it."

Liz smiled. "I think I can distract young Tom for fifteen minutes."

Chapter 10

"Are you sure you want to go through with this?" I asked. We sat in her car parked in a visitor's spot near the Unit. Liz leaned over to kiss me in the dark. Her lips felt warm, soft, and reassuring. "If you are."

"I are." Our teeth shone in the dim light like two rays of hope. I just prayed hope wouldn't disappear like the smile on that Cheshire cat, leaving Alice on her own in Wonderland.

"Then so am I."

"Let's go over it one more time."

She ran down the story, repeating it from rote.

"Are you sure you can make it believable?" I asked.

"There are three things I'm sure of when it comes to men." She held up a slender finger. "One is that they fall all over themselves to help a beautiful damsel in distress." She held up a second finger. "Two, it has very little to do with the distress part." She waved three fingers over the cleavage of her workout top. "Three, they shun 'woman's trouble' like the black death, preferring execution by firing squad to discussion of menstrual cramps."

"But are you sure you can get Tom out of the way for twenty, thirty seconds? That's all I need."

"You just watch for the signal." Her fists bumped into the roof of the car. "When I stand up and do this, come on the run." Her eyes darkened. "Are you sure that's it? Just one security guard monitoring the cameras?"

"Yep. Tom's on duty till twelve. Then he does a sweep of all four levels before turning things over to the midnight-to-eight man."

"Not much security for a place in the biowarfare business."

"We're not supposed to *be* in that business anymore. When we were, there was probably a half-dozen security personnel inside or patrolling the perimeter." I shrugged. "But now there's not much call for stolen vaccine. So, after business hours they let technology handle it."

"Are you sure you can disable that technology?"

"Just give me thirty seconds. Fifteen maybe. Besides, if you do *your* job, Tom won't be looking at the monitors."

She fanned her cleavage again and smiled.

I kissed her. "Don't take any chances."

"What's he going to do, shoot a damsel in distress?" She kissed me back, then she was out the door.

I watched her Nikes strut toward the building, her body outlined in the entrance light. She was dressed in a sort of black catsuit, Lycra spandex painted on the curves of her body. It looked more like lingerie than workout attire. If Tom had been interested in her little black dress, he was going to love this.

When she reached the entryway, I pulled the binoculars off my lap. She looked even better magnified thirty times. I watched her smile at the camera, reading her lips as they recited her lines to the microphone.

Hi. Tom, isn't it? Is Dr. Creel there? No? Now a cute little pout. *I was supposed to meet him here. Is it alright if I come in to wait?* She paused to listen to his reply. *No, just for a few minutes.* She stood back to let him see the whole outfit. *We're on our way to the gym.* Now she was listening, hand on hip. *No, they're open till midnight. Like my outfit?* Another pause and a lot of dimples. *Why thank you. That's sweet of you to say.*

I could barely make out Tom seated at his desk beyond the glass. I watched as he put the phone down and his outline became larger. Then the distinct buzz of the door carried to the car. She was inside.

I saw their figures retreat eleven steps. Turning the glasses up to forty power allowed me to see more than two blurry images. It wasn't enough to read their lips, but my imagination filled in the rest.

That really is an attractive outfit, ma'am, I mean Liz.

You're a sweetie. More fanning of the cleavage. *But I don't feel very attractive.* Her hand went to her flat stomach. *I'm a little off my feed. I really should have cancelled tonight.* Now the hand cupped her mouth. I could almost hear her whisper, *It's that time of the month.* Even with the distance, I swear I could see Tom blush.

Anything I can do, ma'am... ah, Liz? ...Are you alright?

Now Liz was fanning her face. *Ooh. I feel dizzy.*

Here, have a seat. She slumped down in a visitor's chair. *Can I get you some water?*

Yes, thank you .... Oh, my. I think I might faint.

Put your head between your legs. Want me to call a doctor?

No, I'm a little better. Just the water. Maybe a cold compress. Would you be a dear and get them for me?

Sure, sure. You just rest. I'll be right back. He grabbed a coffee mug off his desk and rushed off.

As soon as Tom's body disappeared down the hallway leading to the restrooms, Liz leaped up; her fists pumped skyward. I pulled down my ski mask and ran.

In college, my best time for the forty-yard dash was four point eight seconds. I met Liz at the door in four, just as the buzzer sounded.

"Hurry, he's in the men's room."

Another two seconds and I was yanking out the breaker under the desk. The monitors went blank. A few more seconds and I was at the stairway, cardkey in hand. I caught a glimpse of Liz back in her chair, head between her legs. I could just hear Tom say, "Here you go ..." before the closing door cut him off.

The dead cameras stared accusingly at me as I hit the steps two at a time. Central records was on sub-three, just one floor above my lab. The cardkey almost slipped from my sweat-slicked fingers, but the green light clicked on at the second swipe. I was across the Rubicon. I hoped I wouldn't meet Caesar's fate.

The smell of grinding paper replaced the normally sterile atmosphere of the records vault. The entire floor was under negative pressure, muffling sound and making my ears ready to pop. Even so, the hum of the cross-cut action sounded louder than jet noise as it wolfed down documents. The big commercial unit could handle up to twenty-five sheets at a time, but you were supposed to remove the staples to protect the blades. "Fuck the blades," I mumbled as I fed quarter-inch packets from the pile next to me. I winced as the shredder groaned under the strain. "Just don't jam on me, baby."

I stole a glance at the wall clock. I'd been at it for ten minutes, another three or four to go. I tried to avoid looking at the security cameras, sure that the red lights would blink back on at any moment. So, I kept my eyes on the prize, knowing that all the cameras would see was a black-clad shadowy figure in a ski mask who might or might not be me. They'd have my keycard registered on the data log, but I could say it was lost. That's why I was meeting Liz at the Unit, to report the lost card. It was a paper-thin excuse, but it added doubt. They could easily rip it apart if they wanted, but I was betting they wouldn't want to.

I grabbed the last folder, tearing the pages out in one big chunk. That's when someone touched my shoulder, robbing me of ten-years life. I froze for a split second, the way a shoplifter stiffens for the KwikMart clerk. Then I spun, a roll of papers in my hand, ready to swat the intruder. Not a great plan, but I hadn't planned on getting caught red-handed. Then my heart started beating again.

"Hurry," Liz said, her face flushed and sweaty.

"What? Where ...? How did you ..."

She held up a plastic card. "I grabbed Tom's cardkey from the desk when I sent him to get a doctor."

"What? Why didn't he just call?"

"I yanked the phone cord when he was getting me more water. He said it must be the same short that blew out the cameras." She smiled a sweaty grin. "I told him I might have appendicitis. He'll be halfway to his car before he realizes he has a cellphone in his pocket."

I laughed. "Cellphones aren't allowed because of the cameras. But you're right, he won't leave the desk for long."

"Then you better hurry. It took me a couple of minutes to find you. I stumbled into someone's lab and busted a vial of somebody's cheap perfume." She wrinkled the cutest nose I'd ever seen. "Then I heard the grinding and followed my ears."

"Almost done ... there. That's it." The shredder swallowed the last of the documents. "Now get your ass back upstairs." I slapped her spandex-covered bottom. It felt smooth and firm, making me wish I had it home in bed.

She kissed me hard. "Give me two minutes, then come up. I'll get Tom to help me into the ladies room, where I'll stage my miraculous recovery."

I kissed her, just as hard. "Will you marry me?"

"Too late. I'm spoken for." She sneezed.

"God bless."

Another quick kiss, then she was gone.

Chapter 11

Back in the present, the after-work crowd at Woody's had thinned to stool-perch regulars. On the juke, Dwight had given way to Reba, George, and Willie. Barroom conversation had shifted from work to politics. And tears had begun rolling down Deacon's cheeks.

"We thought it was a cold," he slurred. "Thought she had a cold. Or maybe hay fever." He waved a hand in self-dismissal. "Not that I noticed much. Not me. I was too busy. Holier-than-thou Dr. Creel was too busy. Busy with stonewalling FBI interviews. Busy with boards of inquiry. Busy with cold rebukes from Bunsen Honeydew. Too busy to notice Liz's sniffles morphing into atypical lethargy and sullen silences." He downed the rest of his whiskey, then waved for Jazzelle. "Cheap perfume."

"What?"

"What Liz said when she broke that vial in Joe's biolab." Deke wiped his eyes. "That's the first thing I thought of working with 606 — the pure drug, not the weaponized monstrosity Joe was developing. I opened the Snyder Laboratories container and thought it smelled like my mother's perfume, the cheap stuff she wore when she went out drinking."

A sad grin flashed over his eyes. "Funny things you remember from childhood. Later, you go nose blind. Then you forget."

He finished the beer, tapping the glass against the table. "Then you're too busy to remember. Too busy with sanctimonious pride. Too busy dodging a shitstorm of bureaucratic inquiries. Too busy looking out for your own hide."

The thunk of glass nicking wood made Amy flinch. "Where's those drinks?"

Jazzelle scurried back over. "Hi, folks. How about we switch to black coffee?" She looked at her father behind the bar. Daddy nodded. "On the house."

Deacon held up a finger and turned bleary eyes to the server. He spoke in the deliberate, constrained cadence reserved for the very drunk defending their sobriety. He pointed at himself. "Maker's Mark, Miller back." He pointed to Amy, holding his fingers halfway up an imaginary glass. "Highland Park ..." His fingers filled the glass. "Water."

Amy looked at Jazzelle, waving her hand flatly over the mostly full scotch and water still sitting in front of her. Then she pointed to Deke's glasses and spun her fingers indicating another round. Jazzelle started to protest, but Amy mouthed, *Just one.*

The young server glanced at her father scowling behind the bar. Amy met the big man's glare, pointed to herself, and nodded. The young marine and ex-marine held their gaze for a moment, then the ex-marine shook his head and started pouring whiskey.

"Too busy." Deacon smeared snot across his shirt sleeve.

"It wasn't your fault." Deke's glare severed her words mid-sentence. She switched tack. "What *did* happen? With the inquiry, I mean."

Deke laughed. "Just what I thought would happen. Nothing. Oh, they huffed and bluffed and threatened. My career would be over. My life would be over. Etcetera, etcetera, ad infinitum, ad nauseum."

"What did you do?"

He shrugged. "Held to my paper-thin, bullshit story. What else?"

"And then?"

"*Then* they went from bad cop to good cop. It was all a big misunderstanding. Just rederive the formula for Creel-1 and all would be forgiven."

A light dawned behind Amy's brown eyes. "That's why you're such a VIP. They haven't been able to rederive the antidote. All the records are destroyed ... except?"

Deacon tapped his head. "Except up here. They thought it would be simple." He shook his head.

"But why the urgency? Unless something has ..." Her brown eyes sparked again.

"You catch on quickly, Specialist Robbins."

"I'm surprised they let you leave in the first place," Amy said.

He shrugged. "They had little choice, once the media got hold of it."

"And then?"

"Then I was allowed to resign for the good of the service. For my *own* good, as well." He sniggered. "I thought I'd won." His eyes welled again as Jazzelle came back with the drinks. Deacon smiled away the tears. "So, I had time off. Time to plan a funeral." He held up his whiskey glass. "Time for a new hobby."

"Do you think Liz would approve of this hobby?"

He started to take a sip, then stopped, shot glass inches from his lips, eyes on hers. Amy thought the rebuke hit home. Then for a moment, just a moment, she thought she saw something else in those steely blues. Perhaps regret, perhaps recognition, like seeing a long-lost friend after twenty years, noting the familiar features under the changes etched by time. Then the look was gone, replaced by a sad cynicism.

"As you were, Marine Force Specialist. That will be quite enough of the ten-cent psychology." He downed half the liquor. "Better minds than yours have tried." He sipped beer. "Well, maybe not better. Better trained, perhaps." The beer glass thunked wood. "Stick with your training, Specialist."

"Yes, sir." Amy snatched up the dram glass and placed it before her. "I'm trained to follow orders and meet the needs of my superiors." The beer glass joined the whisky glass. "Orders from my superiors are to see to your well-being and to assist you in performing your duties." She signaled Jazzelle. "Getting shitfaced instead of tending to those duties meets neither of those objectives."

Jazzelle appeared at her side.

"Clear this table, please, ma'am. Then bring me the check. The Commander and I are leaving."

"And if I refuse?" Deacon said.

"Not covered by my orders, so not an option ... sir."

They stared at each other, tension filling the air like ozone before a storm. Then Deacon smiled, raising his hands in surrender.

As Jazzelle gathered up the glassware, she stole close to Amy and whispered, "Good job, sarge."

Chapter 12

I t was only last year. Back when Liz was alive. Back when Deacon had courage, a purpose, and hope for the future. The deed had been done; the Rubicon crossed.

Deacon sat calmly beside Josiah Metternich as Special Agent Paul Carstairs pressed stop, then play. Two familiar voices emerged from the recorder, their tones slightly altered by electronic hum.

Special Agent Carstairs: "Can you explain, Dr. Creel, how the cardkey signed out to you was used to enter the records vault at approximately the same time that valuable government records were destroyed?"

Deacon Creel: "As I said previously, I had mislaid my cardkey. Perhaps, looking back on it now, it may have been stolen. But regardless, I had intended to return to Unit 13 that evening to report the loss, er, theft. Ms. Adams was to meet me there, which is why she was present there at the time of her illness."

Special Agent: "And this was at the same time when the security cameras and phone were miraculously disabled."

Deacon Creel: "Apparently."

Metternich punched stop. "Dr. Creel? Deacon, my boy. Do you honestly expect us to believe this?"

"It's the simple truth."

Carstairs placed his finger on the record button, but Metternich grasped his hand. "Leave that off for now, Special Agent. And would you be kind enough to step out for a moment? Perhaps get yourself a cup of coffee."

Carstairs paused.

"Just for a moment. Please."

"Very well, Doctor." Carstairs rose, leaving the recorder on the table of the conference room. "Just for a moment."

As the door closed, Joe shook his head. "Deacon, Deacon. My boy. Let me give you a piece of sage advice."

Deacon again thought that the fingers tented over Metternich's shirt looked like five white worms writhing from out of his considerable belly.

"There is no way in hell that anyone is ever going to believe this tale. It will shrivel like a fungus exposed to the purifying rays of the sun. Because like a mushroom, it is bred of so much horse shit."

Deacon sat there, saying nothing.

"Do I have to tell you how this will play out?" Metternich held up one fat finger. "First there will be an investigation, during which the horse shit will be shoveled away." Another finger arose. "Then there will be a series of arrests — you, Ms. Adams, perhaps others. Were there others?"

Deacon just stared at him.

"Then there will be a very public trial, during which I guarantee." He pointed accusingly. "*Guarantee* that you will be found guilty of illegally entering a government facility for nefarious purposes, espionage, treason, destruction of classified documents, and anything else the DOJ can think up." Metternich's hands re-tented over his belly. "Then I suspect that Ms. Adams will be sent to Ashland for three to five years." He pointed again. "You, on the other hand, will likely wind up in Butner, Terra Haute, or Leavenworth for a couple of decades. That is ..." Another finger rose. "If you aren't strapped to a table with a lethal IV in your vein." He smiled. "Treason is a capital offense, my boy."

"What's the advice?"

Metternich shrugged. "Simply this. It doesn't have to end this way. Not for someone with your intelligence and good sense." He paused, letting this sink in. "You made a mistake. An error in judgement." Metternich raised his hands. "Perhaps *we* erred as well. Pursuing a purely exploratory research path that was, shall we say, only *indirectly* in keeping with the unit's mandate." He smiled his Honeydew smile. "That is how it could be perceived, you know. *Will*, no doubt, be perceived. Not exactly illegal, just indirectly legal. You on the other hand?"

"I ask again. What's the advice?"

"Come to your senses. Rejoin the brotherhood." His hands fluttered to rest on their familiar perch. "All these charges could be forgotten. You would be … Ms. Adams would be in the clear. What's more, I can see even bigger things in your future. A future where *Captain* Creel heads his own department somewhere — you decide where. A future of important research, respect, cocktail hours, connubial bliss, in essence the American dream. If …"

"If I just play ball. If I just rederive the formulas for Creel-1. If I keep my mouth shut."

Metternich smiled again. "I see we understand each other. What do you say?"

The conference telephone rang. Metternich picked it up. "I said I didn't want to … Oh? Alright, put him on. Hello, Nelson. What's that? No, I haven't seen the paper today. I have been …" He looked at Deacon. "Ah, busy. Why?" Metternich's face went pale, his look of poised arrogance replaced by clammy fear. He looked at Deacon, who smiled in return. Then color returned to Metternich's cheeks, first a warm pink then an angry red. "That was in *today's* Post?" Another pause. "What? *60 Minutes?* No! No, um tell them no comment. I realize that, but for now it's no comment." He slammed down the receiver, hatred in his eyes, icy words seething from between his teeth. "You stupid, arrogant, sanctimonious little prick."

Deacon's smile widened. "I take it there was something distasteful in the paper?"

"Do you think this makes a difference? This doesn't change anything."

"On the contrary, Doctor. I think it changes everything. To use your own phrasing, 'your horse shit will shrivel under the purifying rays of the sun.' Or should I say, the scathing eye of media and public scrutiny." Deacon leaned forward. "When the dirty little secrets of this dirty little place get exposed for what they are, then I think it is you, and others, who will be facing that extended vacation in Terra Haute. I on the other hand, will be giving interviews. Explaining certain matters in a certain summary report that was not among those destroyed so mysteriously." Deacon raised a finger. "Unless?"

The two men exchanged glares. All the benefits of the doubt, all the pretense that had built up over the years was washed away, leaving only mutual distaste. Finally, after several eternities, Metternich said, "I'm listening."

Deacon leaned back and tented his fingers in an imitation that was not a form of flattery. "Let me give you a little sage advice, my boy."

"Leave a message at the tone." Beep.

"Hi Hon," Deacon said. "It's me. Thought you might be working late. I also left a message on your cell, but you're probably on your way home and don't want to talk while driving. Safety first, good girl." Deacon smiled at the inside joke. "How about I stop over and pick you up. I'm in the mood to celebrate. I faced the devil and did not bend. Anyway, you can stop worrying about wearing prison issue, even though you'd look dynamite in orange. Your job is secure, all charges dropped, as they say on TV. I even got them to throw in separation pay as I shuffle off the government coil. But more about that over dinner."

He glanced at his watch. "I have an 8:30 reservation at Siranella's, so freshen up and I'll pick you up at eight, don't be late. No need to go fancy. This is a come as you are celebration, and you look great in anything. Besides, I'll have to get used to dressing down in my new role as private citizen. See you in a bit. Love you."

Deacon hung up the phone feeling better than he had in days. The proverbial weight of the world had been lifted, or in this case the weight of a prison sentence versus a lifetime of guilt for every death attributable to project Seppuku. He'd need to find a new job but was confident he'd land on his feet. There was always room someplace for a bright, young (maybe not so young anymore, but still) man with two doctoral degrees, government experience, and an IQ in the stratosphere. Perhaps a change of scenery was in order. Maybe a biotech company in California. Plenty of work for tax attorneys like Liz on the West Coast. He kept smiling. A nice change in scenery: vineyards dotting the hillside, golf outings at Pebble Beach, beer and oysters on the bay. A good analogy, he thought. The world was his oyster. He had it all. Most importantly, he had his self-respect, his very soul — intact, inviolable. And he had the greatest woman in the world to share it all with. Who could ask for more?

He pressed the buzzer again, again hearing melodic tones through the townhouse door. Lights were on inside, and Liz's Subaru was parked in the drive. She must be home, but still no answer. He knocked, wondering why people always do that — hear the doorbell working and then knock. Habit I guess, he thought with a smile.

"Liz, it's me. Open up."

Still only silence. Maybe she was in the shower. The thought of her lathering up brought on a new emotion, changing his lighthearted smile to a lascivious grin. Why not, he thought. I'm ten minutes early. We might have time before dinner.

Reaching under the toad statue near the door, he retrieved the housekey. They'd talked about a safer hiding place, but that usually went the way of his admonishments about not driving and talking on the cell. The brass found the keyhole, but before he could turn the lock, the door clicked open.

The small foyer was country quiet.

"Liz?" No answer. "You know you left the door unlocked. Need to watch that."

The family room was well lit but empty.

"Liz, Hon? Your knight in shining polyester is here."

His own words echoed in reply. A quick look to the right showed an empty kitchen. The hallway ahead was deserted.

"About ready to go? Or can I suggest an alternative plan?"

The bathroom was at the end of the hall, past the two bedrooms. The door was ajar, light shining from inside. There was no sound of a shower stream, but steam wafted along with the bathroom light. Deacon could smell the telltale moisture of bath water, along with a hint of something that made him think of pennies. He approached the door.

"I haven't taken a bath in years," he said. Kicking off his shoes, he untied his tie and dropped it to the floor. "What a great idea." He unbuttoned his shirt and tossed it over his shoulder. "Why don't I join you." Now his pants were also on the carpet, leaving him in his jockeys. "What do you say? In the mood for a quickie?" He pushed open the door, a smile on his face.

The coppery smell punched his nose like a well-landed jab. The air felt warm and humid. Ahead of him lay a tub full of water, heat still rising in waves. Liz lay in the tub, her beautiful breasts bobbing in the liquid, her head canted to the side as if she was asleep.

And at first, that's what he thought. That she'd fallen asleep in the tub. Then he realized that the bathwater was pink, actually past pink to rose. What Liz had once called Barbie pink. His eyes followed the various shades as they darkened, turning bright red at his fiancé's wrists.

Chapter 13

"S ir?" Deacon woke suddenly, bathed in sweat, head throbbing. A bright light shone somewhere up above, making his headache pound and his stomach lurch.

"Sir? Commander?"

Hands shook him gently. The voice sounded familiar.

"Deke?"

He opened bleary eyes, the pain spiking then dropping back to a dull throb. Outlined against the light was a familiar set of large dark eyes, black hair framing a beautiful face. Relief washed over him.

He reached out and hugged her. "Thank God. I thought, I mean I had this dream where ..."

"We don't have time for this," shouted a male voice he knew. "On your feet, Creel. Now."

The fog began to lift. The woman in his arms wasn't Liz. She smelled differently, green-apple shampoo instead of rose-scented perfume. And she was dressed in camouflage instead of a soft blouse. He recognized her as she backed away.

"I said now." A hand yanked him vertical, ratcheting up the pain again. He shook the hand away.

"Get your fucking hands off me."

He was back in the present, the mist rising from his eyes. He recognized the woman as Fleet Marine Force Specialist Amy Robbins. The man was Nelson Barzoon, still dressed in natty business attire. He remembered where he was, guest quarters in Unit 13. Then he remembered the dream and crashed down again.

"Leave me alone. Let me die in peace."

The rough handling resumed, pulling him upright and shaking him. "I'd happily grant that request," Barzoon said. "If we didn't need what's in that bourbon-soaked brain of yours. Now on your feet."

Amy firmly pulled the lawyer's hands away. "Excuse me, sir. I'll have to ask you to leave now." Barzoon glared at her. "I'll help Commander Creel and see that he gets dressed and to the meeting."

Barzoon straightened, adjusting his tie and jacket. "The meeting we rescheduled for eight-thirty *this* morning. Rescheduled to accommodate his drunken antics. Rescheduled despite precious time ticking away." Barzoon slicked back his grey hair, his anger momentarily sated. He glared again at Amy. "See that he gets there." Then he left.

"Stupid bastard," Deacon mumbled, hiding his head under the pillow.

Amy drew liquid into a syringe then squeezed out the air while looking into the overhead light. One knee on the bed, she pulled down Deacon's shorts and swabbed the upper buttocks with alcohol.

"Shouldn't you wait till I buy you dinner or something?" Deacon said.

She slid the B-vitamin injection home, eliciting only a minor flinch from her patient.

"Only one sure hangover cure, Specialist." The muffled voice from under the pillow sounded pained but still held that defiant bravado she'd heard on the transport plane.

"Sorry, Commander. No hair of the dog on my watch."

"You're no fun." Deacon repositioned his body into sleeping pose. "Just five, ten more minutes."

"Sorry, Commander. Deke. I've got my orders."

"Go away."

"Can't do that, sir. Here, take these." She held out two extra-strength Tylenol and a glass of orange juice.

"I said, go away." The voice rising from under the pillow sounded far off. "Or I'll bust you back to civilian."

"Take the pills, sir. They'll help with your headache."

"Maybe if I ignore you, you'll leave."

Amy put down the pills and juice, then pulled the sheet, exposing one foot. Fisting her right hand, she separated her index and middle finger into a claw, inserting Deacon's big toe in the gap between them. Without warning, she tightened her hand back to a fist and twisted.

"Son of a bitch!" Deacon bolted upright, bloodshot eyes wide open, pillow thumping to the floor.

"Now, let's try this again, sir."

She popped the pills into his gawping mouth, then tilted in the glass of OJ. He dutifully gulped them down. The natural sugar would help, as would the acetaminophen.

"Where did you learn that?" he asked.

"Old drill sergeant trick. I also brought you up a large, black coffee from the commissary." She took the plastic lid off and handed him the Styrofoam. "Careful. It's hot."

"I know how to drink coffee, Specialist," he said. She smiled inwardly as he burned his mouth on the steamy liquid.

"Yes, sir."

"So, when is this meeting I'm supposed to attend?"

"Zero eight thirty, sir. We have thirty minutes to get you presentable. Why don't you shave and get dressed?" She smiled. "I have no orders to shave you this morning." Then she held up his suit in a dry-cleaning bag. "You can take a shower in the head down the hall. Would you like some scrambled eggs and toast?"

"What I'd like is for everyone to leave me alone."

"Can't do that sir."

"Say sir one more time," Deacon said, "and I'll kick your cute little butt. Then I'll kick that asshole Barzoon's."

"Mr. Barzoon is right, sir."

"What?"

"He said people were dying. If that's so, if people are dying, then you have to help."

"After what they did? I was a fool to let them talk me back to this place." He slipped feet over the mattress and put down the coffee. "They wanted their assassination drug. Now let them stew in it. I hope they all get a dose, especially Barzoon and Honeydew."

"Permission to speak freely, sir."

"I may *technically* be your commanding officer, Amy. But I'm uniformed service, which is only *technically* the military.

So, you really can call me Deke." He reached for the coffee cup, hand trembling. "What's on your mind."

"You're behaving like a child, Deke." He flinched from the unexpected rebuke. "Maybe what they did was wrong, I don't know. And they told me you lost someone you loved, that you feel guilty about that. But drowning yourself in alcohol won't help, and it ignores a bigger issue. There's someone out there killing people."

"What do you know about it?"

"I know I became a corpsman to save lives, to ease suffering. And until they catch the person or persons responsible, you are the best hope for ending this suffering. If you want to feel guilty about something, feel guilty about that." She held out a shaving kit. "Now, while you get yourself together, I'll get you some breakfast."

The small conference table on sub-level two was over half full. All were present on a needs-to-know basis, which left Amy on the outside, despite her briefing. Metternich murmured in private conclave with Carstairs, the special agent running the investigation. Likewise, Barzoon spoke quietly with Cathleen Harris, physician, lawyer, and undersecretary for chemical and biological affairs. Harris was indeed a stunner who caught the attention of the men in the room. Carstairs seemed especially interested, his eyes straying back to her every few moments. Even the other woman in the room took notice, said other woman seated next to Deacon, lean and handsome in a brown pants suit.

"Good to see you again, Lisa." Deacon's hangover had reached manageable proportions, one of the benefits of long practice at the jug. Still, he would kill for three fingers of bourbon right now.

"Surprised to see *you*, Deke. I was sure you'd be off in the south seas, painting pictures of naked ladies. Maybe cutting off an ear over a lost love." Her smiling face darkened. "Sorry about that. Sometimes my smart mouth speaks without thinking."

Deacon shrugged. "How's Ruth?"

"We are no longer cohabitating."

"Oh? Sorry to hear that."

Now Lisa shrugged.

Deacon leaned closer. "So, what's really been going on around here?"

"Haven't they told *you*?"

"Never sure how much to believe."

"Well, I'm a bad source for confirmation. I've been studying tularemia back in my hole at Allergy and Infectious Diseases. They came to me a couple of weeks ago asking if I could whip up more of your wonder cure for the big sayonara."

"What did you tell them?"

"The truth. You were project leader and in charge of synthesis. I was second banana designing protocols. To me it was just powder diluted in normal saline."

Deacon nodded.

"So, now *I* ask *you*. What's really going on here?"

Deacon grinned, a little of the old bravado returning. "Don't *you* know? It's all a big excuse for you to meet Cathleen Harris."

The undersecretary turned at the mention of her name.

"Excuse me," Harris said, flashing Lisa a smile that made a beautiful face gorgeous. "Do we know each other?"

"Um, ah, well, um."

"Smooth," Deacon murmured from the side of his mouth.

"Only by reputation," Lisa finally said.

Harris pointed a manicured finger at Lisa. "You must be Dr. Reilly. I've been hearing good things about you."

"Me?"

"I read your paper on molecular markers of aberrant genetic changes. Very interesting."

"Um, thank you."

"Ahem." Metternich cleared his throat. "Perhaps we should get started. Let me begin by introducing everyone." He pointed to the crisply dressed, middle-aged man next to him. "This is Special Agent Carstairs from the Hoover Building." Deke thought the intro and title were unnecessary. It wasn't the first time he'd met Carstairs, who looked like a dictionary definition of G-man. "Agent Carstairs is running the investigation into the, shall we say, missing bioterror agent."

Lisa looked at Deacon, brows raised.

"Farther along," Metternich said. "We have Nelson Barzoon, legal and legislative counsel from DHS. On his right is Undersecretary Harris. She, ah ..."

"Thank you, Joe." Harris smiled again. She was good at smiling.

The undersecretary spoke as one comfortable with command, but with that feminine gift of making everyone feel that she was just a junior partner to their more important role. And it didn't hurt that she looked like a runner-up for Miss Alabama, sexy southern drawl included.

Deacon remembered back to last year when smitten Lisa had seen Harris on Fox news, thinking that the undersecretary would fit in with that network's sexy anchors. Her bleached-blonde do was quaffed just so, makeup professionally applied, as if she were appearing on a Sunday-morning talk show instead of a shabby conference room two stories underground. A modest amount of décolletage peeked up from her pink, two-hundred-dollar blouse. If he could see under the table, he was sure there'd be shapely crossed legs in a slightly shorter than regulation skirt.

"I asked Nelson if I could come to the meeting today. Given the importance of this, ah, affair." She glanced sideways at Metternich. "And given the delicacy, I thought that my office should provide direct oversight and support. Nelson will still be running the show from our end, but he will keep me closely informed, and I will see to it that he — that you all get whatever you need."

"Thank you, Dr. Harris. Now, I will turn things over to Agent Carstairs to ..."

"Where is Charley Hayes?"

Metternich stopped speaking at Deacon's question.

"Who?" Harris asked, turning to Barzoon.

"Dr. Charles Hayes," Deacon said, looking at Metternich. "Virologist. His name was on that list I gave you. Everyone on that list was supposed to be brought here, kept informed."

"Ah, yes," Metternich said. "He is on sabbatical, so unavailable."

"So was I, but here I sit."

"Um, Dr. Hayes had personal business overseas, as I understand it." Metternich adjusted his collar. "But I have selected a good replacement."

"*You* selected?"

"Yes, I was sure it would be alright."

"*You* were sure?"

Metternich clenched his hands, white showing atop the knuckles. "Yes. Dr. Mila Saponek is an accomplished, world-renown virologist."

Deacon leaned across the table. "I said I wanted Charley Hayes. And I said I wanted him briefed. And I said I wanted him now."

"Forgive me, but I don't understand," Harris said.

"Um, well," Metternich said. "You see, Dr. Creel requested ..."

"Demanded," Deacon said.

"Demanded?" Harris said.

Deacon nodded, his finger tapping morse on the conference table. "As a prerequisite for my cooperation, my participation in this sordid affair."

"Dr. Creel," Metternich said. "Deacon, my — this is neither the time nor the place."

Harris waved Metternich into silence and conferred quietly with Barzoon. After a few moments, she spoke.

"Dr. Creel. I am aware of the importance of your participation in this *affair*, as you call it. Although I was not aware that it was less than voluntary." She stole a glare at Barzoon, then looked at Deacon with softer eyes, eyes that were deep and blue like a gentle ocean a man could drown in. "I am also aware of the tragedy surrounding this project's birth, and of the ill-timed, ill-considered genesis of it." The room was deathly quiet. "I want to tender my personal condolences on *your* loss. And I want you to know that the investigation into the circumstances surrounding that loss is continuing."

She held Deacon's gaze, but from the corner of his eye he thought he saw Metternich squirm.

"But there are bigger issues at stake here. Issues in the here and now. Issues of life and death, perhaps on a WMD scale." Her voice stayed steady, but her eyes pleaded. "Perhaps the affair was sordid, as you put it. Perhaps it should never have been initiated. But we've got a tiger by the tail. And like the lady from Niger, we might very well end up inside."

Maybe it was the southern accent that lent sincerity to her words. If she was acting, , she was good at it. For the first time, he considered the possibility that the undersecretary may not have known. That perhaps she was playing catch-up with a bad situation getting worse. Perhaps she was even a little afraid. Maybe she wasn't the enemy.

"So, I would appreciate it." One soft hand waved to the assemblage. "We *all* would appreciate it, if you could put those feelings aside for now and help us, help the country stay outside the tiger."

The room remained quiet. No one spoke. No one else mattered, only him and Cathleen Harris. She held his gaze, eyes steady, eyes pleading, eyes beautiful. Finally, he nodded. "Alright, Madam Secretary. For now."

The meeting concluded, as the poet said, not with a bang but with a whimper. Harris left after the preliminaries, gracing them with a parting smile. Carstairs outlined the FBI's efforts, which amounted to surveillance on any and all contacts associated with Carla Ortiz, then he left too. Barzoon informed them that the threat level was raised to orange, citing non-specific intelligence of a potential terror threat. Although Deacon could not determine how this color change helped, it was at least something for Homeland Security to do. Finally, Deacon and Lisa were given their marching orders.

"The unit has been closed down until further notice," Metternich said. "Non-essential staff have been furloughed with pay."

"Everyone has been told there is to be routine cleaning and maintenance, which might take as long as ten days," Barzoon added. "So, you and your staff have that long to resynthesize Creel-1."

"And if possible," Metternich said, "Come up with a less invasive delivery system."

Lisa shook her head with a smirk. "All of ten days? What will we do with the spare time?"

"You'll have unrestricted access to all laboratories, computers, and library facilities," Metternich said. "You'll find your staff in place, ready for work."

"More like drinking coffee," Lisa said.

"Dr. Saponek should be here this afternoon."

Deacon raised his hands. "That's all well and good. I'm sure the staff will do their part and I suppose I can make do with

Mila Saponek — she has a good reputation. And I suppose we *might* be able to resynthesize and test Creel-1 in less than ten days, given what we already have." He tapped his skull. "But I doubt that we will be able to come up with an easily deliverable form in that time, even for rats. Then there are human trials, which would require considerable ethical review."

"Already cleared."

Deacon was stunned. "How'd you manage that without even a protocol?"

Metternich smiled. "There are ways."

"We have volunteers standing by," Barzoon said.

"You found people lining up to take a newly synthesized, only partially tested antidote for a suicide drug?" Lisa asked. "How?"

"Money, doctor," Barzoon said. "More than for the usual clinical trial. Considerably more."

"Why the rush, Joe?" Deacon's question cut through the banter like an icepick to the back of the neck. The room was silent. "What's going on?"

"Time is, um, of the essence," Metternich said, exchanging a glance with Barzoon.

"Then why just us chickens?" Lisa asked. "If we got crisis mode here, let's get NIH and CDC cranking on it too."

"Security issues make that impossible," Barzoon said.

"Last I checked," Lisa said, "there are plenty of folks with top-secret clearance at CDC, more at NIH. They all pitched in for the anthrax letters. That was before my time, but that's the word at the institute."

"This is, um, somewhat different," Barzoon said.

"Yeah," Lisa said, "it's smaller scale. That should make it easier, not harder."

Deacon noticed a sheen of sweat on the brow of the nattily dressed Barzoon. A sideways glance showed Metternich squirming, his five fat worms writhing on the table.

"It's just different," Barzoon said. "Let's leave it at that."

"You leave it at that," Lisa said. "I don't like being kept in the dark. Last time that happened ..."

"*They* don't know, do they?" Deacon pointed upward. "No one was told, right?"

"What do you mean?" Lisa said. "No one was told? What about Harris?"

"When the spam hit the fan, you had to tell someone, so Barzoon went to his boss. Right?" Deacon stared daggers at Barzoon. "But that's as high as it goes. I'm right, aren't I?"

"You mean," Lisa said, looking at Barzoon and Metternich, then back at Deacon, "*nobody*? You guys did this on, on your own?"

"What about Carstairs and the Bureau?" Deacon asked.

"They've been told they are pursuing a terrorism suspect," Barzoon said. "Which is true, and all they need to know for the present."

Deacon smiled at Metternich. "Nice feather in your cap, that's how you described it, Joe. Remember?" Metternich studied his fingers. "Hat band getting a little tight, is it?"

"Be that as it may," Barzoon said. "Undersecretary Harris has granted us ten days to get on top of the issue, before she ..."

"Turns the matter over to higher authorities," Deacon finished. "Like the ones at Pennsylvania Avenue?"

"Holy shit," Lisa said.

"That sums up the problem nicely," Barzoon said.

Amy heard angry footsteps thudding down the hall, then a door slam from the room next door. She was knocking on that door before the echoes died.

"What?" The tone of the response did not portend a happy greeting.

"It's Specialist Robbins, sir, um, Deke. Permission to enter?"

She felt more than heard a pause, followed by, "Why not?"

Amy stood at ease before her boss, semi-casual slouch, hands behind back. Commander Creel didn't require the formality, even chafed at it. But habits, like Marines, died hard.

She'd never been an aide-de-camp before and wasn't sure how she was expected to behave. She was only sure that the idle waiting was painful, as foreign to her nature as push-ups to a green recruit. There were no surgical packs to sterilize, no lectures, no calisthenics, no classes to teach. For the last hour, she'd straightened his room, drank three Pepsi's, and reviewed *Navy Hospital Corpsman*, a book she knew by heart. Now her current assignment was back, so she was going to make the most of it.

"Can I get you anything, sir, um, Deke?"

"How about a straight razor and a hot ..." His steely eyes frosted over, fluorescent light glinting off the tears hiding in the corners. "Sorry. Poor choice of words."

"How was the meeting?"

"It was — typical."

"Would you like some coffee or anything?"

He raised his hand toward the ceiling. "I've had it up to here with coffee and *anything*." He smiled a pained grin. "How about a bourbon rocks?"

"Sorry, sir."

Deke waved her off. "I should be getting downstairs, anyway." He started to take off his suit jacket.

"What are my orders while you're gone?"

He turned and looked at her. Not *at* her exactly, more through her, as if he was looking at someone standing right behind her, or perhaps at a spark of memory her face kindled in his mind. He'd looked at her that way once before, no make that twice — once on the Hercules transport and again when he woke this morning. Each time, the look softened him, made him more human, more innocent, almost boyish, with a hurt boy's need for a mother's love.

Who was this man, she thought? She really didn't know. He was something of a genius, she knew that from the way the politicos put up with him. She knew he was a hard drinker, no social tippler who had two martinis before dinner, maybe one at lunch. This was a boozer, the kind who dove into the bottle for the long swim. "Going in the tank," her father used to say. She also knew he'd been married (engaged?) but that she'd died. The circumstances of her death were a little vague, but Amy knew they were connected with his current job, with why he left it in the first place, and with his drinking.

Yes, three times he'd looked at her as if she were someone else. His mother? The wife who'd died? Each time he did it, she saw the joy on his face turn to pain. She saw the longing for memory turn to the need to drown it, drown it quickly so it couldn't surface. And each time, she felt a little of that pain, felt that need to forget, as if it were carried to her on a virus or a filament of thought linking brain to brain. That first time, on the Hercules, she'd been ordered to help him. Now she'd been ordered to help him again. The only difference was, now she wanted to.

She waited as his eyes came back from whatever bittersweet remembrance she'd conjured. Then he smiled, a becoming smile that radiated warmth and a little mischief.

"Go get a haircut."

"Pardon?"

"Have your nails done, too, if you like."

As Amy gaped, he added, "Now if you'll excuse me, Marine Force Specialist, I need to start making my magic."

Chapter 14

The two rats slept in peaceful repose, no doubt dreaming of peanut butter, bacon, and other rodent delicacies. The sleek white fur rose and fell with each respiration. The beady, inquisitive eyes remained hidden, but the lids began to flicker. Pink, velvety ears flicked. Whiskers rose to attention, sensing the coming of a new day.

"Rudolph's nose is twitching," Lisa said, her face at tabletop level. "So is ZuZu's tail. They're coming out of it."

"ZuZu? Rudolph?

Hey, Christmas is just around the corner."

"Sure," Deacon said, "right after Halloween and Thanksgiving."

"Speak for yourself, Dr. Creel. When I was a kid, I started my letters to Santa on Labor Day. Went as an elf for Halloween. Helped with the turkey-day cleanup so I could make the 'good girls' list."

"Good girl? What happened?"

"I grew up. But I still remember. And I still love all the Christmas movies, TV shows, decorations, nativities. All the things modern culture is trying to kill — the bastards."

Deacon shook his head. "Well, don't get too attached to *this* Christmas miracle. Dear old Rudolph and ZuZu are destined for the necropsy table in a couple of days."

"Thank God Snyder refined their rodent model," Lisa said. "Having a quick and predictable time of onset for 606 makes things a whole lot easier."

Deacon peered down from a high-top metal stool. "As I recall, it used to be a three- to six-day suicide run."

"A lot has happened since your sabbatical. Now it's six hours on the rat nose." Lisa checked the clock and started the timer. "Can almost set your Timex by 'em. Snyder still can't cure Alzheimer's, but they've built a better rat trap. Rube Goldberg would be proud."

"Your cynicism is showing, Leese."

"Well, with all the problems this country is facing, you'd think there'd be better ways to spend ..." She caught herself ranting and laughed. "Hell, that's why you love me. My cynical charm."

The initial trial was limited to just two anesthetized rats administered the newly derived Creel-1 and 606, six-hours apart, then kept zonked out for six more hours. If all went as Deacon expected, their two Christmas rats would stumble out of the anesthesia, take a drink of water, then start looking for food. When Rudolph and ZuZu were still normal twenty-four hours later, they'd call the trial a success. That was the easy part.

"How is her highness coming on the viral carrier?" Lisa asked.

"Dr. Sopanek," Deacon said, "claims to have gone as far as she can until she has 'a verking drug vit vich to test.'"

Lisa chuckled. Mila Saponek had turned out to be a sextigenarian scientist from eastern Germany, who probably wasn't too pleased that her homeland had reunified with the bourgeois West. She was partial to grey wool suits, horn-rimmed glasses, and severe bun dos for her white hair. Deacon didn't like her, but she was supposed to be good.

"She's definitely no Cathleen Harris in the looks department," Lisa said, "but get her out of that bun and into a little makeup and leather?"

"You're incorrigible."

"What can I say, I like strong women. Anyway, she's supposed to be top notch in viral vectors."

"She'd better be," Deacon said, as he watched ZuZu rise shakily onto her four legs. "Rederiving the formula for Creel-1 was a snap, given that we've already derived it once."

"And given that your mega brain could spit it back out like a gob of snot."

"I appreciate the compliment, if not the imagery," Deacon said.

"Speaking of which, why didn't you synthesize it yourself? You did last time, before all the, um, unpleasantness."

Deacon ignored the memory of the unpleasantness. "My lab skills are rusty. I wasn't taking any chances. Ray heads up developmental chemistry. He's a ten-times better bench chemist than I'll ever be. I knew he'd have no problem, even with a tricky synthesis." He watched Rudolph take a few stumbling steps toward the water bottle. "But turning my antidote into an easily deliverable treatment will be a tougher nut." He left unsaid the human testing, which he still couldn't believe received ethical approval.

"When these two stay healthy," Lisa said, "we can test another pair, just to make sure. When those two don't buy the farm, we'll pass Creel-1 on to Comrade Saponek — with any luck, a little over forty-eight hours from now. With six days to spare on our ten-day deadline." She smiled. "Wanna go to Disney World?"

Rudolph's gait steadied as he reached the metal nozzle of the plastic water bottle. He sniffed it, then took a tentative drink. Evidently deciding it was okay, he wrapped his little rat mouth around the tubing while his little rat tongue pushed the metal ball to start the flow. Rudolph drank heartily.

"Yeah, buddy," Lisa said. "You must be thirsty after that long nap. Bottoms up."

Rudolph continued to drink, his rodent teeth nibbling at the stainless-steel tube while his tongue held the metal ball at bay. They watched as he drank more, then more still.

"Enough already," Lisa said.

Rudolph gagged out little rodent coughs but continued drinking.

"Something's wrong," Deacon said. He reached into the cage to pull the rat away from the bottle but jerked his hand back as Rudolph nipped his finger. "Shit!"

"You okay?"

"I'm okay," Deacon answered, shaking pain from his finger. "But look at our boy."

Rudolph lunged back to the metal tube, obsessively forcing it into his mouth. Half the nozzle disappeared, but still the rat forced it further. Coughing changed to choking, but still he jammed further, his four incisors now gnawing against the plastic cap.

"Jesus," Lisa said.

"Pull the bottle away," Deacon shouted.

Lisa grabbed the plastic bottle protruding outside the cage, but Rudolph held on tight, both teeth wedged firmly into the plastic of the cap, the entire two-inch tube rammed down his throat. Lisa shook the bottle and pulled until the rat's nose was crammed against the inside wire.

"Shit! The little bastard won't let go."

"I'll pull him off," Deacon said, lifting off the cage top and reaching inside.

"Careful! Remember last time."

Deacon had barely touched the hairs on the rat's haunch when he flinched back, distracted by a large crash to his right. Looking in that direction revealed ZuZu's cage upended on the floor, water, urine, and feces scattered about. Their female rat had wedged her snout into the cage wire, teeth gnashing, blood and foam spittling about as she wrenched her head back and forth in a frenzy that was every bit as violently obsessive as her brother's. Deacon reached down just as ZuZu gave her neck a violent jerk. He could hear the vertebrae snap as she twitched twice then lay still, her head at an impossible ninety-degree angle from her haunches.

"And there goes Rudolph," Lisa cried.

Deacon dragged his eyes from the dead female rat to the male rat dying on the lab bench. Rudolph's nose and tail, which had been a ruddy pink, were now purple. The body stiffened and shuddered, then went limp. Deacon's trembling fingers pulled the already cooling rodent toward him, but it still wouldn't budge.

"Little bastard has nailed himself to the plastic cap like Jesus on the cross." Deacon let go of the rat and said, "You okay?"

Lisa nodded. "Yeah, I'm fine." She pointed. "But *they* sure aren't."

"What the hell happened?" Deacon asked.

"Well," Lisa said, wiping her hands on her lab coat. "At first blush, I would say our Christmas rats had exhibited suicidal behaviors from their dose of SL606. The kind of behaviors Creel-1 was supposed to prevent."

"But didn't," Deacon said.

"That's for damn sure."

"I don't get it. What could have gone wrong?"

"Maybe your gin-soaked brain got part of the formula wrong."

Deacon shook his head. "I could have sworn. Did you change the protocol, add something?"

"Don't point at me, Commander. I just injected the stuff *you* made."

"I know," Deacon replied, waving her off. "I'm just grasping at — you have any left?"

Lisa shook her head. "We had barely enough Creel-1 for the trial."

Deacon nodded. "What could have gone wrong?"

"You *sure* you got the formula right?"

"I'm sure."

"I mean, it's been eight months," Lisa said. "Lot of bourbon under the bridge."

Deacon glared at this second reference to his drinking. "That will be about enough of that, Lieutenant."

Lisa nodded. "Aye, sir."

Turning from Lisa, he stared at the two dead rats and the mess on the floor. "I don't understand. What could have gone wrong?"

"Excuse me for barging in, doctors. I was on my way up to administration when I heard a crash." Metternich's bulk filled the doorway, spectacled eyes looking at the mess. "Everything alright?"

"Um, yes, fine, Joe. Just a little, um, accident."

"So I see, Dr. Creel." His stare at Deacon suggested that more explanation was required.

"Yes, ah, I, that is we were just ..."

"Just testing to make sure our batch of 606 had lost none of its potency," Lisa said. "And as you can see."

"Yes, indeed." Metternich cleared his throat. "But I could have told you that it has not, Dr. Reilly, *if* you had asked me."

"Just being thorough," Lisa said, smiling.

"Commendable. But time is of the essence. Mila tells me she is still waiting for a working antidote to test with her viral vector. So, I suggest you cease rehashing old ground and commence with testing of Creel-1." He looked from Lisa to Deacon. "That's not a problem, is it?"

"No, no, of course not," Deacon said, feeling guilty and hating himself for averting his gaze from those pig eyes.

"That's next up," Lisa said. "Should have results in a couple days."

Metternich looked at his watch. "No more than that, please." His eyes were lost in a grin that made him look like the director of Muppet labs. "Tempus fugit." Then he was gone.

"Well," Deacon said.

"Well," Lisa repeated, "We've got two days to figure out what the hell went wrong."

"Maybe it was something in the production process," Deacon said. "I'll have Ray whip up a new batch, oversee it myself."

"That'll eat up one day," Lisa said.

"Thirty-six hours," Deacon corrected.

"Which leaves us exactly twelve hours," Lisa said. "Just enough time for one more run."

"Keep your fingers crossed," Deacon said.

"And pray," Lisa said.

Chapter 15

Special Agent Paul Carstairs coughed into his hanky, then popped an antacid into his mouth. Tall and handsome, he looked every bit the central-casting version of an FBI agent, right down to the sharp creases of his navy-blue suit and the grey sideburns on his brush cut. Twenty years ago, he'd been a rising star, as committed a G-man as any in the Bureau. But time and two divorces had dimmed his luster. Enthusiasm had turned to impatience, then lethargy, then bitterness. Now he was back on the coast with a chance to soar.

Harris was another rising star who'd been touted as the next Attorney General — maybe VP. She had a keen eye (not to mention a great ass). He wasn't privy to all the technical details, something about a terror plot, needs to know, and some untimely deaths under mysterious circumstances. They'd tried to downplay the implications, but he'd spent enough time in their lab-coat and dagger world to know that things weren't always as portrayed. And with Creel on the scene, it must be connected to that cluster fuck last year.

He didn't know it all, but he knew it was important to Harris, that she'd gone personally to Justice on it. And he knew it was big. If he could break it fast, make some arrests, it'd look good, make her sit up and notice. She'd owe him. With her in his corner, it might be Special Agent in Charge Carstairs. If ... he thought. He coughed again, then returned the hanky to his pocket. If only this wasn't another dry hole.

"Agent Carstairs?"

A plainclothes cop stood beside a CSI tech running a reddish-brown Honda. Carstairs had met a thousand similar county detectives over his two decades. This one happened to hail from Courtland County, Maryland, but he looked no different from those in Macomb County, Michigan, or Somerset County, New Jersey. Average height, shoulder droop, donut gut, shabby out-of-style sport coat.

The FBI agent gripped the outstretched hand. "Paul Carstairs. What have you got, Sergeant Willowicz?"

"Willinski. Conrad Willinski."

"Sorry. May I?"

The Honda's trunk was ajar, so Carstairs opened it. The sickly sweet odor he'd noticed as he walked over bloomed into a death bouquet.

Willinski read from a pad. "Hispanic female, approximately thirty-five to forty-five years of age. Dark hair. Height approximately five feet five, weight maybe one fifty, one sixty. Face rather badly disfigured, looks postmortem, that's why we couldn't match it to the photo. We left the body in the trunk pretty much as we found her, waiting on the coroner."

"ID?"

"No sir. Forensics has done a preliminary on the car. No wallet, handbag, registration, nothing. Even the license plate and VIN were removed."

"Prints?"

"Burned off. But it was a rush job. We still might get a match."

"So, what makes you think it could be our gal?"

"Both body and car match the general description," Willinski said.

"That all?"

"No, sir. This was in the interior, wedged between the seats." He handed Carstairs a red slip of cardboard.

Carstairs hesitated.

"It's okay, it's been dusted," Willinski said. "No prints."

The FBI agent handled the tattered paper.

"You see," Willinski said. "It's a temporary tag for visitor parking, Fort Deidenbach. Looks to be two to three years old. Given the suspect's history, seemed like a probable."

Carstairs nodded, handing back the cardboard tag. "Let's also run the VIN off the chassis, make sure it's her car."

"Will do. What do you think?"

"I think my job just got a whole lot harder."

Chapter 16

"Y ou staring at me isn't going to help." Raymond Treadaway slipped the forceps delicately under the filter, lifting it slowly from the suction flask. "Don't you have someplace to be?"

Deacon watched over the lab director's shoulder. The air smelled of vinegar, potatoes, and sickly sweetness. He detoured from the memory lane it dredged up. He thought how good a drink would taste , or maybe two or twelve. He shook off that thought as well. Some roads were best left untraveled, at least for the moment.

They'd started the run at oh-five-thirty, which still left nearly eighteen hours for the complex synthesis to be completed — if there were no screwups setting them back to zero. The lab director had personally overseen the setup and was now handling the delicate graveyard shift. Creel-1 couldn't be in better hands, but still Deacon couldn't relax.

"Are you following my formula exactly?" Deacon asked.

"Exactly," Ray said.

"Are the reagents fresh?"

"Delivered by Capitol Scientific two days ago."

"Did you check the glassware?"

Ray dropped the filter into the oven and looked up. "The glassware?"

"You know, was it clean? No residues from previous experiments?"

"Dr. Creel. Are you honestly asking if my staff is incompetent?"

"Sorry, Ray. I'm just, you know."

"Why don't you knock off for the day? Get some rest. Do

you good." Ray adjusted the oven temperature, then muttered, "Do us both good."

"How much Creel-1 will I have to work with?"

"Same as last time," Ray replied.

"Can't you get me a bigger batch?"

"Sure," Ray said, plopping his lab-coated bottom on a metal stool. "You get me an industrial pilot plant for two weeks and I'll run you off ten or fifteen grams." He removed his safety glasses. "But with *these* facilities, *your* formula, and two days, you get two hundred milligrams, give or take a milligram."

"But that's barely enough for an N of two. I'd feel more comfortable if we could dose more rats, five or ten."

"And I'd feel more comfortable if you took a nap, or ate a sandwich, or ran in the gym. Anything that takes you out of my lab." Ray yawned, then smiled. "Sorry, it's late. I'll let you know when it's ready, Deke. Try not to worry."

"Buy you a cup of coffee, sailor?"

Deacon held up his half-full cup, then said, "No, but I'll buy you one."

"Thought you'd never ask, Commander." Lisa grabbed a Styrofoam cup from the counter of the break room and filled it from the carafe. "If you can call this sludge coffee." She sat opposite her chief. "What are you doing here? I figured you'd be overseeing Ray whip up more of your baby."

"He shooed me out. Said I was making him nervous. But I could ask you the same question."

"Couldn't sleep," Lisa said.

"Nightmares?"

"Actually, I woke up during the climax of a passionate affair with Undersecretary Harris." Lisa smiled. "Too keyed up to get back to sleep."

"You've got a one-track mind, Lieutenant." Deacon sipped from his cup. "You look tired."

"I could say the same for you. I guess we both have a lot on our minds."

Deacon nodded. "Listen, Leese. Earlier, with Rudolph and ZuZu, I didn't mean to imply that you were to blame."

She waved him off. "Forget it."

"In fact, I hold your skills in high regard, Lieutenant. And your friendship."

"Thank you, Commander. If I wasn't a dyke, I'd blush."

"Mind if I ask you a personal question?"

"As long as it doesn't have to do with my dream about Dr. Harris."

"You're smart, and you're good at what you do. How come you're still a lieutenant, still a GS-12? That's what you were when I met you."

"And for two years before that." She drank her coffee and shrugged. "No ambition, I guess. Not for *management* anyway, at least around this sewer, er, place."

"And why so cynical?"

"You of *all* people are asking me that?"

"Yeah, I know."

Deacon slumped deeper into his chair. Maybe it was his recent failure. Maybe the rebuke from Amy. Or maybe just getting older. But Deacon Creel wasn't feeling like a wunderkind these days. He was feeling introspective.

"But when I think back over my career," he said. "My time at EIS and in Iraq. Some of the GIs, COs, and genuinely interested scientists I've rubbed shoulders with." He shrugged. "I guess what I'm trying to say is not every place in government is Unit 13, and not everyone in government is Josiah Metternich."

"Maybe they *weren't*, but they are now."

Lisa's lackadaisical cynicism mutated into an impatient sneer. It was like watching Jekyll turn into Hyde, if the good doctor of literary fame had been a jaded lesbian researcher.

"Now we worry more about the habitat of the hooded dormouse than about the millions of illegals traipsing across our border, along with their diseases, gang affiliations, and drugs. We spend five times more on *entitlements* than on national defense while gutless politicians from both parties kick the fiscal can down the road and watch our national debt balloon into the stratosphere."

"Take it easy, Leese."

"I've taken it easy," she snapped. "And I've watched political correctness eat away our first-amendment rights, gun grabbers eat away our second-amendment rights, and fat-assed judges make crazy laws from the bench. I've seen a once great nation reduced to begging the world to like us while they pick our pockets and call us the great Satan. I've had it up to here with taking it *easy*, Commander."

Deacon knew Lisa's political proclivities, but he never knew they ran this strong. "What's your solution?"

"My *solution?*" She suddenly quieted, the fire dampered, the apathetic cynicism back. She shook her head. "Is to finish my coffee and try to get some sleep. Or at least stare at the ceiling until I have to get up. But I hope that answers your question why I'm content to be a lowly technical specialist, one who doesn't have to eat at the same trough as the," she added air quotes, "*smartest* guys in the room."

"I hope present company is excepted." Deacon met her eyes and smiled. Lisa patted his hand.

"You are all right, Dr. Creel." She rose and tossed her cup in the trash. "If I weren't queer, you'd be the one for me."

Deacon winked. "Right back at you. Get some sleep."

"You do the same."

Deacon watched her leave. Then he headed to his quarters, his mind cluttered with thoughts that made sleep impossible.

Chapter 17

He'd been barely twenty-four, a double-doctorate punk, when he joined the epidemic intelligence service. Now, a year later, Deacon was on detached service in Iraq. When the call had gone out needing CRBN specialists for overseas deployment, he'd been among the first to volunteer. Hooyah!

Two technical specialists watched him pull body armor from the cab and place it on the hood of the heavy vehicle. They were a few years younger than him, but regular army through and through. One was tall and lean, with brush-cut sandy blond hair. The other was short and stocky with hair black as coal. Mutt and Jeff, Deacon thought. They stood at an attentive slouch, shoulders slack in their sand-colored fatigues and body armor. The short one had an A4 carbine dangling from his chest on a single-point sling.

As Deacon walked over, he noted them eyeing the shavetail lieutenant new in country. Deacon could almost see their thoughts like cartoon balloons over their heads. *Was this guy a greenie needing to be led or was he an inexperienced asshole that was going to get them killed?* Deacon hoped he was neither.

"Ten hut," tall one shouted. They both straightened and saluted. "Lieutenant."

Deke snapped off a crisp one. "It's ensign. But let's make it Deke, OK?"

Eyes wide at the informality, the tall one said, "Um, alright sir."

"You two have names?"

"Um, yes sir."

"Deke."

"Ah, okay Deke. I'm Specialist Walters."

"How about a first name?"

"Ah, Johnathon. Jake." Deacon held out his hand. They shook. "This here is Corporal Jackson. Peter."

"Pleased to meet you, Pete." Another handshake. Deacon pointed to the hut partially submerged into the Baqubah side street. "This it?"

"Yes sir. Um, Deke. Twenty or thirty canisters in there. Not sure what it is. Maybe nerve agent."

"Or maybe motor oil." Deacon smiled.

Jake smiled back; his body relaxed. "You tell us, sir. Ah, Deke."

"How'd it get missed in the big round up? It's been quite a while since the thunder runs."

"Don't know, sir," Jake said. "This place is a bit out of the way. Looks more like a lean-to garage than a weapons cache."

Pete shrugged. "Shit, I mean, stuff still shows up from time to time. Found two drums of mustard only last month."

"Well," Deacon said. "Let's assume the worst and do this by the book." He walked back to the Humvee and grabbed his body armor. "Has it been checked for booby traps?"

"Yes sir. Um, Deke. The corp and me scoped it out. No trips or detonators. Just the canisters."

Deacon shrugged into his vest, then grabbed a respirator off the back seat. "You two wait out here while I ..." His eyes stared past them. For a moment, he wasn't sure if he was seeing what he was seeing, but only for a moment. He'd never seen an insurgent or a grenade launcher outside the boob tube, but it was like your first rattler. You just knew.

Deacon dropped the respirator and grabbed the Beretta strapped at his side. The gun flashed up in one quick stroke, leveled at a short, swarthy man with his head wrapped in a scarf and his hands wrapped around the grip of a rocket launcher.

The two grunts dove aside as Deacon fired, the air filling with yellow flashes and wisps of burnt powder. The detonations still rang in Deacon's ears as a second sound took their place — the unmistakable, butt-puckering whoosh of a rocket motor.

Jake spun into a crouch, his service pistol leveled. Pete Jackson did likewise, carbine pointed toward the dead insurgent. Then they both looked back at Deacon.

Deacon's breath was fast, his face cold with sweat. But his eyes remained on the prostrate Iraqi, his rock-steady gun still poised toward the threat. Jake dashed to his side.

"You alright, sir?"

Deacon nodded, then lowered and holstered the pistol.

"Looks like he was aiming for the hut," Pete said. "I'm guessing it wasn't motor oil in there."

"I think you just saved our lives, Deke," Jake said.

"No." He wiped sweat and grime from his forehead. "I just saw him first."

As he sipped coffee in the small conference room, Deacon's mind returned to the present. Iraq had been a test, in a life full of them. And he'd passed in Iraq, just as he had in vet school, and grad school, and EIS. Being the best got to be a habit. Then it got to be a monkey. Then the addiction blew apart like angel feathers.

Caffeine and nerves had made for another restless night in a series of them. He'd fought a losing battle with guilt, was still fighting it. He'd fought a losing battle with booze, was still fighting it (he could almost taste Maker's Mark melting away by an icy beer chaser). But he hadn't fought doubt about his scientific skills, his mental abilities, his eidetic memory, his intellectual acumen. That domain had been his rock, his anchor.

Deacon Creel had always held onto a little air of superiority. When things were going well, he'd feign an "aw shucks, twarnt nothin'" humility. But when the going got tough, the humility drifted away. The booze helped with the drifting, lubricated the slide past boast to sneers of derision for the lesser beings who could not be suffered lightly, if at all. Through all the travails of last year, Liz's funeral, trying to wash away memory with a river of whiskey, through all of it, a part of him, sometimes a small part hidden in a closet of the mind, he'd found solace in the certainty of that superiority, that intellect, that mega-brain.

When Barzoon pumped him out of the drunk tank, it was still there, a glowing ember of arrogance. Time and tide had not extinguished it. Technical tools may have gotten rusty, human dignity may have taken on the odor of the alley, but the fundamental fact of his superiority, his brainpower, was inviolable. It couldn't be dulled by time or bleached out by liquor. He'd had it since birth, it had never failed him. He'd never failed.

Yet now, if two more rats died, could that still be said? Would that linchpin still hold? Deacon had no doubts about Ray's skill formulating Creel-1. He had no doubts about Lisa's skill administering it. That left only Deacon himself, the man responsible for Creel-1, his brainchild. The drug that had worked before and should work now. If it did not, then either the first time was a fluke, or ... or what? Deacon's eidetic memory was less than eidetic? Or maybe Deacon Creel was less than he'd always believed. Either way, it would be a first, and in many ways a last. Boy, did he want a drink.

"Is Dr. Reilly joining us?"

Deacon jerked aware. "Um, beg pardon, Joe?"

"I said," Metternich repeated, "will Lisa Reilly be joining us?"

"No, no. She's overseeing the latest rodent trial. It's at a critical juncture, so, um, no."

"Very well. Mila must be likewise *occupied*." Bunsen Honeydew morphed briefly into kid petulance. "At least *you* are present, so let us begin."

Mila Saponek entered the room along with a rustle of white lab coat and a stink of tobacco smoke. She was a tall, stern woman, her silver hair tied into a bun that tightened the severity of her features, which, Deacon thought, might have been lovely at one time and which could still be considered handsome.

"Good evening, Dr. Saponek," Metternich said. "I'm glad you were able to join us."

Saponek grunted in reply, then seated herself in an empty chair across from Metternich. Reaching into her pocket, she withdrew a pack of Chesterfield no-filters and deftly slid a white tube between her lips.

"Ah, this is a nonsmoking facility," Metternich said.

Saponek lit her smoke with a well-practiced flick of a stainless Zippo. "Let's get on vit it," she said, blue smoke puffing with each accented word. "I must to my lab be getting back."

"Ah, well, um, alright. Everything going well there?" Metternich asked. "As well as can be expected?"

"I have been sinking on the matter of za carrier," she said, as if lecturing a group of students whose mumblings did not require her attention. "I've determined zat a modified polio-virus vould best be, *if* ..." she poked her cigarette into the air for emphasis. "If, zee drug, zis Creel-vone, is not too large, no more zan eight to nine kilo daltons. The resulting drug-conjugate could be taken orally, zee modified virus vitstanding stomach acid." She smiled, as if remembering a joke. "In a sugar cube vitt ones morning coffee, perhaps?"

"Well, um, well that's very good," Metternich said. "I'm glad to hear ..."

"But verst." The smoldering butt shot skyward. "I must have zee drug vit vich to verk." Her dark eyes latched onto Deacon's. He thought again that she might have been beautiful once, in a dominatrix sort of way.

"That is being worked on," Barzoon said.

"Ah, yes," Metternich agreed, glancing nervously at Barzoon and then Deacon. "So, um, for the time being, perhaps we should turn things over to Agent Carstairs? I believe he is the reason for this after-hours meeting. Please fill us in on the latest, Special Agent." Bunsen Honeydew returned with a pig-eyed smile. "How goes the man, I mean woman hunt?"

Carstairs sneezed into a hanky. "Excuse me. Summer cold." He cleared his throat. "The woman hunt is over, unfortunately."

"How so?" Barzoon said.

"Carla Ortiz was located this afternoon. In the trunk of her car. She was quite dead."

Barzoon tossed his pen on a folder. "Along with our chances of sweating information from her."

"Has the body been identified definitively?" Metternich asked, visibly disturbed.

"The face had been mutilated with acid, but partial fingerprints match her clearance file. There's no doubt."

Deacon's stomach turned at the thought of that pretty face now burned beyond recognition.

"Cause?" Barzoon asked.

"Strangulation," Carstairs said, hankying his nose. "Either that or a fractured neck. The guy who did it had to be strong, or well trained in such things."

"Oh my," Metternich said. "My, oh, my. What do we do now?"

"We," Carstairs said, "continue the investigation. Follow up on contacts, neighbors, lovers, friends, friends of friends. But especially, follow the money."

"Money?" Metternich asked.

"The hundred grand. No doubt it had been laundered thoroughly before reaching Ortiz, but I know a couple of people who are pretty good at sniffing out stains." He smiled. "Following tiger tracks, as it were."

"So, you think there's a chance of tracking it to its source?" Metternich asked.

"Let's say I'm optimistic." He looked at Barzoon. "It would make it easier if I could get my people more on who or what we are looking for, *specifically* that is."

Metternich looked at Barzoon, who stared him down with a cold gaze before turning to the FBI agent. "I am not at liberty to divulge that at this time."

Carstairs started to protest before Barzoon cut him off.

"But I *will* take it under advisement. So, if there is nothing else?"

"Actually, there is," Carstairs said.

"Oh?"

"There may have been another one."

"Another what?" Metternich asked.

"*What* have we been discussing, Joe?" Barzoon asked sarcastically. "Who?"

"The Honorable Angela Putnam."

"The district court judge?" Barzoon asked.

Carstairs nodded.

"When?"

"Body was found in Arlington this morning."

"You say *may* have been?"

"She took an overdose of sleeping pills and scotch. Might have been accidental. She was a recovering alcoholic and had been having marital problems. So, it's possible she was depressed, fell off the wagon. We'll know more when forensics identifies the type and amount of drugs in her system."

"Had friends, colleagues reported her as depressed or suicidal?" Barzoon asked.

"So far we've only spoken with her husband and coworkers. Husband said they'd been 'talking and working on things,' but he'd had an affair, could have been lying. Law clerk said she'd been a little tired lately."

"Had she had any respiratory complaints?" Metternich asked. "A cold or ..." He stopped short after an icy stare from Barzoon.

Deacon thought of Liz in rosy water. He wished the image into the cornfield then wished for a drink.

"Not that I know of," Carstairs said. "But it's certainly possible." He pointed to himself as he blew his nose.

"So, there's no reason to believe it wasn't an accident or ... something?"

Carstairs shrugged. "No, except that she didn't leave a note, which is a little atypical for educated women. Two, she'd just ruled on a rather controversial gun-control bill, a political hot potato that's made tongues wag and tempers flare. Three, she'd once been mentioned as a candidate for the high court. From the little I've been able to glean from all this secrecy, this might have made her a ..." He shrugged again. "High-profile target?"

Deacon saw Carstairs exchange looks with the man from Homeland Security. Barzoon's expression was a mixture of surprise and appreciation for the agent's intuition.

"Well," Barzoon said, "thank you, Special Agent. You *will* keep us apprised, of course."

Carstairs took the hint, nodded, and left the room. Deacon started to follow suit, when Barzoon spoke again.

"I think you can now appreciate the urgency of your efforts, Dr. Creel." He smiled a mixture of genuine respect and crocodile anticipation. "We are all counting on you."

"Prancer and Bailey are coming around," Lisa said.

"What happened to Rudolph and ZuZu?" Deacon asked.

"Figured it was bad luck to reuse those."

"We can certainly use the luck."

Deacon felt like déjà vu all over again. He and Lisa were back in the lab with two sedated rats in Tecniplast cages. Just like before, Rudolph and ZuZu versions 2.0 were sleeping it off, ready to emerge from their twelve-hour nap. They'd similarly been dosed with a new batch of Creel-1, the batch assiduously processed under his and Ray's watchful eyes, before receiving the SL606. The difference was that there was no wire on which to grip and twist; the water bottles and wire tops had been replaced by slotted plastic. The only other difference was that another forty-eight hours had ticked off the clock. Hours that may have cost the life of a woman named Angela Putnam.

"You okay, skipper?"

Deacon only nodded, the tightness in his chest restricting speech.

"Don't worry," Lisa said. "This one will be the charm. I can feel it."

"Your woman's intuition?" Deke managed.

"Hell no. My faith in Deacon Creel."

Deacon returned her reassuring smile with a feeble one.

The two researchers watched as noses twitched, whiskers danced, and tails waved. The Creel-1 had been given six hours to take hold before the SL606 had been administered. That should be more than enough time, if ... The big *if* again, Deacon thought. His life had become a series of ifs, most turning into woulda, coulda, shoulda. Please God, let this not be one of those.

"How goes the battle?"

Both Deacon and Lisa started at the high-pitched nasal voice. Josiah Metternich stood just inside the doorway.

"Um, well, hello, Dr. Metternich," Lisa said, raising her eyebrows at Deacon.

"Can we help you, Joe?" Deacon asked.

"No, no. I just wanted to come down and check on your progress. Please, go on with what you were doing." He squinted at the rats through the beady eyes of a close relative, perhaps an oversized marmot. "Is this the moment of truth? The proof of the pudding, as it were?"

Deacon felt strange, surreal, as if he'd left his body and was watching it. He became aware of his feelings and reactions not in the first person, but by proxy, as if a close friend was observing and relaying the information to him. This friend noted the sheen forming on Deacon's forehead,, Deacon's labored breathing, the rapid heart rate quivering Deacon's lab coat with each triphammer blow. His friend saw Deacon shuffle toward a stool to sit down before he fell down.

Joe Metternich was saying something now, although Deacon couldn't make it out. The words hung in the air but didn't penetrate the cotton filling his head and ears. He caught a glimpse of Lisa, her eyes reflecting the terror in his own, eyes that said, 'uh oh.' She was speaking now as well, her words barely penetrating. Deacon's alter ego saw her turn to Metternich, her face taking on a strained smile that was as fake as a starlet's chest to anyone who really knew her. Fortunately, Metternich did not.

"Um, not quite," Lisa said. "Still a bit to go. Why don't you turn in and we'll give you a full report in the morning?"

Deacon heard the words more clearly now and blessed Lisa for them. He was back, back in his own body, back with his own feelings experienced in the first person. Now Deacon could feel the sweat clinging to his face. He noted the bone-wearying fatigue ratchet down to mere tiredness from the end of a trying day. His lungs managed a deep breath against the strain of tension in his chest. If Metternich would just leave, all would be well.

"Nonsense," Metternich said. "I wouldn't miss it." He waddled over, faux good nature oozing from him like the sweat from his round, red face. "It's good to get back into the lab. I've been riding a desk too long, never in on the kill. No, no. Just pretend I'm not here." He plunked his mass on a steel stool, making that impossible.

Lisa's eyes met Deacon's, the fake smile still plastered to her lips. The 'uh oh' in her pretty browns changed to a question. Deacon's eyes returned the proper answer, although his brain was not sure that he *could* hold it together, not sure at all. Still, there was little else to do.

"Wish us luck," Deacon said, directing the question to Lisa as much as Metternich. Then the three scientists stared at the waking rodents.

The larger of the rats, Prancer no doubt, shook its whiskers and slumped onto its chest, eyes blinking. It took a tentative step forward, paws stumbling once before regaining some semblance of swaying balance. Nosing, no doubt sensing for the water, it examined cage walls, steps steadying.

Now Bailey was awake. She was quicker to her feet, as if the anesthesia had worn down to plain sleep before she'd roused.

She likewise followed the perimeter of the cage, pausing to look up periodically.

Seconds ticked by without anything unusual. Deacon managed an inhalation against the steel bands that used to be his ribcage. His peripheral vision caught Lisa checking the clock. He followed her gaze and watched the secondhand creep around, like it was sweeping through syrup instead of air. He hadn't noticed the time Prancer woke, but he heard Lisa say, "That's one minute." Still the rats explored, twitched, nosed, and poked, apparently normal in every rodent sense of the word.

"Excellent," Metternich said. "Well done. You are to be congratulated, Dr. Creel. And you as well, Dr. Reilly. Now we can pass the good news onto Mila."

"Thwack!"

The cage lurched forward, the force of Prancer's charge jolting it several inches. The white animal leapt into the air, landed, then dashed in the other direction with another titanic thunk of bone on plastic. He reversed course again, and again, the force of the collisions threatening to upend his Tecniplast prison. Lisa reached to steady the cage just as another charge slapped it hard against her hands.

"Ow!" Lisa yelled.

Deacon heard a strangled grunt. His attention turned to the other cage, where Bailey had managed to hook her teeth into the plastic slats on the roof. The female rat flipped her body violently, seeming to time each twist and jerk to the sounds of Prancer's repeated head bashings. Deacon reached over to steady the Tecniplast, wondering errantly why it mattered.

"Oh my God," Metternich said.

Deacon followed Metternich's eyes to Prancer, who was now lying in a pool of blood and brains, gore spattered against spider cracks in the cage walls. Then Deke looked down at Bailey just as she twisted one final, violent time. He heard a soft crack as her neck took on the unnatural, ninety-degree bend he'd seen before. Her body dangled still as a side of beef.

Silence filled the air along with the smell of blood and rodent piss. No one spoke for one full sweep of the clock. Finally, Metternich said, "I assume this was *not* a successful test." His tone was matter of fact, but with an undertone of contempt, as if he relished the notion that they'd failed. "Four days wasted. Four days."

Deacon once more rose out of his body, Metternich's words an echo fading against the blood pounding in his ears. He heard Lisa's distant voice say, "Now is not a good time, Joe." Then Metternich spoke again, the anger of the words penetrating through Deacon's fog.

"When would be a good time, Dr. Reilly? When more have died because our prima donna's whiskey-soaked brain has lost its spark? Maybe the next time he insults me? He who is perfect and without flaw. Would that be a good time?"

Deacon was losing the flow again, the words barely audible against the incessant pounding in his head. Yet they were there. They carried through on a subliminal level, bypassing his ears, going directly to his mind. Like a well-trained deaf mute, Deacon watched the fat lips form them and he knew their meaning.

"What am I supposed to tell Barzoon? Hmm? What am I supposed to tell Undersecretary Harris? What? That the boy wonder we've rested our hopes upon is a fraud?"

Our hopes, Deacon thought. What did Metternich know about hopes and dreams. Deacon had had hopes, hopes for career, for family, for love. He'd also harbored the dreams that went with them. Thoughts of Liz rose like a body in a swamp. He tried to force them back, but his mind refused to turn away. "What about when the next person dies? What am I supposed to tell *their* family?"

Deacon thought, what do you tell them? Tell them who's responsible, really responsible. The clarity of this thought was a revelation. It was a solace, a balm, a bandage against the guilt and remorse he'd lived with night and day for close to a year. Gradually, he was changing. Gradually, oh so gradually, all the frustration, worry, fatigue, doubt, and sleeplessness of the last few days distilled into a new, potent liquor. Insecurity, self-loathing, and guilt were morphing into a new emotion. Oh, they were still there and he'd return to them. But for now, they were subsumed, burnt away like slag, leaving only pure product. Molten metal, hot and hard. The steel of hate.

"Well?" Metternich was screaming at him now. Deacon could feel the blast of coffee breath against his face. "Boy wonder? Ha! It is to laugh." Lisa tried to say something, but Metternich cut her off. "Boy fool. Boy ... fraud. Boy..."

Don't say it, Deacon thought, blood pounding in his ears like the roar of an L train. Hate seething from his gut like acid. If you say it, you'll cross a line. We'll both cross a line.

"Boy ... failure."

The last was said quietly, almost calmly. Yet it struck home with all the power of a lover's curse. Deacon saw the word form on the pucker of the almost feminine lips, he heard it through the bell jar of his head, he saw the letters in his mind, ten feet tall. And he smiled. The line had been transected; the Rubicon crossed. A great weight lifted from Deacon's chest. For the first time in many months, he had purpose, his way was clear.

Metternich turned away, lashing his petty tyranny in Lisa's direction.

"And you? What good have *you* done for this project, this important work? None, as far as I can tell."

Deacon stood, legs planted firmly, his muscles sprung steel. Lisa saw him step toward Metternich's back, her look of sheepish indignation turning to surprise that Metternich, lost in his tantrum, did not notice.

"Well, Dr. Reilly? Answer me. What!"

"Joe," Deacon said, placing his left hand on Metternich's shoulder. "There's something I've been meaning to say to you." Metternich's corpulent body turned from its rage against Lisa, the fat moon-face rotating into view, angry words still spewing from the pouty lips, hate still raging from the beady eyes.

Metternich stopped talking as Deacon drew back his fist. Lisa managed only, "Deke. No!" Then the fist struck home. Self-hatred, insecurity, guilt, had all returned. But instead of caressing them like an old friend, Deke's mind funneled them into his right hand. It felt glorious.

Blood splattered across Deacon's lab coat as Metternich's lip burst like a bloated leech. Metternich's round, Charlie-Brown head flew backward, glasses flying against linoleum with a crack and tinkle of broken pieces. Metternich's chair went one way, his bulk the other. And as some noir novelist once wrote, the good doctor dropped like a bag of hammers.

Lisa gasped and ran to Metternich's side. Deacon stood there, panting and smiling.

He said just two words. "I quit."

Chapter 18

Ten-year-old Amy Robbins sat up in bed. Her eyes flew wide. Something had awoken her, but it didn't feel like it had been a dream. At least she couldn't remember one. Then she saw the hallway light flick a band of gold under her bedroom door. She heard her mother's footsteps in the hallway, hurrying along the runner in bare feet that hadn't had time to don slippers. There was a soft knock on the front door. Her mom's hesitant voice said, "Yes, who is it?"

"Elaine?" the voice answered back. "It's Bob Wainwright. I need to talk to you."

Gunnery Sergeant Wainwright? Uncle Bobby? What was Uncle Bobby doing here at ... She glanced at the bedside clock. A little before four in the morning. Oh-four hundred as her dad would say. She missed her dad, far off in Iraq fighting the terrorists. Yet she was proud as well. Staff Sergeant Robbins, platoon sergeant, Bravo Company, Sixth Marines. He went to Iraq to guard the peace. To guard them all.

Amy's thoughts were broken by her mother's voice. A single word. "No." Repeated over and over in a tone Amy had never heard before. A tone that filled her with menace. Then Uncle Bobby spoke again.

"I'm so sorry, Elaine."

Then her mom was crying. Then Amy was crying.

Amy jerked awake. Had it been a dream? Was the terrible news just a dream? For a moment, she was still a little girl learning about her father's death. Then the moment passed, and Marine Force Specialist Robbins heard the knocking on her bedroom door located in guest quarters at Unit 13. She was fully awake now, bouncing from the bed and slipping into her flannel robe as she hurried to the door. One hand clicked on the light as the other undid the deadbolt. Blinking against the sudden brilliance, she opened the door.

"Hi. Sorry to wake you. But — you seen your boss?"

Lieutenant Reilly was standing there, tall and lean in her lab coat. She and Commander Creel, Deke, had been working down on the restricted floors. Amy hadn't seen either of them for almost twenty-four hours. She blinked away flashbulb dots from the sudden lights and started to answer. Then she noticed Reilly's worried look. Then she noticed the blood smeared across the white coat's sleeve.

"What's wrong?"

"Ah, maybe we should discuss this inside."

"Metternich is okay, busted lip but okay. But your boss is gone."

"Where?" Amy asked.

Lisa shrugged as she paced. "Hoped *you* might know. He's off the premises, anyway. Security desk called to him as he bolted through the door." She checked her watch. "That was forty minutes ago. Guard called downstairs then looked outside." Lisa's thumb and forefinger formed a goose egg. "Joe wants to send out MPs, have him hauled back under arrest, general court, assault, throwing of the book, yada yada. I'm hoping we can avoid that."

Amy had finished dressing, buckling the belt on the khakis that went with her blue polo and loafers, the business-casual uniform reserved for off-base activities.

"His royal roundness was there to witness the failure " Lisa paused, holding up a finger. "Pardon, the *second* failure of Creel-1."

"Creel-1?"

"Yeah. It's the ... how much do you know?"

"Some," Amy said. "Enough, I think."

"It's this antidote to a, well a poison that's been stolen. You understand?"

"Yes," Amy said. "The formula that only Dr. Creel knows."

"Well, that has certainly been the working assumption. But after two failures?" Lisa shrugged. "Let's say Metternich now has his doubts. He was not pleased with the outcome of the latest test. And, well, he let those feeling be known in his own inimitable way." She was pacing again. "Deke of course did not care to be dressed down by the little corporal, especially when such dressing down fueled his own inner insecurities. Hence," She smacked her fist into her other hand. "So," Lisa said, stopping in mid pace, "King Creel stormed out and is currently AWOL. Any ideas?"

Amy said, "I think I know where he *might* be."

The Burrito Brothers were drinkin' Canada Dry on the jukebox. Same shit, different tune, Amy thought as she entered Woody's Place for the second time.

The late-night crowd was just as big as the happy-hour one, but louder. She could barely hear music pulsing from the juke amidst the raucous laughter and shouts pulsing from the patrons. The camos had been replaced by various forms of business casual not unlike what she was wearing.

Instead of Jazzelle, another young girl dashed between tables, but her face held the unmistakable stamp of the Samples line.

Woody was at his old stand behind the oak. He saw her almost as soon as she stepped through the door, waved, then pointed to the back. Amy nodded and headed in that direction amidst leers, wolf whistles, and calls of "hey babe."

Deacon was at his old stand, slumped into a booth bench. His fingers were wrapped around a half-full beer glass, his eyes staring through a half-empty shot glass, vision fixed on some distant point in the past. Amy sat down opposite, watching Deacon continue to stare at the dark liquor, bar lights turning the glass into multifaceted reflections. After a moment, he looked up and seemed to recognize her, his eyes regaining their old, sad smile.

"Fleet Marine Force Specialist Robbins." There was no slur, just the thick, slow language of the moderately wasted, words pouring forth like syrup from a jug. "What an unexpected pleasure." Before she could answer, he held up a cautionary finger. "But I am remiss, remiss I say, remiss in two respects." He tapped the table with his forefinger. "One, I have not offered you a libation." Helicoptering his hand over his head, he shouted, "Angelique! Get your fine self over here." Then he held up two fingers. "And B, I called you Fleet Marine Force Specialist when I have previously insisted that you forego such martial formality and call me Deke. Sooo, I apologize and rephrase." He snatched the dram glass in one swift motion and downed the booze. Wincing slightly, he exhaled and said, "How you doing, Amy?" The sad smile was still there as he looked around. "Where's Angelique with that drink?"

"I don't need a drink," Amy said. "And neither do you, Deke."

"Oh, but that's where you are wrong Fleet Marine — Amy. I most certainly do need a drink. Several in fact. I need a river of drinks. Enough to wash away the taste of that place, what they've done, what they're doing, what they are. Wash it away, so I don't have to even think about it. So I don't have to keep kicking myself for letting them drag me back into this." He upturned the empty shot glass and thunked it on the table.

"Don't have to face your own guilt?" Amy added. "Your own failure?"

His head snapped up, the smile gone. Then it returned, tinged with anger. "Quite the amateur psychologist, aren't we, Fleet Marine Force Specialist?"

"If that's what's needed, sir."

"And you think that's what's needed? Hmm, Fleet Marine Force Specialist?" He stared at his glass, not at Amy, then sighed.

"You are right, of course," Deacon said. "Right as rainy rain. I may have popped old Honeydew in the lips, but I was really popping old Doc Creel, not so young pushing middle-aged boy wonder who has lost his wonderfulness." He gulped beer. "Old Deacon, Doc, Creel." He painted air quotes around the Doc.

"You know," he said, "back in vet school." His eyes softened in reminiscence. "Back in the olden days. That's what we called them. The old farts who soldiered along practicing medicine they'd learned during the Nixon administration, forgetting more than they remembered. We called them *Doc*. Doc Fleming, or Doc Martin, or Doc Poopoofnick. Everybody had a Doc story about quaint ways and continuing-education conferences spent at the golf course." He finished the beer. "I was a boy wonder of course, youngest in my class, but I still knew about Docs. Had worked with one." He cupped hand to mouth, voice lowered as if in secret conclave. "You had to work in the biz before they let you train for the biz, even if you were a snot-nosed Poindexter who was aiming to be a boy-wonder scientist rather than a doggy doctor."

Deacon settled back, eyes half closed. "And I was sooo smug about it. So superior to all the Docs. So superior to all my *classmates*. I who had had a straight 4.0 since preschool." He smiled again. "Voted most likely to be potty trained." His eyes held that half-sleeping look she'd seen on the plane, but now there was a hint of self-loathing mixed with the disinterest. "I who had always succeeded. *Would* always succeed." The smile darkened further. "That was back in the olden days, the good old golden-boy olden days. Before I ever landed in Unit 13. Before I even met ..."

Deacon shook his head. "I can't figure out where it went wrong." His eyes flew open, tears glistening the corners. "I just can't figure it out."

"Mind if I join the party?"

Amy looked up at Lisa Reilly standing by their booth. "Maybe we can figure it out together."

"How did you get here?" Amy asked, as Lisa settled in next to her.

"Followed you, of course."

Angelique showed up, flushed and out of breath. "Sorry for the wait. It is a frickin' madhouse today. What's everybody drinking?" She looked at Deacon. "Coffee?"

"Corona and lime," Lisa said.

Angelique nodded and looked at Amy.

"Scotch and water." She thumbed toward Deacon. "Another beer for Commander Creel."

"Beer and." Deacon held up his empty shot glass.

"Just beer," Amy said, her tone broaching no argument.

Angelique got the message and scurried off.

"So," Lisa said. "This is a pleasant spot. Seems I've been

here once or twice before, although Ruth didn't like it, back when there was a Ruth and Lisa, or would that be Lisa and Ruth, I guess it doesn't matter anymore as Buddy Holly used to say, if that's what he *did* say, I'm bad with lyrics and I can't sing worth a damn. Am I babbling?" No one spoke. "So," she continued, "I talked Señor el Doctor Cerdo out of alerting the gestapo for the time being. Promised I'd bring you back, that you'd apologize." Deacon's teary glare made her blanch. "Well, maybe we can defer the second part. But we'll need to be getting back, after our drinks of course, and after we maybe figure out what went wrong today."

Angelique returned with their order. "Anything else? If ya'll want food, the kitchen is closed, but I could wrangle over cold sandwiches. Somethin' on the belly sometimes helps, you know?"

"No thanks," Amy said.

"Did you remember the whole formula clearly?" Lisa asked. "Was there maybe one part that was hazy?"

They'd been jawing the problem through two rounds of drinks.

"Maybe a snippet lost during an alcoholic blackout?" Deacon shot back.

"Well, I wouldn't put it quite that way."

"I remember it as clearly as I do my street address in third grade — 13898 Charest, Dayton, Ohio, 45458, or my driver's license number — SX3561284, or the number pi — 3.14159 26535 89793 23846 26433 83279 50288 41971 ..."

Lisa raised her hands in surrender. "Okay, I get the picture. And Ray's synthesis was correct, you're sure?"

"I *watched* him do it."

"You watched him the whole time?"

"Yes, well, no, he sent me off because I was making him nervous. Remember? When we had coffee in the breakroom, remember? But come on. You know Ray better than to think *he's* the weak link here."

Lisa sipped her second beer, eyes downcast. Deke recalled their conversation in the break room.

"And I'm not saying *you're* the problem either. Like you said, you just injected the stuff Ray sent you. That leaves us with just one possible answer."

"Barzoon sent me," Lisa said.

"The one weak link that ... Huh? What?"

Lisa smiled. "Sorry. Just my irritating, overly fastidious nature. It was pointing out that I received the sample from the Grand Poobah, not Ray."

"What? Barzoon brought the sample to you personally?"

"Well, no, he had a gopher deliver it. It's a chain of custody thing he set up for added security."

"I'm confused," Amy said.

"Me, too," Deacon said, eyes clearing in interest, his dulled senses sharpening. "Enlighten us, please, lieutenant."

Lisa shrugged. "That's the chain of custody Homeland Security set up. The 606 is restricted access, and the Creel-1 deemed too important to entrust to us flunkies. So, Ray calls Barzoon when synthesis is complete. He sends someone to hand deliver it to me, along with enough 606 to get the job done. And this hired goon watches as me and Stan anesthetize and inject the rats."

Hairs stood to attention on Deacon's neck. "This is how it worked both times? Both times it failed? Today and a few days ago?"

Lisa nodded. "I thought you knew."

"No," Deacon said. "No, I didn't."

"Is this important?" Amy asked.

"Yeah," Lisa said. "What's the big diff who delivers it?"

Deacon was suddenly sober. His confidence renewed. "Do you test the purity or anything when they deliver it?"

"How?" Lisa replied. "I get just enough to do the treatment. And mine is a clinical lab, not an analytical one. I don't have a mass spec. Even if I did, I'm not sure what's in the stuff so how can I tell if it's pure? And again, what's the difference who delivers it?"

"I'm not sure," Deacon said. "But don't you think it odd that we didn't go through such precautions when we were handling 606 and Creel-1 before? It was just as dangerous then. We all had the same clearances then. Why now? And why don't Joe's people deliver the sample? He heads the lab. Why Barzoon, who couldn't tell a virus from a Volkswagen?"

"I don't know," Lisa said. "Maybe because we're directly under Homeland Security now. Undersecretary Hottie more or less said her department was taking over. They're more cloak and dagger, I guess."

They sat in the not-quite silence but reduced din of the ready-to-close tavern. Most patrons had left, the hangers-on awaiting official dismissal. Lisa looked at Amy, who looked back at Lisa. Then they both looked at Deacon. Finally, Lisa spoke.

"What are you thinking, boss?"

"I don't know. Maybe nothing. Maybe ..."

"Last call come and gone, folks," Angelique said. She blew an errant hair from her less harried brow. "Check time?"

Deacon nodded. "Thanks, Angel."

"How'd you know to call me that? My daddy calls me that sometimes, but no one else."

For the first time that night, the clouds lifted the sadness from Deacon smile. "I must have heard him say it. And I've got a photographic memory."

Angel pulled the bill from her receipt pad and dropped it on the table as all three patrons stood. Deacon looked it over, then rummaged the billfold from his trousers. Checking his cash reserves, he frowned, then scanned the bill again.

"Um, does anyone have any cash?"

"I'll get it," Lisa said, shaking her head as she tugged her wallet from her pants pocket. "I notice that your memory is photographic for everything but money."

Deacon chuckled. "I owe you."

"You can buy me a beer sometime," Lisa said, dropping four bills onto the table.

"I owe you more than that," Deacon said with a smile.

The air had been warm and clear when he'd crossed Amber Drive earlier in the evening. Now, an early morning fog was adding a chill, its tendrils goose-pimpling his arms. Turning up his collar, Deacon breathed in gratefully.

He was no longer drunk. Lisa's revelation sobered him like a dip in the Potomac. He still couldn't be sure, but an anxious little knot crept into his gut. It might be nothing more than an inability to accept his own failing. Or it might be paranoia, his distaste for Unit 13 coloring his judgment. Or it just might be an explanation, a reason why. He smiled. "Just because you're paranoid, doesn't mean they aren't trying to get you."

"What was that?" Lisa asked.

He shook his head. They continued walking through the lot, pausing periodically to let unsteady vehicles angle out of parking spaces. The place was emptying fast.

"So," Lisa continued. "You gonna tell me what you're thinking?"

At first, he didn't answer. What he was thinking seemed too outlandish. Then he said, "First thing tomorrow, ask Ray to synthesize a new batch of Creel-1."

"If at first you don't succeed?"

They stopped as a red Ford blew past, barely missing them as it shot from the fog.

"Have it delivered, per previous runs."

"So, we try again," Lisa said.

"No," Deacon said. "We take the sample back to Ray. Me, personally, to have it tested."

"What? Why?"

"Because," Deacon answered.

"You're concerned that the sample has been switched in transit," Amy said. "Aren't you, sir?"

Deacon heard Amy's fog-muffled words, but her presence was reduced to a pair of shoes marching on his right. "Let's go back to Deke and Amy, okay. And yes I am."

"What?" Lisa said, her words likewise muffled, her body completely hidden. "Switched? By who? Barzoon? Why?"

"I don't know," Deacon said. "But it would explain a lot."

"But why would Barzoon want to — whoa. Are you thinking what I think you're thinking?"

"I don't know *what* I'm thinking. Not for sure anyway. I just know that right after Barzoon institutes this unusually cumbersome chain of custody, a drug that used to work now crashes and burns."

They reached the curb. The fog had deepened to the point that visibility on Amber Drive was measured in inches, the streetlight adding glare that reduced rather than aided vision. Deacon looked first one way, then another, cocking his ear for sounds of oncoming traffic. Hearing none, he started crossing.

"Joe isn't going to like a delay of two days just to test out some wild-ass-guess paranoid theory." Lisa's voice sounded distant, as if the night mist was choking off her words. "Especially given that he's already convinced your benumbed brain is the problem."

"I don't give a good goddam what Honeydew thinks. I've stopped worrying about that a long ... before now anyway."

His heels clicked softly on the macadam, Amy's right beside his. That and the green-apple smell of her shampoo were the only indications that he wasn't walking alone. The fog ate everything else, swallowing up sight, sound — even thought. The cover of a noir novel swam into his brain, something by Hammett or Chandler, one of those garish illustrations of a mysterious forties babe, ruby lips gasping, painted nails touching the ample bosom pillowing from her trench coat, a shadowy figure approaching from out of the fog.

"I want a meeting for zero eight thirty tomorrow morning," he said, feeling oddly as if he were talking to himself. "Just me, you, and Ray. Let's keep this ..."

They'd gone halfway through the crosswalk when a noise broke out of the mist as if to say 'here I am, fear me.' It was a noise Deacon immediately recognized — the throaty growl of a muscular engine being unmistakable when heard from the center of a street on a foggy night.

Deacon paused, hoping the sound would doppler away. Instead, it increased in volume until the growl became a roar, like a lion making the killing dash on an unwary roebuck. He froze, the lighting instincts that kept him and others alive in Iraq having fled momentarily. Amy reacted quicker. He felt strong arms push him back and down. He felt pain as his knee hit the pavement. Then he felt the rush of a powerful machine thundering past, a blur amidst the swirl of mist, it's engine whining into the distance.

"Are you alright, sir?" The voice came from somewhere to his right.

"Yeah," he answered. "Drunken bastard." In the distance, the engine noise morphed into a screech of tires. Then he heard it again, the gut-wrenching sound of acceleration.

"What the hell?"

Deacon headed toward Amy's voice. Amy must have headed toward his. Their bodies met with a thud that sent them both onto the pavement. He wrapped arms around the taut, warm smell of green apples and rolled toward the curb they'd left a moment before. There was a second swirl of mist and exhaust, this time preceded by a glare of headlights that Deacon's mind registered as two hungry, flame-ringed eyes, like some dragon straight from middle earth. Once again, there was a screech of tires. Once again, the wail of a big engine getting bigger.

"This way," he yelled, grabbing Amy's arm and heading toward the safety of the tavern lot. The driver, evidently foreseeing this possibility, headed for the curb, the monstrous beams shadowing them in the fog, two specks of humanity fitting for a midnight snack. The penumbra of headlight grew rapidly, more rapidly than Deacon thought possible. He wasn't sure exactly where the curb was but knew it must be close. But the headlights seemed closer, and the roar of the engine closer still. The glare filled his eyes, the roar his ears.

What a way to die, he thought. Then he tugged Amy's arm and yelled, "Jump!"

Chapter 19

Deacon floated, unable to distinguish reality from fantasy. Now he knew how a leaf felt on the freeway, the overpressure of the passing car shoving him forward. He heard a high-pitched squelch, the sound of a tire sideswiping the curb. Then he was landing with a breathless thunk on the strip of grass that separated Woody's lot from Amber Drive. The streetlight seemed to dim, then brighten in several pulses. When his vision stabilized, he realized he was still holding onto Amy. He could still hear the idle of the high-toned engine, which seemed to be pausing to assess the situation. Then the sound of its motor receded into the night.

Deacon lay panting, eyes staring at the glare of the streetlight, his breath rapidly rasping in his ears. All about was fog, or maybe the afterlife, he couldn't tell for sure. Then he heard Amy say, "That kind of hurts, sir."

Deke realized he'd been holding her arm in a death grip, one he had difficulty unclenching. When he finally did, she said, "Thanks." After a pause, she asked, "What just happened?"

Deke took a moment to clear his head, then said, "All in all, I would say someone just tried to run us over. At least, that's how I saw it. You?"

"Affirmative."

"You alright?" Deacon asked. He could smell green apples, although their source was not visible.

"Fine," Amy answered. "A couple of scrapes, maybe permanent nerve damage where you grabbed my arm."

Deacon sat up, still panting, and smiled. "Sorry about that."

"Where's Lieutenant Reilly?"

Those three words tore through his inertia like proverbial excrement through the proverbial waterfowl.

"Lisa," he cried, rising shakily to his feet, aches and pains forgotten. "Yo, Leese!"

"What's all the noise," answered a deep, masculine voice behind them. "Jesus H. Christ. Let's maintain a little decorum."

"Woody," Amy said. Deke could hear her shambling up off the wet grass, although he still could not see her. Nor could he see the man behind them, although he knew that she had correctly recognized the voice of the proprietor.

"Mr. Samples?" Amy called into the fog.

"Who that?" Woody hollered back. "That you, darlin? You find your boss okay?"

"Yes," Amy called back. Deacon could see her now, at least the part of her wiping hands on grass-stained khakis. She was walking toward Woody's voice. Deacon followed.

"What was all that other racket? Sounded like Saturday night at the drag strip."

"We're missing one of our party," Amy yelled. "Lieutenant, er Doctor, Reilly. Did you see her?"

As the voice grew louder, a bear-like image took shape in the klieg lights of the parking lot. "I ain't seen nobody since I turned the cash register over to Angel. She's my little closer, minds the books. What happened? Drunk driver lost in the soup?"

"Maybe," Deacon called out, adding a muttered, "but I doubt it."

"Yo, Deke!" Lisa came stumbling out of the fog, hand to the back of her head, joining Deke and Lisa in the parking lot.

"Where have you been?"

"I must have gotten separated from you two in the fog, angled up country." Lisa pointed. "Next thing I know, something's hurtling by and I dove for it. I don't remember much after that until I came to at the sound of our drill instructor over there."

Woody chuckled. They could see him clearly now, his bulky frame haloed by the parking-lot lights. "You folks need a ride somewhere? My Ford is parked right behind the building."

"No," Amy said. "We can..."

"Thanks, sarge" Deacon said. "That'd be great." Amy's and Lisa's curious expressions carried telepathically through the mist. He sideways whispered, "Where's your car?"

"I'm in the communal lot," Amy said.

"Inside the gate?"

"Affirmative."

Deacon smiled and yelled, "Maybe an all-night diner? Denny's or something? Get some breakfast?" He could still sense his companion's curiosity, but they thankfully didn't voice it.

"The Troubadour is on my way home," Woody said. "Greek place about two miles from here. That suit you?"

"That works like a champ," Deacon said.

Woody huffed toward his car. Before Deacon could follow, Lisa grabbed his shoulder.

"You wanna tell me why we're going out for gyros?"

He shook her hand away, then side-mouthed, "Not here." He looked right and left, fruitlessly searching fog. "We don't know who's listening."

"Coffee?" asked a heavy woman in a greasy apron as she handed menus all around.

The menus were coated in vinyl, with paper-tufted cracks suggesting the Troubadour had not changed its bill-of-fare since at least Bill gave his cigar to Monica on Pennsylvania Avenue. Nor had it replaced the vinyl booths, duct-tape repairs and all. Nor had twenty years of grease and smoke done anything to ease the yellow tinge that the light fixtures cast over everything.

Deacon nodded. Lisa nodded. Amy asked for a Pepsi.

"So," Lisa said, "you want to tell me why we're here?"

Deacon shushed her as the waitress returned with two ceramic mugs and a cold glass. "Food?" asked the face that launched a thousand breakfast orders.

"Later, thanks," Deacon said.

"Bagel, cream cheese, eggs scrambled, hash browns," Lisa called to the retreating figure.

"I don't think she heard you, Lieutenant," Amy said.

"It's Lisa. And I'm hungry." Lisa picked up an old-style glass bottle and dispensed real sugar into her coffee. She then looked inside the cream dispenser and said, "Perfect." As she stirred her cup, she asked, "*Now* will you tell me why we are sitting in a restaurant at three in the blessed a.m.? A restaurant with no cream on the tables and where the eggs are going to taste like oregano."

"Keep your voice down."

"Why?" Lisa asked, looking about. "Woody isn't here, if that's who we're keeping the secret from. Only a few people are in fact *here*, and they're all strangers, at least to me, so we can't be keeping secrets from them. And by the way, what's the secret we are not keeping?"

"That wasn't any drunk driver, or any accident." Amy spoke in a declarative statement, then deferred to authority. "Was it, sir?"

"I don't think so," Deacon replied.

"What," Lisa said. "On Amber Drive?"

"Someone tried to kill us," Amy said.

"Why do you say that? Because when I think two in the morning outside a watering hole where the local wildebeest have just been drinking for five or six hours before operating three-thousand-pound machinery, drunk driving immediately comes to mind."

"Do these wildebeest of yours," Deacon snapped, "screech to a halt, reverse direction, and make another pass after they drunkenly miss a passing antelope on their way home to sleep it off?"

"What? Who did that?"

"Your drunken wildebeest, that's who," Deacon said. "You were evidently out of it, which probably saved your life."

"Come on," Lisa said. "I know you're shaken up right now. But let's be realistic. A lot of people were leaving the bar. A lot of those people were drunk. The fog was thicker than the oatmeal in this place. Don't you think there's a more likely explanation?"

"I know what I know," Deacon said. "And I *know* what happened out there."

Lisa picked up her mug, then thunked it back down. "Okay, say you're right. I'm not saying that, but I'll concede the point for sake of argument. Maybe they were just trying to scare you. You know, put you off the scent."

"Then they succeeded. But I doubt the intent was just to scare."

"But why?"

"That's the sixty-four-thousand-dollar question," Deacon said.

"But, well then, shouldn't we be back at the unit?" Lisa said. "Checking in and reporting this to the cops — to site security?"

"And what guarantees we would make it back to the unit?"

"Now hold on a minute," Lisa said, raising her palms. "That sounds pretty far-fetched."

"If they tried it once," Amy said. "They could try it again. Maybe with guns this time."

"Listen," Lisa said. "It's late. We've all had a couple of drinks — Deke more than a couple. The paranoia is running high right now and I'm having trouble swallowing it. If you want my advice, I think we should finish our breakfast, take a couple of Tums, then head back to Unit 13 where it's safe. In the morning, this will all seem like a case of indigestion. Which I am sure it will be."

"Think about it," Deacon said. "I'm the key to the antidote for an unusually deadly drug, a secret antidote that someone might want to *keep* secret. But suddenly, the antidote no longer works. I'm discouraged, I'm *supposed* to be discouraged. Then I learn for the first time about this fucked-up chain of custody and I reach the same conclusion anyone might, given the circumstances. At that point, someone tries to kill me."

"But who would know about any of this?" Lisa said, lowering her voice. "Who would know what you found out?"

"We discussed it in a crowded bar," Amy said. "Anyone could have listened in. Could have listened in and left early, waiting for *us* to leave."

"I think the fog threw him," Deacon said. "He was expecting a clear night, good visibility for hunting." He waved bye, bye. "Then drive off. Just another hit-and-run."

"I'm sorry," Lisa said. "This sounds too unbelievable, too cloak and dagger, too James Bond." She raised her hand, trying to signal the waitress.

"So does a suicide drug," Deacon said. "But that's what the minds at our beloved unit came up with."

"I still can't believe there is such a thing," Amy said.

"Believe it. And I was the boy charged with developing the antidote. Because no terror weapon or assassination drug is really good until you make it so it can't be used against you."

"Should you be telling her all this?" Lisa asked, nodding toward Amy. "I mean, security, need to know?"

Deacon laughed. "I think the point is moot at this juncture. Don't you?"

"It still seems too Lee Child for me. But okay. *If* you are right, and I am not yet saying you are, who?"

"Who devised the chain of custody?"

"Barzoon? But why would Barzoon want to kill Burke, Lebel?"

"That's another sixty-four-thousand in the kitty," Deacon said.

Lisa sipped her coffee. "So, what now?"

"I don't know," Deacon said. "I need some rest. I can barely think." He backhanded a yawn. "And I don't think it's a good idea to rest back at the unit."

"If we don't show up soon," Lisa said, "Herr Metternich is going to send out the Gestapo looking for us."

"You can rest at my place, sir, um, Deke."

Deke looked at Amy. "*Your* place? I thought you were staying at the Unit?"

"I was, I am, but my family has a place near Monacy, on Hoover's Lake. I mean, it belongs to my uncle, but we can all use it. I spent summers there when we were stationed at Quantico. It's not much, just a fishing cabin really, two rooms and a loft, but it's not that far, maybe thirty miles."

Deke watched her smile. It wasn't anything like Liz's smile. So why was he thinking of Liz?

"Okay," he said. "We'll call Uber, have them drop me a block away from the base, you and Amy at the gate. Lisa heads back to the unit, Amy to get her car. Questions?"

"Who pays for the Uber?" Lisa asked.

"I think my credit card can stand it." Amy smiled again.

Deacon again noticed the dark eyes that reminded him of a famous rock singer he never met, and a not-so-famous lawyer he once knew intimately.

"Who knows about this place?"

"Sir?" Amy asked.

"Is it listed on your personnel file?"

"No."

"What'll I tell Herr Metternich?" Lisa asked, again raising her hand for the server.

"Tell him I was drunk. Let him think I'm in my quarters sleeping it off. I doubt he'll check with security to see if I clocked in. Not before noon anyway."

"And what'll I tell him tomorrow when he wants to see you?"

"Stall him." Deacon's half-shout broke through the early morning quiet, causing the waitress to look over from the counter. She grabbed her coffee pot and walked their way. Deke lowered his voice. "Tell him anything. I'm still asleep, I'm in mourning for my poor behavior, the dog ate my homework —anything."

"More coffee?" the waitress asked.

Deke shook his head.

"You want anything else?"

"Yes," Lisa said, holding up the empty creamer. "Then bagel, cream cheese, eggs …"

"Just the check," Deacon interrupted.

The waitress shrugged, deposited a slip of paper on the table, then left.

"I'll call Uber," Amy said, digging her cell out of a hip pocket.

"I'll pay the check," Deacon said, taking out his wallet.

"Two coffees and a Pepsi?" Lisa said. "Big spender."

Chapter 20

Dawn was just a glint in the horizon as Amy navigated her Corolla down the road to Hoover's Lake. The nameless lane wasn't much, just a dirt and gravel track off CR 113, but Amy navigated the ruts and overhanging branches with a skill born of long familiarity. Hoover's Lake itself wasn't much either, no more than a pond with a glandular condition, although Amy told him you could still catch brown trout and perch in it. She turned in at a dark, weathered sign with Robbins burnt into the wood in childish script.

The house was as advertised, just a hunting/fishing cabin with a combination living room-kitchen, a bathroom the size of a phone booth, and a loft bedroom. But the structure had been built with care, logs well-fit and cement-chinked. An uncle's work of love that Amy and her dad had shared. The front door was locked, but a key was hidden quaintly under the mat.

"My dad and I hung this door," Amy said, smiling in the dim light of early dawn. "I caught a trout that summer that was almost a record." She turned away as she fit the key into the lock. "That was the summer before my dad's last deployment to Iraq."

Inside was dark and quiet, with a smell of long disuse. Deacon found and flicked a wall switch, but nothing happened.

"Wait a minute," Amy said. "We turn the power off when no one's using the place."

Deacon watched her disappear into the shadows. The sound of metal on metal was followed by a soft click and a sudden flare.

Deacon shaded his eyes against a dingy yellow glow that made the place seem warm rather than cheap. The light came from a floor lamp standing beside an old recliner with a mismatched calico patch on one arm. The other furnishings were rustic and likewise homey. The room was dominated by an ancient, plaid sofa with more patches sewn into the arms, and a stone fireplace from which a Franklin stove jutted, its black piping directed up the chimney. The nicked oak coffee table held issues of *Field and Stream* dating back to the 1980s, and the bookshelves behind the recliner held dusty volumes by Verne, Hemingway, Tolkien, and King.

"I need to get rid of some Pepsi," Amy said, closing the bathroom door but continuing to speak. "Make yourself comfortable."

Deacon plopped on the sofa amidst a swoosh of dust and mildew. The smell reminded him of the home place in Dayton, the sofa they had in the makeshift basement rec room. It also reminded him a little of Iraq, no doubt the hint of dried mouse turds mingled with the must.

"Turn the water on, will you Deke? The main is under the kitchen sink."

Deacon rose with a grunt. A few steps and he was in the kitchen, squatting to part the curtains that passed for cabinet doors. He flinched at the gunshot sound of his knees popping, then found the brass shutoff and rotated it vertical.

"You know," he called. "That may be the first time you said my name without a sir, commander, or "um" in front of it."

The toilet flushed then rumbled as bubbles of air were replaced by well water. Then the bathroom faucet came on.

"I guess this is the first time we've been in a domestic situation rather than a business one." Her voice washed in and out as water splashed her face. "You don't seem like my boss right now."

As he turned, he saw her coming out the bathroom door, hands toweling off her face then wiping at the short hair swathed to either side. She placed the towel around the hairs, a hand on each side kneading off the moisture. Amy looked at him, her face fresh and clean, free of makeup, a tired smile replacing the more solemn business face she usually wore. He was reminded again how much she resembled his late fiancée. The thought hurt and was pleasant at the same time.

"Have a seat. I'll make coffee. Or will that keep you up?"

Deke returned to the nostalgic sofa. "Coffee would be great. I'm too keyed up to sleep just yet."

He watched as Amy parted curtain doors and rummaged for coffee and filters. She moved with more efficiency than Liz had, but her actions were just as graceful in their competency. More sweetly painful nostalgia hit as her features pouted up, unable to find something. Liz had looked like that when she was pondering a problem — not exactly, but close enough to raise a tingle along the short hairs on his neck.

"Black okay?"

"Fine."

Amy poured water into the Mr. Coffee. "Coffee might taste a bit rusty." He felt her smile, even though he couldn't see it through the back of her short, dark hair. "Sorry."

He watched as she pulled a can of coffee off the shelf, then blew dust off the filters she placed beside it. Simple domestic chores, done with simple efficiency. "At least the mice don't like coffee." She laughed. It was nothing like Liz's laugh, and yet ...

"I'm not sure I've ever just seen you sit and relax," Deacon said. "Even in the bar, you seemed 'on duty.'"

He caught dimples from the corners of her cheeks. Then his eyes trailed to her other cheeks, lean and muscular inside her khakis. Despite his fatigue (or maybe because of it) he felt himself stiffen. He turned away, embarrassment sending his gaze to the fireplace. Or maybe it was guilt that cast his eyes away, as if even admiring a shapely ass was being unfaithful to Liz. That didn't make sense either, he thought. There had been other shapely asses he'd done more than ogle since Liz passed; shame rising amidst hazy memories of drunken nights when he'd conjured Liz's countenance into the bleary faces of barroom pickups. But this was different.

"I like to keep busy," Amy said. "That's part of being in the corps." She chuckled again, it was soft and feminine, all hard edges gone. "No, I guess I was like that even before. My mom calls me her little overachiever."

Deacon pushed pleasantly unpleasant memories aside and closed his eyes, trying to lose himself in the comfy familiarity of the old sofa. It had been quite a day. Failure had led to violence had led to despair had led to maudlin memories had led to the traditional drowning of sorrows had led to the Barzoon shocker had led to a near-death experience under the wheels of three-thousand pounds of Detroit (or maybe Japanese or German) steel. He should have been exhausted, was in fact exhausted. Considering the booze, he should be passed out. But having someone try to kill you was better than Nodoz.

Stress and spent adrenaline cluttered his brain, along with a dozen questions. What was Barzoon's game? Deke had pegged him for a bit of a prig, a competent bureaucrat, and a cagey politician. Was he more? Perhaps a cagy extremist wacko? Perhaps an operative of a foreign government? Did he have handlers? If so, who? The questions rattled his mind like lottery ping-pong balls, although there would be no lucky winner.

Amy continued speaking as she worked at the coffee, telling him about some childhood experience at the lake house. He barely heard the words, only the lilt of her voice drawing his eyes back to her. The soft cadence worked its way through his weariness and fought its way past the needling questions, altering them to strange sensations that washed over him in a trickle, then a downpour. Things began to change. Her speech blurred into no more than a soft murmur, like the memory of some long-forgotten lullaby. The peace he sought gradually appeared, an almost eerie calmness as soothing as the rhythm of her voice. He felt detached, almost in a trance under the ministrations of a skilled hypnotist, the way you feel when a good masseuse places just the right pressure on just the right muscles as Debussy hums from the sound system. Other feelings rose as well, feelings that warmed yet discomforted. Primal feelings. Primal urges. They weren't worrisome, and yet they were — both excitement and shame, like finding a copy of *Penthouse* in your dad's dresser. Mixed in was a sense of déjà vu or maybe precognition. On some level, he knew what was going to happen next.

His neck hairs tingled as if current were passing lazily from his temples to his spine, current that stimulated but with the threat of danger. Her voice faded to far away, its musical ebb and flow a lifeline that tethered him from drifting off the edge of a waterfall, or maybe oblivion. His body relaxed, the needling worries seeping away like an outgoing tide. He studied the outline of her body, not turning away this time, unable to turn away. His mind drifted into uncharted depths, perhaps dangerous ones. He didn't seem to care.

Then, suddenly he was back in himself, yoyoing to the present with an electric snap. He was back in the cabin. Country quiet hung in the air like dust motes. The spell was broken. But traces lingered, as did the tingling, as did the primal urges, as did the stiffness.

Amy walked toward him with two porcelain mugs, one sporting a black lab with a chip for a left eye, the other the words Semper fi emblazoned above a globe and laurel. He watched her movements, economical yet graceful, like a dancer's. He stiffened further.

"So," she asked, sitting beside him on the sofa and placing the two cups next to the old magazines. "What's going on?"

He didn't know if it was a question related to their current predicament or an attempt at frivolous small talk. It didn't matter. He just stared into her eyes, their darkness wells of comfort. The tingling on his nape intensified. The sense of precognition grew, guiding his movements. He leaned forward as his hands moved to each side of her face. Her weary smile grew more serious.

"I don't think this is a good idea, Deke."

But she didn't pull away as his hands cupped her cheeks, eyes never leaving hers. Then he kissed her. She kissed him back. It wasn't the first kiss he'd had since Liz died, but perhaps the first one that held any meaning.

She tasted of Pepsi. She tasted of the scotch that had come before. Her lips tasted nothing like Liz's rose-colored gloss. Yet the kiss brought a flood of nostalgic feelings that were as sweet as they were painful. He held his breath, as if afraid he'd exhale his soul into hers. He felt her sigh as their lips parted, then pressed in for a second time. But strong fingers applied steady, unrelenting pressure to his shoulders, pushing him back.

"That's where this is going to end, Commander."

Her dark eyes were tinged with doubt or maybe something more. She turned away, roses blooming on her cheeks.

"For now," Deacon said, under his breath. Then things happened with the speed of a traffic wreck.

Glass from the window blew inward while the single light bulb blew outward, fine fragments showering them like shrapnel. The cozy glow was replaced by a gloomy dawn that cast the room into semidarkness amid the ratatat of machinegun fire.

Chapter 21

Deke lunged forward, prepared to cover Amy as he dragged her to the floor. But her reflexes were just as sharp and battle honed. Again, they met in the middle, their bodies joining with a heavy thud, arms wrapped protectively around each other. A split second later, they were on the deck, pain lancing through Deke's knee as it toppled the coffee table onto its side, its thick oak providing some layer of protection as they clung to each other.

More shots peppered the wall, walking their way amidst broken kitchen crockery. Most people would have huddled behind the imagined safety of the oaken table until the shooting stopped, even well after it had stopped. But most people hadn't been in the crucible of combat, where safety was too often an illusion. They lay in each other's arms for no more than three seconds that were punctuated by the coffee carafe bursting forth with hot, black liquid. Then Deke buried his face into her neck, the smell of her appealing despite the danger, and shouted one word.

"Where?"

The Marine did not ask 'where what?' nor did she ask anything at all. She simply disentangled herself and crawled, knees and arms splayed like a spider's, ass low but not unattractive. Deke wondered briefly how the latter thought could survive the current situation, then followed in his own low crouch.

In several quick, crab-like slides she was in the kitchen, hand sweeping broken glass and ceramics from their path. A throw rug fronting the kitchen sink likewise swept away revealing a trapdoor about two-feet square. Amy flinched as the shots worked their way lower, aged stuffing flying from the sofa like off-season snow. Then her finger hooked into a pull ring and jerked the hatch up and off. Deke noted the door's passing, its surface streaked with blood that marked where Amy's hand had met the broken glass. Then the upper part of her body was gone from view, then her khaki-covered legs, the black leather of her shoes. Deke heard a soft groan as she hit whatever lay below, then the fireworks started up again and he followed her into the cave-like opening.

Deke landed hard on a dirt floor. The drop was no more than six feet, but the impact sent a howl through his shoulder. He rolled painfully, his feet banging the small electric water heater opposite the ladder. Amy was already standing, one hand on the wooden rungs below the trap.

The damp air smelled of earth and tree roots. The sound of gunfire faded to distant echoes off the cavern-like walls. But there wasn't a cavern's pitch-like blackness. Light filtered in from the trap and from a narrow window opposite. Not very bright, no more than a flicker, but enough to make out Amy's silhouette lifting something off the floor and swinging it.

The grime-covered window blew outward, letting more light filter into the tiny space. Deke could now see that she was swinging an old axe, sweeping its head back and forth to clear glass from the window frame. With a heave, the axe went through the window. Amy grabbed the sill and chin-upped her body after it.

"This way," she muttered as Deacon watched her disappear. Then he was on his feet, pain lancing his shoulder as he likewise grabbed the sill and vaulted through the narrow opening.

The smells now were earth and forest green. By the morning light filtering in, Deke could see that they were under the porch. He could also see the soles of Amy's loafers working their way to the porch steps. He watched as she rolled sideways to make room for him, his eyes again noting the economy and grace of this simple movement. Then he was beside her, the only sound the harsh breathing that filled his ears.

The gunshots had stopped. All was quiet, 'too quiet' like in the old cliché. Even their breathing ceased as they stared into the gap under the porch. Seconds ticked by, and still there was no sound. No footsteps signaled the departure of their deadly visitors. No car engine roared to life and pealed into the distance. All was quiet.

Suddenly, they sensed more than heard movement to the left. Then the silence was rent by the single, sharp tinkle of breaking glass. Then footsteps retreated, the need for stealth apparently forgotten or no longer necessary. More silence. Then a new sound, like the crackle of wrapping paper on Christmas morning. A new smell, pungent and strong. The smell of gasoline and smoke.

The sharp odor grew, as did the crackle. Deacon felt heat creeping below the floorboards. Amy cast him a sideways glance. Even in the dim light, he could read the fear upon her features, along with the sad realization that the family getaway she had helped to build was going up in flames. Then it was her turn to say a single word.

"Go."

With lizard-like quickness, she squirmed from under the porch and pelted into the nearby woods. Deacon paused for just a moment, then did likewise.

Amy stopped behind the trunk of a huge maple, looking back for Deke. She was about to go back to find him when he lumbered into view. What she saw was a bit of a shock. Pain and fatigue painted his face and body, the kind of look she'd seen on wounded soldiers kept up all night by mortar fire. His sides were pitching heavily, each breath a labored effort.

"You okay?" she asked, her voice almost a whisper.

He nodded, right hand cradling his left shoulder. "Just need a second to catch my breath."

She saw his skin blanch and eyes lose focus as his body stumbled forward. Dropping the axe she'd grabbed from under the porch, Amy caught hold, her support steadying him and sending color back into his face. He even managed a weary smile as he nodded toward the fallen axe, its head outlined against the leaf litter.

"You brought a rusty knife to a gun fight?"

She returned his smile. "Better than no knife at all."

"I guess. Although a Berretta would be better. Or maybe an M16."

She snatched up the axe. "Don't happen to have one on you, do you, sir?"

He shook his head, still smiling. "I'm okay now. Let's move."

They trudged along, flickering in and out of the long, thin shadows of the trees. It felt like hours since they'd reached her family cabin. What used to be the family cabin, she thought, the smell of gasoline and burning logs heavy in the air. Yet the sun that was a hint on the eastern horizon when they'd arrived had barely crested the lip.

Amy paused periodically to let Deke catch up, noting that the blanched grey was returning to his features. At each stop, she looked and listened behind them, but caught no signs of pursuit.

"Do you need to rest?"

Deke shook his head, wincing with pain and gripping tightly to his shoulder. "I'm okay."

Amy could tell that he wasn't. He needed someplace to rest and sleep, along with plenty of fluids and something on his stomach. She scanned from side to side, taking her bearings.

"If we keep bearing left, we should reach CR 113, if I haven't lost my childhood compass." Still no sound of pursuit. "We might be able to hitch a ride. Locals still stop for travelers out here."

"I don't hear a lot of traffic," Deke said.

She heard labored breathing mixed with the sarcasm.

"Where's the nearest town?"

"Caldwell is about six or seven miles. But Miller's store is closer, maybe a mile and a half. I used to walk there for candy."

"I'm guessing you favored hard candy. No mess."

Amy smiled. "Actually, I was a chocoholic. Especially Three Musketeers. Still am."

"I stand corrected." His voice sounded a little steadier. "Lead on, Macduff."

Amy took one step and froze, axe held at port arms. Something rustled up ahead. It might have been deer or even a squirrel. She wouldn't have thought much about it if it hadn't come from the direction of the road and if someone hadn't just tried to kill them. Deke must have heard it too, or at least sensed her wariness. He stopped one step behind and waited.

The noise came again, louder this time, moving closer. It was too loud for a squirrel, which meant it was either a deer heading home to bed or one of their pursuers who had circled back to CR 113. Her short hairs prickled when the rustling brush was followed by a grunt or curse, she couldn't tell which and didn't care. Deer rarely did either.

Deke started to whisper something, but she raised her arm for silence. Then she slid her hands together around the haft of the axe and cocked it over her ear like a Louisville slugger. The sound grew into definite footsteps. Her eyes could now discern movement, someone tromping through the woods, outlined against the slanting rays of the rising sun. She felt Deke stumble back as the axe head touched her shoulder and she shifted feet, ready to swing. Whoever was up ahead must have heard them because he paused briefly before rushing forward. Amy tensed, her body a cocked spring ready to unload.

Chapter 22

A poplar branch peppered with green buds moved toward her. Amy caught a hint of tan, followed by a swarthy complexion that sent visions of Islamic terrorists into her adrenaline-spiked imagination. She gave the axe one final backward cock before sending it toward where the head met its long, slender neck. At the last moment, something in her brain recognized that head and sent a quick message to her arms. It was enough to alter the trajectory of the axe into three inches of trunk instead of neck. The figure fell, uttering two words.

"Holy shit!"

Amy released the haft and stumbled into Deke, who grunted down onto one knee. As Amy helped him up, a familiar voice cursed again.

"What the fuck! You almost killed me with that thing."

Lisa Reilly rocked to a sitting position, then stood up, dusting dirt and leaves off her pants.

"And I just washed these khakis. What the hell?"

"What the *hell* are you doing here — sir?" Amy asked.

"Looking for you. Hey, you don't look so good, Deke."

"Shrewd observation as always, lieutenant." Deke rose unsteadily to his feet, right hand clamped to his left shoulder. "Now do you mind telling me why you're sneaking around in the woods?"

"Like I said, looking for you. I was just changing for bed when Herr Metternich burst into my quarters unannounced. He didn't even notice I was standing there in bra and panties. Anyway, he's fit to be tied and wants to see you immediately. Sounded like Elmer Fudd through that fat lip."

"What did *you* say?"

"What you told me. You'd passed out in your quarters. He was going to go down there and wake you, but I convinced him to wait until morning. Said we'd both present ourselves at zero nine hundred. So, I figured I better come and fetch you back."

"How did you find us?" Amy asked.

"Twarn't hard, ma'am. You said you had a cabin on Hoover's Lake. Tain't but one road leading to Hoover's Lake. Tain't but one sign reading Robbins on said road. Post hoc ergo proctor hoc, here I stand."

"That's not what that means," Deke said, his breath slowing.

"My Latin sucks, sue me."

"So, again I ask, why are you sneaking around in the woods?"

"If you must know, I've joined the Fort Deidenbach branch of the lesbian rangers." She smirked. "Actually, I'd stopped to read the quaint hand-burnt sign for fair chapeau, when I heard gunshots."

"Chateau," Deke said. "Your French is no better than your Latin."

"Whatever. At first, I figured maybe it's hunting season. Then I see this big cloud of smoke. My keen spider senses determined it was time to move cautiously, so I left my car parked on the road to Hoover's Lake — by the way, does it have a name?"

"The road to Hoover's Lake," Amy said.

"Figures," Lisa said. "And entered a deer track that appeared to be angling toward the smoke. The track died out after about thirty yards, so I stumbled along until, let me see, oh yeah … someone tried to kill me with an axe."

"That's nothing," Deke said. "Someone tried to kill us with what sounded like an AK. And yonder smoke is Amy's family cabin."

"What's left of it," Amy said, looking longingly back. "And probably my car."

"No shit?"

"No shit, Lieutenant."

"Where's *your* car?" Deke asked.

Lisa thumbed over her shoulder. "About fifty yards that away."

"Lead on, Macduff."

"I think that's MacGruff, isn't it?"

"Your Shakespeare is as good as your French and Latin."

"Are you alright, sir?" Amy said, perched atop Deacon's lap. "Am I hurting you?"

"I'm fine," Deacon said, his right arm wrapped around her so he could clutch his left shoulder.

In truth, he felt fine, better than he should have, strangely calm. His shoulder pain had ebbed to a dull throb, and the soothing, surreal feeling from the cabin was reasserting itself in the tiny confines of Lisa's Miata.

Instead of the lilt of Amy's voice, there was the rumble of the roadster's engine. Instead of the smell of coffee, there was the hint of green apple mixed in with the potent scents of country forest and post-traumatic sweat. He felt the weight of her small bosom perched shelf-like atop his right forearm, the roundness of her bottom wriggling atop his lap. His ears and neck tingled like before. Soon he knew he'd feel stirring like before.

Trying to think of something else, anything else, he said, "Did you have to bring a two-seater?"

"Hey. It's the only car I own. And I figured I'd be taking *you* back, with Amy following in her car."

Lisa completed her turn, the front end bouncing off the muddy track and onto the cracked pavement of CR 113. "And I'm glad I didn't have to drive further down the quaintly named 'Road to Hoover's Lake' or I might have quaintly broken an axle. You folks out here ever heard of macadam? Or even gravel?"

"That's decades away in the twentieth century." Amy smiled. "Country folks still live in the olden days."

Deacon closed his eyes and tried not to think of the soft, warm weight on his groin and thighs.

"So," Lisa said. "What now? Do I still take you back to the Unit?"

"I think we need to go to the police, sir, um, I mean Deke."

"Who would we even go to?" Lisa asked. "How do we know who else is in on it, who Barzoon has recruited?"

"Maybe Carstairs," Deacon said.

Amy lurched against him as the car hit a pothole. "Take it easy, Leese.

"Sorry?" Lisa said. "But how do you know that Carstairs isn't in on it. Maybe others in the FBI as well?"

"We don't," Deacon said. "But at the last briefing, I got the impression he's been kept out of the loop. On important matters anyway. Got the impression he didn't like it. So maybe he's a place to start."

"Seems risky to me," Lisa said, speeding up to pass a hay truck.

"Got to trust someone," Deacon said, pain lancing suddenly through his shoulder as the car hit another pothole. "Jesus! Mind getting us there in one piece?"

"Sorry."

The car slowed as Lisa pulled back onto the road. Deacon felt Amy relax into him, her body draping his like a warm, funky blanket. "Hmm," he murmured, breathing in the smell of her. Then she stiffened in his arms.

"Am I hurting your shoulder?"

"What? Um, no."

"Where?" Lisa asked.

"What?"

"You said, get us *there* in one piece. Where's there?"

"Some place safe, where I can get some sleep," Deacon said.

"Back at the unit?" Lisa asked.

"No, Dr. Reilly. After what just went down on Hoover's Lake, I would say the unit may not be your best suggestion of the day."

"So? I could take you to my place?"

"First place they'll check," Deacon said, relaxing again as Amy snuggled back into him. Sleep was just around the corner, with the hum of the tires and the warm softness of his aide de camp making it difficult to stay awake.

"Motel is probably best," Amy murmured. Her breathing was getting shallow and regular in his arms, suggesting she was at morphia's doorway as well. "There's one on route 27, the other side of Caldwell."

"On my way," Lisa said.

"I don't get it," Amy said, dreamily. "If what you think is going on is indeed going on, and they, whoever *they* are, want this antidote, why are they trying to kill you before you give it to them?"

"*If* — what we think is going on is indeed going on," Lisa said. "We've already given them what they want. Twice. And Ray Treadaway has the formula."

"So why try to kill him at all?" Amy asked.

"Maybe because they don't want anyone else to have it," Deacon said.

A loud pop like a jester's ball landing in his wooden cup, and sharp pain gave way to a general soreness. His vision tunneled momentarily, then returned quickly. His shoulder once again felt as if it was part of his body.

"Sorry," Amy said, releasing his arm. "Better?"

Deacon nodded. "I'm guessing that wasn't the first time you've set a dislocated shoulder."

Amy smiled her nothing-like-Liz's smile.

"First time when there was no one shooting at me," Amy said.

Cabin six of the Country Inn Motel was behind the office, about fifty yards off State Route 27. The furnishings were old, but the room was clean without the musty, basement smell of Amy's family place. The wood paneling was dark with age yet cozy in a woodsy sort of way. Antlers hung above the faux fireplace, with miniature versions adorning light fixtures and switches. A single double bed sat next to a bedside bureau, a larger chifforobe under a painting of a fox hunt on the opposite wall. The bathroom was small, but the porcelain tub and toilet were clean and functional.

Deke leaned back in the armchair with a sigh, hand still holding his shoulder but without the knife stab from before.

"Why don't you lie down?"

"No," Deacon said. "I'm good here. You take the bed."

"Un uh. I'm going to be in that chair looking out the window. You're all done in, so I'm on guard duty."

"*You* shouldn't even be here."

"Let's not have that argument again, Commander. You've already lost it in the car."

Deacon smiled, eyes closed, body enjoying the pleasure of a located shoulder. "Yes sir, Marine Force Specialist."

"And if I *am* to stand guard, I'll need a shower to wake me up and to remove several layers of Maryland countryside. I feel like I've got stuff growing on me. You okay while I take a quick one? Won't be five minutes."

"I think we're safe for the moment."

"Okay. But call me if you see or hear *anything*."

Deacon saw only the backs of his lids as he snuggled into the chair. He heard the bathroom door close and the shower click on, distinct sounds, like the horn blare of the semis on SR 27. After that, things got hazy. Amy softly hummed something as she bathed, sounded classical. Part of him marveled at the equanimity of this woman who'd been through a hard night and one hell of a morning, yet hummed in the shower like any other day. Another part was captured by that old feeling, the one that had overtaken him on Hoover's Lake and again in the car. That sensation of being a cobra in the hands of a snake charmer, the music of her voice soothing and guiding him. The shower clicked off and all was quiet except for her song, hummed soft and gentle. The old tingling returned. The light grew dim. The sound of the traffic died away, ebbing and flowing like waves on a sandy beach. Her voice dropped to no more than a background murmur, a sweet lullaby. His head nodded, his breathing steady. The soft music and lapping waves carried him off.

"BANG!"

Amy reveled in the warm ping of water on flesh. The day's (and night's) worries drummed away with the water, at least for the moment. It was a trick she'd learned in her overseas deployments. Set aside some alone time. Time when you could let the outside world go away. Time to live within yourself, your memories, dreams, fantasies. It wasn't real, and it wasn't that long (not usually, anyway), but it was still a respite, some mental R&R. It didn't change the reality in which you lived, but it made it livable. At least it did for her.

The current fantasy was one she'd had for years, a recurring theme in which she was waiting for her husband, lover, boyfriend, fiancé — didn't matter. She was making a romantic dinner, always spaghetti and meat sauce, her mother's recipe. The table was already set, candles lit, room lights lowered. Breadsticks sat in a glass tumbler on a checkered tablecloth. A single rose sat in a small, crystal vase next to an open bottle of chianti. She was wearing her little black dress, the one with cold shoulders and décolletage. The air smelled of meat sauce, Dior perfume, and vinegar from the salad she was tossing. Ravel drifted from the stereo. She was working steadily but unhurriedly. He would be home soon, but she had things in control. She'd greet him with a kiss, just one for an appetizer. Then they'd have a leisurely meal. They were in no rush. They'd eat slowly, chatting, flirting. They'd sip wine. She'd enjoy his eyes on her while they talked, the desire in them. They'd both know what was coming afterward, when the dishes were stacked, and she'd preceded him into the bedroom. But they wouldn't rush it. At the right moment, she'd ask if he was ready for dessert. Then she'd head to her boudoir, the scene already set, light muted from a scarf draped across the bedside lamp. The air rife with the heady aroma of perfume and possibilities. She'd slowly undress, changing into a sheer, black chemise. He'd enter while she was slipping it over her head, her back to him. Then his arms would wrap around her waist, his lips finding her neck.

The setting was always the same, as was the dinner, as was her outfit. Only the man changed. He was never a man she'd dated or gone to bed with. Always it was an older man, an authority figure. In high school it was Sergeant Robert Wainwright, her Dutch uncle Bobby. In college, the cute TA in first-year biology (his name was already forgotten). For a while, almost a year, it was Gunnery Sergeant Chris Watkins, the PE and self-defense instructor at Quantico. For a long time after that, it had been no one. Now, it was Deacon Creel. Commander Deacon Creel.

She found herself thinking of his rank, even in her fantasy. Somehow, that made it better, sexier, almost taboo. An illicit trip into officer's country. He wasn't really military, she knew that. He was a doctor, a scientist. Yet he had the title and bearing of an officer, the flaws of an officer. The same flaws she'd seen in her father, in many men in the Corps — remorse and booze. Flaws that made her want to care for Commander Creel — Deke. Flaws that made her want to submit to him, at least in a fantasy.

She wanted to stay in the shower forever, reveling in the tingle of hot water and make-believe. But she'd promised five minutes, and so she took five minutes. Semper fi. But this was more than just a jarhead promise. She'd meant what she said about standing guard. And she *would* stand guard, even if it meant biting her lip to stay awake. Nothing would happen to Deacon Creel on her watch. Not if she could help it.

Clicking off the tap, she slid the opaque curtain on its tarnished brass runner and stepped over the rim of the clawfoot tub. Grabbing a towel, she dried off, the room hugging her in a foggy mist. The towel moved lower, the terrycloth tickling her nipples to attention. Semper fi, she thought with a giggle; not that they needed much after the shower. Then she dried her legs, left then right, always left then right, like cadence.

She didn't know everything that was going on, but she knew they (whoever they were) were playing for keeps. The shootout at the cabin proved that, proved it even stronger than the car outside Woody's. Then...

"BANG!"

Chapter 23

Deke jerked awake. He snapped around toward the outside door, the source of the shotgun blast. His mind envisioned wood fragments bursting into the room, shards and buckshot pelting across the floor and bed. But the sturdy wooden portal stood intact, deadbolt turned, safety chain engaged. Then his ears recognized the drone of a log-hauler shifting gears, its load settling again amidst a second gunshot pop. He barely had time to register this before Amy burst into the room, a bath towel held protectively across her chest.

Water flew from her short hair. Her bare feet flew to the chifforobe, her free hand snatching up a porcelain figurine, Cupid and his bow pointing toward the bed. She held the cherub as she had the axe, feet planted.

As Amy stared at the door, Deacon stared at Amy. The towel barely covered her. The short, shapely legs veeing to either side of the white cloth ended in planted feet on one end, a small, taut ass on the other. Dripping hair plastered to the curve of her neck sent droplets running down the smooth skin of her back, skin that held the rosy glow of recent hot water and adrenaline.

Deacon was wide awake, his senses acutely aware, his emotions keenly aroused. As before, he was struck by a feeling of preordination. He rose from the chair as if guided by invisible hands, the ache in his shoulder forgotten.

He saw Amy relax as she recognized the truck noise. "Semi on the highway," she said. "I'm turning into a regular nervous Nellie."

Deacon placed his hands on her shoulders, the taut yet soft flesh indenting with his touch. He pulled her to him.

"No, Deke. I don't think we should do this."

"You're probably right." He whispered into her ear.

His mouth found hers. She resisted for a moment, half-heartedly. Then she returned the kiss, her hands on the back of his neck.

The towel held momentarily against the pressure of their bodies. Then it tumbled to the floor as they tumbled to the bed.

The highest Russian operative ever placed in America massaged shoulders that refused to relax. "What's the matter?" she asked.

Her lover hesitated, then said, "Things are ... wrong. They've gotten out of control. It wasn't supposed to be like this. I don't like it."

"Shhh. You worry too much." The strong hands continued forcing tension from the tight muscles. "You should learn to relax."

"But you said we were only going to frighten them."

"And that's all we did."

"Fog-blind car chases? Bullet-riddled walls? A fire?"

"Quiet." The hush was almost a command. "Keep your voice down."

Her lover obediently lowered the volume. "A cabin burnt to the ground? You call that a scare."

"No one was hurt. Were they?"

"Well, no. But they might have been."

"You need to leave things in my capable hands." As if for emphasis, those hands massaged from shoulder to neck.

"Mmm."

"Everything is going according to plan. We knew Creel might figure it out eventually. But he'll be too busy worrying about his own safety. And the safety of the little marine fluff he's brought along. Not sure what he sees in her."

"Mmm." The hands massaged shoulders and neck, then continued down the chest, expertly teasing. "She's a tough bit of fluff, for one thing," her lover said. "For another, she's a dead ringer for his late fiancée."

"Ah, ha. Good. We can use that. Play off it."

"I don't know." Her lover's words were almost a whisper, the shoulder beginning to relax. "It doesn't seem right. He's pretty messed up about it." The taut muscles relaxed further, head lolling from side to side. "Mmm. He, ah, still carries a lot of guilt."

"Better and better."

"But ..."

"Shhh." The strong hands slid lower, soft tissue stiffening to the touch. "You believe in the mission, don't you?"

"Ahh." Her lover's neck rolled, savoring the pleasure. "Yes. Oh, yes."

"Then leave everything to me."

"Ahhh. I'll have to ..."

"Shh. Just leave it to me." The fingers lingered, squeezing, massaging, "Cast aside your doubts. Alright?" Her lover was beyond responding. "No one has gotten hurt, except those who brought it on themselves. Soon, very soon, we'll be in position to change things. To erase the stain that has been painted across our great land." She leaned forward, nibbling her lover's neck with tiny rabbit kisses. "Very soon." Sliding forward, their bodies melded, merging into a writhing mass of pleasure.

Deacon woke to the smell of fresh coffee and the sound of faint humming. Liz was up early. He smiled. As he rolled onto his side to call to her, a dull pain throbbed his shoulder. His eyes popped open, registering the motel room, daylight peeking around the edges of the curtains, coffee steaming from the two-cup complimentary carafe. He remembered where he was. He remembered yesterday. He wanted a drink.

Amy emerged from the bathroom. She was dressed in yesterday's dirty clothes. Face clean, but tired. She smiled. "You slept well."

Deke thought for a moment. He had slept well. Better than he'd slept in months. Then he remembered who he'd slept with. No, that wasn't quite true. He remembered who he'd made love to. But had she slept? He studied the haggard features, a suitcase under each eye.

"What about you?"

Amy shrugged. "Okay."

"You don't look okay."

"I'm fine. I don't need much." She smiled.

Deacon sat up, ignoring the soreness in his shoulder. "Please don't tell me you stood guard all afternoon? All night?"

"Not *all* night. I dozed a little."

"You need to get some rest."

"I'm fine, I said." She held up a steaming paper cup. "Coffee helps, although I'd rather it was Pepsi. How's the shoulder?"

He tentatively rotated it. It hurt, but only with the dull ache of a healing sprain. "It's, it's okay."

Amy poured coffee into a paper cup. "We, um, didn't hurt it yesterday?"

Deacon slipped his legs over the side of the mattress and snatched his underwear from the floor. He kept his eyes on the curtains as he slipped them on, wanting to say something but not knowing what or how. Finally, he cleared his throat. "Listen, um, about yesterday. It ..."

"Shouldn't have happened," Amy finished.

He turned to face her.

Amy's smile was tired or sad, perhaps both. "But maybe it had to. We both carry ... ghosts. Ones that had to get acquainted eventually."

He met her gaze. "Do you regret it?"

She didn't turn away. "Do you?"

Deke paused before answering. He thought about last night. Then he thought of Liz. She had been there too. But not like before. Not completely. Not a substitute. He said, "I don't know."

Amy smiled again. "An honest answer." She handed him the cup.

"And these ghosts getting acquainted," Deacon said. "Is that all it was?"

Amy sipped her coffee, paused, then answered. "I don't know."

Deke nodded. "An honest answer."

Alone in his bargain-basement apartment, Special Agent Paul Carstairs poured three fingers of bourbon into a juice glass. He grimaced as he shook his head and downed half the liquid. "Middle aged, divorced — twice — and drinking expensive booze from a juice glass. Ain't bureau life glamorous." He loosened his tie and dropped into his bargain-basement chair. "What's the point?"

The leads, his one lead, had dried up nicely. Carla Ortiz had been a faceless government bureaucrat — in the full sense of the word. He thought of her body lying in the trunk, features indistinguishable from seared hamburger, and took another gulp. Her Federal Civilian Personnel Record was unblemished and complete, outlining her pay raises, honorable mentions, and clearances. It detailed her Social Security number, addresses (going back fifteen years), college degrees (bachelors in English and associates in administration), height, weight, fingerprints, and distinguishing characteristics (none noted.) It did not list her friends, of which there appeared to be few, her lovers, of which there appeared to be fewer if any, or her motivations for absconding with top-secret government property. Her brother in Kansas City had not seen her in ten years. Her mother in Baltimore said she rarely talked about work or her personal life. There was the financial trail, being tracked as he sat there, but ...

"Optimistic?" He shook his head and downed the remaining liquor. "What's the point?"

He considered getting up for more bourbon but didn't have the energy. 'Lethargy' was the watchword lately. He chuckled grimly at the enthusiasm with which he had initially approached this assignment. Back when he'd entertained hopes of becoming Harris's fair-haired boy. Now those hopes were running out like the snot from his summer cold. He sleeved back a sneeze then struggled to remove the paddle holster from where it was digging into his hip.

He thumped the holster onto the coffee table, staring at it for a moment. Then he reached over and pulled his Glock out and placed it alongside the holster. Glock 19, standard bureau issue, he thought. Dark, simple, unadorned, dangerous, even sexy. The little black dress of pistols. So much power in such a little package. Fifteen rounds, each capable of stopping a heart, crippling a spinal column, or rupturing a femoral artery. Each capable of turning a skull into a Halloween jack-o-lantern, it's mushy insides replaced by vacant space. But, as he thought about it, it only took one for that. One bullet delivered at close range. Close enough that you couldn't miss. Just one. And all his problems, concerns, worries, and regrets would be over. Just one.

Shaking his head, he got another drink then sat back down to stare at the pistol. He'd stared at it through three more bourbons, eyes fixed on the black shape as he blindly poured the liquor into the juice glass. With each trip to the bottle, the idea became a little less ridiculous. With each trip, the solution seemed a little more reasonable. Practical even. It brought a little more comfort.

He didn't have much to live for, not when you thought about it. And he had been thinking about it, more and more each day. This idea, this fixation, no longer frightened him. Instead, it brought a sort of peace, almost a longing.

His two ex-wives might be a little upset but would hardly grieve. Not after the acrimony of the divorces. He thought about those burned bridges and wiped away a tear. There were no children to worry about, or to worry about him. Hell, he didn't even have a pet. He'd leave life without so much as a ripple. His own FCPR would be examined, stamped 'DECEASED,' and filed. Case closed. In a year, maybe two, he'd be forgotten. "Paul who?" they'd ask.

He emptied the whiskey glass and put it next to the pistol. As his fingers left the glass, they sought out the Glock, lingering there. It was cold, hard, reassuring. His fingertips caressed it as one would a woman. He stroked slowly along the cool, elegant lines of the slide, the curves of the trigger guard, the roundness of the butt, its knurls needling his fingertips. His fingers ceased their caress and settled on the grip, letting it lightly fill his hand. The pebbly plastic felt familiar against his palm, like an old friend. Old friends? He smiled. I guess we are, he thought. We've spent more time together than both ex-wives and all the girlfriends and hookups combined. His fingers tightened until the knurled plastic settled firmly against his palm.

Paul's index finger toyed with the trigger guard, tracing along its curves. Back and forth. It ducked inside the guard then out again, like a scared kid petting a strange dog. When nothing bit, it ducked back inside, lightly nudging the trigger safety. Still no bark. Still no bite. It settled gently against the curved surface. It felt good to settle there. It felt right. It felt peaceful.

Paul hefted the instrument of peace. Only about a pound and a half, fully loaded. Fully alive, he thought. He'd come to think of it as a living thing lately. A corporeal being. A quiet companion. "An old friend." The words echoed through the empty apartment and through his head. A friend that could solve all his problems. "What are friends for." He thought he knew. All at once, he thought he knew exactly what this friend was for.

Paul placed the barrel against his temple. It rose slowly, steadily, until cold metal rubbed the hair of his regulation sideburns. He closed his eyes. The feeling of peace descended like a cool, dark veil. He felt better than he had in days. Calmer. At a crossroads no longer. His finger tightened on the trigger safety until he felt the click. Almost there. His finger tightened further. Any second and the peace would be there. It would be final. It would be eternal.

Chapter 24

B rrrrng." The ringing telephone jarred away Carstairs' peace just as it jarred the pistol from his temple. The heavy metal chunked to the table, bruising where fingers met wood. Paul released the Glock as if it were a snake, the click of the reengaging safety sending another shiver through him. He shook the pain from his hand, then shook the trance from his face.

"Brrrng."

He reached into his pocket for his cell but remembered he'd turned it off (a no-no in a bureau that wanted twenty-four-seven access to its agents). He also remembered that the cell played a musical tone, not the old-style buzz of a landline that was also bureau policy.

"Brrrng."

"Yeah, Hold your horses."

Paul reached for the receiver, but his quivering fingers almost knocked it from the cradle. He pulled his hand back, shaking the palsy from it, then snatched up the phone.

"Carstairs. What?"

"Agent Carstairs?"

"Yeah. What the ... I mean, what can I do for you?"

"I'm, ah sorry to call so late. Your office, that is the lady at the Hoover Building, said I might find you at home, but I was expecting to leave a message, like I did on your cellphone."

He walked toward the bourbon bottle. "Well, you got *me* instead. Now who are you and what can I do for you?"

"That's not important. Just say I'm one of the scientists at the, I mean, involved with, I mean at um, Unit 13."

"If that's how you want it." Paul uncapped the bottle. "What can I do for you, Dr. X?"

"I'm calling because I'm worried about Deacon Creel. Commander Creel."

Paul paused, bottle tilted, as his brain tried to register all this. His head was still coming out of the trance. He found himself missing that warm, peaceful feeling of resolution. He thought about pouring that drink, regaining its warm glow. He even thought about having a cigarette, although he hadn't smoked in ten years. Instead, he said, "Right. The project leader on the ... the project leader. What about him?"

"He's disappeared. Him and his assistant, aide de camp, whatever you want to call her. They skipped out of the Unit and no one can find them."

"Skipped out?" He thunked the bottled down.

"Well, left. Disappeared."

"Without telling anyone where they were going?"

"Right," the caller said.

Paul grabbed a pad and pencil off the table. "When was this?"

"Late last night."

"*Last* night? Why didn't anyone tell the bureau?"

"Well, um, yeah, maybe they should have, but they, well, Dr. Creel is a bit mercurial. And we figured he'd show up, you know, maybe a little, well, tipsy."

Paul jotted details on the pad. "What's the assistant's name?"

"Amy. Amy Robbins. She's Army or Marines or something. A corpswoman I guess you'd call her."

"And no one has seen them since last night?"

"No. That's what has everybody worried."

"Anything else?"

"Well, now that you mention it, there are some files missing."

He dropped the pencil. "Files? Which files?"

"Ones pertaining to, you know, the project."

"Would anyone have reason to take these files home?"

"No. They are never to leave the building. Not even copies."

Paul snatched up the pencil and jotted 'more stolen documents' on the pad. "This Robbins. Is she just, well, *just* his assistant? I mean, do you think they're more than that?"

"Well, I don't know, not for sure. But um, they kind of seemed... The way they looked at each other? I guess the answer to your question is, I think so."

Paul twirled the pencil deftly with one hand. "All right, Doctor. I'll contact Mr. Barzoon and Dr. Metternich."

"*No*. I mean, I'd prefer that you didn't. Not right away. You see, they, um, they might not appreciate my coming to you. They've been trying to keep this within the unit, because, well, they both brought Dr. Creel into it, and they'd, well, they'd look bad."

"Okay. I'll check into it first, on my own. But I'll eventually need to question them. And you."

"No. I understand. Just not right away. And please, don't mention that you heard it from me."

"That'll be easy since I don't know who you are. Goodbye, Dr. X."

He'd moved the phone halfway to its cradle when he heard the caller say, "Oh. Agent Carstairs?"

"Something else?"

"Yes. One more thing. Actually, two more."

"I'm listening."

"This Amy Robbins. She's a dead ringer for Dr. Creel's late fiancée."

"Oh? And what's the other thing?"

"He's done it before. Stolen files, that is. Back when he left the service. They hushed it up."

"Yes," Carstairs said, tapping the pencil against the pad. "I'm already aware of that."

Carstairs pulled his nondescript Ford onto Nebraska Avenue. He'd agreed to forgo talking to Metternich or Barzoon for the moment but hadn't said a thing about Barzoon's boss. The undersecretary had been surprised to hear directly from him but had agreed to the meeting. At her office. After hours. Just her, him, site security, and the cleaning staff.

Paul was nervous — and not just about seeing Harris again. The trance (urge, fever, fixation, whatever you wanted to call it) had passed, leaving in its wake both disappointment and relief, the way an underconfident athlete might feel when the big game gets rained out. But the urge hadn't gone far. It still lurked in the background, in a dark, little-used corner of his mind. Twice on the drive over he'd found himself accelerating over ninety. Once, he'd angled directly for a concrete abutment, jerking the wheel back at the last moment. All he had to do was let his mind wander into that dark, musty corner. He tried not to let it roam.

He thought about the new lead. He didn't know what game Creel was playing. Was he seeking revenge, like last time? Only now maybe with more than just press releases and ruined careers. Paul needed to know what sorts of files had been stolen. He needed to know what type of bioterror agent he was dealing with. He needed to know why high-profile politicians were dying under mysterious circumstances. Barzoon had refused to divulge the information. Maybe Harris would. Either way, Paul had a lead. He was on a trail. His mind had something else to concentrate on.

Paul tried not to think what would have happened if Dr. X hadn't called. That thought left him cold, gooseflesh rising. The feeling wasn't fear exactly. More like — wonder? Awe? How could that be? A shiver raced through him, and he found himself driving faster. Slowing, he turned into the gate and showed his credentials. The guard told him Harris's office was on the second floor of the red brick building that dominated the site. He parked out front. Light from a three-quarter moon bathed him as he walked toward the building.

The shadows reminded him of a graveyard. He found the thought comforting.

Chapter 25

A my woke suddenly. The dream faded just as quickly. Even
before she recognized the motel room and remembered
how they'd gotten there, it had begun to disperse. In the
dream, she'd been running from something or someone. Some
threat. She'd been frightened. But the fear wasn't for herself.
She feared for the life of the person she'd been running with.
Who was it? She could no longer recall.

She rolled off the bed, fruitlessly brushing at two-days-
worth of dirt and wrinkles in her dress casuals. Looking
around, she saw Deacon coming out of the bathroom.

"What time is it?" she asked.

"Almost six."

"You shouldn't have let me sleep this long."

"You needed it," Deacon said. "After standing guard duty."
He shrugged. "I figured it was my turn to watch. I think we're
safe enough here until dark."

As he came into the bedroom, she headed for the lav.

"What do we do now?" she said from her seat on the
commode. "Do we call Lieutenant Reilly? Or should we go
directly to Agent Carstairs?" There was no reply.

Amy flushed the john and ran the sink. A faint smell of
rust and rotten eggs accompanied water as cold as Valley
Forge. The vestiges of sleep swirled down the drain with the
splashing water. "She must have contacted Carstairs by now."
There was still no answer. Towel in hand, she headed back to
the bedroom.

Deacon was standing by the window, peeking through the
drapes at the parking lot.

"I said, should we go directly to Carstairs?"

"What if he's part of it?" Deacon continued to stare between the parted curtains.

"Carstairs?"

Deacon nodded and let the drapes fall back into place.

"Isn't that a little, well, paranoid?"

He smiled. "Just because you're paranoid, doesn't mean ..."

"They aren't out to get you. I know. But you yourself said he probably wasn't part of it. And if he *was* part of it, wouldn't they have come for us by now?"

Deacon looked back out the window. "I told Lisa to tell him the story, but not where we were. Not until she heard from me."

"Who else can we go to?"

"There may be someone," Deacon said, again scanning the back lot. "Someone who was maybe taken by surprise as much as I was when I first heard about their famous project seppuku."

"Who?"

He shook his head, then turned and smiled. "Let's get some food. I don't know about you, but I'm starving."

Deacon dug into country ham and eggs, the eight-ounce slab of meat taking up most of a manhole-sized platter. Amy bit into a burger. Ripping a paper napkin from a stainless-steel dispenser, she wiped her mouth then washed the food down with cold Pepsi.

"You know it's dark outside," she said. "Most people are having *dinner*. Have had dinner."

"Yeah," Deacon answered around a forkful of home fries. "But there's a reason diners serve breakfast twenty-four-seven."

After they'd left the motel, he'd had her drive north toward the Pennsylvania border. It felt odd driving Lieutenant Reilly's Mazda instead of her old Toyota, but the car handled well, and they made good time following lesser roads and pikes to the little diner east of Hagerstown. She wondered again if he was just being paranoid. Then she remembered the smell of spent gunpowder and burning logs.

"So, what now?" she asked.

Deke gulped from a large coffee mug. "I think we need to split up."

She put down her burger. "That's a hard negative, sir."

"At ease, Marine Force Specialist. It makes the most sense."

"It does not make sense for an aide de camp to desert her commanding officer. Semper fi, remember?"

Deke reached out and took her hand. "Think about it, Amy. It's easier to track a couple than just a single person. And as long as I'm with you, you're in danger."

"Been in danger before, Deke. I'm not abandoning you in the wilderness just because you draw fire."

"You won't be abandoning me in some wilderness. You'll be dropping me off in D.C."

"Washington? No. That's crazy. It'll make it easier for them."

"No, it'll make it harder." He squeezed her hand once, then went back to his eggs. "I should have seen it before. Every time they tried to take me out, to take us out, it's been in a secluded setting. The dark road. Your cabin in the boonies. I don't think they'll take a chance in a crowded city where hit-and-run drivers get stuck in traffic and where gunshots attract attention and kill bystanders."

"Sounds logical, Deke. But with all due respect, I'm not about abandon you."

"That's an order, Marine Force Specialist."

Her dark eyes bored holes through his head. "I thought you told me you weren't really Navy, Deke."

"I'm not. But I've got a sheet of paper that says I am. It also says I'm your commanding officer."

Amy paused, face warm. "Aye, *sir*."

He squeezed her hand again. "I'll be fine."

She shook her head and picked up her burger. "Why D.C.? The belly of the beast. Why not, I don't know, Baltimore? Annapolis? Richmond, Virginia?"

"Because the belly of the beast holds possible allies. After you drop me off, I want you to find Agent Carstairs."

"But Lieutenant Reilly, I mean Lisa, should have contacted him already."

He drank coffee, nodding. "And we should have *heard* from her already. I don't like the fact that we haven't. She hasn't called. She doesn't answer her phone."

Amy bit into her burger and didn't respond immediately. She gulped more Pepsi, then asked, "What do I tell him?"

"Tell him everything except my suspicions about Barzoon. If I'm wrong, if Carstairs is part of it, no sense tipping him off that we know about Barzoon."

"What about you? You keep saying 'after I drop you.' Where am I dropping you?"

"3801 Nebraska Avenue Northwest."

"The Nebraska Avenue Complex? But that's Barzoon's home turf."

"It's also the home of Undersecretary Cathleen Harris."

"Who's she?"

"Big shot from Homeland Security, in charge of biological and chemical affairs. In a nutshell — Barzoon's boss."

"But if she's his boss, won't she be in on it, too?"

Deke shook his head then forked ham into his mouth. "I got the feeling, the strong feeling, that she was as much in the dark about this as I was. More so, maybe. I'm convinced that Barzoon and Metternich went to her as a last resort. Panic mode. I'm pretty sure about Barzoon. I could be persuaded that Joe is involved, although he seems more like a tool than a traitor. But Harris?" He shook his head and finished his eggs. "I'm betting no."

"But it's pretty late. She probably won't even be there."

"She will. I'm betting on that, too."

"How do you know?"

"One, because high-powered bureaucratic bigwigs work long hours. And two, because I already called her and set it up." He laughed then answered the question she'd been too surprised to ask. "While you were sleeping." He checked his watch. "So, we better get a wiggle on if we're going to get me to Nebraska Avenue by twenty-one-thirty hours." He raised his hand. "Check?"

The gate guard handed Deacon a temporary pass. Evidently, he was expected. The scuffed plastic card allowed him after-hours admittance to the main building, which was still called "The Rectory," a title dating back to its original life as The Mount Vernon Seminary for girls. It had been part of the Navy Department during World War II, an isolated facility where code breakers plumbed the depths of Nazi encryption. Now it was the headquarters of The Department of Homeland Security, a government agency that sounded more like it belonged in Moscow than D.C. — just put "Peoples" in front of it.

Deacon followed the blacktop road to the large, red-brick building, walking up stone steps that seemed more appropriate for a public library than a cabinet-level department headquarters. Waving the cardkey at the entrance elicited an electronic chirp and a flash of green before the door clicked open.

The first thing he noticed was that the place didn't smell like a government building. It didn't have that banal, institutional odor of cheap carpet and pressboard furnishings. Instead, the interior smell matched his exterior impression of a library, or maybe a museum. The air was rife with age — whiffs of mold mixed with decades of floor polish, dust, and paper. Unlike the prominent, high-ceilinged entryways common to building in the political hotbed of the city, this out-of-the-way lobby was just a small foyer of well-worn ceramic tile and wood paneling.

Deacon walked past a reception desk that currently housed no receptionist, then made a sharp left to follow a winding staircase to the second floor. The stair runner swallowed the sound of his footsteps as his mind ran through what he needed to say to Harris. Things that would convince her of the seriousness of the situation, without sounding like a nut.

He felt the stubble along his jaw, wishing they'd stopped for shave cream and a razor. He sniffed his pit and thought a deodorant stick would have also been a good purchase. He'd cleaned up as best he could at the motel, but rolling away from cars, crawling under porches, and running through the woods did little for clothes he'd worn two days. Had it been only two days?

Deacon caught his reflection in the glass of a hanging photo, Tom Ridge shaking someone's hand. The image did not inspire confidence. He'd seen similar reflections in store windows and street puddles only a few weeks ago. He wondered if that's all Harris would see, a paranoid bum who smelled of BO and burning cabin. Beautiful women whose appearance was always *just so* could be that way. But he reminded himself that the undersecretary was also a savvy politician, and as such would need to look beyond appearances. "I hope so," he mumbled as he approached another empty reception desk in front of a door holding Harris's name plate.

He paused at the closed door and listened. Harris was talking to someone. He couldn't make out the words, but it was a one-sided conversation suggesting a phone call. Still taking calls at 9:30, he thought. Bureaucratic bigwigs really did work long hours. His hand poised over the door until there was a break in the monologue. Then he knocked.

Now the pause was on the other side of the door. Deacon waited. A sultry southern accent said, "Come in."

Chapter 26

A my waited down the road from the Nebraska Avenue Complex, drinking Pepsi and watching the gate for signs of Deacon. She'd called the Hoover Building and left a message on Carstairs' phone. Then she'd finagled his cell number from the duty operator, saying he'd given her instructions to call day or night, but that she'd lost his card. She got another voice mail. So, with nothing to do until he called back, she'd driven back to Nebraska Avenue to wait for Deacon.

Amy stifled a yawn, then took a sip from the large plastic bottle. Caffeine and sugar were poor substitutes for rest, but she'd have time enough for that if everything worked out. If Deacon's meeting went as planned, he'd be placed under protective custody. She'd see a dark sedan enter the site, then leave a few minutes later, her boss (her lover?) inside.

He seemed certain of Harris and was confident that's how it would go down. But Amy wasn't so sure. Something didn't feel right. Maybe it was caffeine nerves, but she felt the hairs on her neck stand up. The same feeling she'd gotten in Iraq when an out-of-place package showed up near the barracks or when an RPG was on the way. Maybe she was being paranoid, but it seemed like Deacon was walking into the lion's den. So, she waited.

Finally, a dark, late-model Ford, the type you associated with the bureau, appeared. But it was leaving the gate, not entering. Probably just a late worker going home, she thought, smiling at Deacon's quip about big-time bureaucratic hotshots. The car paused at the end of the drive, then turned in her direction. She found herself ducking low when the headlights swept the Miata, force of habit after the last few stressful days. Feeling foolish, she sat up again before the Ford had passed. Its tinted window was partly rolled down, revealing a passenger. She only saw him in profile for a second but was sure it was Deacon. Mission accomplished, she thought with a smile.

She watched in the rearview as the car stopped before entering the traffic circle. To her amazement, the passenger door burst open, and Deacon rolled out onto the pavement. His movements were awkward because his hands were manacled together at the front. Before he could rise, the driver was out of the car grabbing him by his injured shoulder. Deacon stumbled. The driver, whose suit, brush cut, and drawn Glock screamed FBI, didn't seem to care about his passenger's pain. He just manhandled him back into the car, banging Deacon's head against the jamb. Then he slammed the door and reentered the driver's side, still holding his Glock as he closed the door.

Amy sat, unable to move, her eyes locked on the Ford's headlights rolling around the traffic circle.

Deacon held his cuffed hands against the goose egg rising on his forehead. His shoulder hurt like a son of a bitch, but the head pain was fresher so got first chair in the suffering symphony.

"Sorry I had to get rough, Doc. But you broke your promise."

"I never promised not to try and escape."

Carstairs clicked the Ford into drive and headed for the traffic circle. Deacon saw that he still held the black pistol, its sharp angles arcing along with the steering wheel, the muzzle sometimes pointing Deacon's way, sometimes at Carstairs himself.

"Don't give me that shit, Doc. You promised to behave if I didn't force the bracelets behind your back. What does *behave* mean to you?"

"Semantics," Deacon said, noting with relief that the pistol was now pointing at the road. "You want to holster that thing, Special Agent?"

Carstairs looked shocked, as if he hadn't known he was still holding it. Then he replaced the Glock in a strong-side holster. Deacon noticed Carstairs wasn't wearing his safety belt, an ingrained habit for everybody, especially government agents. Deacon clicked his into place.

"Just don't make me draw it again. I'd hate to have to use it on myself … I mean, you."

Ignoring the pain in his head and shoulder, Deacon studied Carstairs. Something wasn't right with the FBI agent. The relaxed, almost bored look he carried into a conference room was gone. Maybe it was just the stress of Deacon's escape attempt, or maybe he was tired, but he looked … agitated. His breaths came in the short gasps of someone being chased by an angry mob. In the light of the passing streetlamps, his face looked pale and drawn. Drained. Deacon had seen such looks in combat, on the faces of lonely men who had gone days without sleep.

"Are you okay, Special Agent?"

Carstairs flinched. "Huh? What?"

"I asked if you were alright."

"Me? I'm, ah, fine."

"You don't look fine."

"Never mind how I look, Doc. My worries are limited to a summer cold." He sleeved his nose. "You've got bigger problems."

"Look Carstairs. I don't know what this is all about. I didn't take any files. And I wasn't running away from prosecution, I was running from somebody trying to kill me. To kill both of us, me and Amy. I mean Marine Force Specialist Robbins."

"Where is your partner in crime, by the way?"

"She's not my partner in crime."

"Fine. Lover. Stooge. Whatever. It'll go easier on you if you tell me."

Deacon could hear that Carstairs was trying for bad-cop bravado, but it wasn't working. The experienced agent sounded as nervous as a rookie patrolman making his first arrest. He also seemed oddly distracted. He fidgeted with his tie and flinched as the streetlights flashed by.

Deacon raised his hands to massage his injured shoulder. Leaning back and closing his eyes, he gave up trying to convince the agent. "I guess I'll wait for my lawyer." He expected a retort from Carstairs, something along the lines of 'no lawyer is going to get you out of this.' But the agent said nothing. He just kept driving. In fact, he drove faster. It felt like they were doing at least sixty, the overhead lights strobing past Deacon's lids like a disco ball. The Ford suddenly swerved to the side then back again, a car horn angrily greeting the maneuver. Deacon opened his eyes.

"Hey. Take it easy, Special Agent. I'd like to be alive when I talk to ..."

The words locked in his throat as his eyes locked on the speedometer. The Ford was doing seventy-five — on Massachusetts Avenue. And it was still accelerating. Deacon looked out the windshield. Traffic was light, but there were still cars to avoid — the most immediate two stopped at a red light directly ahead of the onrushing Ford.

"Slow down," Deacon yelled. But the look on Carstairs face said he wasn't going to. That look was not panic or even plain, ordinary fear. And that's what scared Deacon most of all. Carstairs' look was one of peaceful acceptance. Fear was only visible in the agent's bone-white knuckles on the steering wheel.

The stopped cars grew uncomfortably large in the windshield, but still the Ford didn't slow. Deacon had seconds to act, or they'd be staring at either airbags or eternity. The fight or flight he'd experienced during his recent escapes kicked in again. He hoped he hadn't used up nine lives.

Deacon's cuffed hands grabbed the wheel and pulled it sharply toward him. At first it wouldn't budge, Carstairs' determination locking them dead ahead. Doubling his efforts, Deacon managed to jerk the wheel to the right, sending them hurtling down another road, the street sign little more than a blur.

The immediate danger had passed, but there was no time to relax. Determined hands pulled the wheel out of Deacon's grasp, sending them toward parked cars and storefronts. Deacon fought for control, managing to straighten the wheel before Carstairs wrenched it left toward oncoming traffic. Again, Deacon wrested control, again only for the moment. The FBI agent had the strength of a berserker on Benzedrine. A snatched look at the speedometer said they were doing eighty. Deacon had bought time, but something needed to happen soon — or their trip would end suddenly and badly.

Deacon took a split second to run the possibilities. He couldn't reach the the brakepedal while belted in and wresting the wheel. Pulling Carstairs' leg off the gas was also out of the question; even a first-year anatomy student knew you couldn't pit injured arms against healthy legs. Punching Carstairs' in the balls would probably force his foot harder on the gas pedal. That left one choice, and one slim chance.

Deacon released the wheel and grabbed the gear shift, jerking the trans into a lower gear. The car slowed abruptly amidst a grating roar, the sudden deceleration pinning Deacon and his injured shoulder against his safety harness. Carstairs had no safety harness against which to pin, so his chest struck the steering wheel and his head the windshield. The rest was a blur as the Ford veered.

Jamming the Miata into gear, Amy sped after the taillights that were already through the traffic circle as she entered it. By the time she was back on Massachusetts, the little red lights were distant specks. She accelerated to keep pace, but the lights continued to dim. In seconds, she was doing sixty, veering around an old Cadillac. A blat of a horn up ahead said that the Ford was also recklessly weaving through traffic.

"Shit. What's with this guy?"

Traffic was heavier as she approached the Naval Observatory. Amy had trouble distinguishing the Ford among the many taillights and the glare of headlights and streetlamps. Just as she feared she'd lost them, two red lights veered from the pack and sped erratically onto Wisconsin Avenue. Amy pulled around a Prius and gunned the engine, following the Ford.

She broke into the turn, then punched the gas, the needle climbing past seventy. Moments later, she was jamming on the brakes again. The Ford had changed from a diminishing image in her windscreen to one that filled it, having suddenly gone from freeway speed to runner's speed. As the Miata squealed to a stop, the other car skidded to the left, then jumped a curb. It banged to a stop against a light pole, steam rising from the engine, the grill and hood dented in a rictus smile.

Amy leapt from the sportscar and ran to the Ford's passenger door. It opened before she reached it, Deacon stumbling out.

"Deke!" She wrapped her arms about him for support. "Are you alright?"

His body shuddered. "Ow. Easy on the shoulder."

Amy loosened her hug and backed away, her hands still steadying him. "Sorry. Are you okay?"

"Yeah. I think so." His cuffed hands tucked against his shoulder. "Check Carstairs."

Amy didn't want to leave, but she was a medic with triage training. Treat the more serious injuries first. So, she ran around the trunk and opened the driver's door.

The driver was slumped over the wheel, blood pouring from a gash above his left eyebrow. She gently but firmly placed her hands on either side of his head, stabilizing the neck as she pulled him back into his seat.

He groaned.

"He okay?" Deacon asked.

"Not sure," Amy said. "I think so. Doesn't feel like any vertebral fractures." Pulling a hanky from her khakis she applied steady pressure to the wound. "But I gotta stop this bleeding. Head wounds bleed like a motherfucker."

Deacon chuckled. "That may be the first time I've heard you curse, Specialist Robbins."

Carstairs groaned again and tried to swipe her hand away.

"Easy, sir. Let me keep pressure on this cut."

The FBI agent's hand stopped trying to push her away and instead reached down to his side. Before she knew what he was doing, he'd drawn his Glock and raised it to his temple.

"Jesus!" Amy pushed away the pistol just as it went off with a flash-bang that temporarily blinded and deafened her. Carstairs groaned again as the pistol clattered into the cabin and his shoulders slumped into the seat.

Amy's eyes met Deacon's staring in from the open passenger door. She read his lips.

"You okay?"

Amy nodded, reapplying pressure to the wound.

"Looks like he's passed out," Deacon said. "Did the son of a bitch try to shoot you?"

Amy shook her head in disbelief. "No sir. At least I don't think so. I think himself."

"What?"

"I'd swear he was trying to shoot himself." She stared at Deacon. "Why the hell would he try to shoot himself?"

Deacon thought for a moment, then reached over and wiped snot from Paul Carstairs' nose. "I think I know."

They were at the corner of Wisconsin and Thirty-Fifth. A sign along a cement and steel wall read Holyrood Cemetery. "That fits," Deacon mumbled.

"What?" Amy said, wrapping her hands around Paul Carstairs' leg. A siren droned in the distance.

"Nothing," Deacon said. "On three." With a groan, he laced his fingers against the FBI agent's chest. "One. Two. *Three*."

"I'm not sure we should be moving him," Amy said as they lay the unconscious form on the grass. "He may have a head or neck injury. Better to wait for the ambulance."

"Can't wait for an ambulance. And we need him."

"Need him? For what?"

Deacon placed his cuffed hands against his shoulder and leaned against the steaming car. "See if you can find the keys to these handcuffs while I try not to pass out."

Amy snaked her hand into the pocket of Carstairs' suit jacket, striking pay dirt the first time. "We *need* him? He *needs* an ambulance. And why are you handcuffed?"

Deacon shakily held out his hands and she unlocked the bracelets. Deke placed them in his pocket. The sirens grew louder.

"Evidently, I am wanted for stealing government documents. Maybe espionage, treason, and whatever else they can pin on me. You, too."

"Me?"

Deke nodded. "Pull the car over and we'll put him in?"

Amy stood her ground. "Why do they think we stole documents?"

"That's what I want to ask Carstairs. Now get the car before the cops get here."

Amy pointed toward the Miata. "How we gonna fit all three of us into *that*?"

"We'll have to make it work," Deacon said. "Oh. And take this." He tossed the agent's Glock to her.

"For protection?" she asked.

"Maybe," Deke said. "But mostly to keep Paul here from blowing his brains out."

Chapter 27

U ndersecretary Cathleen Harris rolled kinks from her long, slender neck. It had been quite a day. And she hadn't liked a lot of it. This project, this assignment, was taking on unpleasant dimensions.

Deacon Creel was no doubt brilliant. Harris could see why Barzoon and that fat ball of dough, Metternich, had brought him into it. But a man who was uncontrollable once would be uncontrollable again, no matter how brilliant that man might be. She smiled. Well, she thought, tidying the papers on her desk, at least he's safely in custody now. She reached a well-manicured finger and flicked off the reading lamp.

Harris had just risen from her chair when a soft knock on the door stopped her. With a sigh, she returned her pert bottom to worn, comfortable leather.

"Yes?"

The door opened slowly. A familiar face entered. The face looked a little sheepish. Maybe even a little guilty, like Judas reporting to the Pharisees for his thirty silver cartwheels.

"Come in. Please, have a seat."

"I, um, I hope I'm not interrupting anything."

"Not at all. I was just on my way after a long day, but I always have time for you."

Harris pointed to the chair in front of her desk. "Please sit." Then she crossed to seat herself opposite her guest. She moved with slow, sensual steps, raising her tight skirt so she could shimmy onto the lip of the polished mahogany desk. She crossed her legs. "I guess I owe you, that is, Homeland Security owes you thanks for alerting the Bureau about Creel. That showed a great deal of courage and, well, loyalty. I know he's a friend of yours, so it must have been difficult to do the right thing."

"Yeah. That's what I wanted to talk to you about. I'm trying to figure if it *was* the right thing."

Harris tilted her head quizzically. "Well, I must admit having Special Agent Carstairs walk into my office was a bit of a surprise. But the more I think about it, the more I'm sure you were correct to do it."

"What happens now?"

"Now?"

"To Deke, I mean. And to that Amy. What happens to them? Jail until things resolve?"

"Perhaps," Harris said, taking her visitor's hand. "Perhaps." She gently stroked the tawny skin with her soft, slender fingers. "Or perhaps, well, something more permanent."

Her guest flinched from her touch. "What do you mean?"

Harris gently retrieved the fingers and delicately kissed them. She could feel warmth rise in the flesh.

"Well, Carstairs appeared quite agitated when he was here. Haggard. Preoccupied. As if he'd reached the tertiary stage." She gently pulled the hand to her inviting thigh and rested it there. Her guest sighed. "I wouldn't be a bit surprised if he met with an accident on the way to the Hoover Building." The fingers on her nylons quivered, then inched northward. She allowed them to. "Dr. Creel might share that accident." The fingers on her thigh hesitated.

"But we were, well, we were only supposed to, you know, scare them. Let them create a ..."

"Shhh," Harris said, reaching forward to gently stroke the handsome features. "My darling, I know how you feel." Her fingers gently teased along the neck, tickling behind the ear. Her lover responded with closed eyes and shuddery breaths. Harris smiled. "You know him. Of course, you have divided loyalties. But make no mistake, you chose correctly." Her fingers trailed down to the top button of the khaki shirt, flicking it undone. "You chose wisely." A second button flicked between expert fingers. "You chose courageously." Her fingers trailed down to tease the nipple. "I'm proud of you." Her lover moaned.

Harris continued gently stroking the hairs along the tawny skin, letting her fingers tease lower. Rising from the desk, she sat in her lover's lap. "I'm so, so proud of you." She gently tweaked a nipple, producing more shudders. "Believe in the mission." They gently kissed. "Believe in our country." She kissed again, their lips touching longer. "Believe in me." Her lips locked over those of her lover.

Lisa Reilly responded as she always did. With total abandon.

Agent Carstairs groaned and rolled toward his side, the handcuffs stretched over his head jangling against the metal bed frame. Then he slipped back into unconsciousness.

"He must have a concussion," Amy said. "Otherwise, he'd have come around by now."

"I was more worried he'd come around while we were crammed together in the front seat."

"We should have left him for the medics," Amy said. "He could die."

Deke drained the dregs of his paper cup. "And *if* we'd left him, that's just what would have happened."

"What? How so?"

"He'd been complaining of a head cold."

"So."

"That's one of the first symptoms. Liz ..." He choked up, then continued. "My fiancée had one, just before she, um."

Amy touched his hand. "It wasn't your fault, Deke."

"It sure as hell was somebody's. And I was the one who was supposed to love and protect her."

Amy squeezed his hand. "I still can't believe there's a suicide drug. When you first told me, in that bar, I don't know. I thought it was just another version of ..."

"Pink elephants?" He smiled sadly. "I wish it were."

They both started at a knock on the door. "Housekeeping."

"No ahora," Deacon yelled at the Hispanic accent.

"Bueno," the maid replied.

Carstairs groaned again, louder than before.

"Tiene usted un problema?" the maid asked.

"No," Deacon yelled. "No problema. Me duele el dedo."

"Lastima. buenos dias." The maid trolley trundled down the outdoor passageway.

"I didn't know you spoke Spanish," Amy said.

"Spanish, French, Latin, and German." He pointed to the TV. "Let's make a little background noise. I'll check on our boy."

Deacon heard the TV come to life, CNN filling the air. Then he pulled the desk chair over to the bedside."

"How you doing, Special Agent?"

Carstairs managed a smile. "I've been better."

"How's the head?"

"Hurts like a sonofabitch."

"Yeah. I guess it would have hurt less if we let you put a bullet through it."

The agent flinched, as if Deacon had read his mind.

"How long have you been having these thoughts, these urges?"

"I don't know what you mean."

"Like hell you don't."

"You wanna take these cuffs off?"

"You wanna tell me who told you that I'd stolen documents?"

Carstairs snorted, then winced at the effort. "Didn't give me a name. Just said one of the scientists on the project."

"Project Seppuku?"

"Is that what it's called?"

Amy came over with a wet washcloth. "Here, this should help." She placed the cloth on his forehead. "Commander Creel. Can I have a word?"

"In a minute," Deacon said. "This person who told you. Was it a man or a woman?"

"Now, please, sir." Amy motioned to the bathroom.

Deacon nodded, then turned up the volume on the TV. "Don't go away."

Carstairs rattled his chain and smiled.

Amy closed the bathroom door so that Carstairs couldn't hear them. "You better take it easy, Deke. A concussion is a very tricky thing. He needs rest and fluids. He doesn't need browbeating."

"First off, I was asking questions, not browbeating. Second, we probably saved his life by bringing him here instead of leaving him."

"Even so."

"Even so, I need to find out who told him this fable about the stolen documents. I don't think it was Barzoon or

Metternich; Carstairs would have recognized their voices. So, we must have someone else to worry about."

"Who?"

"That's the million-dollar question, isn't it? And Paul in there has the answer. And it's my job to get that answer. A job I might have accomplished by now if you hadn't pulled me in here. Alright, Marine Force Specialist?"

Amy flushed crimson. "Alright *Commander*. But *my* job is medicine. There is an injured man in there who has at least a concussion and possibly a slow bleed. A man who should be in a hospital instead of Gestapo headquarters. A man who at the very least needs rest and fluids." She paused before adding, "Sir."

Deke kissed her lightly on the lips. "You're awful purty when you're angry, ma'am."

Amy smiled. "Just take it easy. Okay, Deke?"

He winked. "Bring him some water ... please."

Deke opened the door. "Alright Agent Carstairs." He'd barely reached the foot of the bed when he stopped. He wouldn't have believed it possible. What he saw looked impossible.

"Here, Mr. Carstairs. Drink this." Amy stopped short next to Deke, water swishing from her plastic cup. "Oh, my lord in heaven."

Paul Carstairs was obviously dead. But the way he died was unbelievable. The cloth Amy had placed on his brow was now shoved into his mouth. No, more like swallowed, a tiny white tag on a terrycloth corner the only visible bit. Despite the concussion, he'd managed to pull his shoulders up on the pillow, wedge the cloth into his mouth, and wedge his head in the minute space between his manacled wrists. Then he'd evidently twisted his wrists to tighten the slack and choked to death. His dark purple face confirmed the cause of death. But that wasn't the most gruesome part. The look on his contorted features was one of pure contentment.

"I've never seen anything like it. How is that even possible?"

"It's possible," Deacon said. "ZuZu and Rudolph could tell you that."

"The political world was saddened yesterday when Senator Janet Pankovich was found dead in her Chevy Chase townhome. The cause of death has not yet been released. The young senator was often spoken of as presidential material and a pundit favorite for VP following vice-president Brookes' announcement that he would be stepping down due to his wife's grave illness. The short list for his replacement has dwindled to ..."

Deacon shut off the TV.

Amy still gaped at the body lying on the bed. "How is that even possible. I mean, there couldn't have been more than six inches of slack between his wrists. How could he have? I mean, even the rag. How could he have swallowed it? It just doesn't seem possible."

Deacon tapped the cup of water in her fingers. "Drink that."

Amy obeyed, eyes still staring at the figure on the bed. "I'm looking at it, but I don't believe it."

She turned to him, pupils the size of platters. There were those Ronstadt eyes, Liz's eyes. He took the cup and tossed it in the basket.

"Like I said, it's possible. If someone wants to kill themselves badly enough."

"But the rag," she said. "How'd he get it into his mouth? What about the gag reflex?"

"The Craiglist List killer slit his wrists and stuffed toilet paper down his throat so the prison guards couldn't resuscitate him. Then he calmly placed a plastic bag over his head and died, without making a sound."

Amy stared at him. "Project Seppuku?"

Deacon nodded.

"What do we do now?"

"We get the hell out of here before the maid comes back."

"We can't just, just leave him."

"We're not taking him with us. Now let's go." He shoved the Glock in his waistband then turned to the door.

"But. But. Our prints are everywhere," Amy said. "I used my credit card for the room."

"And we're also wanted for espionage and treason. So, let's get out of here before that card is charged and they track the transaction to the Knight's Rest Motor Lodge."

Deacon threw down the menu. "Let me have a bacon, egg, and cheese on wheat toast. And coffee."

"You want home fries with that?" the waitress asked. "It's a buck fifty extra. Otherwise, it comes with chips."

"Chips are fine."

"And you, ma'am."

"Just a Pepsi," Amy said.

The little diner was in an industrial park outside Garrison. They'd logged twenty miles since leaving the Knight's Rest, stopping once at an all-night Walmart for a few hours sleep in the back of the nearly deserted lot. The sun was red on the horizon when they'd stopped at the diner for food and gas. Deacon figured it was better to have all the credit card slips from one location instead of a connect-the-dots string.

"You should eat," Deacon said.

"I'm not hungry," Amy said. "How can *you* be?"

Deacon's stomach rumbled at the smell of frying sausage and dark-roast coffee. "I'm not. My body is."

The waitress brought their drinks. When she left, Deacon said, "You must have seen worse in Iraq. Being a combat medic."

Amy nodded. "Worse by way of mangled bodies. But I've never seen ..." She shook her head and drank her soda. "What do we do now?"

Deacon sipped and watched her. She was tired, her large eyes sunken with fatigue. Her young face lined with sleepiness and worry. But she still looked beautiful. He hoped for the hundredth time that he wasn't getting her killed.

"I think we need to stop fleeing and start thinking," he said. Amy eyebrowed a question mark. "They've had us on the run. First Woody's bar. Then the cabin. This all seems to be working toward a plan."

"Yeah. They plan to kill us."

"Or keep us moving. Keep us on the defensive. The espionage charges are just another play on the same theme. Why?"

Amy looked around, but no one was listening. "You're dangerous to them somehow, I guess. I'm dangerous by association."

"But how? Because I might foil their plot? What plot?" His food arrived. Deacon took a bite but kept talking. "There's some master plan involved here. I feel it."

"Couldn't it just be a sicko? Someone with a political axe to grind. Like that guy shooting up the congressional ballgame."

Deacon napkinned egg yolk off his mouth. He thought about Lisa's rant while they shared coffee at the Unit. He shook his head. "No. She's too apathetic."

"What?"

"Nothing. Just wool gathering." He sipped from his cup, washing down the grease and egg. "If it's just a sicko who got ahold of weaponized 606, why am I a problem? Why not let me rant and rave while he goes on killing? And how did he even know about me, unless he's someone on the inside?" Deacon shook his head, again. "There's more. Some grand design. There must be. Someone inside working toward a plan, a goal. These don't feel like random deaths to me. They're too high profile. They must have something in common."

"They're all from the same political party."

Deacon bit sandwich. "Something more. I can feel it."

"Well," Amy said, stealing a chip from his plate. "Who are we talking about? What do you know about the victims?"

Deacon ran down the list. "There's Silas Burke."

Amy licked her fingers. "The president's advisor. I heard he'd died in a traffic accident."

"Yes. Suicide by abutment." He held up two fingers. "Then Kristen Lebel, the party chair."

Amy stole more chips. Another Liz mannerism: turning down food then eating his.

"She died in her sleep, didn't she?" Amy asked.

"Yes. From an overdose of pills." Deacon held up three fingers. "Then there was Scott Waters. Rising congressional star in only his second term."

"Good poll numbers?"

"Fabulous poll numbers, from what I've heard. Then Angela Putnam."

"Was she in Congress?"

Deacon was no longer hungry; he was full of questions. "No. District-court judge. Eastern Virginia. Just sent down a controversial gun-control decision." Deacon thought for a moment. It seemed like he was missing something. Something recent. He shrugged. "That's it — so far."

Amy snagged another chip. "So, what do they all have in common, other than political affiliation?"

Deacon leaned back and crossed his arms. "Let's start with Burke. What does a presidential advisor do?"

"Advises the president?"

"Yeah. But about what? In particular. What's important, right now?"

Amy shrugged. "What isn't."

"Then a party chairwoman."

"Same thing," Amy said. "Advisor. Politics instead of policy."

Deacon nodded. "Scott Waters. Congressman. Why?"

Amy snagged another chip. "He was only in his second term. Not much track record."

Deacon raised a finger. "But a rising star. Already lauded as having presidential timbre." The thought nagged at him. It was tied into something he'd heard recently, and something Lisa had said, but he couldn't place it.

"Then a judge?"

"Yes," Deacon said. "Why a judge?"

"Can I have some of that?" Amy pointed to the sandwich.

Deke slid the plate to her.

"Someone," Deacon said, "is working toward a pattern. Some goal. And it must be coming to a head or what I knew, or thought I knew, wouldn't matter. But what? Why me?"

Amy bit into her half. "They needed you to develop the antidote. Don't forget that."

"So that 606 couldn't be used against them? Okay. But why'd they wait? They'd already started killing. That is, the suicides started before I was ever brought into it. You develop the antidote *before* weaponization. That's SOP. Why did they need me now?"

"Maybe..." Amy averted her eyes and nodded toward the door.

Two county sheriffs entered and took the booth near the exit. Deacon caught the server's attention and checkmarked the air. "Finish that. Time for us to scoot."

"Where to?" Amy asked, washing down the last of the sandwich.

"You're off to do research. Find out whatever you can

about our victims. What do they have in common? What sets them apart?"

"And you?"

"See if I can contact our only remaining ally."

The Garrison branch of the Baltimore County library system was a small brick structure of 1950s vintage. Amy expected to find a prim, grey-haired book marm in a dowdy suit, eyeglasses dangling from a gold chain onto a nonexistent bosom. Instead, she got Margeri, a tattooed, twenty-something with a nose ring . But the girl was friendly and escorted her to a computer carrel, internet access available to all.

Deacon wanted to find out everything he could about the deaths so far. Any commonalities or oddities. Amy started in reverse order with a search of Angela Putnam.

As with any recent death, the first thing to show up on Google was her obit. As expected, it was highly complimentary, a cross between Mother Theresa, Joan of Arc, and Madame Curie. The only nod to the nature of her death was a reference to a "heroic struggle with substance abuse." A *Post* article, although still complimentary, dug deeper. The struggle with substance abuse was defined as two stints at Betty Ford. Survived by her husband became "estranged husband." Hints of possible suicide were dropped by reference to "work and homelife stress." Amy jotted particulars on a borrowed legal pad, then read through Wikipedia and a *Times* article published back when Putnam had been mentioned for the high court.

Amy jotted more specifics. The sudden death under questionable circumstances certainly fit this suicide drug. Like all high-powered politicos, Putnam had problems, but the problems described by the media didn't seem to justify suicide or a leap off the wagon into booze and pills. Still, Amy didn't feel satisfied. The pieces felt sterile, sanitized. The Reader's Digest version of a life written by friendly authors. She paged down several screens and found more meat — gristle and bits of spoiled beef.

The alternative media, the bloggers, web-based news, and counterculture pundits, were less sympathetic. Some of their "facts" were more vindictiveness than verity, but a narrative emerged when Amy read between the lines. There were rumors of a third stint at rehab, one in a lower-profile facility in San Diego. Other rumors placed Putnam off the wagon on more than one occasion in between dry-out sessions, including a raucous argument with an Armenian waiter in a fashionable Arlington restaurant.

Amy also discovered that the last stay at Ford was presaged by a DUI arrest her handlers had successfully hushed — this "rumor" backed up by a police report. The "home life" stress was a philandering husband and a path to divorce, one that was likely to be rancorous and costly to both Putnam's pocketbook and her political aspirations, aspirations that had dimmed considerably in the long years since her mention for the high court. Finally, the kicker — she'd done it before. Prior to her first bout of rehab, she'd been rushed to the hospital with enough alcohol and sodium seconal in her system to make a rhino drowsy.

"This woman didn't need a suicide drug," Amy mumbled, jotting down notes. "She was getting there fine all by herself."

Deacon sipped his umpteenth cup of coffee and waited. Lisa's parking spot was empty and the windows of Building K, apartment 102 showed no signs of movement. He'd backed the Miata into the shade of a blue spruce, so that he could watch the building. Forty minutes later, the only activity had been a woman and her lab entering 103 and Deacon's trip outside to piss behind the blue spruce. Still, he waited. Where was she?

She wasn't at Unit 13; he'd called from a pay phone outside a Shell station and was told the building was closed for the weekend. The round-the-clock full-court press evidently couldn't survive without him. She might be hooked up somewhere. Lisa had been known to hit the gay bars from time to time but wasn't much for staying the night — more the cuddle for ten minutes then split amidst a proclamation of an early morning meeting. So, where was she?

He'd just rolled down the window for air, the warmth of the Miata's cozy cabin drawing him toward sleep, when a car entered the parking lot. Deacon heard it before he saw it, its pop, pop, pop suggesting bad plugs or a dirty fuel filter. He ducked down into the Miata's interior as a used, lime-green PT Cruiser pulled into Lisa's designated spot. Blue smoke puffed from the tailpipe and the smell of burning oil filled the summer air. Deacon smiled. It had rent-a-wreck written all over it.

The engine quit after a few final knocks, and Lisa Reilly got out. She was dressed in nice but rumpled pants and blouse, all in black so that her whip-thin frame looked particularly elegant. His guess about a hookup must have been right, but it probably wasn't something casual — not if she'd spent the night. Deacon watched as she yawned then dug keys from her pants pocket. He waited until she was turning the key on apartment 102, then exited quickly and dashed across the lot. Before she'd closed the door, his hand was on the knob pushing it open.

"Hey! What the ... Deke?"

Deacon ducked inside the door and closed it. "Howdy, ma'am. Mind if I come in?"

"What the hell are you doing here?"

"Found myself in the neighborhood and thought I'd drop by." Deacon pointed to the door. "I like your car."

"Yeah? Well, thanks. Not only does it look like something Linda Blair threw up, but it sounds and smells like a school bus."

"Good gas mileage?" Deacon grinned.

Lisa grinned back. "No. But it was cheap. All they had at the bus station you dropped me at was Sam's Discount Used Cars. I had to buy that eyesore. Cost me seven-hundred bucks. Your running away from prison is putting me in the poor house."

"I'll pay you back."

Lisa embraced him.

"Seriously, great to see you. But what are you doing here? The cops have already grilled me once about you and might be back anytime."

"Joe and Barzoon really want their pound of flesh, huh? All this for suspicion of stealing a few files?"

"Files? Don't you know?"

"Know what?"

"You're now wanted for murder. You and what's her name, both. An FBI agent."

"Shit. Carstairs? He killed himself."

"That's not what's playing on the news. Here, read it." Lisa opened the door, scanned the parking lot in both directions, then snatched the newspaper off the stoop. "You're front page, *above* the fold."

Deacon read the headline. "Rogue scientist and lover wanted for murder and espionage. Regional manhunt underway."

"The unit is closed. I've been furloughed along with everyone else. The FBI's talking to everybody. Joe has gone into hiding. Barzoon is ranting about killing you, then Joe, then himself. So, how was *your* day?"

Deacon tossed the paper aside just as Lisa's landline rang.

She looked at the number. "Probably a telemarketer. Baltimore area code."

"Better answer it," Deacon said. "It could be Amy. I told her to call me here. By the way, why didn't *you* call me?"

Lisa held up a restraining hand, then picked up the phone. "Hello? Oh, hi. Yeah, he's here." She handed him the phone. "It's Linda Ronstadt."

Deacon snatched the receiver. "Hi, Amy. What you got?"

Amy filled him in on what she'd learned. Deacon listened, nodding. Then he said, "What about Putnam?" He listened some more, then nodded again. "Okay. Keep at it. I'll stop by and pick you up before they close."

"Close? Where is she?"

"The public library in Garrison. I had her do some research about our suicides. See what they had in common." He picked up the paper again. "There's some plan at work here. I can feel it. 606 is being used to target specific individuals for a specific reason."

"Could Amy find out what that reason is?"

"Not so far. All she's got is that Silas Burke and Kristen Lebel were particularly close to the President. Burke was a law-school pal at Harvard, and Lebel managed his first run for the White House."

"Waters?"

Deacon kept his nose in the paper. "Political shooting star. Spoken of as a presidential hopeful in four years. Maybe even a VP candidate now."

"Putnam?"

Deacon's eyes continued skimming the story. "No. Looks

like she may be a red herring. Amy said that her personal and political life were both in the toilet. She'd fallen off the wagon before and probably this time as well. Most likely an accidental overdose. Or run of the mill, unassisted suicide." He finished the front-page story, then turned to its continuation deeper in the section. "By the way, why didn't you call me like I asked?"

"Oh, sorry. But with this manhunt, well, man and woman hunt, I didn't think it was a good idea to contact your cell. Plus, there wasn't much to report. I wasn't able to get in touch with anybody who might help."

"Janet Pankovich is dead?" Deacon's eyes latched on the third-page headline.

"Uh huh. A day or two ago. Your fifteen minutes of fame pushed her off the front page."

"Suicide?" He stared at Lisa.

"Yeah. I thought that, too. Could be a coincidence though."

Deacon read the story, his eyes growing wider. "She was mentioned as a VP pick, just like Waters."

"Hey, a lot of people are on that list."

"Yeah, but she was on the *short* list. They both were." He stared through her, thinking out loud. "And how would a president decide between them? He'd seek advice from trusted advisors. Close personal and political confidants."

"Like college friends and former campaign managers?"

Deacon's head went back into the paper. He read aloud. "Beltway insiders opine that the tragic deaths of both Waters and Pankovich have reduced the President's short list to just two names." He read them silently. "I'll be a son of a bitch."

"What?"

"I think I know who's authored this hit list. And who's next on it."

They'd sat in Lisa's kitchen, sipping coffee. Deacon would have preferred a shot of Maker's Mark (maybe ten of them) but not now. Not yet. He smiled. At least the last few days were keeping him on the wagon.

"Why don't we just go to the cops?" Lisa said. "Lay it out. Bypass all the cloak-and-dagger bullshit."

"Okay," Deacon said. "*Lay* it out. Run it by me. See how it sounds."

"Alright." Lisa cleared her throat. "Excuse me, officer."

"Detective," Deacon said. "You'd probably be talking to a detective."

"Okay. Excuse me, *detective*. My name is Dr. Lisa Reilly. I'm one of the scientists over at Fort Deidenbach. You know, the research labs?"

"Go on."

"Well, we were working on, I mean the unit I was with developed a kind of, well, a suicide drug. You see, we were working with a drug company to improve their Alzheimer's drug, which has this side effect of causing suicide, and somebody at the laboratory, my laboratory, not the drug company's, turned it into a suicide drug, you know, for assassination, and now we think, that is, Commander Creel and I think, they are using it to kill off the …"

Deacon smiled as Lisa trailed off. "Any other great ideas?"

"Okay. So, we can't go to the cops. And we can't go to the FBI?"

"Not with me the prime suspect in the death of one of their agents." Deacon's fingers rasped the stubble on his chin. "Who does that leave? Who in authority? Who might be able to act?"

"Ray?"

Deacon shook his head. "He may be lab director, but he's still basically a tech. I don't think he'd carry much weight. And I'd prefer not to get anybody involved who isn't already."

"Well, Barzoon is out. How about Joe? Or do you think he's working with Barzoon?"

Deacon thought. "Yeah, he's working with Barzoon. But maybe not against us?"

"How so?"

"Joe is a prig, a jerk, and a shamelessly selfish, self-important bureaucrat. If it was underhanded dealings to beat somebody out of a promotion, Joe's my man. Top of the list. But treason? A plot to kill off highly placed, high-octane politicos?"

"So, you figure Barzoon is using him? *Has* used him to get the 606 weaponized and cover his tracks for him? Never told him the real purpose?"

"Yeah," Deacon said. "Joe is just a stooge. That would be my guess."

Lisa nodded. "What are you going to do now?"

Deacon pulled the Miata's keys from his pocket. "First, I pick up Amy."

"Then?"

"Save the next victim of Project Suicide."

Chapter 28

Deacon drove to Garrison, an upper-middle-class suburb of Owings Mills, itself a bedroom suburb of Baltimore. The town evidently thought a lot of itself with street names like Royalty Circle, Majestic Court, and Countess Drive proclaiming the regal nature of the eight thousand Garrisonians. The public library was near the corner of Craddock and Countess.

The plan was simple. Deacon would pick up Amy, then head back to Lisa's. They'd swap her Miata for the puke-green Cruiser, a vehicle ugly enough to defy suspicion as a getaway car. Deacon and Amy would contact the next intended victim, at least assuming that Deacon's insight was correct. Lisa would head to Unit 13 and try to find someone with whom they could confide. Their list of potential allies was getting small. Misjudging a foe as a friend could be dangerous, even deadly. But Lisa said she'd risk it.

Lisa agreed to find Metternich and enlist his help. He was supposedly hiding out from Barzoon, but neither of them rated him as a very good hider — probably at home, gardening. Deacon hoped she'd find him. He hoped Metternich would bury the hatchet and help. He also hoped he wasn't sending Lisa on a wild-goose chase or suicide run of her own.

Traffic was light as he turned off Craddock. The little community's Norman Rockwell image was shattered once he'd turned onto Countess Drive.

A dozen gawkers were lined up by a state police car blocking his way, wigwags flashing. Through a gap in the crowd, Deacon could see an identical two-toned cruiser blocking Countess just past the library, a nearly identical group of rubberneckers lined there as well. Unmarked cars were parked between the two cruisers. State troopers milled about the central area, holding back the crowd and steering clear of the suits moving into and out of the library.

One of the troopers walked toward Deacon, his young, six-foot frame stiff as the Stetson on his head. One powerful arm helicoptered the air, then pointed. Deacon nodded and three-pointed a turn back the way he'd come. As he popped the Miata's stick shift from reverse into first, the soft babble from the crowd became continual chatter. The low-slung sports car prevented Deacon from seeing much, but he waited expectantly just the same. Like good sheepdogs, the troopers herded back the gawkers, opening a line of sight to the front of the old building.

"Shit," Deacon muttered.

Marine Force Specialist Amy Robbins was led from the facility by a blocky woman in a dark-blue pant suit. Amy's hands were behind her in the traditional arrest posture. Despite the strain and lack of sleep, she still looked beautiful, reminding him once again of his late fiancée and churning up a series of emotions. There was angst seeing her led away like a common criminal, a chained animal. There was anger at the one (ones?) responsible. But mostly there was shame. Again, he had gotten a loved one into a mess, led her into danger. Thoughts of Liz flooded him with regret. Tears welled in his eyes as his knuckles whitened against the gear shift.

A heavy thud shook the car, knocking Deacon back to reality.

"Move it," yelled the trooper who'd just banged the Miata's hood.

Deacon nodded and popped the clutch. The little car jerked forward and drove off, slowly picking up speed. Deacon looked into the rearview, but the crowd blocked his sight again. He started to cry.

Deacon's left foot slammed the clutch, while his right hand jerked the Miata into second. His other hand was busy wiping tears from eyes that blurred reality into nightmare, or maybe the other way around.

The shame and remorse that drove along for the ride drifted into the back seat. The shotgun seat was taken over by an old friend, someone who'd comforted him many times. Mr. Booze. He'd get drunk. And not just drunk—gloriously, uproariously, rip-roaringly, mind-numbingly drunk. He could stop by a liquor store and use his emergency cash to buy a quart of cheap bourbon. Then, he could light somewhere, some pretty spot. He pulled his foot off the gas as he drove past a wooded development. That would do. Some pretty, secluded arbor. It would be just him and the bottle, their love affair continued. A romance that didn't heal old wounds but provided a temporary Band-Aid. Then, after waking to a four-alarm headache and a thorough vomiting, he could turn himself in. He'd explain that Amy was guiltless; maybe they'd let her go. Maybe someone would even believe his story. Stranger things had happened. Or maybe he would die trying to escape or be found hanging by the neck in his cell. That wouldn't be so bad, either.

And that's what he wanted to do. What he would have done — except. What about Amy? And what about that new occupant who would reside in Number One Observatory Circle? Whether a foreign operative, or just a ruthless, power-hungry sociopath, this new vice president would be only a heartbeat away from the White House. And this new VP would have access to a suicide drug with which to stop that heart. And it would be Deacon's doing. Commander Deacon Creel would have another sin to answer for, perhaps the greatest sin yet. So, he pressed the accelerator and drove on.

Lights flashed from the rearview like diamonds glinting in his shiny eyes. The law-enforcement parade, Amy's motorcade, was right behind him. He pulled the Mazda onto a tree-lined circle and slowed. In the rearview, Deacon watched the reflected line of cars move past, the lead cruiser followed by a dark-blue Ford sedan, then a brown SUV, then another cruiser. To Deacon's surprise, the cruiser riding drag did not follow the crowd. That cruiser slowed, then turned down the same road Deacon had taken. The flashing lights grew larger in the mirror as the powerful vehicle picked up speed, closing the gap between them.

Deacon's first impulse was to run, just tromp the gas pedal and go. But the cop most likely wanted to pass. Probably on his way back toward the library and using the park-like circle as a turnaround. Deacon slowed and pulled to the curb. But the trooper wasn't about to pass. Instead, the brown cruiser broke sharply to a halt behind the Miata.

Deacon's eyes glued to the rearview as the cruiser's door popped open and the same cop who'd told him to move along popped out. The trooper didn't move in the lazy way they do when your taillight is out or you've been doing fifty in a thirty zone. Nor was he smiling. His face was grimly set, his movements quick and efficient. There was no citation book in his hand. Instead, he held a blue-black automatic pistol. The trooper ducked behind the protection of his open door and levied the pistol at the Miata.

"Out of the car. Hands over your head. Now!"

And just like that, another of Deacon's old friends was back, that adrenaline surge. Fight or flight. In Iraq, it had been fight. But then he'd been the one holding the pistol. His brain pondered this equation for only a moment before firing a nerve impulse to his feet on the clutch and accelerator. A flashbulb popped in the rearview, followed by a thunk against the little car. Then Deacon was flying down the tree-lined street.

Chapter 29

Amy sat on a molded plastic chair, its dull tan matching the brown gloom of the walls. Her left hand was cuffed to a shiny bolt protruding from the top of the grey metal table in the interrogation room. She watched the bolt, fascinated by the yellowish light glinting off its surface, the only sign of life in a room designed for lifelessness. A soulless room that had seen the beginnings of many soulless journeys behind iron bars and plexiglass. Now it was her turn.

She'd been offered cigarettes and coffee. She'd declined but accepted a Pepsi. Then she'd been left alone to marinate in fear until ready for grilling. She had one consolation — Deacon was not here. He was evidently still at large, which was no doubt why they were so anxious to talk to her. She didn't know where he was, not exactly. But even if she did, she wouldn't say. He was the only hope of proving their innocence, of getting someone to recognize the danger. The only hope of foiling what was taking place. For that reason, she wouldn't tell them anything, not even the truth, which sounded more like an insanity defense than an explanation. She also couldn't betray Deacon Creel. He was her boss and protecting him was her duty. Semper fi. And there was one other small reason. She was beginning to think she loved him.

Time ticked by as Amy sipped her drink. There was no clock to mark its passing, the powers that be wanting 'interviewees' lost in time. There was only the table, the plastic chairs, the dull brown walls, and the eye in the sky. Amy looked at the dark camera orb situated above her. She found herself wanting to wave to it. She didn't.

A woman entered the room. She was short, blocky, and dressed in a drab brown suit that matched the interrogation room. She was not attractive. In Amy's experience, pretty women knew they were pretty, even when being pretty was an impediment, as in the corps. Likewise, homely women knew they were homely. This knowledge either raised insecurities that led to sad, uneventful lives, or heightened determination and resolve, which might land someone in law enforcement.

The woman pulled up a plastic chair and straddled it, man fashion, bust against the seat back. She smiled. "I'm Detective Antonelli. But you can call me Angie, okay?"

Amy said nothing.

Angie pointed to the camera. "Want to wave? Tough ones always want to wave, like they've discovered the big secret that we videotape suspect interviews. I figure you must be one of the tough ones, gyrene and all."

Amy didn't answer.

"They read you your rights?"

Amy nodded.

"You want to speak up?" She pointed to the camera again. "For posterity."

"Yes," Amy said. "In the car."

"You want a lawyer?"

Amy shrugged.

Angie pointed to the camera, still smiling.

Amy cleared her throat. "It doesn't matter. I'm not going to say anything."

"Lawyer might advise you different."

Amy didn't answer.

"Okay. Suspect has indicated that she does not wish legal counsel." She looked hard at Amy, raised brows daring her to say different. Then she shrugged. "Would you like to tell me how I can get ahold of your boss, Commander Deacon Creel? Or is he your handler?"

Amy didn't answer.

"Your lover?" She watched Amy's face, then smiled again. "I hit the nail, didn't I?"

Angie leaned her chin onto the plastic seat back. "Listen, Amy. I'm going to call you Amy, okay?" She paused a beat. "Amy, if you care about this guy, tell me where I can find him. It'll be better for him — really." She watched Amy, no doubt looking for chinks in the armor.

"Amy. He's stolen government files. Which is bad. He's killed a government agent, which is much worse. FBI is going to be *real* angry about that. It won't take much for him to wind up dead."

Amy only stared at her.

Angie switched tacks. "It'll go better for *you,* too. No one wants to send you away. You're just a stooge. That's what I think. Used by Creel. You know you're being used, right?"

No answer.

"Tell me where Creel is, and I can pretty much guarantee you no more than a year. A little twelve-month vacation at some nice place like Allenwood. Maybe less."

No answer.

"Otherwise, it's going to be hard time at Leavenworth. Years of hard time. A lifetime of it. FBI is going to see to that." She smiled. "And you're pretty. They like pretty fish in women's stir." A beat. "Nothing to say?"

"I think you're confusing me with someone else."

"Am I?"

"I never stole any files. Commander Creel never stole any files."

"And Agent Carstairs?"

"He ..." Amy thought how ludicrous it sounded to say he killed himself. She shook her head.

Angie nodded. "So, you never stole any files. Well, I have someone next door who tells me different. The one who reported the files stolen. They sent her down from your Unit 13 to try and talk some sense to you."

Amy stood pat, eyes unflinching, but still she wondered. Who? What woman at the unit might be able to sway her? She hardly knew any of the women there. She'd walked by a couple of bench scientists in their white lab coats. They'd say hello, but that was all. She didn't even know their names. One admin named Nancy was nice. Amy had gotten her coffee once, but they were hardly close friends or confidants.

"Who?"

Angie smiled and spoke to the eye in the sky. "Send her in, please."

Amy turned to the door, her stare boring into the smooth grey metal. The knob turned. Her eyes widened when Lisa Reilly entered.

"Lieutenant Reilly?"

"Oh, Amy. Why did you and Deke do it?"

Deacon shifted gears smoothly and quickly. The Mazda flew around the curve in the little road, the state cruiser disappearing from the rear view. The young trooper had been prepared, but he'd also been surprised, which was good. And he'd screwed up, which was better. Had he skewed to a stop in front of the Miata, Deacon would have been trapped. Instead, he was able to run for it. If Deacon could just make the main drag, the freeway was a half mile. With luck, he could be lost in the flow of traffic before the rookie threw up a radio cordon.

The little car roared down the suburban circle, the line of ranch homes and concrete drives strobing by. Deacon glanced at the review, but saw no cop, not yet. Dead ahead was the traffic on Reisterstown Road. Deacon relaxed, almost there. Then his knuckles whitened as a black Mercedes backed into his path, evidently neither seeing nor expecting the little roadster traveling sixty in a twenty-five. Deacon swerved, barely missing the sedan, then slewed back toward freedom. He glanced again in the rearview but saw only the Mercedes pulled partway onto the lane, the driver's head poking out the window in astonishment.

Relieved, Deacon looked forward again, then instinctively slammed the brakes and screamed into the car's tiny interior. Immediately ahead, filling the windshield, was the state cruiser. Its rookie occupant savvy enough to know that there were only two exits to a loop.

Chapter 30

The Miata decelerated rapidly, tires squealing amidst the smell of burnt rubber. In the last moment before the crash, Deacon could see the trooper's head across the cruiser's hood, his gun hand once again pointed at the little roadster. The pistol popped, the sound dull as wadded cotton, the flash a little white dot against Deacon's retina. A spider crack appeared on the windshield, the bullet buzzing past Deacon's ear. Then the world was reduced to a loud crunch and a blinding burst of white that jolted Deacon backward.

Reality returned as suddenly as it had fled. Deacon was still belted in the Mazda. But now a deflated airbag sat in his lap, both he and the bag covered in diamonds of broken safety glass. Through the missing windshield, he could see the inside of the police cruiser, its radio babbling away in a series of words and bleeps. His vision carried past the car to the young trooper, his body prostrate on the road, hands over his head, gun several feet to the side of his extended arm.

Deacon's door opened suddenly, and hands grabbed his arm.

"Are you okay?" a voice asked. "You're bleeding."

Deacon dabbed at the dull pain throbbing from his nose, his fingers coming back slicked with blood.

"Here," the voice said, handing him a handkerchief.

Deacon placed the hankie to his nose as arms helped him out of the Miata.

"I'm Bob Burns. I was just showing that house to the Steinmetzes over there when it happened. I saw the whole thing. Steady, now."

Deacon stumbled out of the car, his head spinning. He looked where Burns had pointed, a sign for Commonwealth Realty stood proudly on the neatly trimmed lawn of a small cape cod. Then he looked at the Steinmetzes, a handsome couple in their thirties who gawked as if he'd just stepped out of a flying saucer.

"I saw the whole thing. That cop car pulled right in front of you. I never saw anything like it. And you were going so fast. Why were you going so fast? I, I never saw anything like it."

Deacon stared at Burns, a man in his fifties who looked like an ad for Grecian Formula. Then he stared blankly at the Steinmetzes, who stared blankly back. Then he stared at the black Mercedes, engine idling in the street.

"I'll need to borrow your car," he said, the words sounding oddly distant and foreign, as foreign as the distant sound of sirens growing louder.

"What?" Burns said. "What you *need* is a doctor. You must be pretty shook up. Here, let's lay you down on the lawn."

Deacon jerked out of his grasp, stumbling forward past the dented cruiser.

Burns rushed to steady him. "Hey. Careful. Take it easy."

Deacon reached down and retrieved the trooper's pistol, swinging it at the man standing next to him. "I said I'll need to borrow your car."

Burns backed away, realization dawning. Deacon could see the wheels of the man's mind finally turning to the truth behind the bizarre crash he'd just witnessed. Burns raised his hands.

"Hey. No. Wait. I didn't see anything. Really."

I need to borrow your car," Deacon repeated.

"Sure. Hey. No problem." Burns dug his keys from his sport coat. His hand dangled them at Deacon, fingers barely gripping as if the keys were diseased. "Here."

Deacon grabbed the car keys, blood from the hankie smearing them. "Thanks. I'll try and keep it in one piece for you."

"Hey. No problem." Burns kept babbling as he backed away. "Really. Whatever. It's insured. So, whatever."

Deacon walked unsteadily to the Mercedes, the Steinmetzes eyes following him every step of the way. He stopped at the open door and turned to Burns. "Please see to the trooper." Nodding toward the unconscious officer, he entered the big black car and drove off.

Detective Antonelli placed a hand on the doorknob, then turned toward Amy. "Why don't we give you a little time to think before the feds get here? Time to reflect on your options. Who knows, you may realize that your loyalty is misplaced. That your *best* option is to stop acting like a horse's ass." The detective winked, scanned her cardkey, and left.

Amy stared at the grey, steel door. She heard the lock click. She heard her own heartbeat. Then, only silence. Nothing to focus on except her own dark thoughts.

Her original plan had been simple. Keep her mouth shut and play for time. Time for Deacon to get to the bottom of this cesspool and clean it out. It hadn't been much of a plan, now it was nothing at all. Lisa's appearance put paid to that bill.

Amy still couldn't believe that Lieutenant Reilly, Lisa, was part of the conspiracy. Her mind kept trying not to believe it, coming up with scenarios where their ally had been duped, the victim of false information planted by someone higher up. But each time her reasoning ran into Reilly's own words, her bald-faced assertions that Deacon and Amy had just disappeared with classified documents. Her method-acting sincerity pleading with Amy to come clean. There was no mention of burning cabins and firefights in the woods. No mention of hairs-breadth escapes from hit-and-run drivers. And then there was the fact that Lisa's complicity explained so much. It explained why Deacon's antidote hadn't worked, the antidote that Reilly was charged with testing. How the bad guys had been able to track them every step of the way. Deacon's arrest at the NAC. Amy's arrest at the library, when only Deacon knew her whereabouts, him and whoever he confided in.

No, Plan A had to be dumped. Amy scanned the room trying to come up with Plan B. Some way to escape to warn Deacon. But what she saw wasn't encouraging.

There was no window, just four walls and the steel door. There was an air duct, but that couldn't be more than eight by twelve inches. Only on TV were ventilation ducts the size of mine shafts. There were two other chairs (both molded plastic like hers), the metal table, and the solid metal door. The door was locked. The table was bolted to the floor. Amy herself was tethered to the table. And if all that wasn't bad enough, there was the eye in the sky watching everything she did.

Her training had taught her there was a way out of any trap, even if that way risked death. So, she tried to put all her obstacles to one side and concentrate on what she would do if she did escape. She thought back on the journey to this locked room. Closing her eyes, she took several slow, deep breaths. She tried to relax, clear her mind, allow it to drift back, to relive the event. As her breathing slowed, her body calmed. A mental movie played in her head.

They'd turned onto Fayette Street to a greyish blockhouse of a building. Her mind's ear heard overhead doors clanking open as they pulled inside. She saw a mental image of several vehicles in the garage, unmarked cars and a few cruisers bathed in diffuse fluorescent light. She continued taking slow, deep breaths; mental images projecting across her closed lids. Now she was travelling up three, no, it had been four, steps to a concrete platform with a rust-colored, steel door. The door was equipped with cardkey entry, she heard the soft chirp and saw the green flash of recognition. The door led to a narrow hallway that elled to the left. She'd seen no electronic keypad on the interior side of the door, suggesting the lock restricted entry from outside but not the other way around.

The hands gripping her shackled arms had led her past two restroom doors, before turning right into a second hall. They walked past a break room, she'd seen soda machines and hot coffee through the open door, to a second door, this one metal on the bottom and wired glass on top. Then twenty more yards to the grey, metal door she was now facing. She remembered the words Interrogation 1 posted on a placard above the door.

That was all that separated her from freedom, three steel doors, one of which was cardkey access. *All*, she thought. Add to it the fact that she was locked to a table under constant surveillance by the eye in the sky.

Amy glanced at the camera watching her. It was no more than eight feet up, its shiny black bubble protruding through suspended ceiling tiles. She found herself again wanting to wave. Instead, she finished her Pepsi and set the bottle down. As the plastic softly snicked against the rubberized metal of the table, an idea snicked into her head. She had little notion where it came from or even if it was real. But it arose full form, as fantastic ideas typically do.

Amy looked at the plastic bottle, then she looked again at the camera. She thought for a bit, letting seconds tick by, then nodded and spoke.

"Hello? Can I have another Pepsi?"

More seconds ticked by. Amy counted to sixty, then spoke again. "Hello? I said, can I have another ..."

The door clicked open. The same skinny matron who'd cuffed her to the table entered, Pepsi in hand. Unsmiling, she set it down, then used the cardkey around her neck to chirp the lock and leave.

Amy rested her hand on the cold bottle, beads of condensation coating her palm. She tried to relax, to keep her breathing steady, nonchalant. That became more difficult as she thought about Plan B.

Like Plan A, it was simple. But this backup plan was much more difficult to carry out. *Impossible* to carry out may have been a better description. Maybe she should wait, she thought. A better opportunity might present itself. But she knew that was fear talking. If she waited, she'd be in the hands of the FBI, and it could be only a matter of minutes until they arrived. They'd take her to the Baltimore field office, or more likely the Hoover Building. She'd be surrounded by federal agents and locked doors in endless corridors. The time was now.

Raising a hand to her mouth, she feigned a yawn. Then she snatched the Pepsi and feigned a stretch, both arm and bottle fully extended. As she brought her hand back, she let it drop below the table. Trying to stay as nonchalant as possible, she rolled her neck and shoulders, making it look as if she was easing away the kinks. What she really wanted was distracting motion, someplace for the watcher to watch. Someplace other than her hand under the table vigorously shaking the full soda bottle.

She closed her eyes and kept rolling her shoulders. She let her free hand roll as well, all the while shaking the soda and counting silently. At ten Mississippi's, she straightened up and stopped shaking. She stretched again, the bottle at full extension. She paused for a beat, wondering if she was really going to do this, then swung the bottle back to the table, grasping the cap in her shackled hand. She said a silent prayer and twisted the top.

Amy reacted in mock surprise even before the liquid geysered up. Her chair capsized to the floor as she bolted erect, arm extended toward the camera, hand squeezing the plastic. Sticky, brown liquid exploded from the mouth of the bottle, showering her head and clothing as she gasped and cursed. More importantly, it showered upward, painting the ceiling tiles a bleary tan. When she was sure the flow had stopped, she tossed the bottle down and swore again. Wiping cola from her face, she turned to face the camera.

She smiled as she saw the sticky, brown liquid dripping off the lens. But no one could see the smile. The eye in the sky was blind.

Chapter 31

The president is set to announce his decision within twenty-four hours, with most beltway insiders suggesting it will be one of the remaining two names from the original short list. Chief among these is Simon Bolivar Hernandez, former high-tech CEO and two-term Mayor of Santa Fe. Other possibilities had included Senator Jim Breacher of Pennsylvania and Governor Judith Hayward of Florida, both swing states important to the president's reelection, until these candidates withdrew citing personal reasons. Pundits and the public alike wonder if *personal* reasons is code for the so-called 'second-slot scourge,' the name given to the untimely deaths of several candidates in the selection process."

Deacon clicked off the radio. "The second-slot scourge," he said. "If they only knew."

He watched the little townhome from the stolen Mercedes, which now sported a stolen license plate courtesy of a parking-lot Chevy. His stomach grumbled. His only meal since his half sandwich with Amy had been a drive-thru muffin and coffee; he'd been afraid to go inside. Even so, the kid in the window looked at him askance, as if he'd seen the face before. Deacon had exactly sixteen dollars and fifty-eight cents to his name, a credit card he couldn't use, a stolen car with stolen plates, and a driver's license photo plastered all over the news.

"Sounds about right," he said.

A D.C. cop car pulled slowly down the street. Deacon buried his face in the map on his lap, playing the scruffy tourist finding his way around, his three-day growth and dumpster ball cap helping the charade. He could feel the cruiser slow to look at him before driving on, no doubt wondering about the grunge behind the wheel of a Benz.

Hernandez had recently rented the townhouse instead of settling into the Mayflower, a sure sign that he at least was convinced he'd be the next VP, the first Hispanic VP, a PC coup. Age and demographics seemed to be the only qualification for higher office, Deacon thought. Someone who was young and looked good on TV, with the right gender or ethnic credentials. Simon Hernandez fit the bill.

Deacon had called Hernandez's office claiming to be a reporter for the *Times-Picayune*, a real New Orleans paper if a fictitious job. His faux southern drawl and southern charm had been convincing enough for the receptionist to divulge that the Honorable Mr. Hernandez was resting at his Georgetown residence and not taking questions from reporters. A couple more calls, a couple more lies, and he had the address. That was a nice thing about an eidetic memory, you knew lots of numbers for lots of leads. The bad thing was that you remembered the past just as clearly. Deacon wanted a drink.

He'd passed two package stores on the drive over, his foot easing off the gas at each. His current bankroll would support a pint of Beam or a fifth of Ten High. But each time he drove on, thinking of the mission. Thinking of Amy. The two were interconnected, both equally important. Well, maybe not equally. But she was safe for now. He didn't think anything would happen immediately. They'd use her to try and find him. Nothing would happen at all if he could convince Hernandez of the danger. A tough task but doable, if Lisa had gotten through to Metternich, if Joe wasn't part of it, and if Lisa had convinced him to act. A lot of ifs, but no sense going down that road. It led to a liquor store.

He looked at the townhouse windows again. A light came on the second floor. *Someone* was there. He knew it wasn't Hernandez's wife or kids; the receptionist had revealed they were still safely in New Mexico. Deacon waited. A faint light flashed downstairs, then dimmed again. Definitely there — and moving. Deacon craned his neck up and down the street.

Hernandez wasn't under Secret Service protection yet. But the cops made frequent drive-bys. The police were at least convinced he'd be the next VP. If Deacon was going to do this, he'd better do it. He took a deep breath, paused, then stepped into the street.

Deacon felt naked and exposed even in the narrow, empty lane. He reminded himself not to run (running attracted attention) but walked briskly and purposely to the front door. He breathed a sigh of relief once his face was hidden from the street. Grasping the handle with one hand, he raised his fist to knock. Before he could, the door clicked open. He'd been prepared for lots of things — Hernandez not answering, Hernandez recognizing a wanted man, a sudden appearance by D.C.'s finest. But not an unlocked door. He scanned the street again, then stepped quietly inside.

He cleared his throat. "Mr. Hernandez?" His tentative words echoed off the marble of the foyer. "Sir?" No reply.

Deacon eyed the living room, which was empty from its sunken stepdown to its polished-brass fireplace, no tread marks on the white carpet. The curtains were drawn, casting gloom over the cheery furnishings. Deacon didn't like it. The room felt antiseptic, lifeless, unlived in. And it was so quiet. No sound at all. No one spoke. There were no footfalls. No background TV or radio prattle. Not even outside road noise. Only the sound of his own breathing. It was the silence of the grave. A feeling of déjà vu swept him. It was an uneasy feeling, one that raised hackles. It reminded him of another unlocked door, a bitter memory poking its head from a subbasement in his mind.

His eyes shifted back to the hallway tiles, following them past the stairway to the kitchen. The kitchen door was ajar, the yellow glow around the edges revealing the source of the light he'd seen outside.

Deacon hesitated, then walked slowly forward, his footsteps echoing faintly down the hall. As he neared the kitchen, a soft sound broke the silence. It was so soft he probably wouldn't have heard it without the preternatural quiet. But he did hear it. And he recognized it as the low, sad sound of weeping.

Deacon walked faster, not trying to muffle his steps. "Mr. Hernandez?" He spoke loudly. The sobbing ceased. Deacon paused, waiting for the answering, "Yes?" or "Who's there?"

There was only the quiet, which frightened him more than the unlatched door or the idea of barging in on a total stranger.

Deacon was at the door in two quick steps, pushing it open. He raised a hand to his eyes, squinting at the sudden brightness. As he adjusted to the light, he could see more floor tile leading to high-end appliances that gleamed like new, their stainless-steel surfaces reflecting the overhead glare. His eyes fixed on the Sub-Zero fridge and the large erasable board magnetted to its surface. Written there in smeary purple were two words — "I'm sorry."

Deacon turned toward the kitchen table. A youngish, middle-aged man sat there. He had the handsome, dark features of a Latino, hair neatly combed, white shirt buttoned to the top, red tie tightly knotted. He did not look at Deacon, did not even seem to notice he had entered. He just sat there, eyes closed, tears dribbling down his shaven cheeks. His demeanor was calm, but his jaw was set in determination. The man's right hand lay on the table, the purple marker in his fingers, the solvent from the felt tip sweetening the antiseptic air. His left hand was raised, holding a black revolver. The short barrel did not point at Deacon. It pointed at the temple of Simon Bolivar Hernandez.

Deacon froze, unable to move or even look away. The image burned into his retinas seemed to magnify, to zoom in on every quivering hair, every pore on the dark features. Deacon watched in horror as the man's grip on the weapon tightened, color draining from the trigger finger blanched with strain. Once more, it was fight or flight. The damn broke, and Deacon leapt forward.

"No," he cried as he sprung off the hard tiles, arms raised to push the gun away. It was man against machine, a race between Deacon Creel and a bullet. Deacon was fast. The bullet was faster.

Deacon's hand gripped the gun the same instant the muzzle blast deafened him with thunder, blinded him with lightning. The sweet scent of the marker was erased by the reek of burnt powder. Gunshot residue stung Deacon's eyes as blood and brains spattered over his face and hands. The force of his leap sent both men to the floor, Deacon landing atop Hernandez, his hand wrenching the gun from the lifeless corpse.

Deacon tumbled from the gore and heaved the heavy weapon against the wall.

"No!" he repeated. "Not again."

Amy shook like a wet dog, drops of cola flying from her hair and fingertips.

"Can I get someone to take me to the bathroom? I'd like to clean up." Petulance oozed from her voice, capping a barely disguised disgust. "Maybe *then* I can get a Pepsi that isn't booby trapped?"

She waited, playing the injured party while praying that her desperate plan might work.

"I said, can someone take me to the fucking bathroom." The shouting and f-bomb added a nice touch and let her vent the anxiety building inside her like gas in that shaken bottle. After a few more seconds, the door clicked open and the skinny matron entered carrying a towel. Amy snatched it from her hand.

"Thanks," she snapped. "'Bout fucking time." She one-handedly wiped her face and head, then rattled her cuffed wrist. "Can you at least take off the goddam handcuff?"

The matron hesitated.

"I'm in a fucking police station. Where am I gonna go?"

A male voice from a hidden speaker said, "Go ahead."

The matron's neck and face flushed crimson, clearly displeased with her charge. But she no longer hesitated. Pulling a small key from her pants pocket, she unlocked the cuff. "Now if you promise to watch your language, I'll take you to the lav." That's all she was able to say.

As soon as Amy's arm was unshackled, it was around the matron's neck. She wrist-locked it with the other arm while stepping behind the woman and applying steady, unrelenting pressure, biceps and forearms working together against both sides of the neck. The matron might have been able to break the chokehold — Amy had been taught a method in the Corps — but surprise worked against her. All the jailer could manage was ineffectual clawing at her attacker's hands. Amy ignored the painful gouges and pressed harder. After five Mississippi's, it was all over. The jailer slumped into dreamland without making a sound.

There was no time for self-congratulations or even reflection on her current course of action. The die was cast.

Amy lay the unconscious guard on the floor, then snatched up the fallen key and uncuffed her wrist. Ripping the cardkey off the sleeping matron, she dashed to the door, pausing to listen for sound in the hallway. Hearing nothing but her own panting, Amy placed the card against the reader until she heard the characteristic click. Before the flash of green died, she was in the hallway.

Chapter 32

A my scanned in both directions. The hallway was empty. As she began to gently close the interrogation-room door, a voice asked, "Is everything alright in there?" Her heart began beating again when she realized it was the disembodied voice of the eye in the sky, blinded by the Pepsi but no doubt curious by the sudden silence. Amy said, "Fine." and quietly shut the door.

She retraced her earlier path, heading for the garage, hoping that the cars were unguarded and that at least one had keys in it. A cop exiting the break room almost bumped into her, then smiled and said, "What happened to you?" Amy smiled back, adding a little extra dimple, then raised her arms and shook her head. The man laughed again as they went their separate ways.

Amy passed the ladies room just as a young woman in short skirt and plunging neckline exited, face flushed as she tucked her blouse into her skirt. The girl kept her eyes down as they passed. Amy glanced over her shoulder, to make sure the girl kept on going, and saw a male cop exit the ladies room, recoiling from Amy's gaze before heading in the opposite direction. Amy had time for a brief grin, then she was at the steel door to the garage.

She'd been correct in her original assessment that there was no key access in this direction. Tossing down the cardkey she'd carried from Interrogation 1, Amy opened the door and stepped onto the concrete platform in the garage.

She'd been expecting more diffuse fluorescents but instead had to shield her eyes from the glare of afternoon sunlight. One of the steel rollup doors was open, traffic noise filtering in off Fayette Street. Music was coming from somewhere, a country singer crooning, "I sang Dixie as he died." A cop and a mechanic chatted over the innards of a black police cruiser with its hood open.

"Turn her over," said the young, skinny mechanic in coveralls. The cop, a few years older and about thirty pounds heavier, grunted behind the wheel. The engine fired up. A couple of seconds later, the mechanic hollered, "That's enough." The engine died and the cop grunted back out.

Amy paused for a second, then walked over deliberately, like she knew where she was going and why.

"Hi," she said, dimples sparkling.

"Hi yourself," the mechanic said, eyeing the short, pert beauty with drying syrup in her hair. "What happened to you?"

"Got mauled by an excited Pepsi bottle," Amy said, still smiling.

"Well," the mechanic said, "I can see how you might get somebody excited."

The cop joined them, hitching his pants and smirking.

Amy kept her prettiest, dimplest grin on her face. "I was on my way to the ladies when they asked me to come get you." She spoke to the cop.

"Me?"

She nodded.

"*Who* asked you to get me?"

Amy paused. She could see the cop was curious and a little dubious. She needed to come up with something quick. "That,um, sergeant. The one at the desk. Sergeant ..."

"Washington?"

"Yeah."

"What does *he* want?"

Amy shrugged. "Something about paperwork."

The cop shook his head. "Son of a bitch. I told him I'd have that report this afternoon." He looked at Amy. "How am I supposed to be on the street and make out a report at the same time?"

She shrugged again.

"Shit. I better see what he's got up his ass." He turned back to the mechanic. "It only does it at speed, Lee. Kind of a shimmy when I get her over fifty."

Amy continued smiling, but let her eyes travel downward to her bosom. She undid the top two buttons on her blouse, acting as if she were wiping off cola that had creeped into her cleavage. Then she looked back at the mechanic and winked.

Lee kept watching her, a grin plastered on his face, as he spoke to the cop.

"I'll run her down to the freeway in a few minutes. See if I can duplicate it."

The cop nodded and trudged up the steps.

When the steel door clicked shut, Amy looked at Lee again, still smiling. "You sure know a lot about cars."

He smiled back. "I know a lot about lots of things, sugar."

She pouted and leaned under the hood, the two halves of her open blouse separating. Pointing hesitantly, she asked, "What's this?"

"Transmission fluid, darlin." Lee leaned under the hood as well, his hip butting hers.

"How do you ... put it in?" Her eyebrows raised as if she was asking about more than tranny fluid.

"Well," Lee said. "I generally just twist this here." He reached in and twisted the cap. "Real gentle like. Then I just ease the hose over ..."

Amy ducked out of the engine compartment and brought the hood down hard, driving Lee's head and shoulders into the motor. As she raised the hood again, the mechanic staggered back, eyes dazed. Before he had a chance to recover, she landed a two-handed hook into his temple. Pain lanced through her knuckles as they met greasy skull. Lee stiffened, a look on his face like he'd just had a terrific idea, then slumped against the cruiser and onto the floor.

Amy quickly scanned the garage, grabbed the limp mechanic under the arms, and dragged him away from the cruiser. A second after she'd slammed the hood, she was in the police car. As she'd hoped, the electronic key was sitting in a cup holder. She found the ignition button and fired the engine.

"Don't worry," she called softly to the unconscious Lee. "I'll keep it under fifty."

Then she drove through the metal door and onto Fayette Street.

Deacon's first impulse was to check for a pulse. But one look at the lifeless body with the side of its head missing said that was a useless exercise.

Simon Bolivar Hernandez. Deacon had never met him. Had never gotten to know if he was a good man who might have made a good vice president. He'd certainly never grown to care for him. But in a way, looking at the dead man was like looking at Liz all over again. Once again, an innocent had been sacrificed. Once again, the great Deacon Creel had been unable to stop it. But there was one important difference. This time, it had not been a senseless accident. Deacon couldn't blame himself for this one. This time Deacon knew exactly where the blame lay. This time, instead of the sight driving him to drink, it filled him with grim determination. If someone had dropped a bottle of bourbon in his lap right now, he'd have thrown it against the wall. He didn't want whiskey. He wanted revenge. Revenge for this poor man. Revenge for the others who were guilty of no more than being successful politicians. Revenge for his late fiancée, who'd been the first victim in this misguided endeavor to create a new weapon of cold war, an assassin's dream.

Instead of reaching for a bottle, Deacon reached for the revolver. Its cold metal was slick with blood as he held it in his hand. This felt as it should be. It stood for the blood of so many. Deacon caressed the weapon, an instrument of death more corporeal than the one known only as 606. He had the means in his hand to end this, and he knew exactly who he needed to use it on. He had means and motive as the prosecutors said. All he needed was opportunity.

"Freeze!"

Deacon spun to face a cop, a service automatic pointed directly at him. The guy looked young, no more than twenty-one or so. His muscular arms shook as they left the short-sleeved navy-blue uniform shirt and clutched the black pistol. He must be more scared than I am, thought Deacon.

"Drop the gun!"

Deacon looked at the revolver he was holding, then looked back at the cop as if to say, 'who me?'

"Toss it over here. Now, you son of a bitch!"

Deacon held the gun up. "Toss it?"

"Now! Unless you want me to blow you away."

It was fight or flight again. Just as it had been in Iraq and all the scrapes since. But a whole lot more was riding on it than just escaping capture or even stopping an RPG. Perhaps the future of the country. A strange calmness descended on Deacon. He smiled. The cop looked confused, as if he wasn't sure what to make of it. "You want me to toss it?"

"Yes, goddammit. Toss it over here. Now!"

"Whatever you say."

Deacon hefted the blue steel high, arcing it right at the scared cop. Before the guy could do more than duck, Deacon leapt toward him, his head striking the cop's groin with a satisfying thud. The force carried them both down in a mass of arms and legs, the cop's gun skipping off the kitchen table as it flew from his hand. Deacon scrambled to his feet. The cop stayed down, curled into the fetal position.

Deacon paused for a moment, panting and kneeling, hands on lap. "Sorry about that." Then he scampered to the fallen cop.

He pulled the cuffs from the cop's tactical belt and snapped one end onto the kid's left wrist. Then he pulled hard against the chain, causing the prostrate form to grunt and obligingly roll onto his chest, knees and belly still twisted into the familiar bend produced by testicular torture. Deacon snapped the other cuff onto the cop's right wrist.

His assailant secure, Deacon rose unsteadily to his feet. The world tilted for a moment, then swam back into focus. Deacon wiped sweat from his brow, then walked to the cupboards. It only took two drawers to find the dish towels and rags. He grabbed a handful, then turned to the cop recovering on the floor.

"What's your name?" Deacon asked.

"Please," pleaded the cop, his eyes taking on the wretched gleam of a trapped animal. "I got a wife. I got a baby on the way. Please don't kill me."

"Your name?" Deacon repeated.

"Um, Wilson."

"First name."

"Terrence. Terry."

Deacon squatted next to the cop and said, "Okay, Terry. Open."

It took a second for the cop to realize he wanted him to open his mouth. Then he complied.

Deacon shoved a dish rag between his teeth, the cop grunting 'please' as Deacon tied a towel around his head. Another towel sinched up the cop's ankles. Satisfied with his handiwork, Deacon grabbed Hernandez's revolver from the floor. He didn't bother with the cop's automatic, he already had one in the Mercedes, courtesy of the trooper he'd collided with. And neither service automatic seemed right. He hefted the revolver, caressing the blood-spattered surface. This seemed right. This seemed like the proper instrument of vengeance.

Terrence Wilson's eyes grew wide with terror at the sight of Deacon lovingly holding the cold, deadly steel.

Deacon smiled at him. "Don't worry, son. This isn't for you. This gun and I have more important business this day." Then he rose and left, his face grim as death.

Chapter 33

Amy walked swiftly but didn't run. She tried to keep the same nonchalant pace she'd used in the police garage. She'd dumped the cruiser in the parking lot of a strip mall near the University of Maryland campus. Now she was moving through what appeared to be student housing, the euphemism applied to tenements adjacent to any college campus. She'd used the bottled water inside the cruiser to wash most of the Pepsi from her face and hair. The warm, early evening breeze felt good as it dried her. The breeze carried the smell of traffic exhaust and frying onions. Her stomach grumbled.

"Hey honey?"

She ignored the cat call from a guy with a scruffy beard seated on a porch, a can of Coors in his hand.

"Hey," he called again, his equally scruff buddy giggling like a coed. "How about a date?"

She considered ignoring him completely but noticed he was easing out of his chair, as if he might stumble down the steps to chat her up. Beer had a way of instilling courage into boys trying to be college men. She also noticed her buttons were still undone. Buttoning her blouse, she said, "No thanks. Ask me again when you graduate."

The retort had the desired effect. The guy slumped back into his lawn chair and laughed, his buddy slapping him on the shoulder.

She needed another car if she was going to find Deacon. But where to look for him? Based on their previous conversation, she figured he'd be hiding out in a big city. But which one? D.C.? Arlington? Here? She stopped walking and started thinking. No, he wouldn't be hiding out. He'd be trying to get to the bottom of this, if he wasn't already captured — or worse. She brushed the latter thought away as she wiped a tear from her eye. She wouldn't think about that now. She'd believe he was still safe somewhere, figuring out this whole mess. A mess that wasn't centered in Baltimore or Arlington or even Fort Deidenbach. A mess that was centered in the seat of the government. Our nation's capital. And that's where he'd be. She was sure of it. But, how to get there? A siren sounded in the distance, then died away as a second siren joined it. However she was going to get there, she'd better get going.

A few junkers were parked on the street, but they didn't look like they'd even start. And anyway, she had no idea how to hotwire one. The Corps had neglected to give her a course on stealing cars.

Her eyes made another complete circle before stopping on a car slightly less beat than the others. A silver Nissan Sentra, maybe five years old. It was parked on her side of the street, directly in front of her recent cat-caller and his pal. Amy took a deep breath, undid her buttons again, then walked back.

"Hey," she shouted.

The guys stopped talking and looked at her. Then the one she'd called to smiled. "Hey yourself."

She pointed to the Sentra. "Know who that belongs to?"

"It's mine," said the guy sitting next to the scruffy beard. "Why? You want a ride?"

"Maybe." Amy smiled, giving him some extra dimple. "Why don't you buy me a beer and we'll talk about it."

Chad tottered off his seat. "I gotta tap a kidney." He smiled at Amy. She smiled back. His friend Bryon was talking to another pal over by the pool table. They kept giggling and pointing her way.

Chad winked at her. "Don't go away." Then he stumbled off.

They had driven to a local hangout called unoriginally, "Local Hangout." It was a typical college pub, grease seared into the tables along with hundreds of initials and naughty limericks. The menu consisted of such appetizing fare as "greaseburgers" and "cornhole dogs." Sure know how to treat a lady, Amy thought, but she still wolfed down a burger and fries while nursing a beer. The two boys split a pitcher of Corona and slipped deeper into drunken adolescence. The crowd was small for a Saturday, summer recess apparently hurting the trade. Amy was glad there weren't more people, especially when the baseball pregame was interrupted by beaking news.

"We interrupt *Baseball Tonight* for a special report," a voice on TV announced.

A familiar news anchor popped on the screen.

"Police are searching for a suspect in the murder of former Santa Fe Mayor Simon Bolivar Hernandez, who was found shot earlier today in his Georgetown home. Mayor Hernandez was the leading candidate for vice president following George Brooke's announcement that he was stepping down from that spot."

The anchor checked his notes.

"Capitol police are requesting assistance in apprehending Dr. Deacon Creel, the prime suspect in the shooting."

An old photo of a younger, smiling Deacon popped on the screen.

"Creel, already suspected of stealing sensitive government files, was seen at Hernandez's residence, where he escaped from authorities. He is thought to be armed and highly dangerous."

"Wanna shoot some pool?" Bryon was standing next to her, a glint in his glassy eyes. He pointed toward the table. "My friend, Chris, is pretty good. We can play rotation, for drinks or ... something."

Amy turned away from the TV. "Okay. Um, but how about dessert first?" She pointed. "Get me a Clark Bar from that machine over there."

Bryon made a circle with his thumb and finger, then staggered off. Amy switched back to the news announcement.

> "The death of Simon Hernandez reduces the list of likely candidates to one."

A picture of a pretty, mid-thirties woman scrolled up.

> "Dr. Cathleen Harris, current acting Secretary of the Department of Homeland Security is thought to get the nod."

Amy had heard the name before. It was the one Deacon mentioned. He was going to recruit her help. He'd gone to her office the night he was arrested.

> "Dr. Harris would bring several firsts to the office. She'd be the first physician to assume that role. Dr. Harris would also be the first openly bisexual vice president."

The screen switched to a picture of Harris entering a Washington club. She was dressed to the nines in a Halston dress that cost more than Amy made in a month. On her arm was a tall, leggy woman dressed all in black, which made her look even taller and thinner. The woman with Harris looked very familiar but out of context, the way a workmate is difficult to recognize in sweats at Walmart. Then she gasped and said, "Lisa?"

"Hey. Put the game back on. I was watching that."

Chad slid back into the booth next to her. He smelled a little like the pee he'd probably dribbled in his pants. He grabbed her hand. "Unless you want to do something else?" His leer mirrored Bryon's. Amy smiled and managed to extricate her hand. Then she turned back to the TV set.

> "The murder of Simon Hernandez marks the second time that handgun violence plucked a candidate from the vice-presidential short list. Rising political star Scott Waters met a similar

> fate only weeks ago. That death was rumored to be suicide, but unnamed sources inside the Justice Department state that the FBI will be revisiting it as a possible homicide, perhaps also attributable to Creel."

Bryon tossed a Payday bar on the table, then slid into the other side of the booth. "They didn't have Clark Bars, so I got you that. Hokay?"

Amy nodded.

Bryon pointed to the pool table. "Chris says he'll spot you a ball. He said he couldn't spot you two balls, because he was hoping to need them later."

Chad and Bryon both sniggered. Amy smiled and turned back to the TV.

> "Creel was last known to be in the company of this woman." Amy's ID photo flashed on the screen. "Although not implicated directly in the murder, she is thought to have aided and abetted ..."

"Instead of pool," Amy blurted, "how about we go to my place?"

Both boys looked stunned, too stunned to even leer.

"It's not far," Amy said. "I can make coffee, and we can ..." She ran her fingers gently across the back of Chad's hand, then smiled at Bryon. "You know."

Bryon's eyes grew even larger. "You mean?"

"Mhmm," Amy cooed. "We could play another game involving balls and shafts." She teased her fingers across Chad's hand. "And angles and curves." Her other hand teased the short hairs on Bryon's hand.

Bryon gulped. "The three, um, three of us?"

Amy took his hand, pouting. "Never done that before?"

"Um, well, sure."

"Like hell you have," Chad said. He put his arm around Amy and whispered in her ear. "You lead, we'll follow."

Amy kissed his cheek. "Sounds good. But first you better give me your car keys."

"Huh?"

"The keys. Hand them over. You're in no condition

to drive." She smiled her sexiest. "I'll be in charge of the driving." She undid another button. "I'll be in charge of everything tonight."

Chad fumbled in his pocket, almost ripping his jeans jerking out the key fob.

Both of the boys put their arms around her as they stumbled toward the Nissan. Amy had trouble steadying them as first one then the other inebriated stud fondled her ass. She held the keys but didn't unlock the car, even after she'd reached the driver's door, both guys drooling at her as they leaned against the passenger doors.

"Oh," Amy said. "Chad, honey. Can you run inside and get my candy bar? I left it in the booth."

He looked at her oddly.

She batted her Ronstadt eyes. "I'll need to keep up my strength if we're gonna have a marathon."

Chad smiled and staggered back toward the Local Hangout.

When he was out of sight, Amy said, "Shit. What I *really* wanted was a Snickers. Had a real craving." She batted at Bryon. "Run back in and get me one. I'll make it worth your while. Promise."

Bryon acted like he was going to orgasm right then and there, before stumbling after his compatriot.

Amy sighed, then clicked the car's locks. When she was safely inside, engine running, she said, "Another time, boys. I've got a date right now."

Chapter 34

Deacon sat by the side door of a church on Nebraska Avenue. He'd ditched the Mercedes in Wesley Heights, then walked through a light rain. Along the way, he'd spent some of his dwindling cash on a second-hand hoodie at a thrift shop and copped a pair of low-power reading glasses via five-finger discount at CVS. They made an okay disguise when added to his grease-stained ball cap and three-day stubble. Just another bum waiting out the rain. .

Peering over the top of his glasses, he could watch the entrance to the NAC on the other side of the street. But that was all he could do. The pistol was safely tucked in his hoodie pocket, five rounds still live in the chambers. He knew where he needed to take it, and what he'd do with it when he got there. Right now, getting there was out of the question.

Deacon had no sure way of knowing she was even in there. But something in his gut said she was. The steady flow of vehicles coming and going seconded the notion — it was too much traffic for a Saturday evening. The types of vehicles made it unanimous. Some were the dark sedans and SUVs driven by the FBI and Secret Service. There was also a dark van, no doubt to load files and personal effects being transported just down the road to One Observatory Circle — the new home for a brand new Veep. A police cruiser was parked in the street out front, a cop in rain gear directing traffic.

Deacon watched the other cars trickling down the street, a red pickup, a white SUV, a light-colored VW Beetle. Some slowed to rubberneck the activity before being waved on by the cop. That's what I'm doing, thought Deacon. I'm rubbernecking. That's all I can do, for now. He touched the gun in his pocket. It felt comforting.

The traffic cop blew a whistle, then jumped in front of a silver sedan, his hand held like the Heisman Trophy. The car obediently stopped, its driver looking down for something on her lap as the big van he'd seen earlier pulled into traffic. The cop's whistle sounded again as he waved the car on and scampered back to safety. The driver of the silver sedan glanced Deacon's way, her eyes briefly visible below the brim of a ball cap, then drove on. She looked familiar, but at this distance could have been Selena Gomez.

Deacon couldn't sit still any longer, restlessness and cold cement driving him to stand. He stamped life back into his feet, bending his legs one after the other. Then he started walking.

This is stupid, he thought. Disguise or no disguise, he should be staying out of sight. But he kept walking. He wasn't sure where he was going, he just followed his shoes. They led him opposite the cop car and then they stopped. He stood in the drizzle, looking across the street at the NAC. No other cars had followed the van. He thought about crossing the street, asking the cop what all the fuss was about. That would be really stupid, he thought. His picture was plastered all over TV and the newspapers, and his current disguise was best viewed from a distance. Up close and personal, even a traffic cop might recognize him. So, he stood in the mist, hands in pockets, watching. He didn't have to watch long.

The cop spoke into a mic on his lapel, then scurried to the NAC entrance. He peered into the gate, then ducked into the road. No cars were coming, but he stood there just the same, arm raised, whistle in his lips.

A dark-blue SUV pulled into traffic, followed by a black, lower-slung limousine. The limo paused halfway onto Nebraska Avenue, then a man jumped from the shotgun seat. His dark suit and electronic earpiece shouted Secret Service. Another man jumped from the lead SUV, his hand tucked into his jacket clutching a Mac-10 sub-gun. Machine gun Mike took up a position in the middle of the road, while the guy from the limo opened the rear door. A curvaceous leg poked out, followed by a body to match. Deacon's jaw dropped as he watched Cathleen Harris step from the car.

She walked purposely toward the traffic cop and held out her hand. The flustered cop tentatively shook it. Deacon could hear bits and pieces of a conversation.

"Thank you so ..." Harris said, smiling. "I know it's tough ... rain, but I appreciate ..."

The cop stammered back, "My pleasure."

She held his hand with both hers for just a moment, smiling her patented man-melt smile. The agent from her limo spoke softly in her ear and turned her back toward her ride.

She's got the common touch, Deacon thought. Then a second thought forced its way into his head — this might be his only chance. He didn't think about doing anything. If he'd thought about it, he wouldn't have moved. Instead, he placed his gun hand on the reassuring metal in his pocket and let his feet do the walking.

Chapter 35

Deacon moved quickly toward the street. Harris smiled and thanked the Secret Service agent, then let herself be led toward the car. Deacon reached the curb when Harris was still halfway to the limo. He felt the steel of the revolver and took a deep breath. Fight or flight. Time to act. The world around him dimmed to a tunnel around Cathleen Harris, each step toward her limo as slow as molasses dripping from the jug. The night noises dropped away, replaced by a cottony silence filled only with the pounding of his heart. Now or never, he thought. Then he whispered, "Fuck it," and stepped off the curb, hand grasping the butt of the snub-nosed revolver.

Before he'd taken another step, the silver sedan he'd seen earlier pulled directly in front of him, screeching to a stop. Machinegun man pulled the sub-gun from his coat as the other agent shielded Harris.

The door to the sedan opened, hitting Deacon in the leg. A voice from inside spoke loudly.

"Sorry I'm late. I had to drive Jen home."

Deacon looked inside. It wasn't Selena Gomez. It was Amy Robbins leaning into the passenger seat. He'd recognize that face, those eyes, anywhere.

Her voice quieted. "Get in."

Deacon hesitated.

"They'll kill you, and you won't accomplish anything. Is that what you want?"

Out of the corner of his eye, he saw Harris hustled back inside the limo. The machinegun-toting agent was staring at him.

"Get in," Amy whisper-shouted.

Deacon cleared his throat and spoke loudly. "About fucking time."

Amy drove off before he'd even closed the door.

They sat in a McDonald's parking lot, Deacon drinking coffee, Amy a Pepsi. She'd been afraid the drive-through kid would recognize them from the news, but she needn't have worried. He didn't look old enough to watch anything but MTV, sports, or anime.

She studied Deacon. He looked worn and gaunt, years older than when she first met him. Maybe it was the last-week shadow on his face, maybe the sadness and grim determination behind the beard. Amy had seen him drunken, sobbing, amused, disinterested. But the cold set to his features was new. It frightened her.

"You sure you don't want a burger or something?"

Deacon shook his head.

"When was the last time you ate?"

He shook his head.

"I can go back in the drive through. I don't think they're going to recognize us."

"I'm not hungry." The words came through slow and crisp but not annoyed. Just that cold resolve again, as if food was no longer important, his only concern being what he had to do.

"You'll never get close to her," Amy said. "I heard they've taken her to Blair House to await the formal swearing in on Monday. Full Secret Service protection."

Deacon nodded, seemingly unpersuaded.

"It's suicide," she said. He didn't answer. "We've had enough of that, lately." His cold resolve remained. She considered making a personal appeal, telling him how she felt about him but held back. Then he spoke.

"I'm not thinking about her. I'm thinking about *her*."

At first Amy didn't understand. Then she said, "Lisa?" She'd filled him in about her stay with the Baltimore PD. About everything.

"*She's* not under Secret Service protection," he said.

"But what can she do but call the cops on us."

"Maybe nothing except give me the satisfaction of slapping her lying mouth." He took the gun from his pocket. "Or maybe she can give us access to Madame Vice President." He placed the gun in the glove box. "And a better weapon to use against her."

Amy shook her head. "No. Absolutely not. This is ridiculous."

They'd driven the forty miles back to Frederick and were now parked behind the memorial hospital. Deacon had filled Amy in on his plan, which seemed as impossible as trying to gun down Cathleen Harris.

"You're a trained corpsman, aren't you?"

"Yes, but ..."

"Fleet Marine Force Specialist?"

"Yes. But that doesn't ..."

"You've done it before."

Amy pounded the dashboard. "But that was on laboratory animals. Rats and dogs. Research animals. Not a person. Not you."

"The anatomy is a little different, but the process is basically the same."

She shook her head again. "No. I can't. It's, I can't do it."

"It's my risk," Deacon said. "And my bad luck if something goes wrong. I won't hold you responsible."

She thumped her chest so hard it hurt. "But *I'd* hold me responsible. I'm trained to save lives, not experiment on them. And we're not just talking about *any* life here." She hesitated, wondering if she should say more. "I don't think I could go on if I, well if I hurt *you*." Her eyes locked into his, her gaze portraying what she was feeling better than any words.

He smiled, but it wasn't the old Deacon smile. This one held a hint of understanding but with that cold resolve she feared. "Let's take first things first. I'm not asking you to do anything to me yet. I'm just asking you to steal a laceration pack and an LP pack."

Amy started to answer, then sighed. "Listen, it's one thing to dumpster dive some surgical scrubs." She pointed to the ones she now wore, blood splotches staining the right breast. "But hospital emergency rooms look askance at people walking off with their equipment."

"Hospital emergency rooms are busy places," he said, scanning the parking lot. "Especially on Saturday night. People don't tend to notice another pair of scrubs walking into a treatment area. Not if that set of scrubs acts like they know what they are doing."

"But," she said.

He took her hand. "This is bigger than you or me, Amy." He squeezed her hand. "Bigger than you *and* me. They must be stopped. We're the only ones who can do it."

"But can't we, can't we go to someone? The FBI? A newspaper?"

His cold smile returned. "And tell them what? I'm a murderer, remember? I *murdered* an FBI agent. I murdered the presumptive VP. You're my accomplice. We've stolen government secrets and whatever else they can frame us with. *We're* the threat."

"But if we told them, told them everything."

He touched her face. "Who are they going to believe? Two escaped felons with a crazy story? Or the Vice President of the United States?"

Chapter 36

Lisa paced, phone in one hand, cigarette in the other. It hadn't taken her long to reacquire the habit, a habit she'd thought she'd lost after graduate school. Blue smoke curled around her as she snubbed the Lucky onto a saucer.

"Come on, come on," she said, grabbing another smoke from the half-empty pack. She walked to the stove and lit a burner, lighting her smoke from the blue flame. "What the fuck's taking so long?"

This was ridiculous, she thought. She was seeking reassurance like a scared little kid. But isn't that what she'd morphed into? A little, infatuated kid in the throes of puppy love. No, it was more than that, it had to be. But was it enough? Enough to justify the intrigue, the deaths, the risk to Deacon and what's her name? Was it enough to justify the treason?

She flung the last thought from her mind. It was not treason, she thought. Treason was what was happening to her country, the country her grandparents had struggled so hard to reach, sacrificing to it like a god. Sacrificing so that her parents could inherit the American dream, her birthright. A dream that was now being perverted and spat upon, ridiculed and besmirched. What she was doing, what Cathy was doing, that was patriotism, not treason. That was setting things right. The bitter medicine that made the cure. The darkness before the dawn. She puffed on her smoke. She'd made her decision, and it was the right one. There was some mess along the way, sure. You had to break eggs to make the omelet. But at the other end was a better country. A saner country. And at the other end was her and Cathy. She smiled briefly before the knot returned to her gut.

"Then why do I feel like such a shit?" Shaking her head again, she snubbed out the butt and drew forth another.

"Dr. Reilly?"

The voice in her ear startled her into dropping the unlit cigarette. "Yes?"

"Thanks for holding. I'm sorry, but Dr. Harris can't talk to you right now. Things are a bit hectic, as you can imagine."

"Yeah, sure. But it would only be for a second. I just need, um, I mean, I just want to, to congratulate her on the appointment."

"Well, that's very nice and I'll pass it on to her. I'm sure she'll appreciate it. Goodbye."

"Wait. I just need ..." The phone went dead. "Fuck." Lisa bent down and retrieved the cigarette from the floor. Then she walked to the stove. "I gotta buy a lighter," she said, bending forward. Before the cigarette struck flame, the doorbell rang.

"What now?" She tossed the unlit smoke on the kitchen table.

Lisa walked toward the front door. It didn't take her long. The whole apartment wasn't very big. It was the first place she'd looked at when she hit town, and it was good enough. As were the IKEA and Walmart furnishings. As was the small kitchen with its Melmac dishware and well-used microwave. The only item that was big and nice was the bed. The bed where she and Cathy slept. The doorbell rang again.

"Hold your livestock, I'm coming."

A snick of the deadbolt and the door was open. Astonishment struck her like the warm night air. "Deacon?"

"Surprised to see me?"

"Yeah. I mean, no. I mean, well, I figured you must have been picked up by now. I mean, your picture is all over the news. How did you get here?"

"*Happy* to see me?"

"Well, yeah. Of course." She hugged him. He didn't hug back.

"Can I come in? I feel a little naked standing in the porch light like this."

"Sure. Yeah. Come in." She locked the door again. "Are you okay? How did you get here? Have you seen, um, you know, um."

"Amy?"

"Yeah. Amy. The cute Marine. I don't know why I can never remember her name. Have you talked to her?"

"No," he said. "I guess the police still have her."

"Un uh. She broke out. Knocked out a guard and flew the coop like Johnnie fuckin' Dillinger." She pointed to the small TV. "It's all over the news. Baltimore cops got egg foo yong on their faces."

"Did you talk to Joe? Is he on board?"

"Joe? Um, no. I, I haven't been able to find him. No one knows where he is. The unit is shut down, except for security and skeleton staff. Information is hard to come by." She walked into the kitchen. "Get you some coffee?" She grabbed the smoke and lit up off the burner.

"I thought you gave those up."

She flinched. He'd followed her into the kitchen. "Oh, well, you know how it is. Stress. What's been happening. You and, um, Amy in danger. Old habits, as they say. You know?"

He smiled. "Yeah. I know."

"You want one?"

He shook his head.

"Want anything? Coffee? A drink? Food? Anything?"

"Yes."

"What?"

"Information."

Lisa puffed and shrugged. "I'm as much in the dark as you. Maybe more so. Information is a commodity I ain't got right now. Wish I did. But I can let you have some food." She opened the fridge and looked inside. "Well, eggs or a yogurt, anyway." She closed the door. "Need money? Anything?"

"Anything?"

"Mi casa is Sue's casa. Or in this case, Deacon's casa."

"Okay," Deacon said, reaching into his pocket. "How about shutting the fuck up."

Lisa had time to register the gun in his hand before the lights went out.

Deacon slapped Lisa's face.

"Take it easy," Amy said. "You want to wake her, not kill her." She handed him a cold cloth. "Hold that against her face."

Then she walked to the kitchen cabinets.

"What are you looking for?"

"Smelling salts." Amy rifled through the upper cabinets, which held only cheap plates and glassware. Then she tried the lower ones.

Deacon tossed the cloth on the kitchen table. Part of him didn't want Lisa awake. Most of him wanted her dead. But he needed her. He grabbed the cloth again.

Amy brought over a pint-sized plastic bottle.

"What you got there?"

"Parson's ammonia," she said. "From the age of the label, I'd say a bottle that has never been opened." She twisted the cap, a pungent scent filling the room. "Not exactly smelling salts, but the next best thing. She held the open bottle under Lisa's nose.

The dark lean features grimaced, the cheeks moving back and forth to escape the smell. Amy followed every movement, never letting the neck of the bottle wander from a nostril.

Lisa's eyes fluttered open. At first, they registered surprise and disorientation. Then panic. Lisa jerked against the duct tape that bound her to the kitchen chair, almost toppling it to the floor.

"Struggle all you want," Deacon said. "But if you fall over, I'll have to kick the shit out of you instead of beat it out. Your call."

Amy grabbed his arm. He shook it off.

Lisa quieted. "I, um, I don't understand."

"Like hell," Deacon said, slapping her across the face.

"Deke," Amy yelled, grabbing his hand to prevent a second blow. "She might have a concussion. You could kill her."

"Not a bad idea," Deacon said, the cold smile back on his face. "But one I will forgo the pleasure of for a little cooperation." He smiled at Lisa. "You hear that, you piece of shit? All that's keeping you alive right now is what you can do for me. If I were you, I'd be accommodating."

"Listen, Deke," Lisa said, a fat lip making it sound like 'Lishen Dehke.' "I can explain."

He raised his hand again and she quieted. "I'm talking now." That stony smile slipped across his face like a mask. "All the while, I thought it was Barzoon. Was *sure* it was Barzoon. But never in a million years would I think it was you."

"Just let me explain, Deke."

His stony smile vanished — only stone remained. "How far back did it go? Your treachery? Selling out for some Harris in the hay? All the way back to the beginning? All the way back to Liz?"

"If you'll just listen."

"Nelson Barzoon is just a bureaucratic climber. A cog in the great machine. But you. You're a traitor. You're a fucking murderer."

"No, Deke. Listen."

He landed a savage backhand to her reddened face, the high cheek bones beginning to swell and purple.

Amy grabbed his hand again. Again, he shook free, stabbing a finger in her face before turning back to Lisa.

"I'm going to ask some questions, bitch, and you will be allowed to answer. Otherwise, shut the fuck up. Okay?"

Lisa nodded, a tear rolling down her swollen cheek. "What do you want to know?"

"That's better. Now, the unit isn't really shut down. Is it?"

"Of course, like I said. They ..." Lisa flinched as he raised his palm. "No. At least not all of it. They furloughed some of the staff, but the lab is still operating."

"Making weaponized 606, no doubt."

She nodded.

"And I'm guessing they have Tom making Creel-1?"

Lisa nodded.

"Full-court press? Heightened security?"

"No," Lisa said. "Regular five-day week."

"Business as usual," Deacon said. "Move along folks. Nothing to see here." He shook his head. "Saponek still working on viral conjugation?"

"I guess so."

"How far along is she?"

"I don't know."

He raised his open palm.

"Really! I don't. I haven't been there in a couple days. I just know what I was told by, um ..."

"Harris?" Lisa's face reddened further. "A little pillow talk? The queen bitch doling out a few sips of information to the drooling whelp at her tit?"

"Listen, Deke."

He slapped her, flecks of drool and blood flinging onto the kitchen table.

"Deke," Amy shouted.

He raised his hands in surrender, then turned to Lisa. "Why me?"

Lisa looked confused.

"Why bring me back here?"

She shrugged. "They needed the antidote."

"Yeah. But why the rush, rush. Ten days to find the cure. Then the hit and run, the attack on Amy's cabin. What was that all about?"

Lisa shrugged.

"Trying to kill me? Why? Or was the point just to keep me moving? Distracted?" A thought banged home. "Or use *me* as a distraction. Something to explain the deaths. A loose-cannon whack job run amok. A little tin bear moving back and forth in the shooting gallery. Sleight of hand so that people were chasing *me*, rather than looking at what was really happening." He looked at Lisa. "A patsy?"

She shrugged again. "I really don't know."

Deacon considered this for a moment, then the cold resolve returned. "I'm going to need you to get me into the unit."

Lisa's eyes flew wide. "What? The unit? Why? How?"

"The why is my business. The how is as a visiting researcher. Dr. Campbell, we'll call him. From Vanderbilt. A visiting don from the Harvard of the south."

"But they'll know it's you."

"Dr. Campbell will be disguised. And I think it's fair to say that Unit 13 is the last place they'll expect to find Deacon Creel."

Lisa shook her head, flecks of blood and spit spattering the floor. "I can't do that. *I'm* not even supposed to be there."

"Your clearances and cardkey still work, don't they?"

"Yeah, sure. But ..."

"But what?"

Lisa shook her head again. "I could get arrested just for helping you. And I won't jeopardize ... No. I can't. I won't." Her look of feral fear changed to determination. "The whole idea is ridiculous. I won't have any part in it."

He raised his open palm.

"Go ahead, hit me. Beat the hell out of me. I won't do it."

He lowered his hand.

"Believe me," Lisa lisped. "I'm doing you a favor. I'm doing the country a favor."

Deacon grimaced. "Favor?" Then he shrugged. "Okay." He turned to Amy. "Why don't you clean up, take a shower. I'll make some coffee, try and think up another plan."

Amy looked at Deacon, indecision in her eyes. Then she looked at Lisa. "Is a shower okay?"

Lisa laughed, her fat lip quivering. "Sure. Mi casa is Amy's casa."

Amy looked back at Deacon.

"Go ahead," he said. "I'll come up with something."

When Amy left for the bathroom, Deacon rinsed the washcloth under cold water. He pressed it to Lisa's lip and wiped away the blood. "That's not too bad. Looks like a cold sore with just a little swelling and bruising. We can ice that down, then cover up with pancake."

"You're all heart."

"You bet." He put down the cloth and picked up the pack of smokes. "Cigarette? I'll light it for you?"

Lisa nodded as Deacon looked for matches. "Use the stove," she said.

Deacon lit the paper tube off the burner. He coughed up a blue cloud. "How can you smoke these things?"

Lisa smiled. "You get used to 'em."

He held the cigarette to her lips, and she took a long drag that cherried the tip.

Deacon held up the smoldering cigarette, studying it. "You know, they say these things are the perfect consumer product — at least from a seller's point of view." He blew on it, the end glowing angry red. "An addictive substance that burns itself up. Even if you set it down, it keeps burning."

Without looking down at Lisa, he deftly lowered the tip to the back of her hand. The sizzle and smell of burning skin filled the air even before her yelp of pain. He smiled.

"You're lucky I didn't burn your face. But that would be tough to explain when you take me to the unit. A burn on the hand?" He shrugged. "Curling iron? Oven rack?"

"Listen, Deke. You'd never get away with it. Trust me."

"I used to," Deacon said. "I used to trust you." He blew on the tip again. "No, can't have places that show." With his other hand, he reached over and undid the top few buttons of Lisa's shirt. "But it should be someplace sensitive. Sensitive and hidden." His fingers grasped her front-loader bra and deftly undid the clasp.

Lisa gasped, her eyes wide.

"You've got nice tits. Know that? Small, but nice. I used to think it was a shame you reserved them for women. Now?" He smiled. "They're just for me." He lowered the tip of the burning cigarette.

"Alright. Alright. You win. I'll get you into the unit."

"I thought you'd see things my way." He put down the smoke and rubbed his chin. "I'll keep the whiskers, maybe trim them up a little, add some grey. Clean up." He spread the sides of his hoodie. "Wouldn't happen to have a suit that fits me, would you?"

"Sorry."

He shrugged. "I guess I can send Amy out. That pawnshop on Claridge still open all night?"

"I think so. Listen, Deke."

He touched the mole on his forehead. "Then we have a little something to take care of." He looked at his reflection in the kitchen window. "I've always meant to have this removed."

"Listen, Deke. Let me explain."

He ignored her. "Tomorrow morning. That's when we'll go. Get some food, a good night sleep. Head out early Sunday morning. The Unit should be quiet, no one around. Good time for Dr. Campbell to tour the facility."

Lisa looked away, as if she was studying the kitchen doorway. "What's to stop me from blowing the whistle?" A little of the determination was back in her voice. "Pick myself up a reward instead of a jail sentence."

"That's easy." Deacon held up the revolver, its cold metal still spattered with blood. "I'll kill you. I've killed before."

Lisa's smile drooped on the swollen side, making her look like a lopsided emoji. "War's one thing, my friend. But you're no cold-blooded murderer."

His stony smile returned. "Now don't you bet your life on it — *friend*."

Chapter 37

Deacon scanned the lobby appraisingly, then looked at the security guard. The guard looked back, studying him. As hoped, the guard's focus was not on the steely blue eyes behind the thick reading glasses, the rumpled suit that screamed academic nerd, or the greying whiskers that were mostly Wite-Out. His focus was on the fresh, one-inch incision and four polypropylene sutures rising from Deacon's forehead. Deacon winced as he held a tissue to the wound, drops of serum soaking into the white paper.

"Band-Aid came off," Deacon said in his smooth southern drawl.

The guard nodded, then looked at his computer screen. "I'm sorry, I don't see any mention of Dr. Campbell's visit."

"Cathy must have forgotten," Deacon said. "I'm sure she's quite busy these days."

"Cathy?"

"Dr. Harris."

"The new *veep*?"

Deacon smiled. "I wanted to stay for the festivities tomorrow after her swearing in, but I'm addressing the UN biowarfare summit Monday and my plane leaves tonight." He placed a hand on the gun in his jacket pocket, then nudged Lisa.

"Yes," Lisa said. "This is the only chance that Dr. Cre ... I mean Campbell will have to tour the facility."

"I don't know," the guard said. "Maybe I better call someone." He reached for the phone.

"Why not try Joe Metternich," Deacon said. "No, he's on sabbatical, isn't he?" He frowned. "Perhaps Chuck Schumer, but he'll be as busy as Cathy right now." He snapped his fingers. "I know, Jake Greene."

"The Surgeon General?"

"Yes. I'm sure Jake will confirm it." Deacon patted his pockets. "I have his number here somewhere."

"Well, I guess ..."

Deacon reached over to grasp the guard's nametag, his eyes peering above the lenses. "Oh, beg pardon. I just want to remember your name, Mr. Temple. Mention your kindness when I talk to Cathy."

"Oh," the guard said. "It's, it's my pleasure." He handed Deacon a temporary ID. "This will get you into all but the restricted areas. And Dr. Reilly's clearance will open those doors. Of course, standard security measures are still in effect."

"Thanks, Phil," Lisa said. "We won't be long."

They'd taken the stairs down to three and made a cursory pass through the halls, stopping at a couple of offices to make it look like an actual tour. Then down one more floor to the lab areas.

The camera on the ceiling watched as they walked along the sub-4 corridor. Deacon kept one hand in his pocket, the barrel of the revolver angled toward Lisa. When they reached the junction of two corridors, Deacon stepped toward the right, which led to Tom's lab. Lisa hesitated, her eyes plastered on the surveillance camera, her face a mask of tension. Deacon recognized the adrenaline surge in her features, the flight or fight reaction he'd seen in others and felt so many times himself. Moving casually to her side, he clutched her arm then pulled the gun from his pocket and buried it in her kidney.

"I really don't have any compunction about shooting you."

"I don't think so," Lisa said. "The guard would see."

"Maybe, if he's looking. Maybe not. Certainly, he wouldn't hear from way down here." He cocked the hammer. "And I could be halfway up the stairs before your body hit the floor. Then it's just a matter of telling old Phil that you've collapsed. Then, Dr. Campbell is gone."

Lisa hesitated.

"I have nothing to lose," Deacon said.

Still, she hesitated.

"Believe me, Leese. I could kill you as easily as I'll kill Harris."

He felt her body relax. She pointed right. "This way."

"I remember."

In ten steps they hit a reinforced-glass door with Main Synthesis lettered on the surface. Lisa's cardkey clicked the door open. Ten more steps and they were at Tom's lab.

"Where are they keeping the Creel-1?" Deacon asked.

"I'm not sure," Lisa said. He jabbed the gun into her kidney. "Probably the safe. But I don't know the combination."

Deacon smiled. "I do. I've watched Tom dial it often enough."

Deacon walked her to a black box the size of a small file cabinet, his back to the camera, shoulders hunched as if he were only studying something interesting. Then he punched 02-05-68 into the keypad. "All this fancy security, and the combination is his birthday."

A light flickered green. The door popped open. Rows of small vials sat along two shelves. Some had red caps. Deacon ignored them and examined the green-capped vials, reading the little labels pasted on each.

"How much have they produced?"

I don't know," Lisa said, glancing up at the camera.

"Ah, here we are." He picked up a vial containing a small quantity of reddish-brown powder. "Creel-1. Batch eight." He casually dropped it in his pocket, then repeated the process with batches four through seven. "That should be enough."

"Enough for what?"

"Human testing," he said.

"Human? Now wait a minute. You're not using me as any guinea pig"

"Don't worry. It's not for you." He nudged her with the gun, keeping it hidden from the camera. "Now let's get to Joe's lab."

"What do you want there?"

"A little hair of the dog." He tapped her with the gun. "Move."

Deacon smiled and nodded. "Very impressive. I'm glad I got a chance to see it." He handed Phil the temp ID. "I'll be sure to mention your kindness to Cathy."

"Thank you, Doctor Campbell."

"Isaac," Deacon said, reaching out to shake the guard's hand. "Thank *you*, Phillip. Please give my best to your family."

"Um, sure. Take care, ah, Isaac." He pointed toward Deacon's forehead. "Hope your, your *thing* gets better."

"Everything will be better soon," Deacon said. Then he and Lisa left.

The Nissan met them at the curb. Lisa got in the front seat, Deacon the back. He placed the gun to the back of Lisa's head as they drove toward the gate, pressing it harder as Lisa nodded to the gate guard.

Amy drove them off. "Everything go okay?"

"Fine," Deacon said. "I got what I needed."

"Then I guess you won't be needing *me* anymore," Lisa said.

"No," Deacon said. "No, we won't."

He raised the gun and struck at the base of Lisa's skull.

Chapter 38

His blow was intended only to render Lisa unconscious, at least that's what he'd tell himself later. Just a tap to shut her up, put an end to the petulance in her voice. Just a respite from her chatter, a time-out until he could figure out what to do with her. But at the moment of striking, he'd conjured an image of Liz lying in tepid bathwater, her pale breasts bobbing like waterlilies on a pond of Barbie pink. He saw Hernandez, blowing his brains against the shiny stainless steel of high-end appliances. Carstairs' death mask swam into view, a look of contentment on his purple features.

Maybe it was these images or maybe something Lisa had said about doing him a favor, but whatever it was, he felt the old adrenal surge. His measured tap turned into blood and pieces of bone spattered against the side window. Short, black hairs were pasted amidst the mess. Lisa's unbelted body slumped forward, then accordioned down.

"*Deacon*," Amy shouted, swerving as she slowed the car. Popping the trans to park, she felt for a pulse on the inert form collapsed into the knee well. "I think you killed her."

He clutched the gun to his chest and closed his eyes. "Probably. I hit her hard enough." He squeezed tighter on the cold metal, as if that would turn back time. Then he put the gun away. "We need to lose this car. It's probably been reported stolen. Drop me at Lisa's, then dump it a few blocks away. Someplace they won't find it for a couple days. That should give us enough time."

Amy stared at him, wall-to-wall pupils in her Ronstadt eyes.

"I know," he said. "Let's go. We've important business to tend to."

Deacon sat bare chested, his butt propped on two pillows, his arms hunched over the back of a kitchen chair. Vertebrae formed a series of small hills along his arched spine. "You're too thin," Amy mumbled as she sponged away remnants of soap.

"Did you say something?"

"I said, I wish we had surgical scrub—chlorhexidine or povidone soap."

"Dial works almost as well," Deacon said.

Amy swabbed the area with alcohol, then her latex-covered fingers spread iodine along it.

"I don't like doing this without a lidocaine block," Amy said.

"I took a couple of Codap from Lisa's medicine cabinet." Deacon yawned. "I'm liable to fall asleep on you, so don't worry."

She wiped her fingers on a sterile towel from the LP pack. Then she wiped her forehead against her shoulder. "That's as good as I can make it. Are you sure you want to do this?" She poked a finger on the scrubbed area. "Deacon?"

"Huh? What?"

"I said, are you sure you want to do this?"

"No. But I'm sure I *have* to. Go ahead."

Amy handled the long, twenty-five-gauge needle as if it were broken glass. With her other gloved hand, she located the space between the fourth and fifth lumbar vertebra, painting an 'X marks the spot' in the iodine. Holding the needle over the space, she hesitated.

"Are you *really* sure?"

"It's a spinal tap for Christ sake. Just do it."

"Is that an *order*, Commander?"

Deacon's body relaxed. "No. It's a request, Amy. Please."

Amy took a deep breath, then slid the needle at a ten-degree angle, as if she were aiming for Deacon's belly button.

Deacon flinched, his body tense.

"You okay?"

He nodded, letting out a long breath. Then he took another. "Yeah, go ahead."

She advanced the needle slowly, withdrawing the stylet every few millimeters to check for fluid flow. He didn't flinch anymore, his only movement the steady expansion and contraction of his rib cage. Amy recognized the regular breathing of a relaxation exercise, causing her to relax as well.

Amy concentrated solely on the task at hand, trying not to let him down. Trying to think of him in the abstract, as just another patient. But he wasn't another patient. He was Deacon — Deke. And his life was in her hands. If her needle slipped, she could paralyze him. If her technique wasn't clean enough, she could introduce rip-roaring infection directly to his brain. Then the biggest if of all. She shook her head and advanced the needle slowly.

Her hands moved in a smooth cadence — advance, withdraw, reinsert, advance. A well-choreographed ballet, one she had practiced on lab animals and anthropomorphic dummies. Advance, withdraw, reinsert, advance. Her fingers felt stiff and tired, as if she'd been working for hours, although she knew that less than a minute had ticked by. She'd just decided to stop for a second, to flex tension from her hand, when yellowish fluid squirted from the end of the needle. Her fingers froze. Deacon's breathing froze as well.

"I'm there."

Deacon nodded.

"You sure you want me to go on?"

He nodded again, the rhythm of his breaths returning.

Amy reached to the syringe laying upon the sterile drape. She placed the tip into the needle well, being careful to keep everything steady. The she looked at the reddish-brown liquid filling the barrel of the syringe. It looked like rust or diluted blood. It looked evil. And she had to inject it into the man she loved.

"Has this *ever* been tested in people?" she asked. Deacon's only response was a quickening of breath, like a woman in Lamaze. "I said ..."

"Do it," he grunted.

Amy froze momentarily, then made the sign of the cross and slowly injected the Creel-1.

Deacon slept uneasily, pain in his back and legs interrupting fitful dreams. In one, Liz and he were on their honeymoon —

Greece, just as they'd discussed in their post-coital moments of drowsy conspiracy. They were at a sidewalk café in a seaside village. Liz was beautiful in a white toga, sipping coffee from a demitasse. The air was hot and dry, a bright sun rising from the east. Then the skies darkened with a cloud of ash and dust. Deke heard the roar of an erupting volcano. Then Liz was covered in fallout, her beatific smile frozen in the eternal grey of statuary.

He woke with a chill. Someone was placing a cool compress on his feverish forehead. He looked briefly into eyes as large and dark as black olives. Her death had been a dream, he thought, before drifting back to sleep. The relief was short-lived.

He was at Liz's funeral. He'd had too much to drink, removing his emotional governors and sending him to a men's room stall for long periods of sobbing amidst the muffled footsteps and whispers of mourners passing in and out to relieve themselves. Finally, a voice spoke, asking if he was alright. He recognized Lisa Reilly, briefly brightening his mood. The stall door opened, and she smiled at him. She was dressed in the dark suit she'd worn that day, looking beautiful but somehow manly, not at all out of place in the men's room. She nodded, still smiling, then turned. The back of her head was caved in, bits of flesh and blood smeared into her short hair.

He woke again, his fever broken. Warm fingers stroked gently across his face and closed his lids. A voice said, "Sleep." He slept.

Deacon was home in Dayton, returning from college. It had been the last day of classes. The garage door rumbled open, the creaking of its metal frame reminding him of a coffin with rusty hinges. The ghoulish imagery sent a chill that dampened his high spirits. He shook it off and headed into the house, the rumble of the overhead descending like a summer storm. He knew something was wrong even before he'd put his keys on the hook. The air smelled strangely stale, like sour feet or puke.

He stopped in the kitchen doorway, yelling out, "Mom? Hey Mom, I'm home." No reply. The chill was back, icing his spine from the bristling short hairs on his neck to the belt of his beat-up jeans. He walked through the empty family room. The smell grew stronger, its odor more defined, more familiar. He broke into a run, dashing past the guest room where they stored the winter clothes, past his room, to the master bedroom. He paused for a moment, hand raised to knock, heart yammering in his throat. He opened his mouth to yell her name again, then stopped, the words frozen on his lips. Slowly, as if in a dream, his hand lowered to the knob. The world swam in and out of focus as the door opened slowly and the odor slapped him. His eyes registered the grisly scene, but his mind refused to see. He vaguely remembered the feel of soft carpet as he passed out.

Deacon jerked awake for the third time, this one for keeps. Pain throbbed from the back of his skull like a familiar friend. He raised his head slowly from the pillow, causing the pain to flare then ratchet down. It took a moment to register where he was. His eyes scanned the room, the furnishings unfamiliar. The one familiarity slept soundly in an old easy chair, her face reminding him of Liz. Then he remembered where he was, and the task he still had to perform. Then he remembered the dreams, their vague imagery. His heart raced, his mouth as dry as cat litter. He needed a drink, and he wasn't thinking of water.

Deacon dropped his feet over the side of the bed, the room spinning as he stood. When it all settled, he crept past the sleeping Amy and out the door.

He'd been to Lisa's many times. He knew where the liquor cabinet was, that place of honor above the refrigerator. It contained about three ounces of gin, half a bottle of vodka, and an unopened bottle of Evan Williams. Deacon snatched the bourbon off the shelf, ignoring the cerebral gymnastics that spun the room. He clutched tightly as he fumbled the wrapping off the cap and the cap off the bottle. The sharp, crisp scent of whiskey greeted his nose like a floral bouquet. .

A thousand doubts and reproaches inundated him like a flash flood, dunking him under its turbulent flow. He thought about the plan — ridiculous, chances of success slim to none, death or capture a near certainty. Who did he think he was, Jack Reacher? A cold killer who was going to stop the evil forces at work? He shook his head. You can't stop evil. He raised the bottle. The glass felt smooth and soothing against his lips, the comforting smell of the liquor pungent in his nostrils.

He hadn't stopped Joe Metternich or Nelson Barzoon, and they were just tools that the evil system used to perpetuate itself. He *had* stopped Lisa, her dark-skinned face filling his mind's eye, the feel of the gun as it crushed the life from her. But what did that matter, her life was over when she decided to exchange a lifetime of principles for a shapely body and a fantasy about cleansing the country of evil. His thoughts spun further.

Lisa's almond eyes were replaced by dark orbs, as large and round as anime. Amy. He'd gotten her involved and now she could end up dead or in federal prison. More human carnage to lay at the feet of Deacon Creel. Another failure to drown in the sweet oblivion of drink.

He paused before taking that first, erotic sip, his mind fixed on Amy, the look in those Ronstadt eyes if she saw him now. His arm stopped in mid raise as Amy's eyes became Liz's eyes. There the image froze, just as his arm was frozen, just as he was frozen at the edge of the abyss. Liz's eyes were just as dark as Amy's, her look just as reproachful. It was a look that said, 'You let me down. My death was for nothing. You let us all down.' Deacon wanted to tip the bottle back, let the booze wash the look from his mind, wash his conscience clean. Instead, he lowered it, a single drop of brown liquid striking the kitchen tiles as he set the bottle on the counter, his hands shaking. Then he found the cap and screwed it in place with all the urgency of a man wrestling a poisonous snake. With a steadier grip, he placed the bottle back on the shelf and turned around.

Amy stood in the doorway, staring at him. At first, he saw reproach in her dark eyes, the same reproach he'd known he'd see, or perhaps was expecting to see and wishing makes it so. Or was it something else? He let it go for now.

"You shouldn't be up," she said.

"I'm fine. Just a bit of a headache. What time is it?"

"11:45 — *a.m.*" She pointed to the sunshine beaming between the window curtains. "Monday."

"You shouldn't have let me sleep so long."

"You needed it." She walked to the refrigerator. "Looks like the *late* Dr. Reilly left us the fixings for an omelet."

This time the reproach was undeniable. He let it pass as he'd let pass the half-dozen veiled comments in the car. "Sit down first. Let's chat about the plan." He held out a chair for her.

Amy walked stiffly over, grabbed the chair back, and crashed it to the floor.

"I don't want to sit and *chat*. I want to stand and *fight*!"

"About what?"

"About *what*?" She kicked the chair, its metal arm skittering into Deacon. "What the fuck do you think? About you killing your best friend as if she were an annoying insect. Some mosquito to swat."

Deacon sighed. "Do we have to do this *now*?"

Amy planted hands on hips. "Yes," she spat. "Now. I couldn't do it when I thought you might die from that stuff." She hesitated, lip quivering. "When I thought I might kill you by injecting it." Her eyes regained their confidence. "But you didn't die. I didn't kill you. So, yes. *Now*."

He was in no mood to argue but felt one coming on. He let it come. "I told you it was an accident." He closed his eyes and rubbed headache from his neck. "Anyway, I guess it needed to be done."

"What need? I didn't see any need."

Deacon looked at her. "In the end, there was nothing else to do."

Amy threw her arms to the ceiling as she paced the tiny kitchen. "We could have, I don't know, tied her up."

"And then what? I couldn't watch her. You couldn't watch her. What if she got loose? What if her screams brought the neighbors over? She knew we were going to take out Harris. That we'd be heading to D.C." He shook his head. "Couldn't risk it."

"You mean you didn't *want* to." She glared at him, storms raging behind her dark eyes. "You wanted your pound of flesh. You wanted somebody to pay for Liz." She jabbed a finger at him. "You made yourself judge, jury, and executioner. Then you came up with this rationalized bullshit."

Deacon let the tirade sting. He deserved that. Then he answered calmly. "We're at war, Amy. I made a command decision. She was — collateral damage."

There was no humor in Amy's answering smile. "Sounds like something *Harris* might say."

"As you were, Marine Force Specialist."

Amy laughed. "So, it's *Commander* Creel again. I'm getting seasick with all the ups and downs, *Deke*. You're either a soldier or you're not. And killing in cold blood wasn't the act of a warrior." She pounded the table. "And it wasn't right."

Deacon raised his eyebrows. "What does that mean?"

"*Excuse* me?"

"*Right*? What right are you talking about?"

"You know damn well. Just like you know the difference between right and wrong."

"Right and wrong?" He stood, his voice rising, blood pounding in his ears. "You want to tell me *anything* that's right about this whole fucked-up mess? We've been lied to and manipulated from day one. Is that *right*? They've shot at us, aimed cars our way, framed us. Is *that* right? They've killed at least five people." He paused, throat tightening, eyes tearing. "Six if you count Liz."

Amy's voice softened. "That wasn't their fault, Deke. Or yours."

He slumped down into the chair. "Maybe. Maybe not. But one thing's sure. It wasn't right." He leaned toward her — hands white against the table. "The government, *our* government has turned a potentially life-saving drug into a weapon of mass destruction. The same government that's not even supposed to be in the business of biowarfare. Now Harris, or her minions, or her handlers are using this, this assassin's dream to kill off everyone that stands in the way of her being appointed VP. *Appointed*, mind you, not elected."

Now he stabbed a finger at Amy. "And once she *is* appointed, how long do you think it will be before the president has a summer cold that turns into the winter of his discontent? How long before we have a horse-drawn coffin and a nationally televised interment at Arlington?"

His steely blue eyes locked onto her dark brown ones. "And here's the kicker. The million-dollar question. Why? What happens after Vice President Harris becomes Madame President?" He paused, as if expecting an answer. "Yeah, I don't know, either. But I know it can't be good. And I know it won't be *right*."

Deacon leaned back, drained, spleen vented. His shoulders slumped.

"Lisa's dead. I killed her. Maybe I was wrong. But maybe, just maybe, that's something that *is* right. Because even though I ended her physical life, her dying started long ago when she thought that something evil can beget something holy."

His face softened.

"Funny. She was the one who saw the evil in the whole, while I argued for the good of the individual. In a way, she was right, and yet she bought into that evil, was seduced by it, corrupted. She thought she could *cure* it." He shrugged. "Maybe I killed her for revenge. Maybe a fit of pique. Maybe convenience; tying up a loose end. I don't know, and maybe it doesn't matter. But maybe it was right. Maybe it was merciful." He flew his hands wide. "Or maybe this is so much rationalized bullshit, as you put it. But, please Amy, don't tell me about right and wrong. Lately, the subject has lost its meaning."

Amy replaced her chair and sat quietly opposite him. The storm still raged behind her eyes, but he could see the dawn breaking. "I still say you shouldn't have killed her."

He cocked a finger at her. "Now, *you* are probably right. Maybe I *shouldn't* have killed her. Maybe Cinderella could have been my date to the ball."

"What?"

He pointed to an envelope on the kitchen table. "Open it."

Amy picked up the plain white sleeve, gilt-edged script addressed to Dr. Lisa C. Reilly. An equally formal-looking engraved invitation slid out onto the kitchen table.

"Read it," Deacon said.

"Dr. Lisa Reilly and guest are cordially invited to the inaugural ball of Dr. Cathleen Harris." She looked at Deacon. "A party for the new vice president?"

"Of course. After you're sworn in to protect and defend the constitution you plan to shit on, it's customary to have a party. I'm sure Lisa got all warm and runny at the invite. Probably one of several paramours, male and female, that Harris has on a string."

"So?"

"So, instead of Lisa, you'll be my date."

Amy chuckled and waved the invitation. "How? This is addressed to Dr. Lisa Reilly."

"That's where you come in. You're going to be Lisa Reilly."

"But I can't pretend to be Lisa. I don't even look like her. I'm not tall. And I'm certainly not half Asian. Not even one-sixteenth."

"And if her last name were Wang or Xiang, it would be a problem. But it's Reilly. And you could pass for a Reilly."

"But won't people *know* her there?"

"Unlikely," Deacon said. "Lisa was pretty much of a low-level techno nerd. Never mixed with the bureaucratic big shots. No ambition for it, at least that's what she said. A science outsider. Probably one of the reasons it was easy for Harris to manipulate her. Attention from somebody that high up — and that attractive to boot." He shook his head." Must have been heady stuff for old Lisa. Real nosebleed territory."

"But surely *Harris* knows her."

"Surely. But Harris will be too busy to visit with everyone. Probably two or three hundred everyones, maybe more. If she tries to locate Lisa, and that's a big if, she'll figure she's in the ladies room or couldn't make it or something. She won't check all the invitees to see if one of them is pretending to be Lisa."

Amy held up the invitation, waving it again at him. "But this won't be enough. This is the new VP we're talking about. There'll be Secret Service. They'll want to see ID."

"We have Lisa's purse with Lisa's ID."

"But the *picture*?"

"A quick trip to a photobooth, in disguise of course, and that will solve itself. Pick up a pair of reading glasses, the bifocal kind. Plain glass up top, coke bottles underneath. With that and the wig. Piece of cake."

Amy tossed the invite on the table and paced away. "But a photo glued onto a driver's license won't fool the Secret Service."

"No," Deacon said. "But it *may* fool door security."

She turned to him. "Huh?"

"I've been to these kind of things before," he said. "Secret Service will be glued around the VIPs. Door checks are handled by rent-a-cops, who'll be at ease because of all the high-powered security inside and because things don't *really* start hopping until the guest of honor arrives fashionably late. Just leave the ID in the wallet. They'll only give it a quick look. Never know the difference."

"But how about you? Won't they want to see your ID, too?"

"I have an old driver's license, expired and suspended if they care to check, which they won't. Picture is a dead match." He rubbed his chin. "Scruffy beard and all."

"But Deacon Creel?"

"That's even easier than your ID." He pulled his old license from his wallet. "Type a new name, Isaac Campbell, say. Print it out on photopaper and glue it in place." He shrugged. "A cursory glance through old plastic in a wallet window? At night?"

"But it'll be *your* picture. You're wanted by the FBI and every other federal and local agency."

He smiled. "I'm not wanted by rent-a-cops."

"But won't *someone* recognize you?"

"Doubtful. The Secret Service will be looking for terrorists and suspicious gunmen, not Deacon Creel. And the last place the FBI will be looking for me is the Harris inauguration. Besides, I'll be in disguise as well. Glasses. Scruffy beard. Rumpled suit." He tapped the incision on his forehead. "Band-Aid. Just another nerdy academic out of his depth. I'm sure Harris knows tons of them."

"But ..."

"My, we are just *full* of buts today."

Amy paused, holding her breath. Then she shrugged. "Say we pull it off. What then?"

"Then, I see to it that Cathleen Harris's tenure as vice president is the shortest on record."

She sneered at him. "Make yourself judge, jury, and executioner again? You're getting pretty bloodthirsty, Deke."

"It's necessary."

Amy pounded the table. "How the hell do *you* know what's necessary? Maybe, maybe ..." She shrugged. "I don't know. Maybe we could expose her."

"How?"

She glanced about, as if expecting the answer to come from some imaginary wiseman. "Go to the FBI."

"I killed one of their agents, remember? And we have no evidence. They'd give more credence to Ted Bundy." He paused, looking at his fingers splayed against the table. "And we most likely wouldn't survive long in custody."

"Well, we could go to the Washington Post."

Deacon spread his hands to newspaper proportions. "I can see the headline. Murderer and fugitive from justice Deacon

Creel claims vice president part of a massive conspiracy to force people into suicide." He nodded. "We'd have better luck with the *National Enquirer*. Anything else?"

Amy sat, mouth moving, trying to say something. Deacon could see ideas flash behind her pretty eyes, each vanishing like a puff of smoke hit by the cold air of reality. Finally, she slumped back into her chair, defeated.

"Even if you're right about killing Harris, there's a bigger issue. How? You can't bring a gun or even a knife in there. There'll be metal detectors."

"No, but you *can* bring breath spray."

"Breath spray?"

Deacon reached into the inside pocket of his suit coat and pulled out a red-capped vial of brown liquid. "A proper vehicle for this."

"What is it?"

"Formerly known as Snyder Laboratories formula 606. Now, the assassin's dream."

"But doesn't that have to be given into the spinal cord? Are you planning to ask Harris to bend over for a lumbar puncture?"

"Attractive imagery, but no need. The original SL 606 had to be given intrathecally. The drug couldn't pass the blood brain barrier. But the weaponized form Joe developed is conjugated to a virus that *can* pass, probably parainfluenza. The victim just experiences mild cold symptoms." He paused.

"What?" Amy asked.

"I just remembered Carstairs complaining of a summer cold."

"So, how do you plan to administer it?"

"That," Deacon said, "will have to be worked out on site. I'll need to look for an opportunity that gets me close to Harris or her food or water glass or something."

"What about other people in the same general area of her? How will you protect them?"

"Same answer."

"How about you? How do you protect you?"

He smiled. "I'm immune. Remember?"

"How do you know, Deke? Creel-1's never been tested on people. You said so yourself. How do you know the dose I gave you worked?"

"I don't," he answered. "But I'll know if it didn't."

Chapter 39

Amy followed the black limo to the next available parking attendant. But instead of opening her door for the keys, he tapped on the window. She lowered it with a soft hum.

"Sorry, Miss. But regular valet service is suspended. The Empyre Club is closed for a special party. You'll have to move."

Amy handed him the invitation.

"Oh, sorry." He opened her door. "Beg pardon. I didn't know. I just thought. I mean, you don't see many PT Cruisers at the club. Especially this color. I mean. Um…"

Amy handed him the keys as she got out. "Feel free to park it in the back."

"Thanks. I will. I mean, not that it needs to be kept out of sight. I mean."

She patted his hand and said, "It's okay." Then she took a step and stumbled into his arms.

"You alright?"

She smiled. "New shoes."

She was wearing a pair of wobbly, knee-high boots that were probably calf-high on Lisa. The three-inch heels didn't help. Last time she'd worn heels was senior prom. But the boots hid the excess black-satin pants hemmed up inside. A soft, white blouse fit surprisingly well, except Amy was larger in the bust, making her thrust out from the tuxedo jacket she'd chosen. Overall, she felt like a groomsman at a lesbian wedding, but didn't think she'd stick out too much at this gala. Especially *this* gala. Her date on the other hand? Deacon exited from the shotgun seat, then stepped over to take her arm, saying thank you to the attendant in his soft southern accent. Amy thought he looked like an ad for send this professor to camp. She'd had a chance to press his black thrift-shop suit, which helped a little, but there was no way that gala-ites weren't going to stare.

Deacon steadied her as they followed the crowd toward the entrance, walking behind tuxedos, suits, and gowns that cost more than the car they were driving.

"See," Deacon said, still in character. "We blend right in."

"The waitstaff will be better dressed." She spoke out of the side of her mouth. "I don't have a good feeling about this."

"Relax," he whispered. "A little notice is fine. Hiding in plain sight as it were."

Capital police held back the paparazzi, their camera flashes glaring painfully off the reading glasses Amy wore. A man in a green blazer with an Irongate Security patch on the shoulder hurried by, repeating, "Please have your invitations and ID ready, ladies and gentlemen."

Amy retrieved the wallet from the clutch she was carrying. Deacon pulled his from the breast pocket of his suit.

The partygoers had split into two lines leading to two archway metal detectors. Amy followed a fiftyish man in an Armani suit, a twentyish girl on his arm. The girl showed her credentials, then passed through the arch. The man followed suit. The detector flashed and squawked.

"Would you please empty your pockets, sir?" said another man in Irongate green. Mr. Armani placed keys and a lighter into a plastic tray, laughing as the attendant wanded him. "He must think I'm Deacon Creel."

Amy froze and tried not to look at Deacon.

"Relax," Deacon mumbled.

"Next," the attendant said.

Amy said a silent prayer as she showed her invitation, a phony smile plastered on her face. From above the bifocal line on her reading glasses, she watched the man pass a flashlight over the invite, then similarly pass the light over her ID. He looked at her face. He looked back at the ID. He looked at her face a second time.

"Could you please remove your glasses?"

Amy hesitated, then complied, smile still glued in place. The man checked her ID again, then looked up.

Amy held her breath, smile still masked onto her cheeks.

The man looked at the ID again, then nodded and smiled. "Have a good evening."

Amy handed her clutch to a second attendant who quickly searched the interior. Then she stepped through the detector without incident and the man handed back her purse, repeating the phrase, "Have a good evening."

Amy stopped before the revolving entry door, waiting, trying to hear Deacon's interchange with the security guards. Sweat trickled from under her wig; she brushed it out of her eyes, almost knocking the glasses from her nose.

Through the laughing and chatter, she heard Deacon say, "I'm escorting Dr. Reilly," his southern drawl hard to miss. Then the sweat poured more freely as she heard the detector squawk.

"Would you empty your pockets please, sir?"

Amy turned slowly, the world spinning in the flashing lights. She watched as Deacon placed the breath spray and some spare change into a plastic bowl. He made eye contact with her as he stood, arms outstretched, the metal wand humming over his body. Amy held her breath. The wand moved down one leg, then up the other. It buzzed for a moment, causing the man to redo the right ankle. The attendant rose and looked Deacon squarely in the eye. Then he smiled and handed him his wallet, coins, and breath spray. "Have a good evening."

Amy almost collapsed against his arm as he stepped to her side. "Easy, Lisa," he said. "Piece of cake."

They entered the inaugural party.

The Empyre Club was an odd mix. Outside was clean brownstone befitting a Victorian gentleman's club. Inside was more like Planet Hollywood. Darkness surrounded neon glare rising from art deco appointments that seemed alive. Rows of Lucite and steel tables flanked a large dance floor where laser lights replaced the disco ball of *Dance Fever* days. A raised platform equipped with mics, amps, and drum set dominated the far end of the dance floor.

The club was trendy. It was fashionable. It was a popular DC nightspot, especially among the LGBTQ community.

Amy guessed Deacon had underestimated the guest

list by at least a hundred. The club was packed. At first, the hustle and bustle shocked her. Then she felt lost. Then she felt anonymous. Then she relaxed.

Deacon held her arm, smiling, as they nudged their way through the throng. There were older, academic types in 1990s fashions, and hipper clientele dressed to the nines and higher. There were lesbians in tuxedoes, transgenders flaunting decolletage and Adam's apple, and run of the mill heteros sporting designer gowns and snake tattoos. It was like a high-priced gong show.

"See," Deacon said, still in southern character. "We blend right in."

Deacon had been correct that the guest of honor was not yet in attendance. Still, security was high. Amy noted men and women in conservative suits scanning constantly while mumbling into lapel mics. They didn't seem to pay particular attention to her and Deacon, but she still felt naked as their eyes passed by. The all-seeing eye, she thought, although it was the Secret Service not the dark lord doing the looking. And there was an eye in the sky. Looking up, she noted the black, snow-globe–sized orbs on the ceiling. No doubt, more Secret Service or rent-a-cops were watching on a remote screen in some back room. She felt like she just stepped from the shower into a room full of TV cameras.

She and Deacon milled around, keeping on the move, each with a white wine from a proffered tray. She sipped occasionally, trying to fit in. After about thirty minutes, they'd settled against a side wall, hiding in the shadows of the other guests.

"Why, hello there."

Amy started. A thin, sixtyish man swallowed by an old tuxedo smiled at them over wire-rimmed glasses. He turned to Deacon.

"You look awfully familiar. Do we know each other?"

"Ah, no," Deacon said. "I don't believe so."

The man held forth a yellowed hand. "Miles Silverman. Johns Hopkins." They shook.

Deacon started to say his real name, then froze as the D left his lips. Amy froze as well. Silverman raised eyebrows at the pause. Finally, Deacon replied.

"Um, Campbell. Isaac Campbell. Tulane."

Silverman's smile widened. "You must know Charles Hartwell. Dean of the med school?"

Deacon paused again, then smiled. "Only by reputation."

Silverman nodded. "So, how do you know Dr. Harris? Or should I say Vice President Harris."

"Um, I don't." Deacon kept smiling. "Except by reputation." He pointed to Amy. "I'm here as Dr. Reilly's escort. She's a friend of Dr. Harris."

Amy's jaw dropped as Deacon nudged her.

"Say hello to Dr. Silverman, Lisa. Johns Hopkins."

"Miles," Silverman said, taking her hand.

Amy shook hands limply, turning to Deacon with pleading in her eyes.

His eyes pled back.

She turned to Silverman, swallowed, and said, "Hello."

The old academic held her hand longer than needed, his other hand joining atop it. "Cathy and I go way back. I'm one of her professors from medical school. How do you know her? You weren't in her class. I'm sure I'd remember. And you're much too young."

From the way he spoke of Cathy, Amy thought maybe they'd had more than a student-professor relationship. From his smiling grope of her hands, Amy thought maybe he wanted the same with her.

"Lisa worked under Cathy," Deacon said. "I mean Dr. Harris, at Homeland Security."

Silverman squinted up in thought, his hands still holding Amy's. "Reilly. Reilly? Seems to me I read a paper by a Lisa Reilly on viral vectors of disease transmission. Fort Deidenbach, wasn't it?"

Lisa froze again, tongue swollen to five times its normal size. She was well versed on CPR, hospital sterilization, and triage under mass casualty situations, but viral vectors of disease transmission? Deacon saved her.

"You must be thinking of another Reilly. Lisa's in epidemiology."

Silverman smiled down at Amy, his hands still caressing hers. "My ex-wife was an epidemiologist. Fascinating topic. We should discuss itover a drink." Then his smile wavered. "Fort Deidenbach! Of course. That's who you remind me of." He released Amy and turned to Deacon. "Did anyone ever tell you that you bear a striking resemblance to Deacon ..."

"Ladies and gentleman, may I have your attention please?"

Deacon raised his finger to his lips, silencing Silverman, then faced the raised platform from where the amplified voice had spoken. A man stood in the halo of a spotlight. He was a dapper man, looking as fit and well-tailored in his tuxedo as Silverman looked lost in his. It took only a glance before Deacon's mouth hung open almost to the knot of his Walmart tie.

"Good evening, ladies and gentlemen. I'm Nelson Barzoon, Dr. Harris's chief of staff. I want you to know that ..." He paused for a moment, finger raised. "the vice president will be here shortly."

There was a burst of applause from the gathered guests. Barzoon raised his arms for silence.

"Quiet please." The din scaled back. "After she and her *date* arrive, and you're going to love him, we'll serve the rubber chicken." Laughter and boos from the crowd. More Barzoon hand raising. "For now, please arm yourselves with another cocktail as fortification against the obligatory speeches." More cheers mixed with boos, followed by more Barzoon arm raising. "I'm told they will be short, after which, feel free to eat, drink, and dance the night away to the music of Red Harem." More cheers that Barzoon ignored as he departed the platform and walked directly toward Deacon.

Chapter 40

Deacon ducked, losing sight of Barzoon but sensing his approach. "Pardon me," he mumbled, nudging his way through the crowd, heading away from the dance floor.

Deacon dodged left and right, moving without direction, needing to get away. Part of him knew it was crazy; Barzoon couldn't have recognized him in the shadow of a sea of faces. His heading toward Deacon had been sheer coincidence, a random choice along the rows of the compass. Yet something in Deacon panicked. The shock of seeing Barzoon was the last straw, the one that broke the back of the dromedary already burdened with the stress of the past hour added to the stress of the last week added to the stress of concealing his anxiety from Amy. He wondered briefly where she was, then kept moving.

After what seemed an eternity, he was at the bar. He steadied himself against the rail, sweat slicking his palms against the cool steel. He needed a drink.

"Cocktail, sir?"

Deacon flinched. A cute female bartender was smiling expectantly at him.

"Cocktail?" she repeated, a bit of 'I'm really busy' creeping into her smile.

"Um, yes. Maker's Mark, straight up." He didn't even bother with the southern accent.

She nodded, moving away.

"Make it a double," Deacon called after her.

Deacon gripped the metal tighter, trying to quell the tremor in his hands. The cold steel felt comforting. The fact that it was a bar made it even better. Like visiting an old friend, one he'd spent many happy hours with. Well, maybe not happy, but comforting. Soothing. Forgetful. Time killing. Hours where he didn't have to remember, or if he did, where he could wash the memories back into sweet oblivion. He wanted to do that now, although he knew he couldn't. No, he'd have just this one to steady up. Just one to deal with the stress, control it, tame it to his will, his mission. Just one to get the taste of the mass-market champagne from his mouth. Just one.

"Here you are, sir," the cute barmaid said.

Deacon snatched the glass from her hand, its not quite circular shape soothing in his own. He downed half in a gulp. Relief flooded through him with the warmth of the whiskey. The shakes settled. The clammy sweats turned cool and heartening. He gulped the remnants and said, "Again."

The barmaid's smile dimmed, but she nodded and walked off.

"Enjoying the party, Dr. Creel?"

Deacon turned sharply to face Nelson Barzoon smiling beside him. It was the smile of a hunter facing a trapped animal. Deacon took a deep breath, feeling the after-rush of the liquor. "I'm sorry, I think you've confused me ..."

"Must we, Deacon?"

Deacon's shoulders slumped. "You saw me from the stage?"

"No. *I* didn't see you. They did." He pointed toward one of the surveillance cameras. "Surveillance has been following you for the last half hour. You and your *date*." He looked right and left. "Wherever she's gotten off to." He smiled. "Did she desert you, my boy?"

Deacon shrugged. "Must have had a previous engagement."

"Well, I guess we needn't worry about her. No doubt they'll pick her up outside." He patted Deacon's shoulder like an old friend. "But I knew sooner or later *you'd* end up at the bar." Barzoon shook his head. "Technology is a marvelous thing. In this case, face-recognition technology. Cameras at the door scanned everyone and fed the images through FaceLift, proprietary ID software. Almost as good as fingerprints." He squinted at Deacon. "Although I have to say your disguise is good as such things go. The Band-Aid to cover the mole is a nice touch."

Deacon removed the bandage, revealing the sutures.

"Bravo," Barzoon said. "You know, you remind me a little of

a logic professor I had in law school. Scraggly beard. Glasses. Cheap suit. Always some little injury or other." He smiled in remembrance. "Quintessential academic."

"That's what I was going for," Deacon said. "Best I could do on a limited budget."

Barzoon nodded. "Purchased in Frederick so that the FBI would track you there. While all the while, you were coming here." He frowned. "Why, I wonder? Why would you show up here, of all places?"

"Hiding in plain sight," Deacon said.

"I doubt that. No, I think you have some ulterior motive. Perhaps a lethal one." He grinned. "It may be that I was wrong about you, Dr. Creel."

"Could be," Deacon said. "I was certainly wrong about you, Mr. Barzoon. More than once."

The barmaid brought the whiskey. Barzoon turned his charming smile in her direction. "Scotch rocks, please, Suzette. Highland Park." Then he pointed at Deacon's bourbon. "Please, enjoy your drink. Have another." He signaled Suzette. She nodded.

Deacon sipped the bourbon. "So why did you wait? Why not pick us up first chance?"

Barzoon shrugged. "Why bother. I know you're not armed. No knife, gun, bomb." His hand shaded his face in the universal sign of confidentiality. "You were wanded with a threat-detector that would have picked up nitrate traces." Barzoon chuckled. "So, I figured, why make a fuss. No real danger until the new vice president arrives. Why not let you relax a bit before coming over to chat." He shrugged again. "And I was curious about what you had in mind." He leaned his hip into the bar so he could look directly at Deacon. "By the way, what is that?"

Now it was Deacon's turn to shrug. "Just wanted to congratulate Dr. Harris."

Barzoon laughed heartily. "I'm sure you did. But how?" He patted Deacon's pocket. "With that?"

Deacon reached in and withdrew the breath spray. He puffed a blast into his own mouth, managing not to grimace at the taste. "Just wanted to be at my best when I met the vice president." He puffed a blast at Barzoon, the air filling with a solvent sweetness. "See? Nothing lethal."

"I see," Barzoon said, squinting.

Suzette brought the drinks, and Barzoon dropped a five-dollar tip on the bar. "Thank you, my dear." Then he raised his glass. "Well, what shall we drink to?"

"The new vice president, of course," Deacon replied.

Barzoon nodded and they drank. "Speak of the devil." He pointed to the stage where the lights were coming up. Then he waved to a man in a dark grey suit. "If you'll excuse me, I have another little speech to give. But Agent Haggarty will keep you company."

Haggarty planted himself next to Deacon while Barzoon dashed off. Deacon felt a vice close around his arm.

"Would you please follow me, sir?"

Chapter 41

The amplified voice sounded familiar. Then Amy heard the name and looked sharply up at the man speaking. She didn't hear what he was saying, her mind occupied with seeing Nelson Barzoon. She'd gotten the impression he was a mid-level bureaucratic functionary. Now he was the vice president's chief of staff? She didn't know much about politics, but she knew enough to know something smelled fishy. The crowd cheered, and Barzoon left the stage. Amy tried to signal to Deacon, but he was gone. She moved left looking for him.

Even with the heels, she wasn't tall enough to see over the backs in front of her. She flinched as a hand cupped her ass. Turning, she saw Silverman smiling at her.

"Terribly sorry. Accident." His aged shoulders rose and fell. "This crowd. Hard to move. Nowhere to put one's hands." Now his eyebrows raised. "Can I buy you that drink?"

"Sorry," Amy said. "I'm looking for Dr. Cr ..., my escort, Dr. Campbell."

Silverman pointed over his shoulder. "He went that way. Toward the bar. How obliging of him. Shall we?" He stepped to the side, allowing her to edge in front of him. She felt his hand once again on her butt.

"You know, my dear Lisa. May I call you Lisa?"

Amy nodded as she edged forward amidst talking and laughing people; their mass moving her and Silverman toward the bar. "You seem far too young to have a doctorate. And far too pretty to be in epidemiology." Silverman chuckled. "Did you skip grades in school? Or does youth and beauty run in your family?"

She felt more cupping. Fighting the impulse to show him the Marine Corps thumb-break hold, she said, "That's very kind of you to say, but actually I'm almost thirty."

"I never would have guessed."

Amy stopped short and rose to her toes, as if she were seeing above the backs and shoulders obstructing her view of the bar. "I think I see Dr. Campbell. Awfully nice to have met you, but I really need to ..." That's when Silverman pinched her. And that was the last straw. Spinning quickly around, Amy grabbed his pinky in one hand and his thumb in the other, bending each in opposite directions. The shock, pain, and surprise in his face made her smile.

"I may seem too young for a doctorate, but I'm not too young to know martial arts. Now, you have a choice. I can break your fingers. Or you can stop pinching my ass and stay here when I leave. You pick."

Silverman's knees sagged so that his face was even with hers. He nodded quickly, agony written on his features, and gasped, "Go. Please."

"Right choice." Amy released her grip. "I'll take a raincheck on that drink.."

Amy moved with the crowd like a leaf in the current. She looked about at the suits and gowns that blocked her vision. She felt anonymous again, just one more bit of flotsam in an ocean of the rich, famous, and infamous. She doubted that even the eye in the sky could pick her out. She relaxed, going with the flow, listening to canned elevator music.

Just before the bar, the crowd parted like breakers on the beach, each wave heading to a gap in the humanity lining the stainless steel. Amy could now see more than ten inches in front of her. At first, nothing seemed unusual. Then, from the corner of her eye she saw movement. Not that this was unusual; the entire room was alive with movement. But this movement was synchronized, like soldiers on a drill field. Two men, marching in lockstep, one an obvious government agent replete with dark suit, earpiece, and Secret-Service demeanor. He had his hand locked onto the arm of a second man, a skinny academic type in a cheap suit. Dr. Cheapsuit had a small incision on his forehead. The two men were headed toward a side door marked, 'Staff Only. Not an exit.' After a moment's surprise, Amy scurried after them. Dodging partygoers, she grabbed the grey metal 'Staff Only' door before it clicked shut.

She was in a narrow corridor, the sights and sounds of the party dampening behind her. Deacon and the Secret Service man were just ahead in the glow of overhead fluorescents. She stopped, not knowing what to do, but knowing she needed to do something before they reached a second door with cardkey access.

"Oh, sir?" Her own voice seemed loud within the confines of the narrow space.

The pair stopped, the agent spinning suddenly but not losing his grip on Deacon's arm.

"You're Secret Service, aren't you? Agent ..."

"Haggarty," the man replied, his body tense, ready for action.

Amy didn't look at Deacon, afraid her eyes might give away something. She kept her gaze on Haggarty. "I'm glad I caught you." She approached him casually. "That man, Mr. Barzoom or whatever?"

Haggarty's brows raised. Amy thought his grip lessened just a bit.

"He wants to see you. Told me to run and fetch you back."

"And who are you, ma'am?" His grip relaxed a little more.

"Me? I'm, um, I'm Dr. Riley. A good friend of Cathy Harris."

The agent relaxed further, mention of the new VP having the desired effect. His grip on Deacon was now only perfunctory. Amy allowed her eyes to meet Deacon's, flashing him a coded message she hoped he'd decipher. His eyes flashed back. Now or never.

"But I'm supposed to take this man to security."

Amy lashed a vicious kick directly into Haggarty's knee. But before the agent's leg even started to buckle, his hand was in his suitcoat. That's when Deacon struck a hard right fist into Haggarty's temple.

Amy heard a crunch of bone on bone. She saw Haggarty's eyes startle. Then they were all white as he slumped to the floor, a Glock pistol clattering beside him.

Deacon snatched up the gun and shoved it into the waistband of his suit. "Good job, Marine Force Specialist." He smiled as he shook pain from his hand.

"Corps training, sir." She smiled back. "Now what? We won't get far."

Deacon shook his head. "No. Barzoon is onto us. They've been following me via surveillance cameras." He looked up. "Which, fortunately, don't seem to be fitted into the service corridor. I think they lost track of you."

"One of the benefits of being short."

They both turned toward the door they'd just entered through, crowd noise ratcheting up behind it. Then the speakers started playing "I am Woman."

"Guest of honor must be here," Deacon said.

"That'll make it harder," Amy said.

Deacon thought for a moment, then said, "Maybe not." He looked down at Haggarty. "How tall would you guess he stands?"

Amy shrugged. "Maybe six foot, six one. Why?"

"About my height," Deacon said. "What would you say he weighs?"

"Maybe two hundred. A little more."

Deacon nodded. "His clothes may be a little baggy, but it might work."

"What might?"

"And if I'm not mistaken, those look like size eleven shoes."

"What are we talking about, sir?"

Deacon squatted to pat down the unconscious agent. From an inside coat pocket, he withdrew a small electric razor no bigger than a penlight. "Perfect."

"Why would he carry a razor?" Amy asked.

"Did you ever see a secret service agent with five o'clock shadow?" Deacon rose and clicked on the razor. "Start undressing him while I shave."

"Shave? Isn't that part of your disguise, Dr. *Campbell*?"

"Is now Agent Haggarty," Deacon said, fuzzy hair tumbling off his cheeks in strips. "Complete with G-man clothes, earpiece, lapel mic, gun, and credentials."

A loud cheer rose from the crowd, forcing Amy to raise her voice from a whisper to a shout. "Credentials? Your photo isn't even on them. And I'm willing to bet that the Secret Service knows its own agents."

"I'm sure they do," Deacon said. "But I doubt each agent knows every single other agent on a detail. And I'm betting they scan a room looking for threats, not other people dressed and acting like them."

"So okay. Fine. Maybe you'll fool them for a *minute*."

"I only need a minute. I just need enough time to get close to Harris. Her food. Her water glass. Just enough time to spray some happy-hunting-ground juice."

"But won't other agents be assigned that task, staying close to Harris? You'll look suspicious approaching when you're not supposed to. Especially if they don't recognize you."

Deacon raised his chin to shave the hair from his neck. "I wish I had a mirror."

"But how will you ..."

"Enough," Deacon semi-shouted. "I don't know. Okay, Amy? In case you haven't figured it out, I'm making this up as I go along. Now will you please undress Haggarty before he wakes up."

Amy unlaced one of the agent's shoes, pulling it off and tossing it to Deacon. She looked up at him, worry beaming from her dark eyes. "What if you can't get close enough for the spray?"

Deacon put a hand on the Glock tucked into his waist. "Then I'll go old school."

"You'll never survive."

"Neither will Harris."

Haggarty lay in socks and underwear, curled in the traditional roped-calf posture. His own cuffs pinned his wrists behind his back, plastic ties bound them to his ankles. Deacon's cheap belt held a handkerchief gag securely in his mouth. His eyes were open, blinking anger and anxiety.

"It's okay, Special Agent," Deacon said, clipping the lapel mic onto Haggarty's jacket, which was now Deacon's jacket. "I'm doing your job. You just don't know it."

Deacon licked his palms and slicked back his hair. "How do I look?"

"You might pass," Amy said, "except for the stitches. Can you comb your hair over them?"

"Ever see a Secret Service agent with boy-band bangs?" Deacon reached into the pocket of his new, slightly baggy suit. He handed Amy a small leather case of grooming essentials they'd found on Haggarty. "There's a pair of nose-hair scissors in there. Let's remove the sutures."

"But the wound?"

"It's been nearly three days," Deacon said. "And you used good surgical technique. It should be enough time."

Haggarty grunted loudly. Deacon's foot nudged him into silence. Outside the band played light rock, something from the eighties.

Deacon leaned down so Amy could stretch up. She neatly and quickly snipped the four thread loops, pulling each free by its knot. A small bleb of serum oozed from the side of the red incision, but otherwise it held. She stepped back and eyed her boss. "Still too noticeable."

"Got any makeup?"

Amy pointed to her small purse lying in the corridor. "Makeup will help. But it'll still be noticeable if you look close."

"Maybe in here," Deacon said. "Maybe not out there." He pointed toward the club. "And maybe no one will look close."

"That's a lot of maybes."

Deacon shrugged. "What choice do we have?"

Chapter 42

Deacon clicked on the powerpack in his breast pocket. High-pitched sound howled through his head. Wincing, he adjusted the squelch, and the painful noise from his earpiece coalesced into recognizable chatter, one voice louder than the rest.

"Agent Nine, come back."

Deacon ignored the female voice obviously perturbed at Agent Nine and stood up straight, walking confidently through the crowd, trying to mimic the agents he'd been watching since he and Amy entered the club. The guests were seated, chatting over their rolls and wine glasses, awaiting the salad and rubber chicken.

"Agent Nine, respond *please.*" Agent Nine was in for trouble, Deacon thought. Then he walked on.

He moved along a side aisle, heading in the general direction of the bandstand. A single table had been placed on the raised platform. The band set up was beyond, although all that was playing now was piped-in Harry Connick Jr.

Cathy Harris was seated in the center of the single table. She was dressed in a designer gown that almost made Deacon stop walking and stare. It had a red, semi-see-through beaded top. Her hair hung over the spaghetti straps, a French braid holding it back to reveal her elegant neck and dangling diamond earrings. The seat on her right was empty, a bureaucratic-looking man and woman Deacon didn't recognize just past the gap. On Harris's left was a tuxedoed man who might be Robert DeNiro, seated next to someone who could only be a supermodel. Finishing off the table were Barzoon and a matronly woman in silver, probably Mrs. Barzoon. Behind the group, a slim, hard Secret Service agent kept watch. Nearby, a pretty female server with short hair stood ready with a water pitcher like Gunga Din.

"Agent *Nine!*" Deacon was glad he wasn't Agent Nine. "This is Zelewski. Respond, Haggarty. Now."

It took a moment for Deacon to realize he was Haggarty. Panic threatened. Fight or flight. He wanted to run or pull the Glock and end things now. But then he got himself under control, took a couple deep breaths, and tried to remember Haggarty's voice.

Deacon cleared his throat and talked to his lapel. "Haggarty. Go ahead."

"Well, nice of you to join us. About frickin' time."

"Sorry. Um, comm trouble."

"Did you deliver the package?"

Deacon stood at the edge of the dance floor, puzzled. Package?

"Well, is Creel with Capitol PD?"

"Um, affirmative. Roger that."

"Fine. Now let's see you back in position."

Position? What position? He knew he couldn't ask that. But he also knew that assignments to presidential details rarely remained static, changing as needed to fit the situation. He cleared his throat again. "Roger. Do you want me at my originally assigned position or the alternate?"

"Alternate? What? What the hell's the matter with you? I want to see you at the eastern bandstand exit, controlling that aisle. Copy?"

"Copy. Affirmative. Roger that. Haggarty clear."

Deacon locatedthe two exit ramps flanking the bandstand. He wasn't sure which was east and which was west. But he could see an agent in a navy-blue suit standing tall at the right-hand one. The left one was vacant. More importantly, it was closer to the guest of honor than where he stood now. He headed toward it.

Amy took a final look at Haggarty on the floor, trying to ignore the desperation and anger in his eyes. Another career ruined, she thought. Before leaving, she paused to snatch the wig from her head. "They'll be looking for a blond," she softly said. "And if I'm going to die, I'll do it as Amy Robbins." Tossing the wig to the floor, she reentered the club.

Deacon had tried to talk her into staying put to guard the hogtied agent, but she'd refused. Haggarty wasn't her assignment, Creel was. Besides, what was she supposed to do if someone came in? Kill them? Run? Pretend to faint? She did agree to wait sixty seconds before following Deacon out, so it wouldn't look suspicious if both exited the corridor together.

The crowd had thinned, with everyone either seated or enroute. She thought she saw Deacon heading up the left-hand aisle, walking purposefully. He was on mission. But what should she do? How could she stay on mission, protecting his mission, and him? In a minute, she was going to look conspicuous, just her and the Secret Service standing while others sat.

Stepping out of the trickle of foot traffic, she took the invitation from her purse. The glasses she didn't need made it difficult to read, so she took them off. Table 65 was her assigned seat. She looked left and right, finding it in the middle, near the back. Not exactly a place of honor, she thought. And too damn far to lend assistance if needed. She looked back toward Deacon, his silhouette standing stiffly by the left emergency exit. Then she noticed the traditional skirted figure that indicated the ladies room. It was halfway up the aisle Deacon was guarding.

"Can I help you?"

A Secret Service agent was standing beside her. She hadn't even seen him approach. He looked calm, pleasant, professional, and more interested in what she was up to than in providing her assistance.

"Yes. I was looking for the bathroom."

He pointed up the aisle to the left.

"Thank you."

The agent smiled back. "My pleasure, ma'am."

"Ladies and gentlemen, may I have your attention?"

From his perch atop the exit ramp, Deacon couldn't see Barzoon, but he recognized the amplified voice.

"I regret to announce that Dr. Harris's *date* ..." He paused to let scattered giggles peter out. "Will not be able to attend."

Boos and groans filled the room, gradually falling back to silence. "Yes, unfortunately the president was called away to an important meeting. A national security issue." He paused again, no doubt smiling his Barzoon smile. "And I'm sure we all want his very capable hands on any world crisis. Right?" Cheers and applause rising again then petering away. "And I know you're all eagerly awaiting the rubber chicken." More laughter. "So, we are going to go ahead and serve dinner." Scattered cheers. "After which, our new, highly esteemed vice president will make a few remarks on restoring decency and rationality to our doleful political process." Cheers and much applause. "Enjoy your dinner."

Almost immediately, an army of waitstaff with salad trays descended from the back of the club. Deacon scanned the servers as if he were a real federal agent. But his mind was occupied with other things. His current position was concealed in the shadows, the dim light making him unlikely to be recognized as a faux Haggarty. But he was also concealed from the head table, couldn't even see it. Wandering over there was out of the question. Secret Service manned the steps at both ends of the raised platform, with another one in the middle facing the dance floor. Then there was the one on the platform itself. The waitstaff had a better shot at Harris than he did.

The staff were clad in white jackets and black slacks — except for one man in a maître d's tux. He was about Deacon's height and weight. Same color hair. He walked proudly down the center of the dance floor, tray held high, heading directly for the agent in the middle. There he paused while the agent checked under the napkin covering the rolls, poked and prodded, then signaled him to the left. Deacon watched the waiter start to climb the steps at the end of the aisle Haggarty had been assigned to watch, then he disappeared from view. A minute later he returned with an empty tray and headed down the side aisle toward the kitchen. Deacon paused for a moment in indecision, then followed him, trying not to run or look unnatural.

As he walked through the door, Deacon was hit first with the blast-furnace heat of gas jets and broilers running nonstop.

Then he was assaulted by combined smells — the pleasant aromas of cooking mixed with the not-so-pleasant stink of raw fish, vinegar, and body odor. Noise added to the assault on the senses, the steady din of metal on metal, the sizzle of steaks, both beef and salmon, the chatter of several dozen voices. Cries of "I need three more NY strips," "that's my salmon," and "clear these dishes" filled the air.

A single agent guarded the kitchen, although Deacon suspected more had sealed off the back entrance. To Deacon, the agent looked young, maybe mid-twenties. He was dressed in the traditional dark suit, with the traditional dark glasses. It dawned on Deacon that this was the only agent he'd seen wearing the shades the Secret Service was famous for. And after three steps, he could see why. The glare of the overheads was almost as overpowering as the heat, noise, and smell.

Deacon's eyes followed the maître d, losing him momentarily in a sea of waitstaff, then picking him up as he approached the largest of the several stoves operating full bore. He made a mental note of the location, then walked toward the on-guard agent, dodging staff members with loaded trays.

The agent raised his brows at Deacon's approach. Deacon nodded in response.

"Zeleski wants to see you. She's been calling for you."

The agent tapped his earpiece. "I didn't hear anything."

Deacon shrugged. "Must be having comm trouble."

The agent hesitated, then bent toward his lapel mic.

"She said *now*. Sounded pissed."

The agent straightened up.

Deacon nodded. "I'm supposed to take over here."

The agent wiped sweat from his brow and said, "You can have it. Drink plenty of water." Then he exited the same door Deacon had just come through.

Deacon wiped his own brow, then took up the same on-guard stance, grabbing a water bottle from a nearby counter. He waited. He sipped. He listened.

"I need five strips, three medium, one med-rare, one med-well. Baked potatoes on all."

"I said, clear these goddam dishes. How am I supposed to find anything?"

"I'll take that salmon. Remember, light cream sauce for Harris."

Deacon's ears perked up.

"She watching her figure?" A chuckle.

"No, I am." A bigger chuckle.

Then the maître d was moving past him on an errand to pick up a pepper mill. Deacon moved to his side, grabbing his arm.

"Excuse me, sir. I'll have to ask you to step this way."

The waiter put down the grinder. "What? Why? I've got people to feed. I've got the *vice president* to feed."

"It'll only take a moment, sir. In here please."

"The broom closet?"

"Please. Just for a moment. Don't make me ask you again." Deacon put one hand on Haggarty's Glock, the other guiding the waiter's arm to the closet.

The headwaiter muttered something and entered. Deacon followed him, closing the door.

Deacon moved through the kitchen, adjusting the maître d's bow tie, which was fortunately a clip on. He still wore Haggarty's dark slacks, but now with a short, tuxedo jacket. He'd retained Haggarty's earpiece and powerpack but tossed the mic next to the headwaiter who now lay in the broom closet, hands trussed behind his back with his own belt, Haggarty's tie doing the same for his legs. An apron gag muzzled the D's cries, although Deacon thought the threat to shoot him if he spoke was almost as good.

Deacon hurried over to the central stove where the waiter's tray was now loaded with plates.

The chef didn't look up, just plated the last steak and said, "Hurry along, Alf, before it gets cold. Hope her majesty likes the salmon." He looked up and smiled as Deacon hefted the tray shoulder high. The chef's eyes clouded. "Hey. Who the hell are you?"

"Change of plans," Deacon said, as he whisked the heavy tray toward the door trying not to spill it. The swarm of servers parted for him like the Red Sea for Moses.

Once out the door, Deacon readjusted his load. As he switched hands, he noticed two salmon on the tray, the rest steak. Both pieces of fish had only a dribble of sauce; one had rice and broccoli, the other only broccoli. The latter was no doubt Harris's, he thought. He could have sprayed it down as Haggarty and let the maître d deliver it himself. But he didn't know that then. And what if he was wrong? Amy had demanded to know how he was going to protect innocent bystanders from 606. He'd punted on "deciding on site." He was now on site, and delivering it himself was the only sure way. Whatever else he'd become, Deacon Creel was still a man of his word. At least when he gave it to Amy Robbins.

Besides, either way the chances of escaping alive were slim to none. His immediate future was either in handcuffs or bleeding out from a hollow-point to the pump.

Deacon found himself wishing for the latter.

Chapter 43

Amy ducked inside the ladies room. She stumbled to the sink, steadying herself against the cold porcelain. She looked in the mirror. Outwardly, she looked no different. Inside, her heart was racing amidst a pending panic attack. She splashed cold water on her face, dabbing herself dry with a paper towel. She wanted to crawl into a stall and collapse, maybe curl up against the cool commode and seek the peace of sleep. She was no killer, and she couldn't abet one. At least she never thought she could. She became a medic to save lives. But Lisa was dead. If she hadn't abetted that, she certainly had abetted Deacon.

For the thousandth time, she searched for a flaw in Deacon's logic, some way that they could expose the conspiracy without killing. But each time she came up empty. No one would believe it. It was too fantastic. She still wasn't sure she believed it. Yet, here she was at the inaugural party for the new vice president, who most likely would soon become the new president. And then what?

Amy splashed more water on her face, then stood watching the droplets hit the sink. She'd joined the Corps to serve her country, just as her father had done and his father before him. Duty, honor, country. She wondered what Harris had in store for her country — she doubted it was honorable. It might be (probably was) catastrophic. And then there was her duty. She was assigned to protect Deacon Creel. Commander Creel. Her CO. Perhaps the man she loved. Duty, honor, country.

Amy dabbed towels against her face. "Do your duty," she whispered to the empty room. She looked at herself in the mirror. "Do your duty Marine Force Specialist. Semper fi."

Then she left the bathroom before she changed her mind.

The scene in the club had changed considerably. Instead of people milling about, laughing and drinking, there was the click and clack of metal on china as the seated guests attacked their salads and chatted amiably. The only movement was the army of waitstaff dashing on their conveyor-like journeys to and from the kitchen.

Amy looked for Deacon, but he wasn't under the exit light at the head of the ramp. She scanned the club, picking out individual Secret Service agents but seeing none that looked like Deacon. Panic threatened to return. Where was he? What should she do if she couldn't find him? Had he been picked up? Was his mission now hers?

She couldn't move, frozen in indecision. Then a clatter of plates snapped her from it.

In the direction of the noise, a tall headwaiter was struggling with a loaded tray of dishes balanced on the railing at the foot of the ramp below her. It was the maître d in charge of serving the head table; she'd seen him before she entered the bathroom. She resumed her search for Deacon, eyes darting about the room as her feet moved down the ramp. She'd taken only a few steps when her peripheral vision caught the waiter taking something from his pocket. It was about the size of a fountain pen or a cigar tube. She watched as he glanced about self-consciously, then palmed the cylinder before taking up his load again. Amy looked at his face and suddenly knew where Deacon was.

Deacon lifted the tray high, then almost dropped it, the clatter of plates causing nearby diners to look up from their salads. The monotony of background chatter in his ear was suddenly replaced by the angry voice of Agent Zelewski.

"Why isn't Agent Nine at his station? Haggarty, report in."

Deacon hefted the tray again, balancing it on his right hand, the breath spray cupped in the left hand used to stabilize the load. He walked as confidently as he could, trying not to rush, trying not to spill. No one seemed to pay attention and the other waitstaff continued to stay out of his way like good little underlings. He headed straight for the center Secret Service agent below the podium.

Deacon stopped before the center agent and lowered his tray for inspection, eyes straight ahead, sweat dripping through the makeup hiding the incision on his forehead. The center agent didn't look at his face, only at the food on the platter. The agent started to poke around the plates when they both flinched, no doubt hearing the same angry female voice snap through their earpieces.

"Yulin," Zelewski said into Deacon's ear. "Haggarty's not at his post, and no one has seen him for almost ten minutes. And I've got Upshaw here telling me I wanted to see *him*. I don't like it. Find Haggarty. Now!"

The agent at center stage keyed his lapel mic. "Roger. En route."

Deacon waited, tray lowered for inspection, but the agent just shoved past him and hurried down the center aisle.

Deacon walked quickly to the stairs, the agent guarding them likewise not seeming to notice him. The agent's hand was on his gun, his eyes scanning the crowd, not the headwaiter whose passage had become routine. Familiarity breeds contempt, Deacon thought, as he stepped atop the raised platform and walked toward the honored guests.

Deacon lay the tray on a folding stand set to the side. No one seemed to notice him here either, not the agent behind Harris, not the seated guests. It was as if he was a moving piece of furniture. And as long as he didn't screw up too badly, he should stay that way. At least he hoped so.

Keeping the sprayer cupped in his left hand, he picked up a steak and set it before the bureaucratic gent seated at the near end. Then he picked up the empty salad plate and placed it on the tray. The man mumbled "Thank you." Deacon placed another steak before the bureaucratic-looking woman in the plain blue gown.

"I had fish," the woman said. She pointed. "That one, without the rice."

A wave of relief swept Deacon. He'd been wrong about which one was Harris's meal. Had he sprayed 606 earlier and let the maître d deliver it, this woman would have been dead in a few days, the president a short time later.

"Sorry, ma'am," he said, returning the steak, bringing her the salmon and taking away the empty salad plate.

The room spun in a surrealistic mosaic of canned dinner music, indirect lighting, and background conversation. Deacon felt as if he were living a dream as he slipped the sprayer from his palm to his fingers. He took a deep breath then spritzed twice, sending a fine mist over the remaining salmon dinner. Sliding the sprayer under a used napkin on the tray, he brought Harris her plate.

The new vice president was focused on DeNiro, laughing at something he'd just said. The Barzoons were leaning over, trying to hear, laughing when Harris laughed. Bobby's date looked beautifully bored. Everyone ignored Deacon. So far so good.

Deacon placed down the salmon and reached for Harris's salad plate.

"Thank you, no," Harris said, still smiling at Bobby. "I haven't finished."

"Pardon, ma'am," Deacon said.

Just take a bite, he thought. Just one bite of salmon. Then he placed steaks before DeNiro and his date, swapping them for empty salad plates. Two to go.

Deacon glanced at Harris, still slowly eating salad. He lay steak plates before Barzoon and Mrs. B, saying a silent prayer that they would remain focused on Bobby's amusing stories. Taking their empties, he sighed. Almost done. Just whisk the tray back to the kitchen, then figure out a way to disappear. It might be possible to get away yet. But first he wanted to see Harris eat her fish. After that, it really didn't matter if he escaped or not.

He was just picking up the now lighter tray when Barzoon spoke.

"This is medium. Perhaps medium well." He said it calmly, but sternly. "I ordered medium rare."

Deacon froze. He started to say something, then Bobby interrupted.

"I think I've got yours, Nelson. Here, let's switch."

Barzoon and Bobby raised their plates simultaneously in front of Bobby's date, the china colliding with a clack. They both laughed. The date did not.

"Hey," the supermodel said, clearly offended at the invasion of her space. She glared at Deacon. "What do they pay *you* for?"

Bobby chuckled. "Yeah, I guess that's why central casting hires waiters." He handed his plate to Deacon, smiling. Deacon tried to stay calm as he accepted the plate. Then a voice exploded in his head.

"Code red. Intruder alert. Haggarty is down in the service corridor. Someone took his gun."

Startled, Deacon's thumb missed the plate edge and slid atop the fat on Barzoon's steak. His slippery hand flinched up, the steak flying off its plate and onto Harris's salmon, grease and sauce spattering her dress.

"Awk," Harris cried through a mouthful of salad.

Barzoon rose, throwing down his napkin. "Clumsy oaf!" His angry eyes met Deacon's. "You'll never work … *Creel.*" He cried the name like a fire alarm.

Deacon stepped back amidst an old, familiar feeling. Fight or flight. He couldn't run far this time. And that wasn't his job. Buttons flew off the tuxedo jacket as he ripped Haggarty's Glock from his waistband. Before he'd even leveled it, the agent behind the table screamed, "Gun!"

The rest happened with both dreamlike slowness and the speed of a wicked thought. Deacon leveled the gun, then hesitated, his mind frozen, his finger as well. Then he thought of Liz, and his finger tightened on the trigger. But part of him knew the pause had cost him. It was already too late.

The lean, hard agent on the dais tossed Harris down and vaulted across the table, food and water flying. He grabbed Deacon's arm just as the first shot rang out. Deacon fired three or four more times, as if his trigger finger was trying to atone for his brain's cowardly hesitation. The gunshots were muffled in his ears. But his eyes registered the flashes, his nose the smell of burnt powder. Then he went down, the Secret Service agent's charge carrying him back and off the stage, the two of them crashing to the dance floor. Deacon felt a sharp pain in his side. More agents piled on. The world went dark. His last conscious thought was self-loathing. He'd blown his chance.

Amy lingered within the shadow of the ladies room door watching Deacon ascend the steps to the dais, then he passed from sight. A few steps down the ramp and she could see him again, placing the tray on a folding table.

She waited, watched, and hoped she wouldn't need to act. She wasn't sure what she would do or even how she would know. But if needed, she would act. She would do something. He had his mission. He was hers. She would act. She would probably die.

Now Deacon was handing out plates, as if he'd been a waiter all his life. She couldn't believe it, but no one had spotted him. They expected Deacon Creel to be in the hands of Capital PD, or maybe in academic disguise: rumpled suit, thick glasses, Band-Aid. They weren't expecting him to be a headwaiter; weren't even looking at the waitstaff. The staff had already been inspected. Like the club itself, they'd been run and cleared. They were now equipment, like chairs, tables, and glassware. No, she thought, like servants, which meant anonymous.

Amy flinched as a hand gripped her arm. A dark-haired female agent was beside her. The woman looked young, perhaps younger than Amy. Yet her grip was strong. The set of her eyes, determined. Overachiever, Amy thought. Trying to make it in an older, male-oriented world. She knew the feeling.

"I'm Agent Kutchins," she said. "You'll need to come with me, ma'am."

Amy paused. "I, um, I think there's been some mistake."

"No mistake, Ms. Robbins. Will you come with me please?"

Amy tensed, unsure what to do.

"There is nowhere to go, Ms. Robbins. Don't make me hurt you."

Amy relaxed, which made Kutchins relax. The grip on her arm loosened. Then all hell broke loose.

Kutchins stepped back, releasing Amy and placing a hand to her earpiece. Secret Service agents hurried across the dance floor. The ones at the side stairways jerked to attention, pistols drawn. A crash at the head table drew Amy's attention there. Someone yelled "Gun!" Deacon was firing. Then both Amy and Kutchins were running.

Pandemonium reined as diners dashed for the exits or dropped under their tables amidst the clatter of upended chairs and falling dinnerware. Amy saw this in her peripheral vision, but her focus had shifted to a tight circle, like focusing on blood cells under the microscope. But instead of neutrophils, Deacon was the center of the small, magnified halo that encompassed the table on the dais.

As Amy and Kutchins crossed the dance floor, Deacon's gun popped four, maybe five times. A woman at the head table went down, a red blotch splurting from the shoulder of her plain blue gown. Another shot hit the actor's date in the gut, jerking her upright then onto the steak plate before her. The actor shreiked. The agent standing behind the table had vaulted across it in less time than Amy thought possible and was struggling with Deacon. They fought as the gun fired, then they both tumbled off the platform. Other agents swarmed over them.

Amy stumbled across the dance floor cursing the high-heeled boots that slowed her. Kutchins evidently remembered the job she'd been assigned before the melee started and grabbed Amy's left arm. But she evidently hadn't reckoned on Marine Corps training, or she would have tried for a more effective hold. Amy brought her left arm up, as if trying to break the grip, then used her right to chop across Hutchins' throat, remembering at the last second to take some energy off a blow intended to fracture the larynx. Hutchins released her and went down gagging.

Deacon was still the center of her focus, now trapped beneath three Secret Service agents. Amy didn't know what she'd do when she reached him, but he was her job, her boss, her man, so she dashed toward the pile. But before she could reach it, another young agent tackled her, this one a man. They both went down, his grip on her leg loosening as they hit the floor. Amy brought a knee into his chin and his grip loosened further. As she wiggled free, she kicked full force into the agent's face, her efforts rewarded with the satisfying crunch of broken nasal bones. Then she was up, vaulting onto the platform.

She pivoted, intending to fling herself from the platform onto the pile of agents holding Deacon, when Barzoon yelled, "She's choking."

Amy turned, leaning over the plates and food scattered across the head table. There, on the floor beyond, Cathleen

Harris stared bug-eyed, face purple, hands to throat. Barzoon's hand locked on Amy's wrist. Their eyes met.

"I'm a medic," Amy said. "Let me help."

Barzoon stared at her, lost in indecision, then released his grip. Amy scooted past him and his startled wife and hauled Harris unceremoniously to a sitting position. Then she got behind the choking woman, placing her arms around the slender waist.

Amy had practiced the Heimlich maneuver several dozen times, once on an actual choking person. Her hands obeyed without having to think about it, giving her time to think of other things, thoughts that bounced through her head as her hands worked mechanically. Reason versus reflex. Duty versus country. Trying to maintain her honor in the process.

Amy's left fist balled up tight.

Harris was responsible for the deaths of half a dozen innocent persons.

She brought the thumb-side of her fist between Harris's umbilicus and ribcage.

Harris had murdered her way to the vice presidency.

Amy's fist sought the hollow just below the sternum.

Harris was no doubt "managed" by an outside agency, some foreign government bent on American destruction.

Amy's right hand locked over the left.

She'd tried to have Deacon killed.

Amy's shoulder's hunched, ready to jerk up and in.

If she lived, Harris would no doubt see to it that Deacon was dead.

Amy paused in indecision. Duty versus country. Love versus honor.

No one would ever believe them. Harris would win.

Amy jerked down weakly into the abdomen. It went against her nature, but she paused for a count of two then repeated the process using even less force than before. She continued like this, each two-second pause followed by ineffectual movements with only the appearance of lifesaving. Her reflexes tried to rebel, to save the life as she was trained to do. Amy forced her head to intervene, forced her heart into a stone. She continued like this, two seconds pause, ineffectual umph, until Secret Service pulled her away from Harris — well after life had left the pretty blue eyes.

Chapter 44

Amy sat in a bare room, her left hand chained to a bolt in the table, her right hand holding a Pepsi. Déjà vu all over again. She looked up and there was the eye in the sky, it's polished black surface saying 'Hello again. Glad you could stop by.' The chair was just as uncomfortable as the one in the other interrogation room she'd sat in — hard plastic sans padding.

It seemed like she'd been here for over an hour, perhaps longer. Time was difficult to estimate when you were alone, without a clock, and with the chair slowly deadening your butt. The Pepsi was almost gone, and she knew she'd soon need somewhere to deposit the twenty ounces of fluid she'd just consumed. But she was okay for right now, so she sipped and waited.

Amy was puzzled. She'd figured they'd question her hard, question her early, question her often. Yet still she waited for someone to come in. Someone besides the matron who'd cuffed her and given her the drink. A lean, hard matron who looked considerably more with it than the skinny one at Baltimore PD.

She was still in her party clothes from last night, which also surprised her. She ought to be in prison garb by now. Maybe a shower and delousing, then the orange scrubs and soft rubber shoes. In a word, processed. Processed through the system.

They knew who she was. There was no doubt about that. They knew what she was accused of. They probably also knew that she deliberately took the life of the vice president. Or at least, didn't save it. Either that, or she was the most inept Marine Corps medic that ever said "Oorah."

Amy felt the first stirrings, the initial impulse to pee. Not urgent yet, but soon. She looked at the camera lens above her. "Ah, excuse me? Somebody?" As if in answer, the door opened. A man entered. She had never met him but had heard about him. From Deacon's description, it could only be him. She couldn't recall the name, so she spoke the description. "Bunsen Honeydew?'

The fat man cleared his throat. "Ms. Robbins? My name is Josiah Metternich. Unit 13. May I sit down?"

Amy rattled her handcuffed wrist. "I can't stop you."

"Ahem. Yes." Metternich sat. "We can have that removed shortly." He leaned back, took off his glasses and rubbed his eyes. They were beady, like the eyes of a pig. But Amy noticed a weariness there as well. Perhaps the suffering of Job, or at least the self-perception of it. For a moment, she felt sorry for him.

"Yes. In a moment, they will remove the bracelet and you'll be free to go."

"Free to go?" Amy had expected a long FBI interrogation. A little good cop, bad cop perhaps. Then a jail cell, followed by more waiting, followed by a long court case, followed by more waiting, followed by another jail cell, this time in Leavenworth, Marion, or Petersburg. What she got was an hour and "you're free to go."

"I don't understand."

He replaced his glasses and smiled. Deacon was right, his fingers were like fat worms, his smile like the Muppet doctor.

"Yes. That's why I'm here. I wanted to, well, explain things. And to ask for your cooperation of course."

"My cooperation doing what exactly?"

"Well, um, keeping your mouth shut, exactly. Not to put too fine a point on it."

Amy nodded. "I see."

"No, I doubt that. But hopefully you will. Let me explain."

The ten fat worms joined in front of him, writhing nervously.

"I'm not sure how much Dr. Creel has told you. So, I don't want to divulge any secrets."

"I know about the suicide drug. And I know about the antidote he was developing. And I know that somehow the woman who became vice president was using the former to eliminate her competition. I don't know how. I don't know why. I don't know who else was involved, besides Lieutenant Reilly and Barzoon." She turned her Ronstadt eyes on Metternich. "Do *you*, sir?"

He squirmed like an ant under a magnifying glass. "Well, let me just say, I may know more but am not at liberty to divulge all of it. What I *can* tell you is that 606, the um, suicide drug, was developed as a lifesaving pharmaceutical, then weaponized in the interests of national security."

Amy smiled. "National security? That's become a tired phrase, doctor. The last resort of the corrupt, criminal, or incompetent."

Metternich cleared his throat again. "Be that as it may. I wouldn't have been involved with its development if I hadn't believed in the, shall we say, national importance of it." He met her eye. She stared, unblinking, until he lowered his gaze to his twisting fingers.

"Go on," Amy said.

"Ahem. Yes. Before his untimely death, Agent Carstairs had been working a line of inquiry. More specifically, specialists in the bureau had been working a line of inquiry at his behest. Financial inquiry. Following the money, so to speak." He tried for a smile, but Amy's stony stare wiped it from his face. "More specifically, the money paid to Ms. Ortiz."

"Who?"

"A woman, a government employee in fact." He shook his head. "Never mind. Suffice it to say that a rather large sum of money had been paid to an administrative staffer for nefarious activities. Or so it appeared."

"And?"

"And money leaves a trail. In this case, the trail was well hidden behind shell agencies and cash transfers. But the boys at the bureau were able to track it down. Although not until after the unfortunate incidents at the Empyre Club."

"To?"

"Pardon?"

"The trail. Where did it lead?"

"A wire transfer from a clandestine operative of a foreign government to a Washington bureaucrat." More throat clearing. More hand staring. "In point of fact, one Nelson Barzoon. Unfortunately, Mr. Barzoon is not available for comment, as he boarded an Aeroflot flight for Moscow several hours before the FBI raid on his townhouse."

"And Harris? What was her status, her role in all this? The mastermind? The tool?"

He looked her in the eye. "Cathleen Harris did not exist. That is to say, the person who became vice president was not the one who graduated from Duke as Dr. Cathleen Harris."

"Are you sure?"

He nodded. "DNA had been taken as part of a child identification when she was six. It does not match that taken from the body of the late vice president."

"How is that possible?"

Metternich shrugged, again studying his fingers. "Plastic surgery. Dialect coaching. Intensive background history. Document forgeries. Lots and lots of money directed at making it happen."

"But surely her parents could tell. Her siblings?"

"Both parents were killed in a car accident ten years ago." He smiled. "Or so it appeared. She was an only child."

"Barzoon couldn't have done all that. Not without help."

"That is being pursued. Arrests are being made, quietly, as we speak. More will follow."

"How deep?" Amy asked.

"Let us say, deep enough that it would be quite embarrassing if all the particulars came out. Which brings me back to why I was sent here."

"Which was?"

"To request your cooperation."

Now Amy smiled. "Why should I?"

"Let us say it's in the nature of a quid pro quo. You accept an honorable discharge from the Marine Corps along with *considerable* mustering-out pay."

"How considerable?"

"Say, something in the nature of an early pension? Anyway, enough to keep you free of financial worries for quite some time."

"So, they want to buy my silence?"

"In a word, yes. But not just with money. All pending criminal charges against you will be dropped. Against Dr. Creel as well."

"Where is Deacon?"

"I honestly don't know. I only know he was treated for his injuries and released."

"Released? Did he sign up for this deal as well?"

Metternich shook his head. "As I understand it, he asked only for five hundred dollars and a bus ticket."

"To where?"

"That I don't know."

They stared at each other. Metternich met her gaze without looking away. There was a sadness behind his beady eyes. Amy found herself feeling sorry for him again.

"What about the suicide drug?"

He shrugged. "My understanding is that the project is to be dropped. All traces of it expunged from the files. But that's a job for the new director."

"New director?"

"Yes. I'm to remain on sabbatical for the time being. Afterward?" His sad smile returned. "Well, Ms. Robbins. What do you say?"

"I have to go to the bathroom."

Nelson Barzoon leaned back into his spacious first-class seat and pulled the envelope from his breast pocket. He smiled as he felt the girth of twenty-five-thousand dollars in U.S. currency. Just traveling cash, he thought, returning it to the pocket that also held a passbook for a Swiss bank where one point five million waited. In the other breast pocket was a valid Dutch passport in the name of Karl Bakker, a likeness of Barzoon smiling in one corner.

A female voice drifted from the cabin speaker. It was first in Russian, then in Dutch, then in English. Nelson understood all three.

"Ladies and gentlemen. On behalf of Captain Volkovich and the flight crew, I would like to welcome you aboard Aeroflot flight 196 to Moscow. Travel time from Amsterdam approximately three hours and fourteen minutes. We have reached our cruising altitude of thirty-one-thousand feet, and the captain has turned off the fasten seat-belt sign. Feel free to move about the cabin, but be careful when retrieving carry-on items, as they may have moved in flight. Again, thank you for choosing Aeroflot, and we hope you enjoy your flight."

A pretty flight attendant named Karyn brought Barzoon a glass.

"Here is your scotch rocks, sir," she said in heavily accented Dutch. She placed it down. "Glen morg nee."

"Glenmorangie," he corrected, smiling. "Dank u."

"Have you decided on your choice for dinner?"

Barzoon sipped his drink and nodded. "I'll have the salmon. With a glass of the Pascal Jolivet sauvignon blanc." He handed her back the menu, then unexpectedly sneezed into his napkin.

"Bless you," Karyn said. "Are you all right?"

Barzoon nodded. "Just a summer cold, I think."

"This session of Municipal court 182 is called to order. The honorable Pleasant Webster presiding."

"Be seated," Judge Webster said. The intervening weeks had done little to diminish his size or presence. "Call the next case." Webster waved his hand before his nose and added, "And open a window."

The bailiff called out, "People versus Deacon Creel."

Webster looked at the unkept defendant in the ratty clothes and shook his head.

"I wish I could say it was nice to see you again, Dr. Creel. But I was hoping that Cleveland Municipal Night Court was rid of you." He leaned forward. "I'll be honest, sir. When I heard about the murder charges on you, I was quite surprised. I took you to be a relatively harmless, if irritating, pain in the ass. Kind of like piles." He chuckled. "But I see you back here, free to be a pain in my not inconsiderable behind once again. Your federal problems get straightened out, did they?"

Deacon leaned on one foot, eyes closed, smug grin once again upon his face. "Let's say I'm just *your* bad penny."

"Well, I see that your fifteen minutes of fame, or should I say infamy, hasn't done anything to improve your attitude." He turned to the assistant DA. "Charges, Mr. Simonetti?"

"Drunk and disorderly, your honor." The DA cleared his throat. "On the night of ..."

Webster waved him off. "Let's dispense with the wherefores and heretos, shall we? Suffice it to say that Dr. Creel was swacked and started a fight. Where?"

"The Tune-in Tavern, your honor."

Webster shook his head.

"Your honor," the public defender said. "I'd like to point out that this is only an allegation at this point. It is not clear who ..."

"Maybe not to you, Mr. Thompson. That's what you get paid for. Not being clear *who*. I get paid to keep drunks that start fights off the streets. Or in this case, out of the Tune-in Tavern. And if this was Dr. Creel's first time before my bench, I might listen to the who started what when. But it's his third time."

"Fourth, your honor," Simonetti said.

The judge nodded. "I stand corrected." He turned to the DA. "How much damage?"

Simonetti looked at a clipboard. "Dozen bar glasses. One quart bottle of Ten-High bourbon. One fifth of Finlandia. One eighteen by twenty-four-inch mirror ..."

"Just give me the dollars and cents."

Simonetti eyed the bottom of the list. "Roughly, three hundred dollars, your honor."

Webster nodded again. "I'm gonna save us all some time here." He turned his bulk toward Deacon, hands folded. "You like western stories, Dr. Creel? I do. I like the simplicity of them. I like the quick justice that fits the crime." He smiled as if remembering a favorite tale. "And when the unruly drunk is brought before the judge in western stories, the judge metes out quick, simple, justice. Something like, 'that'll be ten dollars or ten days.'" He shrugged. "But western stories are set in 1880 or so, when ten dollars was a week's wages. This is the twenty-first century, and we got us three-hundred dollars in damages. So, taking inflation into account, and taking a third strike into account, I'm gonna say that'll be four-hundred dollars or forty days." He pointed to the lady with glasses seated nearby. "You can either pay the clerk or accompany the bailiff — quietly if you please."

Deacon's grin became a smile. The smile became a laugh.

"I'm gonna take that to mean you don't have four-hundred dollars." Webster waved to the bailiff. "Take him to the lockup, Stanley."

"I'll pay the fine," said a voice from the back.

"And who are you, Miss?"

"Amy Robbins, sir." She stood. "Marine Force Specialist Amy Robbins. Retired."

The judge raised his brows.

Amy looked at Deacon. Their eyes met. "I'll pay the fine. And I'll accept responsibility for Commander Creel."

"Do you know what you're letting yourself in for, young lady?"

Amy smiled. "I have *some* idea."

John Bukowski is an accomplished writer in both fiction and nonfiction. His short stories have been published in numerous notable venues such as *Dark Secrets, Makarelle*, and *Land Beyond the World*. In a previous life, he wrote hundreds of medical publications, including handbooks, websites, and radio scripts, translating technical topics for the general public. He leverages his expertise in scientific research and public health in his debut novel, *Project Suicide*, blending medical authenticity with suspenseful fiction for an exciting ride.

When he isn't tapping his computer keyboard, he's tapping his feet to music, singing pop, Broadway, and opera—in multiple languages. Originally from Detroit, he resides in eastern Tennessee with his wife and a dysfunctional dog named Alfie.

Made in the USA
Columbia, SC
22 March 2022

57936554R00186